D0108596

WE ALL FALL DOWN

PRAISE FOR *WHAT BIG TEETH*

"With a layered mystery, a haunting setting, and thrilling tension, *What Big Teeth* has an otherness to it that pulls you in and forces you to keep reading."
—TRICIA LEVENSELLER, *Publisher's Weekly*–bestselling author of *The Shadows Between Us*

"Deliciously gothic and wonderfully creepy."
—*The Bulletin of the Center for Children's Books*, starred review

". . . one part haunting mystery, one part dark fantasy . . . This darkly thrilling gothic fantasy will appeal to fans of Karen McManus and Maggie Stiefvater alike." —*School Library Journal*

"A tale so gorgeously twisty, it'll turn you inside out."
—*Tor.com*

"Gazes into [the] darkness to face the monster that dwells within."—*NPR Books*

"A complete ghostly chill that deserves ten stars."—*The Nerd Daily*

"Has bite—and will leave you feeling dazed."—*Forever YA*

"A hauntingly thrilling read."—*The Lineup*

"A fascinating debut."—*PopSugar*

"[An] inventive concept."—*Den of Geek*

"Not your typical YA fantasy."—*Culturess*

ALSO BY ROSE SZABO

What Big Teeth

WE ALL FALL DOWN

ROSE SZABO

FARRAR STRAUS GIROUX
NEW YORK

Farrar Straus Giroux Books for Young Readers
An imprint of Macmillan Publishing Group, LLC
120 Broadway, New York, NY 10271 • fiercereads.com

Our books may be purchased in bulk for promotional, educational, or business
use. Please contact your local bookseller or the Macmillan Corporate and
Premium Sales Department at (800) 221-7945 ext. 5442 or by email at
MacmillanSpecialMarkets@macmillan.com.

Library of Congress Cataloging-in-Publication Data is available.

First edition, 2022
Book design by Aurora Parlagreco
Printed in the United States of America

ISBN 978-0-374-31432-3 (hardcover)

1   3   5   7   9   10   8   6   4   2

For my beloved,
who knows that words are not enough

WE ALL
FALL
DOWN

BEING AN ACCOUNT OF
THE LIVES OF FOUR YOUNG PEOPLE
OF RIVER CITY

As told to R. L. Emblem

In the Year of Queen Zara 42.

PROLOGUE

In the secret city at the hub of the world, the revolution was over. King Nathan the Giant was locked in his own dungeon, waiting to stand trial. But the heavy rains would not stop falling in cold sheets as Astrid made her way to the palace.

People wanted to be in the streets, but the pounding rain drove them back, and so they huddled in archways and under awnings. Yellow squares of light stained the water that pattered ankle-deep in the street as Astrid scurried along. On a wide porch, teenagers in palace livery sang the city anthem in four-part harmony. They stopped as she passed, and some of the boys gave her ragged salutes. She dipped her umbrella forward, a kind of nod, and kept going. No matter who saluted her, she was alone out here in the middle of the street, as she sloshed her way through the puddles. Nobody else had any reason to venture forth tonight. Nobody else's life was coming apart in their hands.

At last, she came to the palace. Its front gateway was unguarded, and the iron gates lay crumpled in a slag heap on the cobbles, so she traveled uninterrupted through the sentryless double doors into the atrium with its great mural of Otiotan fighting the serpent with his flaming sword. Here there was a party. And when they saw who stood in the atrium shaking the rain from her umbrella, the crowd let up a cheer. Astrid, the small brown witch they'd known since they were children, who was now their champion. Astrid, who had blown the gates off the palace with her powerful witch-craft. Astrid, with a sprig of wild mint pinned to her coat, to signify that she was one of the people. Astrid, whose pager was always on to answer the calls of the sick and the needy.

She had to be careful. This was supposed to be a people's revolution. She didn't want to draw too much attention to herself. Didn't want to risk becoming a Hero. She almost laughed at the thought: a flaming sword in one small hand. Any blushing Maiden would have to bend down to cling to Astrid.

Still, it was useful that no one would stop her. Why would they? She was on their side. They'd let her go wherever she pleased.

Where she wanted to go, of course, was the dungeon.

She picked her way through the clusters of revolutionaries who cluttered the halls and vaulted rooms of the palace, stripped to their underwear or wrapped in towels made from torn-down banners. They'd broken into the vintage, and now they were getting smashed on wine older than their grandparents. She made her way down through the winding levels of the palace, past the kitchens, where a bunch of drunk ten-year-olds were trying to roast a pig on a spit under the direction of the palace's old cook, who winked and grinned at her as she passed.

The guards at the edge of the dungeon saluted her. Kyle and Pete, of course. They'd joined the revolution for the same reasons they'd joined baseball games and bar fights: They liked to feel part of something. They were sloshed, too, but trying to hide it behind good posture.

"What of the prisoner?" she said.

"He hasn't spoken or taken food this past day."

"I'll try to get him to eat," she said. "We need him to be strong enough to stand trial."

They nodded fervently.

"Will you execute him, Astrid?" Kyle asked. "It would be fitting."

"No, dummy," Pete said. "It has to be all of us. We'll throw rocks at him or something."

She tossed her head. "Leave me."

They glanced at each other briefly, and then hurried out of the corridor and up the stairs. She knew she'd find them in the kitchen when she was done, drinking with the kids.

The king was in the last cell at the far end of the hallway. Of course he was. It was almost laughable, how things always went exactly the way you would expect. On the table just outside the cell was a dented plate with a few slices of stale bread on it; no wonder he hadn't eaten. She slid back the iron partition that covered the little barred window. "Nathan," she said.

He stood up perfectly straight, his arms folded behind his back as though he were examining a piece of art. His red beard was streaked with blood from his chin, and more blood was crusted on his eyebrow. He smiled when he saw her. Oh, they'd broken his front teeth. She winced, and tried to hide it.

"Astrid," he said. "It's good to see you."

Astrid's heart swelled in her chest. Her king, now and forever. A great thinker, an inventor, big like a tree. Thirty now, with wrinkles blooming at the corners of his eyes. A man with a voice that could lead armies. She had to steady herself against the door to stop her knees from buckling, seeing him like this.

"There's no need for your bluster, tyrant," she said. "We're alone." She hoped he would take her meaning: that they were alone, but to still be careful.

"My apologies, old friend."

"Hardly friend to you these days."

He shook his head. She knew what he meant, so he didn't have to risk saying it out loud. They'd always been like this, even after Marla. Always knew the other's mind.

"Where's Marla?" he asked.

"The people blame her," she said. "They are saying that without her, your excesses would not have been possible. She has fled."

Nathan's brow furrowed. "Is she hurt?"

"Rest assured," Astrid said. "She'll be found."

He put a hand to his mouth.

"Please," he said. "You have to do something about the baby."

"That's up to me now, isn't it?"

He managed a smile. She smiled back.

He mouthed to her through the bars: *Come here.* She took a step closer to the grate, and he approached it from his side. Then: *Shut your eyes.*

In the darkness behind her eyelids, Astrid stood close to King Nathan the Giant. She took her hands off the cold door so that she could pretend there was nothing between them but air. He was right in front of her, so tall that her head only came up to his chest. She could smell his cologne from here, and behind it his breath, sour from hunger and tinged with blood. And something else, too: a metallic smell.

He'd been standing when she approached, she realized, because he'd been standing all day.

She opened her eyes.

"It's getting worse, isn't it?" she said.

He laughed a little, and she could see him flinch when the air hit his broken teeth. "It's bad today. I can't bend my knees."

Astrid's stomach dropped. "But you're not king anymore."

"We knew there was a chance it wouldn't work that way."

Astrid's heart sank. Everything they'd done to make things different, and it still wasn't enough.

Astrid tried not to let her fear show on her face, although they both knew what would happen to him soon; what happened to every king. She'd need to do something about that, and soon, but she wasn't sure yet what. She had no plan. She—

"I really thought it could be different," he said. "I thought *I* could be different. But I'm like all of them, aren't I? I can feel myself going mad. And now—" He looked down at his legs.

"Stop that," Astrid snapped. "This isn't over yet."

He was looking at her again with those clear eyes. Astrid had a hard time with his eyes these days. He was right. He was entering his madness. But he wasn't there yet.

She'd been working on this spell without telling him for some time. He wouldn't have approved, would have told her that they should focus on their plan, that if it worked, they'd both be free. But Astrid was never one to count on a single plan. And now she was frightened, but relieved.

She quietly said a word or two, and felt a little ping on her scalp as one of her braids undid itself. It would take a few minutes to work, if she'd done it right. And by then she'd be long gone. She looked at Nathan, trying not to cry.

"You should eat something," she said.

He nodded, looking weary. "I will," he said. "Just make sure this is over."

She fled from the dungeon. In the kitchen, she told the spit-turning guards to fix the prisoner a plate, a good one this time. And then she went upstairs, through mazes of corridors, stole a raincoat, and let herself out through a side door into the rainy night.

As soon as she was out of sight of the palace, she said the four words that would release another spell she'd braided earlier. It came undone, and she was no longer walking but skimming low across the ground. It was faster this way, and she needed to be fast. She needed to get to Marla before it was too late. Luckily, she knew the queen well. She knew exactly where she'd go in a crisis.

She slid over the wet streets, the rain quickly soaking her skirt, and over the edge of the hill that led down to the riverbank. When she reached the river, her heels dipped just below the surface, soaking through her worn-out boots. She swore and skidded on. The water was raging tonight, and the magic that kept her just above it could barely keep up with it. She stuttered along the waves, picking up her feet to avoid logs that were tossed as easily as kindling in the torrent. She kept her eyes ahead as she ran, on the island that loomed ahead, and the crude stone castle built directly into the island's cliffside. The summer palace. No light came from it that she could see. Good. Marla had enough sense to hide.

When she reached the island, she found herself running sideways up a wall of debris: churning logs and branches that battered against the palace's battlements with every surge of the river. Her foot got caught and she heard something snap. Before she could feel it, she unleashed another spell she'd saved in a braid, the one that killed pain completely. This was too important for her to be distracted. She cleared the wall and floated down into the courtyard beyond. She glanced down only briefly before deciding that pain or no pain, she didn't want to look at her foot just yet.

When Astrid opened one side of the great double doors, she spotted the heap in the corner immediately. A Black woman was huddled under a plaid blanket against the far wall of the great feast hall, next to a battery-powered lantern draped with a scarf. Her legs were splayed out in front of her and she clutched her belly with both hands. As Astrid got closer, Marla looked up at her with those wide, lovely eyes that swayed everyone who saw them.

She was beautiful, Astrid had to admit. Even with rivulets of sweat running down her forehead, even with her mouth locked in a grimace, she was the most beautiful woman who had ever lived. And more than that, she glowed from the inside, a font of living magic. It drew people to her; everyone wanted a little bit of what she had.

"You came," Marla said.

"Of course I did," Astrid snapped. She didn't like the implication that she might not. "Them turning on you was a surprise. What happened here?"

"I was running, and I fell," Marla said. "I think something's broken. And they're not coming."

Astrid let go of the spell that held her aloft, and even with the numbing, she instantly regretted putting weight on her foot. "Let me see," she said, and dropped to her knees. She realized the floor wasn't slick with water, as she'd thought, but with blood. A lot of it. Oh no. "Are you in pain?" she asked.

"Not anymore," Marla said. And then, seeing the look on Astrid's face, "That can't be good, can it?"

"It's not." Astrid put her hand on Marla's thigh, and it came back red. "How long have you been bleeding like this?"

"I don't know. A while."

Marla was a problem, Astrid thought as she worked. The most beautiful woman who had ever lived, a living fountain of love and magic, wife of the king, and she was so—so passive. How long had she been lying there while her life ebbed away, without doing anything, without tearing rags, without trying to save herself? Maybe that was why people lined up to do what Marla wanted. Maybe that was—

It was then that Astrid felt what Marla had already known. There wasn't one baby. There were two. And something else was wrong, too.

"Marla," Astrid said. "They're twins."

Marla smiled patiently. "I know."

"One of them is . . . wrapped around the other. It doesn't feel like the cord. It feels like—"

"One of them is special."

"I'm not sure—"

"Do whatever you need to do."

She made Astrid feel stupid. Damn her. Astrid worked by the light of the lantern until time grew hazy. She talked to Marla the way she'd talk to any laboring mother: making jokes, getting her to tell stories, keeping her awake. She undid spell after spell, feeling the braids burst loose on her aching head: a spell for more blood, a spell for a weak heart.

Everyone loved Marla. Even Astrid, who could barely stand her, loved her. It was impossible not to love her. Astrid fought back tears; she had to work.

"What do you think about names?" she asked when Marla fell silent for too long, when her breathing got too shallow.

"I don't know about the girl," Marla said. "But the boy's name is David."

"David," Astrid said. "That's a good name. How'd you think of that?"

She felt Marla's breathing change, and then stop. "Shit," Astrid said. She hated this. She undid a braid she'd been saving, one that was probably a bad idea: a spell to separate things that were stuck.

And then, all at once, there was a bundle of sticky flesh in her arms. One baby, and one tangle of boneless red snakes wrapped around it. She should have saved the spell. The baby wasn't crying, and his—his!—face was turning blue. Astrid screamed and dug her fingernails into the shape that wrapped around the baby's neck, and the thing made of snakes hissed and fell backward onto the floor in a heap. And then in the light from the lantern, Astrid saw it plainly.

It had a body like a child: two arms, two legs, a head of dark hair. A face that already looked like Marla's, wide-eyed and innocent. But it also had eight horrible long arms like an octopus, longer than its body, growing out of its back and sides, lined on the underside with rows of red suckers. Its hissing mouth was filled with rows of tiny teeth like a piranha. Astrid clutched the wailing baby to her chest and stared down at the thing lying on the floor in the puddle of Marla's blood.

It was horrible. Horrible, horrible. And Marla—Astrid looked down.

Whatever force had animated Marla, that had drawn witches and street sweepers and kings to her, had deserted her. She was dead. And Astrid's heart sank. If Marla was dead, they had no Maiden. And without a Maiden, no magic.

Astrid could feel it receding already, that current that she had always dipped into to make order in her world. To heal and to hurt. With Marla gone, it was like the tide had gone out and left her stranded.

There was nobody here to see her cry, so she let herself cry while she wrapped the baby in Marla's old scarf. David. He looked so much like Nathan. Beautiful. What would he become without parents?

The other thing was trying to drag itself onto its belly. Astrid hated to look at it. She shuddered, and limped away. She had to do something with this baby. She had to keep him safe.

For a moment, she had a vision of keeping him. Astrid the revolutionary and her beautiful son. But she shook the thought from her head. It would raise too many questions, her going off into the night and coming back with a baby. She swallowed the lump in her throat. He wouldn't be safe anywhere in this city, not with his mother dead and his father locked up. They'd want to kill him, too, just to make sure that the whole business didn't start up again. The son of a dethroned king and a dead queen was a good bet for a Hero.

A tiny, desperate hope bloomed in Astrid. She tried not to think of Nathan saying *You have to do something about the baby.* Surely, he didn't mean it like that. And even if he did, he was in his madness. And Marla was gone. There was no one here to make a decision but her.

So she had to get him out of here. She'd need to get him to the mainland, somewhere no one would recognize him. And maybe if she was lucky, he'd be back before Nathan was dead. Before the last of the magic had ebbed from the world like blood from a wound. Heroes always came just in time.

She staggered from the summer palace, into the driving rain. She undid one last braid. She hoped it would be enough. She tried not to think of Marla dead. There would be plenty of time in the coming days and weeks to feel the losses of tonight.

The baby in her arms wriggled, and for a moment, she thought of the other thing, the thing she had left on the floor. But between the pain blooming in her foot, the driving rain, and the warm baby sleeping in her arms and breaking her heart, Astrid blotted it from her mind.

THE
FALL

ONE

It was still August when Jesse ran away.

He'd been a good son, stopped asking questions about where he was allowed to go or when, looked down when Paul called him faggot, and mumbled *yes, sir, yes, ma'am* at the dinner table. He'd given his paychecks to Paul, and had hidden an envelope of tips, skimmed a dollar or two at a time, in the gap between the floor and the baseboard where he'd kept the postcard his best friend had sent him when he was eleven. He'd turned eighteen and sat quietly through the argument where his mom said he was just a kid and Paul said he was a man and should be fending for himself, and he'd waited for them to go camping for their anniversary, and he'd bought a ticket to the place on the postcard: a gleaming jeweled island city, like the Mont-Saint-Michel, with a great iron suspension bridge connecting it to the mainland. *Greetings from River City*, said the postcard. And on the back, in crabbed tiny boy handwriting, a note.

One by one, all Jesse's other secret places had been found: the shoebox in the back of his closet where he kept a girl's black T-shirt and a pair of soccer socks. The loose floorboard under the bed where he'd hid a magazine or two for a while. One at a time, like fortresses under siege, those hiding places had fallen. But the gap in the baseboard hadn't let him down yet. It had saved him $200 and that postcard. And so that was what he had when he left his house at 11:45 p.m. on a clear night, right at the end of summer when the heat was starting to break. He walked to the bus station, his big backpack heavy with packed sandwiches, clean underwear, and library books he felt a little guilty about planning to never return.

He'd done some research on the internet about River City. It wasn't supposed to be real; he'd only found it on old message boards, most of which were full of random nonsense about ghosts and games you could play with elevators and time travel. They'd said that to get a ticket, you had to go to a bus station at midnight on a clear night with a breeze in one of a handful of towns, and get on the bus that pulled up, and pay them whatever they asked for. Some of the older stories said that they'd ask for weird things, like blood, or hair, or a sigh, or the name of your true love. Other people said that was bullshit, that they'd been on the bus this year even, and all they'd wanted was cash. Jesse wasn't sure, but he was ready to give them whatever they asked for. It couldn't be worse than staying where he was.

The bus station was closed, so he huddled outside against the wall, hiding in his sweatshirt. He hoped that nobody would see him; Paul drank with cops, and they'd ratted Jesse out before. He pulled his hood over his face and folded his arms across his chest, hoping he looked tough. Tough was hard for him. He was too skinny, his face too soft and round for it to really carry off well.

From outside of him, we can see how beautiful he is. A little bit lanky and awkward, but with a good gentle face. A scar on his forehead, usually hidden by a soft shock of hair, that he got from Paul, with some help from the sharp edge of a coffee table. Until he was fifteen, he'd told people it was a witch's mark.

He checked his watch. Midnight. No bus. He waited. Buses were late, right? But minutes wore past, and he started to feel like an idiot. Maybe he should just come back in the morning, get on a bus to New York, or wherever it was that kids like him went when they ran away from home. Not that he was a kid anymore. Paul said it often enough.

He was about to shoulder his backpack and go home when he saw a bus coming down the road.

It wasn't a bus like the kind he was used to. It looked like a silver bullet trailer, with red trim, and windows set on an angle, giving the impression of speed, and big wide headlights and a wide front fender that looked like a cartoon mouth. He laughed out loud when he saw it. This was more like it. This was a magic bus to a city that only people on the internet knew about. One hundred percent.

It came to a halt, and the shadowy bus driver pulled a lever to hinge open the doors, and Jesse shouldered his backpack and stumbled up the steps. "Hi," he said. He looked around. There were only a few other people on the bus. A mother sitting near two girls wrapped in a blanket, falling over each other to press their faces to the window. A middle-aged couple and a dog. Jesse grinned wildly at all of them. And then the bus driver, an impossibly jowly and warty man, stuck out his hand.

"What do you need?" Jesse asked.

"What you got?"

Jesse rummaged around in his wad of cash. "I can do . . . fifty?" he said.

"Looks like more than fifty."

"What's the price? Is there a price?"

"Give me all of that."

"You've gotta be kidding me."

"Do you want on the bus or not?"

Jesse felt a stab of fear. Every bit of money he had seemed like a little too much, even for a journey into a magical world. But what choice did he have?

"Or I'll take that postcard," the bus driver said.

Jesse wondered for a second, fearful, how the man had known about the postcard. And then he realized he'd gotten it out with the money. It wobbled in his trembling hands.

"Uh," Jesse said. "Why?"

"Maybe it's valuable."

Jesse swallowed. "I'll give you the cash," he said.

The driver took the wad from him. "Sit wherever."

Jesse stumbled to a seat and fell into it, dazed and panicking. This wasn't at all what he'd planned for. Now he was on a bus with no money. He clutched the postcard for a while before stuffing it into his backpack. Nobody was taking that from him.

The bus rumbled along for hours, through small towns. Jesse wondered vaguely why the lore said the bus came at midnight, when it was clear that it was on a regular damn bus schedule, picking people up between something like 11 p.m. and 4 a.m., and late to each stop by the impatient, desperate looks of the people getting on board. The bus driver extorted all of them, although some people managed to talk him down to something reasonable. One guy didn't have any money, and Jesse watched the driver barter with him for his hat and his jacket and eventually his pocket square. The man sat down in the row opposite Jesse, looking lost and bereft. He kept putting his hand to something under his sweater that jerked periodically. Jesse watched, fascinated, until they stopped in another small town and a woman got on with a scarf wrapped so tightly around her throat that it almost hid the lump bulging from the side of her face.

As the bus filled up, Jesse realized that about half the people who got on had something they were hiding. He started scoping out the people who'd been on when he'd boarded, and realized that the girls sitting by the window were fused at the hip: two girls, one pair of legs. They were fighting over whether the window was going to be cracked open or shut.

Eventually, Jesse drifted off to sleep in the warm darkness of the bus, knocked out by the hissing of the hydraulic brakes and the rumble of the engine. He rocked from side to side, his legs tucked up and braced against the seat in front of him, his head propped on his knees for a pillow. The murmur of voices talking quietly entered his dream in dribs and drabs. *What if it doesn't work? This hospital is the best—they'll know what to do. Girls, stop hitting. I'm hungry.* Snores. The sound of the girls hitting each other and giggling while their mother shushed them angrily. He felt a kind of vague kinship with all of them. After all, there was something wrong with him, too.

He had to go now because he had to get away. He had a feeling that if he stayed, he was going to die. Not of sickness or accident, but because he would get himself killed. Maybe wanted to get himself killed. That feeling had been building in him for months.

It'd hit a peak in the last few days of junior year, when a kid he kind of knew—a starter on the football team—had been in the bathroom at the same time as him. Jesse usually got out of the way of guys like that; he was skinny, they were big. But for some reason he'd stared at him, and the guy had seen him staring, and before Jesse knew what was up, he'd been against the wall, the guy's palms grinding his shoulders into the cinderblocks, the guy's hips against him, too. Jesse wasn't sure in that moment if he was about to kiss him or murder him in cold blood, but the bathroom door had started to open, and the guy had let him go, and he'd escaped, for now, the fate he seemed to be courting. He had to fix himself, before something worse happened.

The sun slanting through the window woke him up at last. It was morning, and they were rumbling along an empty, straight country road, corn on both sides, waving in the breeze, as far as he could see. Trees behind the corn. It was like a corridor of nothing, a long, empty drive.

The man sitting opposite him saw that he was awake, and winked at him. Jesse realized it wasn't pocket square guy, who had moved several seats back and was eyeing them warily. This was a massive white guy wearing a greasy black raincoat, with a wild white beard like a feral Santa Claus. He was younger, though, than most of the men Jesse had seen who had beards like that. He also had a milky right eye, like a cataract, under which his pupil swam, just barely visible. Something about the guy looked familiar to Jesse, but he couldn't place him.

The man fished around in his pocket, and Jesse winced, until the man pulled out a hard candy in a crinkled yellow wrapper. "Want one?" he asked.

"No," Jesse said. "Thanks."

"This bus used to be faster."

"You taken it a lot?"

"Not in a long time," the man said. Jesse realized he smelled vaguely of piss, and also something else: a coppery smell like corroded metal. The guy took out a bottle from somewhere inside his coat, and uncapped it, and took a swig. He was missing a few teeth in the front. "I like to ride it now and then. Scope out what's going on."

"Huh."

"Here's a history lesson," the man said. "People used to come to River City because it was where they could be the way they are without attracting much attention. Then the hospital opened. Now they come here to get themselves cut up and put back together in the shape of ordinary people." He tipped the bottle in Jesse's direction; Jesse shook his head. "Is that what you're here for, girl? To get yourself cut up and sewn into something that makes sense?"

Jesse looked around to see if anyone else had heard. No one else appeared to be listening at all. The mother with the twin girls was checking her phone, over and over again, while the twin girls slept tangled in each other's arms. The middle-aged couple was petting their increasingly nervous dog. He'd sometimes had this happen before, people mistaking him for a girl. He didn't like how happy it made him.

"I don't know what you're talking about," he said to the old man.

"I don't have time for your feelings," the man said. "I got on here to warn you about something."

Jesse felt a prickle, like he might have to sneeze, or like he might be about to explode. And something else, too. The thrill of impending adventure.

"Tell me," Jesse said.

The man looked somber, like he was about to say something. And then he twitched, and his expression buckled. "Oh, shit," he said, groaning. His voice changed, and so did his demeanor, and all at once he looked stupid, helpless. He looked down at the bottle in his hand. "Fuck," he said, and took a big gulp of it, spilling some of it into his beard. Jesse had thought earlier that it was all white, but now he saw it was streaked through with red. The big man swallowed, wiped the back of his mouth with one hand, and tried to focus his one good eye on Jesse.

"I have a hard time," the old man said. "I have a hard time staying present."

Ah, okay. This was the kind of guy who always tried to talk to Jesse. It was something about his open face, he guessed. He had one of those faces that said, *Please, tell me everything bad that's ever happened to you.*

Jesse sighed. "It's okay," he said. "You called me a girl. How did you know?"

"I said that?" Jesse started to give up, but the man chewed on a fingernail. "No, I wouldn't call you *a* girl. I would've said *the* girl."

"What's that mean?"

"Ugh." The old man clutched his head. "Fuck. Okay. Important question. What time are we upon?"

"What?"

"Have y'all killed the monster already?"

"What monster?"

"How about the Hero? Have you met him?"

"Uh . . . no? I don't think so?"

"Do you know you're the girl?"

"You just told me."

"Jesus." The man shut his eyes, and took a big sniff, like he was trying to swallow a booger. He popped his eyes open and the milky one rolled around in his head. "You got anything I could eat? That helps."

"You've got some hard candies."

"Right on." The man dug around in his own pocket. "Huh, maybe I don't have them yet . . ."

"River City ahoy," the bus driver called out.

Jesse looked away from the old man, and up through the bus's bulging windshield. They must have been slowly climbing, because now they were cresting a hill, and below them, spread out, was a great and winding river.

It was called the Otiotan, he knew from the forums. They'd placed the river's origins somewhere in Virginia, or Tennessee, or Kentucky, but no one could say where it met the ocean. It lay across a valley, wider than any river he'd ever seen, like an unknown Mississippi. And in the middle of it was the island, shaped like a great teardrop, low at the upstream end, with a great hill on the downstream side. Gleaming with great silver buildings, and covered in trees. Jesse had never imagined a city could be so green.

"Wow," the old man across from him said.

"I thought you said you'd been there before."

"What are you talking about?" the man said. He glanced over

at Jesse, and smiled, showing a mouthful of perfect teeth. Jesse blinked, not sure what he was seeing, or what he had seen before. "You going there, too? Maybe we can seek our fortunes together."

"Uh," Jesse said. "Look, man, I—"

"Hey, don't worry about it," the man said. "More fortune for me." He propped his arms behind his head, flipped his hat down over his face, and appeared, to Jesse, to be getting ready for a quick nap.

Jesse studied the man. Even with his face covered, there really was something familiar about him that was hard to place. Something about his large square frame, the elasticity of his smile, even his weird way of talking, reminded Jesse of someone he'd known before, a long time ago. Or maybe it was just because they'd both called Jesse a girl without meaning it as an insult.

But Jesse lost the thread of that thought as the bus descended the hill and hit the bridge that led to the city. The wheels switched from a low rumble to a sharp staccato. The wind rushing through the metal bridge sounded almost like a harmonica, and below them in the river was a smaller island with a ruined castle on it, and Jesse lost himself in imagining being down among those rocks. And then, before he could breathe in to will it away, he felt that prickle again, and then a sharp *pop*.

It hurt, like having all your joints dislocated and jammed back in at new angles, like growing new organs, like a total bodyectomy, and the accompanying dizziness as his inner ear tried to compensate and the cramps, good god, the cramps. And Jesse sat there stunned. She knew without looking exactly what had happened to her, even though it was impossible, or at the very least, unlikely.

The old man in the seat glanced over at her. "Huh," he said. "I thought so."

Jesse widened her eyes at him. "Don't say anything," she hissed.

"I'll be quiet," the old man said. "But will you?"

They'd crossed the bridge, and were suddenly on a long boulevard with low old buildings on one side, and on the other, towering new ones. The bus was slowing. The old man jerked a thumb at the bus driver.

"He's gonna sell you to the hospital if you stay on this bus," he said, not bothering to keep his voice low. "They'd pay great for someone like you."

The bus driver turned in his chair as the bus stopped for a light. "Who said that?"

The old man winked his blind eye at Jesse. "Go find the baker's on God Street. Tell Astrid I say hello."

"Astrid," Jesse repeated.

"Yup. Watch your back."

The bus driver put on the hazard lights, and stood up. "Huh," the driver said, looking at Jesse. "Good tip, old man."

The old man stood up and blocked the bus driver's path. "Run," he said. And Jesse snatched up her backpack and ran for the back of the bus.

"Stop that kid!" the bus driver yelled. Stunned passengers stared, doing nothing, as Jesse sprinted past them. She ran for the back of the bus, found the emergency exit door, and flung it open. An alarm went off. Behind her, she saw the driver shove the old man out of the way. And she leaped.

Jesse had always been good at thinking on her feet, but now she was off of them, and careening toward the hood of an old Cadillac. She bent her knees, like they learned in track doing the high jump, and let them buckle under her as she rolled off the hood backward and hit the ground. It hurt, but adrenaline had her up in a second, backpack still on, sweatshirt hood flapping as she ducked through the next lane of traffic. Stunned, she noticed it was mostly bicycles and mopeds that flew around her, riders screaming at her, as she flung herself at the far sidewalk, where she scrambled away into a park on the far side. She glanced back just long enough to see the driver hanging out of the back door of the bus, yelling at her to get back there.

Jesse had always liked running. She wasn't the fastest in track, but she showed up and ran and liked the feeling of being alone, just her and her feet and the wind.

As she sprinted away, she thought briefly that this was the first time in her life she'd run quite like this. Running into the unknown, with no idea what was on the other side to catch her.

TWO

When Astrid closed up the bakery that afternoon, she stepped out the back door and found Nathan waiting for her. He was upright, his legs stiff under him, in the alley behind the shop. He had an urgent look about him. It was going to be one of those days, then.

"I saw her," he said.

Astrid pursed her lips. "Saw who?" she asked.

He sighed in exasperation. "You know who," he said. "The Maiden."

"Where is she, then?"

He looked around. "Lost her."

Astrid resisted the urge to roll her eyes. She reminded herself that he was doing his best. It was not a great best, but she could hardly blame him.

"Are you sure it was her?" she asked. "Could it have been some-one else?"

"Well, it *was* a boy," he said.

She stepped up to him and gave him a once-over. He was look-ing the worse for wear, one hand dangling limp and heavy from his shoulder. She reassured herself that he wouldn't stay that way. The next time she saw him, he'd be as young as he was the day she met him, most likely.

"I have an errand to run," she said.

"I'm serious," he called after her. "He's here. It's time!"

"Then hurry it along!" she called over her shoulder. "If you find him, bring him straight to me."

She kept walking, hoping she'd make it to her stop in time to catch the last bus bound downtown. But when she got there, it had already left, or maybe it wasn't running today—she could never master this new bus schedule, and she was sure that was on purpose; the hospital had bought out the bus lines, and they didn't run regularly between the Old and New cities the way they used to. Now she'd have to hoof it.

Long walks weren't good for her foot. It had never quite healed right, two bones fusing. If this were the old days, she'd break it and reset it with magic. Her friend Didi, whose nephew was a hospital orderly, had suggested that she go to their free clinic and see if they could arrange a surgery. But the idea of going downtown to those horrible white towers growing like mushrooms out of her landscape filled her with unspeakable dread. They might be willing to help out an old lady, and maybe take her picture for an advertisement, but they killed people down there. She wanted nothing to do with them.

She managed to hitch a ride; Astrid Epps standing on the side of the road with her thumb out was a compelling sight. The cop who picked her up was, of course, Pete McNair. He made his partner, a younger man, climb into the back to let her sit in the front. She appreciated it. Pete was a bully, but he respected witches, and her in particular.

"How's your mother doing, Pete?" Astrid asked.

"She's hanging in there," Pete said, his eyes fixed on the road in front of him. "I'll tell her you asked after her."

"Hanging in there doesn't sound so good," Astrid said. "She still living on Pine?"

"Yes, ma'am."

"I'll talk to Didi and have her swing by with some Saint John's wort."

"'Preciate it."

"It's no trouble," Astrid said. "Who's this young friend of yours?"

"That's Officer Mannering," Pete said. "He's a good kid. Right, Matthew?"

Matthew looked up from the back seat. He was a lanky white boy with soft eyes. He wasn't from around here, Astrid realized, because if he were, she'd know that last name. She'd be able to place him in a genealogy, name his grandparents, extrapolate his likely address based on how much money his father made and how protective his mother was. It was uncanny to her, sometimes, to meet people from the New City. Like the feeling when you'd just had a tooth capped, and it didn't yet feel like a part of your mouth.

"You must have come here for college," Astrid said. "What'd you study?"

He looked unnerved by the question. "Uh, biology," he said. That was the other thing. They were so cagey, these out-of-towners, when she asked them questions. As though they didn't understand that she was trying to place them, figure out how they fit into her cosmology, so that she could be more useful to them. Didn't he understand that now that she knew that, she knew also that he'd dropped out of school to join the police? That meant that either his grades were bad or he'd run out of money. A few more questions and she'd be able to set him up on dates, refer him to an appropriate witch for services, bake him a cake for his birthday. He didn't know what his suspicion was cheating him out of.

"Astrid's the mayor," McNair said. "She just likes to know who all her constituents are."

"Thank you, Pete," Astrid said. The boy looked even more confused, though, so she added, "Not a real mayor. People just call me that because I'm in everybody's business."

The boy relaxed. "Oh. Okay," he said. "My mom's like that back home."

"Where's back home for you?" Astrid said. "If you don't mind my asking."

"Kansas," he said.

She nodded. "That's a long way to travel."

"I really wanted to go to school here," Matthew said. "It was the best program."

Probably money, then, or something else beyond his control, had made him leave. Maybe he was born under the star of scattering, or melancholy. Astrid made a note of that. As long as she was having Didi brew some Saint John's wort.

"Where are you getting out?" Pete asked.

"If you can just drop me at the Boulevard, that's fine."

They let her off where God Street intersected with the Boulevard of Bells. That was a fine enough walk. She had to let Matthew out of the back of the cop car, and he got back into the passenger's seat with just a little bit of attitude she didn't like. She'd want to watch him. He had a lot of authority for someone who didn't know the city. She hoped Pete wouldn't get him into any trouble. Pete was fine by himself, but bad news when he had someone egging him on. She'd been relieved when he and Kyle had gone their separate ways.

She was definitely late as she headed for the bridge that led off the island and toward places she didn't particularly care about. The underside of the bridge was her aim. She veered off the sidewalk and onto the dirt track that led to a steep incline. The city had sunk logs into the side of the slope with rebar to make a kind of rough staircase, but it was often half-covered with eroded dirt, and it took all her concentration to pick her way down it. When she reached the bottom and finally looked around, she realized that the boy she was waiting to meet was already there. And when she focused on him, she gasped in spite of herself.

It was him. She almost couldn't believe it.

He was a young light-skinned Black man, as spectacularly tall as young Nathan had been, and with that auburn hair, those freckles, that square jaw, he could be no other man's son. But he looked like Marla, too: a little chubby, and with deep, serious-looking eyes behind smudged, wire-rimmed glasses. He wore a blue Oxford shirt that strained across his broad shoulders, and khakis that had red dirt on one leg. He must have slid, coming down the slope. He stood hunched in his clothes like he was embarrassed about something. She felt the bottom drop out of her life.

"Hi," the boy said. "Are you okay?"

Astrid squinted. "Sorry," she said. "You reminded me of someone."

He gave a single, bitter *hah*. "I haven't heard that one before."

She put her hand out. "I'm Astrid," she said.

He shook it. "David."

So whoever had taken him had kept his name. He looked down and scuffed one of his boat shoes into the dirt. He was so New City, she thought. Amazing that he could be born here and still look so out of place.

She thought maybe she should give him the book for free. But no, if things were starting back up again, she needed to buy herself some time to think about how she was going to react—she couldn't have him getting suspicious. So she said, "Do you have the money?"

He pulled out a wad of cash from his pocket, held together with a binder clip. She undid the clip and riffled the money with her thumb before sticking it into her dress pocket. She took the book, wrapped in brown paper, from her bag, and passed it over to him.

He was the Hero. He had to be. He was the son of the last Hero and the city's king, taken from his home, and he'd found his way back. He fit into the slot like a coin. And look at him. Tall, powerful, the spitting image of his mother and father. He'd look good in the crown of freshwater pearls that was gathering dust in the museum downtown. She tried to keep the pride off her face, the triumph of knowing that he was alive because of what she had done.

"All right," she said. "Good luck with it. I'll see you soon."

"Wait," he said. "Who are you, really?"

"Nobody important," she said. "And if anyone asks, you didn't get that book from me."

Her foot sent shooting pains up through her calf as she climbed back up the steep slope. But she ignored it. A part of her was worried. But a part of her was filled with boundless joy.

If it was starting up again, and David was going to be the Hero, maybe things could be different this time. After all, they'd nearly won last time, would have if Marla hadn't—well. Astrid could help him. Especially, she thought, if they had magic to work with.

She stuck out her thumb again and caught a bike cab belonging to Laurie, whose mother was prone to migraines. As the wheels jostled along the cobbles, she thought about finding a moment to talk to David again. But not now. She needed to get home, and not be too late. If the girls found out she'd sold a book to a university student, they'd have opinions. And of course, they couldn't know about David.

She'd have to do it just right. The cycle could be capricious, latch on to any old nobody. Like King Frank, who'd only been the Hero because, on Carnival Night, he happened to smash the right guy over the head with a beer bottle. A terrible choice, but he'd right-place-right-timed his way into history. Astrid would have to be absolutely sure she set David up to win. It was the least she could do. For him, for magic, for Nathan, mad and wandering. Maybe with David's help, she could get him back.

She had Laurie drop her off outside her shop—if anyone was early to her house, she didn't want them asking questions about where she'd come from. As she turned from waving goodbye, she spotted Nathan a little bit down the street. He was waving his arm at some white boy in a sweatshirt. And then he looked up and caught her eye and mouthed obviously. *Found him.*

Any other day, Astrid would have waved him off. But today she'd seen David. Today was a day for coincidences—and coincidences, as every witch knew, were the harbingers of fate.

THREE

Watching the woman limp back up the slope, David felt a twinge of buyer's remorse—that book had been most of his biweekly stipend. But he had it now. He wanted to tear the wax paper wrapping open like a Christmas present, but he forced himself to put it into his backpack. He slung the pack over his shoulder and trudged up the hill to follow the Boulevard of Bells back into town.

David liked walking, especially in the city, where there was so much to see. But he hated the stares. All around he felt eyes on him, especially now with his shoes and pants stained red with mud from tripping and sliding down the hill under the overpass. People on foot got out of the way to let him by, something he'd never really gotten used to. He tried not to see them seeing him, to just relax and enjoy the walk. At the next intersection, he admired the scenery while he waited for the light to change.

From the Boulevard, it was easy to see the line drawn down the middle of the city. To his left were the packed little neighborhoods of cramped brick-paved streets and scrawny row houses, all buried under a canopy of old-growth trees that threatened to knock through roofs and sidewalks. On the right side were the clean stone and glass buildings of the New City, and in the middle distance, the gleaming steel towers of the University Hospital. Once, downtown had been mostly empty, a low swamp between the two hills of the island. David hadn't been here when the university moved in ten years ago, buying up all that cheap land and building their own whole city: draining the lowland, reinforcing the ground with concrete and steel bulwarks, raising the five white towers of the University Hospital Research Complex. David liked seeing those towers from out here; their windows gleamed in the afternoon sun.

As the light changed in his favor, David started crossing. A police car slid across traffic and pulled onto the shoulder near him. The car flashed its lights, the siren chirping at him. David went back to the sidewalk and stood there, arms at his sides, waiting. Dread materialized in his stomach. The window rolled down, and the officer beckoned him closer. David shrugged off his backpack and waited with his hands half-raised.

The officer driving the car was an older white guy. His partner was younger, and looked uncomfortable, like he knew this was weird. That didn't relax David much.

"Why'd you take your pack off, son?" said the officer behind the wheel.

"I didn't want you to think I was going to take anything out of it."

"Now, why would we think that? You got something in there?"

"No, sir. Nothing at all."

"Don't look like nothing. Where've you been?"

David glanced down and saw that the backs of his pant legs were covered in red dirt, from where he'd slid. Dammit. "I went for a walk."

"Looks more like you went for a fall." The man chuckled to himself.

David made eye contact with the younger guy, who said, "Were you down by the river just now?"

"I was way above it," David said.

"What were you doing there?" asked the older cop.

David tried to wipe the old lady out of his mind and off his face. "Just walking, sir."

The driver nodded, and the young cop got out. He was younger than David had expected. "Can I see some ID?"

David stared straight ahead. "My wallet's in the backpack."

"You mind if I look through it real quick?"

"Go ahead."

David stood there trying to remember what normal people did with their hands, as though there was a normal-person way to stand around while someone rooted through your stuff. The officer rummaging through his bag glanced over at David after a moment, but seemed to have a hard time meeting his eyes. He found David's wallet and held up his university ID card. The picture was from a few years ago, featuring David halfway to an Afro in a T-shirt with an anime character on it. David winced.

"David . . . Blank?"

"Yep, that's me."

"Like the magician?"

David winced. "That's David Blaine."

"What's he got in the bag?" called the officer in the car.

"Notebooks," the guy called, dropping ID and wallet back into the pack. "You go to school at URC right? I think I've seen you around."

"I'm a professor," David said. It wasn't strictly true, but he did lecture. He was going to be late for that now, in fact. He'd built in so much extra time, and then the woman had been late, and now this.

The guy rummaging through his stuff straightened up, although David noticed he didn't zip the bag back up. He smiled a little, but he still didn't meet David's eyes. "Good for you, man," he said, reaching up to give David's arm a congratulatory pat. David tried not to flinch.

The young guy got back into the car. The driver sneered at David. "Have a nice day, *professor*," he said.

The car pulled off and ran a red light, cars braking and honking. David went back to his backpack. He thought about sitting down on the curb for a minute to catch his breath, but there was no time for rest. If he missed his first class of the semester he'd be— well. Better not to think about it.

He stumbled past outlying school buildings, restaurants with flashing signs, movie theaters and bars and the newer, more upscale clothing stores, until he came to the cluster of towers with its cul-de-sac buzzing with traffic. He waited at the light and then crossed the street and stepped through the gleaming silver doors of Tower 4, where he had his lab. The doors slid open, revealing the high atrium of the first floor.

The towers were a city unto themselves. Outside their walls they had spawned a whole network of connective tissue: outbuildings, library annexes, banks, restaurants—but standing inside, it was difficult to see why you'd ever need to leave the towers. After all, they held everything their students might need, and there were rumors that some faculty hadn't left the complex since they'd signed their contracts. A sign directed him up the escalators to the left to the restaurants that lined the terminal, or up the escalators to the right for shopping. He ignored both of these and went to the elevator. He almost always ate at Coffee and Pie, the charmingly unpretentious fake diner on the eighth floor. He liked the ambiance, even if the food tasted exactly like the same Cisco stuff they had on every other floor. He wished he had time to grab a coffee before work—dealing with the cops had left him feeling impossibly tired. He got into the elevator, surprisingly small for such a large building, and felt it whoosh toward his floor.

The elevator discharged him, and he strode across the narrow skybridge to the next building. His lecture was in one of the multistory amphitheater lecture rooms that took up the eighth through twelfth floors of the Sciences Building. He glanced in at the operating theater on his way past. The room was packed to the gills. He couldn't see the operating table from up here at the balcony door, but on the two-story screen they were playing a live feed of it. It was some kind of frog-looking creature, about a foot long, with a bulbous body and skinny legs. The internal physiology didn't look familiar from any frog species he'd seen, and in fact it looked closer to . . . nope. He kept walking. No time to dwell on that.

The physics lecture hall was humming from the outside with chatter. He checked the clock overhead: five minutes late, not his finest hour. He pushed open the double doors with both hands and strode down the ramp toward the stage at the front of the room, through masses of students talking and playing with their devices—in this case, portable tape players and radios and old Gameboys cribbed from yard sales and parents' basements. The island's theta radiation made it impossible to use almost all the devices college students normally loved, cell phones and netbooks, anything that relied on a wireless connection. He'd thought, when he'd come here, that he would miss the internet. But the chance to study here was absolutely worth it. Plus, the school had its own internal net, and people constantly uploaded videos and games to it on the sly, so it wasn't like River City was completely devoid of fun—it was just on a six-month lag.

He stepped up to the podium and shuffled his papers to the sound of bodies shifting in chairs and backpacks zipping.

"Good evening," he said.

"Good evening," some of them mumbled back. Others started giggling. Oh yes, that's exactly what he needed today. That moment of realization that the man running late with his hair a mess and red dirt stains on his pants, the funny-looking giant, *that's* the professor. He forgot, sometimes, that what they saw when they looked at him was not the hotshot youngest member of the school's most competitive department, who had revolutionized the field by realizing that theta radiation was—no, they saw the kid they'd beat up in middle school, before he'd gotten too big for them to risk it. Assholes.

Don't show any fear, he reminded himself, as he mechanically read through the syllabus and attendance policies. He thought about his adviser's only advice after his disastrous first class last spring: *Don't give those little bastards an inch.*

"This is Physics 205, Introduction to the Thetic Principle," he said, realizing he was talking too quietly again. He'd learned to speak softly from his shy yuppie adoptive parents, and now it had turned into a liability. "If you're—" A few people started shuffling out the back, yelling "sorry" and "wrong room." He sighed, and waited quietly before continuing, trying to fill his lungs and project into the back corners of the room. "This class will build on Physics 101, helping you apply the concepts you learned there specifically to the study of theta radiation. Who can tell me what that is?"

"It's the reason my cell phone doesn't work!" someone yelled from the back.

David nodded. "Yes, that's true. Theta radiation is highly disruptive to other wavelengths, because it produces effects that replicate quantum mechanics on a macro, rather than subatomic, scale. Which means that we can get effects like this."

He'd had Facilities wheel in the device earlier. The Theta Projector looked like a large flashlight, he supposed, mounted on the TR-C (Series IV, his rebuild) and projecting onto a slab of rock they'd put on wheels for ease of transport. The granite-like rock that lined the underside of the island had proven to be the only substance that effectively dissipated the particles once they'd been concentrated.

"In this class, we will be frequently doing live demonstrations involving radiation," David said. "If you don't have a waiver on file, I'm supposed to ask you to leave now and not come back until you fill one out. But unofficially, I promise you that as long as I'm not melting into the floor, you're safe. We good?"

Scattered laughter from the tiered seating. Good, he thought. Loosen them up a little.

He pointed the beam of the projector toward the slab of rock.

"This device gathers the ambient theta radiation within the

room by creating a negative electrical charge," he said. "After that, it channels it into a beam, which the stone will dissipate. We'll use the beam to produce some interesting effects. You may smell ozone; this is perfectly normal."

He switched the device on.

A beam of wan blue light floated into existence. It was under-concentrated. It was always under-concentrated; they wouldn't be able to do any real bending of physics until they could distill it more. That woman under the bridge today had been surrounded by a darker, more saturated blue than this. Hell, the first "witch" he'd seen, the old lady at the bootleg DVD stand downtown, had been able to produce a deeper blue than they'd gotten with months of rebuilding the projector. He was going to figure out what they were doing at home that outdid a million-dollar invention if it killed him.

But later, he thought. *Focus.*

"This beam may look like ordinary light," David said to his class, "but it's . . . How can I say this best? It's energy and matter simultaneously. It has mass and can affect other objects." He picked a penny out of his pocket. "For example."

He gently tossed the penny at the beam of light. It bounced off and skidded away across the floor.

"Its surface tension resists abrupt force while being fairly tolerant of force applied over time." He threw a pencil at it; it ricocheted off and bounced into a nearby wall, where it embedded itself point-first in the acoustic paneling. That got a few audible gasps. Then, he held up his hand. The room went silent.

"Watch."

He lowered his hand slowly, pushing it down into the beam of light. He felt a slight resistance at its surface, and then it broke and admitted his hand. He held it there, while the students in the room stared at him silently. It tingled a little. It felt . . . very right.

"You all took Introduction to Physics," he said. "So when I say that this is a shorter wavelength than gamma radiation, you'll understand that I should have no hand right now." He pulled his hand out slowly, regretting that he had to let go of the light. He held his hand up. "And yet, here it is . . . Why?"

He reached over and switched off the beam. He felt an audible sigh of relief run through the room.

"The study of theta radiation is the most pressing question currently in the field of physics," he said. "And URC is the only university doing research into it. This class is math-intensive, it is mind-bending, and it has the lowest pass rate of any course offered at this university. But if you survive it, you will be qualified to participate in the most important scientific problem of your generation."

One of them, down near the front, raised a hand. A girl with big plastic glasses. He called on her. "Yes?"

"Why can't you guys make a class that people can pass?" she asked. "If it's that important."

There was a murmur. The girl sitting next to her, a skinny girl with long blond hair, hit her and looked annoyed. But David was already sinking. He'd only lectured once before, last semester. That time the problem had been that he was too shy and they'd been bored. Now he felt the roots of outright rebellion spreading through the room. He felt panicky; he wasn't sure if he knew the answer—no, that wasn't a choice. He was a lecturer; if he couldn't lecture, he'd be out of a job. He stood up straight, and turned to the girl.

"The material is inherently difficult," he said, "and thetic principle is a new field of study. I'm not a teacher, I'm a physicist who is trying to train other physicists in the use of a highly unstable particle. We have no room here for slackers. I'm sorry, but this is how it works."

He pushed his glasses up his nose and focused on the girl. She sat near the front. She looked Old City: You could always tell them by their faded clothes, patched and embroidered, from a mixture of eras. She reminded him of the woman from earlier today, Astrid. For a moment, he wondered if she was about to show that blue corona. But then she looked down and away, picking at her fingernail, and the feeling passed. He felt a little surge of victory. The rest of the class had shut up, too. Good. They understood his explanation. He was tired, though. He glanced at his lesson plan and felt a surge of helplessness. It could wait, he decided. He'd taken enough shit today.

"Now," he said. "There are copies of the syllabus and the reading list at the print shop down on the third floor, and textbooks under my name available at the bookstore. I'll see you all again on Thursday. If you have a minute tonight, check out the unknown life form dissection in operating theater two. It's important to be cross-disciplinary."

They sat there for a moment longer, staring at him in surprise.

"Go on," he said.

They filed out. The girl with the big glasses was one of the first out the door. He was watching her run away from him, which was why it surprised him when he realized there was one last person in the lecture hall. The girl with the long blond braid, the one who had looked so pissed at her friend.

"Uh, hi there," she said. She was standing up. She was approaching the lectern. She looked a little older than some of the other students, maybe older than him. She was dressed like Old City, too, in patched coveralls rolled up at the elbows and knees, spattered with ink. "I'm sorry about Nita. She's not exactly polite."

"If you're friends with her, please tell her I'm not kicking her out," David said. "I just want her to be sure she's serious."

"We're both really serious," the girl said. "I'm Jackie."

"Nice to meet you," David said.

"I had a question," Jackie said. "So it looks like there's just . . . not much of this theta radiation."

Huh. That was a strange way to put it, but David knew what she meant. They'd had such a hard time concentrating a beam of it. The others in the department seemed, to David, inordinately pleased with what they'd accomplished, but to David it looked wrong somehow. Not that he had anything empirical to tell them about that.

"So, like, what can you do with it?" Jackie asked. "Or, what do you do with it?"

"Well," David said. "It can pass directly through matter, so all kinds of things. Even at the fairly limited concentration we have here, we think we could design a really ingenious surgical laser."

"Surgical laser," she said to herself, as though trying it out.

"Sure. There's also telecommunications applications, especially once we can isolate an isotope. Uh. At higher concentrations it would revolutionize the construction industry, but we're not there yet."

"But you could use it to, like, pass through someone's body and operate just on one part of them?"

"Well, not yet. But soon."

"At this . . . concentration?"

"Yeah. We just haven't designed the equipment. But the principle is completely sound."

"Wow," she said. She leaned forward, still holding her books close to her chest. "That's really cool."

"I'm glad you're excited," David said. "I'll . . . see you Thursday, then."

She gave him a brilliant smile and tossed her hair a little bit. "Yeah. Thanks, teach."

And then she was stepping lightly up the aisle. Once she'd cleared the door, he sighed. He never really liked talking to students one-on-one, especially when they were older than him. But this girl had made him particularly uneasy, although he couldn't really say why.

Alone in the lecture hall, David realized his hands were shaking. He felt like he'd been running ever since he'd gotten stopped by the cops. He took a deep breath, fighting to get his hands back under his control. He packed up his binder of course documents and his instructor copy of the textbook. He was probably just hungry, he told himself. He'd grab something. And maybe some more coffee; he had the sense he was going to be up late.

He couldn't stop thinking about that girl Nita as he made the trek upstairs. She'd looked at him like he was some kind of monster, but not in the usual way. It had been what he'd said.

But what had he even said? That the class was going to be hard? She was just thin-skinned, he told himself. She'd drop out soon enough, or she'd learn. To survive in this place, you had to be able to accept that not everyone was going to make it. He had enough problems of his own without worrying about her.

On the way to the faux diner on the eighth floor, he passed back by the window of the operating theater. They were draping the creature's body with a sheet, and covered up like that, for a moment it looked to him like a tiny human. He shuddered, and kept walking. But the sight stayed with him as he drank a mug of watery coffee and ate a slice of pie, his forearms sticking slightly to the Formica tabletop at the booth overlooking the city. The sunset was staining pink the gathering clouds. He couldn't finish the pie, his throat curdling with disgust. It made him think of that old joke about science that starts: If it squirms, it's biology.

Of course, the joke ended: If it doesn't work, it's physics.

Well, that part just wasn't true. Or at least, it wouldn't be when he was done.

FOUR

Jesse ran.

The twinge came again, and she didn't try to breathe through it; she let it take her, popping back into a more familiar shape, arms and legs extending. Jesse stumbled, caught himself, kept going. He was glad for the longer stride: People kept staring at him as he flew by, and he was sure at this point the only thing between him and a lot of trouble was his own forward momentum. He flew for a long time, down streets of redbrick houses, down alleys lined with broken-down cars and bicycles chained to telephone poles, until his lungs burned hard enough that he stopped, folded in half, braced his hands on his shins, and tried to remember how to breathe. He sank down against a garden wall, his vision red around the edges, narrowing until he thought he'd lose it entirely.

When he could draw a clean breath again, he realized that he didn't know where he was. When he'd been running, he'd had no thoughts other than escape. Now others crowded in: He was alone. He had no money. He had nowhere to sleep tonight.

In a panic, he fumbled in his pack, past the sandwiches and the rolled-up socks and underwear, and pulled out the postcard. He sat down with it and read it again, like he did whenever he knew he was alone and needed to calm down.

Dear Jessie (sp?),

    I'm not here, I'm in North Carolina. They said I can't write to you. This is the only postcard I have, and I've had it since I was a baby. When you grow up, meet me here. If I get here first, I'll wait for you.

[a few words, scribbled out so darkly they were unreadable]

You're my best friend.
David

Jesse took a deep, shuddering breath. And then another. Okay. He tucked the postcard into his backpack. Okay. He could do this. He'd had worse.

He started limping toward the mouth of the alley, and emerged onto a street lined in old oak trees. At the end of the block, he could see a row of shops. Maybe one of them had a HELP WANTED sign. Or a dumpster out back where people would throw away food at the end of the night. He was optimistic. He could do this. Probably.

And then, he remembered what the old man on the bus had said. Bakery. God Street. Astrid.

He asked the first person he saw the way to God Street, and they pointed. Jesse stumbled down an increasingly cracked and tangled street, where vines spread from the backs of abandoned carriage houses and poured over the cobbles to fill every hole. The air was thick with the smell of wild honeysuckle. He'd never seen a place more beautiful than this, and the long, slow afternoon seemed like the perfect time to view it. Finally, the alley ended and he was spat out onto a small city street that had an old signpost on it, the kind you saw at crossroads in movies about Ancient Rome. GOD STREET MARKET, said an arrow pointing to his left.

So he went left, following a brick sidewalk that had seen better days. The trees here were encroaching on the block, the buildings. The road itself bulged and split under the pressure of the roots. Overhead, late summer cicadas buzzed. Eventually he came out onto a street lined with small shops, many of which were single story on the front level and backed onto two-story squarish buildings. Jesse had never seen buildings like these before, sort of hunchbacked.

He kept walking, coming to a plaza ringed with mostly abandoned shops. In the middle was a dead fountain—an empty basin with a slab of rough river rock in the middle of it, but no water. Kind of ugly, actually.

Most of the shops here looked empty. He did spot a bakery, but the sign in the window said SOLD OUT—GONE HOME. So he kept walking past papered-over windows, yellow newspapers on the inside and flyers on the outside. There were signs for concerts, covert-looking advertisements for things Jesse couldn't quite parse (CRYSTAL ELIXIR!), and pasted over top of these layers, large official-looking posters that showed a terrified white woman calling someone on a pay phone while in the background two Black men shook hands. That poster said IF YOU SEE SOMETHING, SAY SOMETHING, and CALL RCPD, with a phone number. Jesse passed a few more abandoned buildings, and on one of them, the IF YOU SEE SOMETHING posters had been torn off, leaving only IF NG at the far corners. In the space where it had been, someone had stuck up a large brown paper poster printed with four words in solid black type that said

RISE
UP
OLD
CITY

And that was it.

Jesse frowned at that one. He was irritated, because his mind collected words, and the rhythm and pattern of these words had already seeped into his head, become imprinted in his skull. He looked at it from different angles. It meant something to someone. He could feel that in his bones, that this message, to the right person, said everything. It felt like someone talking too softly to quite hear.

With that noise in his ears, it took Jesse a minute to realize that someone was behind him.

It was the man from the bus. He was bigger standing up; huge, really, but hunched over like his back hurt him. Jesse found himself terrified that the man had followed him, but at the same time, that little voice in his head, the one that talked about adventures, was whispering *mad prophet*. The man opened his mouth, and Jesse squinted. His front teeth were broken after all. What was going on? If this was a magic trick, what was the point of it?

"Hey, man, are you okay?" Jesse said. "Do you need a doctor?"

The man's milky eye had been wandering away. Now it snapped back to focus on Jesse.

"Oh, it's you," the man said. Something in his voice had changed. He sounded lucid, polite. "Listen, girl. We don't have a lot of time."

Jesse nodded. He felt as though he were in a dream. Some part of him had always known that this would happen. That he would come to the city and find his destiny.

"All right," Jesse said. "Can you tell me what happened to me on the bus? I've—"

The man ignored him. "I bet you think you know why they call this place River City," he said.

Jesse played along. "I guess . . . because of the Otiotan River?"

"No!" the man pointed a triumphant yellowed fingernail at Jesse's chest. "You'd think that! But this place is named for its secret river. You can't see it because it flows between the stones deep under the earth. You cannot see it. You cannot hear it. But it flows, although not with water. And not as much as it once did." He hesitated, a gleam in his eye. "Can you feel it, girl?"

Jesse closed his eyes and took a breath. He didn't feel anything.

"Yes," he said.

The man rolled his eyes. "Liar," he said, but he sounded more disappointed than angry. "Don't dismiss me. You'll have to learn to feel it if you're going to stop the wheel."

Jesse nodded. "Okay," he said. "How do I do that?"

The man opened his mouth—and then let out a burp that stank of tooth rot. After it was over, he wiped his mouth and blinked.

His remaining eye began to wander back off track, rolling independently in his head.

"Hey!"

Jesse and the man turned. Jesse felt both relieved and embarrassed. A woman stood there, hands on her hips, frowning at them.

"Astrid," the man said. "This is the girl. Take care of her."

The woman he called Astrid was compact and brown skinned, with graying curly hair tied up on her head in a loop of purple ribbon and a large-eyed, narrow-chinned face. And Jesse saw her give the man a little terse nod—just a flick of her sharp chin, while her eyes darted around the street, as though looking to see if anyone was watching.

"That's a boy, you idiot," she said. "You're going crazy again."

"But, Astrid."

"Stop scaring people," she said. "Boy, get away from him. He's got lice."

Jesse jumped to obey the woman but as he passed the old man, he felt a hand grab his hood from behind.

"Listen," the man whispered. "Don't make the same mistakes we made."

"Get out of here," Astrid said, and to Jesse's surprise she poked at the old man with one bony finger. It wasn't hard, but that great man flinched and stepped back. He slunk off down the street, occasionally looking back at them, and then disappeared around a corner.

"Who was that?" Jesse asked when he had gone.

"Just an old man," said Astrid. Up close he could see that her mouth was bracketed in deep lines. "Are you all right?"

"I'm fine," Jesse said. "How about you?"

She looked startled by the question. She shrugged. "Fine as I'll ever be," she said. "Come in for a minute. Let him forget about you."

"Is he dangerous?"

"Usually harmless," she said. "But sometimes he gets ideas." She stuck out a hand. "I'm Miss Astrid. You can call me Miss Astrid."

"Jesse Archer," Jesse said.

"Where do you live?"

"Um, I don't—I just got here?"

"Hm." She said it with a little upward flick of her nose, like she didn't quite want to say she'd caught him with his pants down. "Well, come in, then, Jesse Archer."

She went into the shop, holding the door for just a second to let him catch it. He slipped in after her and was blinded by the sudden darkness. Behind him he heard a bell ring, and he was engulfed by the smell.

It was a lot of smells, actually. There was vanilla, to be sure, and a faint lemoniness, and rosemary, and maybe garlic. But what occupied his nose the most were the smells he couldn't place, a whole palette of glimmers and hints of things he'd never sniffed out before. But the shop was just about empty—empty shelves, empty display case. A cash register. It looked like a store that had been entirely cleaned out. Did it sell smells?

"What kind of store is this?" Jesse asked.

"It's a bakery," Astrid said.

"Then where's all the . . . baked stuff?"

"Sold out. You must be new in town. Who's your grandma?"

"No grandma," Jesse said. "Just me."

She frowned. "Shouldn't be here, then," she said.

He bristled. "Look, you invited me in."

She looked taken aback, as though it hadn't occurred to her that he might take it that way. "I meant it seemed unusual. Young people usually don't come here on their own."

"Oh." He couldn't shake the feeling that she was lying to him. That there was something else behind her surprise. But he let it drop. "Well, I came here to go to the hospital," he said. "But I got . . . lost."

"They don't let anyone get lost. You must've made a run for it."

He sighed. "Yeah."

"That was smart." She was working, he could see, closing up the shop; she popped the antique register, pulled out a sparse stack of cash. Jesse noticed a push-broom by the door and went over to it. No sense in not giving the place a sweep. Hey, maybe she'd even have a job for him if he showed he was quick on the uptake. Now that he looked down, he did see a few stray crumbs here and there, although the shop was nearly spotless.

She glanced over at him and then back at her cash, counting out the bills. "People go in that hospital and they don't come out," she said. "Or they come out with almost nothing left of them and a little certificate that says they're all better."

This time there was no warning: just a little pop, and Jesse changed over. It was like blinking, but for every part of him, and suddenly there he was: shorter, rounder, *different* in ways he hesitated to define. She hunched, hoping maybe Astrid wouldn't notice. But Astrid glanced up sharply. "What was that?"

"Nothing," Jesse said. It came out in a squeak.

"Hah!"

Astrid scuttled out from behind the counter and over to Jesse. She looked her up and down.

"You just turned into a *girl*," she said.

"No I didn't."

She gave Jesse a baleful stare and finally Jesse looked away.

"It's never happened like this," Jesse said. "But I think it's been happening for a while, just not—literally, if that makes sense."

Jesse glanced at her face from under the safety of her hair. Astrid's expression had softened.

"You thought the hospital could help you," she said.

"I guess," Jesse said. "But it seems like it's worse here. I never actually . . . changed before. I don't know what's wrong with me."

"Look at me."

She touched Jesse's chin, turning Jesse's face left and right in her hands. Her eyes crackled with midnight blue around the irises, for just a moment, so faintly that at first Jesse thought it was a trick of the light.

"Nothing I can do for you, I'm afraid," she said. "You're not cursed, if that's what you're thinking, so there's nothing there to break. Not blessed, either, I suppose. This is just what you are, says so right on the label. Plain as the nose on your face." She tweaked Jesse's nose with her finger. "To get it out of you, they'd have to take you apart stitch by stitch."

And then he snapped back into being a boy. Simple as that. It was so fast that it left him staggering under the shift in his center of gravity. But now that circling thought he'd had earlier touched down, light as air. Plain as the nose on your face.

"You're a witch, aren't you?" he asked.

"Of course I am," Astrid said. "What else would I be?"

She took him to her house, down a street where tree roots bulged the sidewalks into little cliffs. The houses here were weathered brick, with huge wooden porches that sagged toward the street. There were people sitting on the porches, drinking and smoking cigarettes in the gloom—old men in stained undershirts at one house, a crowd of teenagers at another. A somber little girl rode past on her tricycle, and she stopped when she saw Astrid and gave her a nod. Astrid nodded back.

"You're popular around here," Jesse said.

"I'm the representative of this district on the Board of Witches."

"There's a Board of Witches?" he said. "I always thought witches sort of did what they wanted."

"Of course you know how to do my job," Astrid said. "How foolish of me. Please, tell me more."

He ducked his head a little. "I'm sorry."

"Good," she said. "This one's mine."

They were standing in front of a brick house near the corner, elevated a long way off the street, with a black tin roof on top and on the porch.

"Come on, you," she said. "Come on. Inside, before it gets dark."

"What happens when it's dark out?" Jesse asked.

"Scientists come hunting for people like you," Astrid said. "You'll stay here."

Her house was small: living room in front, kitchen in back, a wall dividing them with a staircase running up it.

"I'm going to make you some tea," she said.

"Thanks," Jesse said. He was thirsty, although he would've preferred water. While she disappeared into the kitchen, he looked around her living room. It looked familiar: afghan on the back of an orange patterned couch, old wingback chair with the fabric worn thin on the arms. There were folding chairs propped up against one wall, though, and a map with pins and string. It was the city, Jesse realized, broken up into sections marked out in different colors. The pins had been moved often; the map was dotted with dozens of holes.

A kettle whistled; Astrid cut it off at one final squeal. A few minutes later, she emerged with a cup of aromatic tea, laced with milk.

"Drink," she said. It was hot, but not scalding, and Jesse sipped at it gratefully. It tasted grassy.

"I need you to get to bed," she said. "I've got the girls coming at six."

"I can help," Jesse said. "I can serve snacks and stuff."

"You'll do nothing of the sort," Astrid said. "Let's get you upstairs. You are not to come down tonight, do you understand?"

She shooed Jesse up the narrow staircase and into her guest room, its wrought-iron bed draped in a big dusty quilt. She set his backpack down on the floor and peeled the quilt back to pat the clean sheets underneath. "Go on." He sat down tentatively, still holding the mug. He sipped again. This stuff was good, actually.

"Why can't I meet them?" Jesse asked.

"They're witches," she said. "And a lot of them were in the revolution, so they'll want to kill you. I don't really have time to explain. Drink up."

Jesse took a big swig. "What revolution?" he asked. "Does this have anything to do with that old guy? He said I had to stop the wheel."

"Did he, now?" Astrid's voice sounded distant, and Jesse realized suddenly how tired he was. He'd been awake awhile, sure, but even a few minutes ago he'd felt fine—

"You drugged me," he said.

Downstairs, someone was knocking on the door.

"Just stay put," Astrid said. "I have to go."

He laid down on the bed, shoes still on. He heard Astrid bustle out, and then, sleep crept in on him from all sides, until he dissolved into it.

FIVE

When David opened the door to his office, it went about six inches and then stuck. He looked in the gap and sighed—the mop had fallen down again. He wedged a foot into the crack and kicked the mop handle, which flopped ineffectually a few times, until he got frustrated and shoved the door hard enough to send the mop bucket toppling, too. He wedged himself inside and picked up the mop. The narrow room had been a janitor's closet before he'd inherited it, with a single plate-glass window and an industrial shelf that used to hold boxes of paper towels. He kept meaning to get rid of the mop bucket, call Facilities or something. But not now. He shut the door behind him, and was fumbling in his backpack when a loud hydraulic hiss from far below made him look out the window.

His office overlooked the bus loop at the heart of the complex. Down below, a bus had pulled up, and was disgorging new patients for the hospital. A woman stepped down and then held out her arms to help a pair of twin girls with only one set of legs. Orderlies came rushing out with a wheelchair. They lined up at the curb out there often enough, waiting to grab people off the bus and rush them to hospital suites, interview rooms, pre-op. David frowned. Physics and chemistry and even bio were honestly different here, worth studying, but the med students were only here to take advantage of the fact that River City was still technically a sovereign principality and mainland rules didn't apply. No malpractice insurance, no legal liability. All the meds had to do was put the word out about that and sit tight, and desperate patients poured in. People who'd given up on getting the treatment they wanted anywhere else. URC med students would do it, and if it went well they'd take their technique to the mainland and publish, and if it went badly, no one ever had to know about it. A pack of jackals, all of them. David had heard one of them talking in the hallway about how he was sure he could take a foot off David's height in one surgery.

David shook his head. He couldn't waste his time worrying about the jackals. There was word that the higher-ups were thinking about slashing the budget for the Physics program, since they'd failed to produce anything more exciting than a faint blue light. He'd be the first to get cut, despite the fact that he was the only one around here who'd made any progress recently. And then—well, he wasn't sure what he'd do. He knew some grad students who volunteered as test subjects for extra cash on the side, but the thought filled his throat with bile. All the more motivation to find a breakthrough.

He double-checked that the door was locked before he undid the brown paper wrapping on the package. He laid it out on the desk: the book he'd spent four hundred bucks on.

It didn't seem like anything special—it smelled like library paste and mildew. It had a brown cover with no type on it, and the spine just said *Planned Magic*. He opened it to the first page. The words *Planned Magic* again, followed by Published by order of His Highness King Mahigan, *Year of King Mahigan 5, Royal Press*.

David sighed; this was starting to look like a hoax. He'd taken History 112 along with everyone else, so he knew that River City was just a little cultural atavism, like Tangier Island or Amish Country. But the true believers, the people who talked about magic, believed that the city was once home to a line of wizard-kings.

David felt a little foolish even entertaining the idea. If he told his adviser that he thought you could produce theta radiation with a magic spell, he'd be escorted out of the building. But the lady who ran the DVD stand had flickered with blue light, and when he'd asked her about it, really pressed her, she'd told him he'd need a book to get started. And then he'd found the newspaper ad. And now he held in his hand a—he almost had to laugh—a magical tome.

He skimmed the table of contents. *Basic Circles. Sample Equilibric Equations. Substituting Variables.* He went to that section and skimmed to the back, to a table that had objects that allegedly had equivalent "masses," although he couldn't fathom what that meant: an unfertilized egg = a kitchen chair, but a fertilized egg = a goat on the brink of death. He frowned. Not a currency exchange. Not a weights and measures, not of any kind he could understand.

He went back to basic circles. It was a two-page spread of symbols surrounding a circle, with branches and nodes inside leading to smaller circles. It was like . . . He squinted.

It was just an equation, he realized, a longhand accounting for objects and effects. It looked like a formula for an exothermic reaction.

He skimmed the directions; it would be easy enough to plug in the variables. All he needed was an object he desired to be the center of the reaction, and an object with enough potential energy to "sacrifice." Well, no reason not to try it. David sketched the shape of the circle and copied the equations onto the linoleum floor with a dry erase marker. He skimmed the table, looking at the row of values that shared the symbols on the diagram. Well, a pencil would do for n, and for q . . . he flipped to the next page . . . a poem? This was ridiculous.

He looked up "poetry" on the school's internal net, but all he found was someone's personal journal, and the poems didn't look good enough to count. So instead he crossed to his bookshelf and took down a volume he hadn't opened in years. It had been a gift from his first—well, his first something. Not a gift, really; a loan he'd never returned when his family moved suddenly. David wasn't even sure why he'd kept it through several moves, why he'd brought it to college with him. Poetry had never been his strong suit. But sometimes over the years he'd opened this book and read a few lines.

His eyes lit on some line he liked, something about rings of bright water. He read them to himself a few times and then closed his eyes so he could savor them. Then he ripped the page out.

(In a bed across town, Jesse sat upright for a moment, startled and disoriented, before sinking back into sleep.)

David put the page down in the appropriate spot in the circle. He set the pencil down in its place as well, and looked back at the book. The last step, it said, was to put in a keystone piece of text that would unite the equation. You were supposed to save it for last, because—he smelled smoke, and looked down.

The pencil was blazing more brightly than he thought a pencil could, magnesium bright. He glanced frantically around the room for something to put it out with, found a thermos of old coffee, and flung it onto the fire. The pencil went out with a hiss. The poem blazed but without any fire, and crumbled into ash.

The smoke alarm went off, and the sprinkler in David's office began spitting on him.

"No, no, no!" he said. He grabbed his laptop from his desk and ran out into the hall with it, ran back in, and opened the windows. He started fanning the smoke outside, and gradually, the alarm stopped, and so did the automatic sprinkler.

All the papers on his desk were ruined. The metal bookshelf had mostly protected the books, but some of their spines were spattered. Nobody had come to deal with the fire, but a few chem PhDs were poking their heads out of their adjoining offices, trying to see what the noise was about.

"It malfunctioned," David said, and most of the doors shut quickly.

He went back into his office. Luckily he still had the mop and bucket. He started cleaning up, but automatically. His mind was elsewhere.

Magic. He'd done magic.

He scoured his mind for alternate explanations. Spontaneous combustion? A trick pencil? Occam's razor told him not to make this more complicated than it needed to be, and both of those options were far more complex than this: He had written out a simple equation for setting something on fire, and something had, subsequently, burst into flame.

Of course, he couldn't publish on this. There was nothing

quantifiable here, nothing empirical, not yet. He needed to make sure the experiment was replicable. But when the time came, this was going to be big. Nobody would tell that stupid joke about physics ever again, or threaten his budget. Nobody would ever again laugh when he entered a classroom, or mistake him for a student, or ask for his fucking ID. Everyone would know who he was before he ever said his name.

INTERLUDE
Power Outage

In the living room at Astrid's house, the witches felt it: the flickering drop in the magic. They looked around at each other, each of them wondering who could cast who was not present with them, except for Astrid, who knew exactly who, but did her best to look surprised.

And in a brick house in the Old City, something stirred. Down past the roofline, down past chimney and gutters all the way to the ground floor, a Small Door set into the side of the wall creaked open.

Maybe you have never seen the Small Doors.

In the Old City, there are often doors set into the outer walls of buildings, usually at waist height, but always somewhere between eye-level and the ground. They are made of iron and usually now welded or painted shut. They sometimes have names engraved on them, or dates. No one uses them anymore, and people speculate on what they were there for in the first place. Coal, probably. Yes, almost certainly something to do with coal.

Late at night, on a deserted street in the Old City, a pigeon strutted along the sidewalk under the eave of a house, where it was nice and dry. It was doing pigeon things, thinking pigeon thoughts, one hungry red eye fixed on half of a sandwich in foil that had fallen out of a trash can. It started for the foil, and was halfway there when the door opened above it.

Pigeons are easily startled. And when startled, they try to fly. This one flew almost exactly straight up.

Several pairs of claws closed around it. The bird let out one indignant shriek and then the iron door banged shut again.

A few minutes later, it opened. There were a few hacking sounds, and balls of shredded feather and bone soon littered the sidewalk. And out came the creatures.

They were small, the tallest no more than a foot high. They looked like little men, at least in general shape—they stood on two legs, usually; they had arms that ended in claws, and they had faces. If that is all it is to be a man, then they were it. But no one who saw them would have really described them that way. Their eyes bulged out of their heads, their teeth were long and snaggled, and they had the scrawniest twigs for necks. They had hungry little rib cages and bulging potbellies and some of them had vestigial tails or the shreds of wings. To look at them was to wonder how they could possibly be alive.

They spilled out of the small door, a whole mass of them, probably about a hundred or so. They never traveled in a smaller group. They did not run so much as they tripped each other, or leapfrogged, so that the end result was like the rolling of a caterpillar tread, with some falling under and reappearing at the back to scramble up and over once again. They moved like particles in a wave, or like an engine, and any bugs or rats that fell into their path were stripped down to inedible parts, which they left in a wake behind them. They flowed over the ground like a tide, sweeping along the cresting ridges of the city, down a steep hill lined with blackberry brambles. So set on their purpose were they that they did not see the two men crouched behind a hedge, wearing dark coats over their polo shirts and khaki slacks. As the horde came tumbling down the hill, the scientists pulled up on a cable, snapping a wire mesh net across a portion of the hillside. It snagged the first ten or so, who began screeching and tearing at the mesh with their claws. The rest of the horde diverted around, scrabbling wildly, while the scientists bundled the net into a dog crate, and together began carrying it down the hill to where their research assistant waited in a van stenciled with the logo of the University Hospital.

The remainder of the horde poured down the slope, seemingly unperturbed. They spilled out into a wide formation as they reached the river. They didn't swim so much as they hydroplaned, skimming over the surface of the water more lightly than any observer could have imagined possible. They leaped from shards of foam to pieces of river debris, and some of them got swept out and bashed to death against the rocks of the rapids, but the horde moved on. The horde couldn't stop, once it had decided on a destination. Soon, they were climbing the rocks that lined coast of the Isle of Bells, clambering through the thick pine forest, and heading for the ruins of the Fortress of the Fourth Tower. When they reached the flag-stones of the old courtyard, they reconvened into a huddle. There was a moment of shuffling, and the horde spat out a single fairy. If anyone had seen, they might have said that it looked like a caricature of Nathan—his wild beard, his milk-white eye.

In one corner of the courtyard was a hut made out of logs and tarp. They streamed toward it, their made leader at the head. And then they slid in a column through a gap in the tarp.

SIX

On the Isle of Bells, in the middle of the Otiotan River, there lived a nameless girl.

The scientists who had captured the girl for a time had named her Turing as a joke, believing her to be a boy. They were wrong, but even she did not entirely know it. She was tall, although not as tall as the last king of the city, and built like a swimmer, with crimson skin and dark eyes. From her back grew seven tentacles, like an octopus, and the stump of an eighth. These lay draped around her shoulders as she read the back half of a paperback book, the front half of which lay in a milk crate at her side, alongside a dozen other books, most in some state of decay.

"We seek an audience with you, son of the river," the old fairy said.

The nameless girl glanced up from her book. Standing before her was a squat creature, with a body like a bullfrog, on two impossibly thin little legs. Behind that one there were dozens, hundreds of them, all around her, in all different colors. The hut was packed with them. They moved and shifted in unison, giving the impression of being inside a beehive, the air warmed by the vibrations of their bodies. The one who had spoken stood in front of her. It was white, and had milky blind eyes.

"What's the occasion of this visit?" she asked.

"You owe us your life, son of the river," said this ancient one.

The nameless girl knew that this fairy was no less young or old than any of the others. Fairies did not have individual personalities or even appearances; this was a guise for Turing's benefit. She suspected that they'd gotten the idea that humans listened more to old people.

"We fed you in your infancy," the fairy said. "We risked our lives to bring you fish and formula. We taught you to speak in our tongue and the human one. We brought you clothes and fire. Without us, you would be dead."

"And I am grateful for my life."

"And so you owe us a favor."

She shook her head at this. "I certainly made no covenant with you as a child. I was too young to speak when you decided to take care of me, so my life was a gift freely given." One of the first books she had asked for, when the scientists taught her to read, was a book about fairies. She knew not to concede points to them, especially not where favors were concerned.

The old one smiled, showing a mouthful of teeth much like Turing's own: small and sharp.

"So all we have from you is your thanks."

"My thanks are all I can give."

"Not so. You have many uses."

"Tell me one of my uses and I will tell you what it costs."

"You're just like your mother."

Turing shivered, as she did whenever they mentioned her mother. "Tell me about her."

"Never!" And a great susurrus rose up inside the hut, as all the little voices cried out in unison: never, never, never. She almost wanted to laugh. She always had to try her luck. The old one held up a hand for silence, and the sound died instantly.

"Son of the river," the old one said.

"What do you know of kings?"

She shook her head again. Nothing to speak of, despite living in the courtyard of a dead castle.

"You know that the secret river runs low," said the old fairy. "You know that it is what sustains us. That once we were bigger. And now we are fewer." Turing nodded. "Tonight, we felt something pull at the river and drink deep."

"A witch?" Turing asked. She knew a little bit about witches. They sometimes came to the abandoned castle to pick herbs. She hid from them out of a fear that she could not entirely explain.

The old fairy made a hocking sound, and all the other fairies hocked, too, and spat. Turing winced as spittle flew in all directions.

"The witches are foul parasites but they know not to kill their host," the old fairy said. "This was no witch. This was a king. We thought the witches had slain the notion of kings when they slew magic twenty years past. But a new King has come. If he ascends, he will take what little we have left."

The creature called Turing had heard all this before from the fairies. From the time she was born until the scientists had captured her, the fairies had lived with her. They had chittered in her ears about how little magic remained in the world, about how they hated the witches, about how at least no kings would ever come again to their city and they would be allowed to die in peace. She let the old fairy's words wash over her until, at least, it said something new.

"But things have changed," the fairy said. "There is a new king. But we have also felt the presence of a new Maiden."

Turing blinked. "Surely not."

"Surely nothing, larva! We can smell her! She is full of magic!"

"But isn't that good?"

"You do not understand. We are all but drained. We have been too long without magic. And we have felt the thirst of this new king. This girl is fragile, and he is strong. He could drink her dry in a year with his ambition. And then all will be lost. But you can help us." The old fairy looked up at her grimly. "You can wait until she gives up her magic. And then you can kill this new king."

Turing put a hand over her mouth to stifle her surprise. "You want me to do what?"

"This is no joke. You must kill him to save magic. To save the city. You are strong, stronger than us. You must." The creature grinned. "It is your fate."

Turing almost wanted to laugh. She shook her head. "I can barely look at people."

"You can deny your desire," the old fairy said, "but you cannot deny your nature. Your body was made for this."

Turing shuddered. Her seven long arms drew close around her, wrapping the rest of her body up.

"Maybe," she said. "But I live in it. And I'm not your champion."

"You are all we have."

"I'm a coward, not a killer. No, I cannot do this favor for you."

Turing felt something cold on her leg. She looked down, and saw that the old fairy had put its tiny clawed hand on her knee.

"Will you do it for a gift?" it asked. "If you kill the king, magic will be saved. When magic returns, the People can give you anything that you want. There is no wish that one person could have that is too grandiose."

Turing's heart quickened. She knew, of course, what she would wish for. But she hesitated.

"Couldn't I just talk to him?" she asked. "Tell him that he needs to stop? Would that be enough?"

"You can try to stop him however you like. But you will need to kill him."

Turing shut her eyes.

"I will promise to try to stop him," she said. "However I decide to do that is up to me. And if I do succeed—"

The old fairy smiled at her. Turing didn't like the smile; it wasn't kind. She knew instantly that in promising she'd made a mistake.

"We already know what you want," the old fairy said. And she leaned in close, and whispered, "We can give it to you. Daughter of the river."

When the old fairy said it, all the fairies echoed it in unison. They kept saying it, over and over, some slower and some faster, until it became a hiss that filled the hut like the beating of hundreds of insect wings. Still chanting, they skittered and crawled down the walls of the hut and poured out the door in a stream, clambering over each other on their way out into the night. Turing looked for the old fairy who had been speaking to her, but it was gone—disappeared back into the mass, just one more body in the iridescent stream of them that flitted over the courtyard wall and out of sight.

The night stretched ahead but she could not imagine falling asleep. This was too much. Surely, the king couldn't be all bad. He was a person, right? If she could find him, maybe she could talk to him . . . She paused. But what if he didn't like the look of her, what if he wasn't in a talking mood when he saw her? She bit her lip. It might be hard to persuade him not to drink all the magic out of that magic girl if he thought she was a monster. No, maybe she had better find the Maiden and warn her.

If *she'd* listen to someone like her. That was the problem. All this would be so much easier if she could get an advance on her boon from the fairies, somehow.

When she had first read the book about fairies, learned what they truly were, she had imagined coming back to them and begging them to change her. To make her into a human girl, like the ones she read about in books. She wouldn't have even dared ask that they make her beautiful, just closer to what everyone else was. That would be enough.

She left her hut. It was not quite dawn, but the edges of the horizon were turning from black to blue. This was the perfect time of day to go and spy on the joggers.

She clambered over the wall of the castle courtyard and down over the heap of debris that the river pushed up against the old ramparts. She dove in and soon was skimming along the shallow bottom, down among the fish and tin cans and churned-up debris. She made her way toward the shore, toward the walking path where, if she held very still in the early morning, she could hide in a shallow bed of reeds and watch people run by. She had a great appreciation for runners, with their brightly colored shorts, their large, pillowy shoes.

But when she put her head above the water, what she saw was something else entirely.

At first, she didn't understand what she was looking at. She'd read about how the Minoans first thought that the Thessalonians, mounted on horseback, were creatures half man and half horse. In the dim light of early morning, the shuffling figure before her initially looked like some great worm, until it resolved itself into four women struggling under the weight of a rolled-up rug.

They approached the edge of the water. She held still, watching. Then, clumsily, they heaved the rug. It hit the bank with a smack and began unrolling, and Turing caught sight of something white. A hand.

She ducked her head beneath. The rug had unfurled completely, and now she could see that it was a man. She swam to him, thinking he might still be alive, grabbed him in several arms, and dragged him up onto the bank. Gasping, she looked up. The women on the bank screamed, until one of them hissed at the others to shut up, and held one hand out between Turing and the others. Her fingertip flickered with blue light, like the flame of Turing's camp stove. Her face and head were covered, but at the bottom of her scarf, Turing could see the tip of a straw-colored braid.

"Stay back," their leader whispered. She backed away slowly. "Everybody, listen to me. On three."

"Wait," Turing said.

The woman with the braid looked shocked to hear her talk. "One," she said, a deliberate step backward. "Two. Three. Run."

The others took off at a sprint. Their leader hung back a second longer. Turing could not see her face, wrapped in a black scarf. But she didn't like her eyes. That woman looked at Turing like she was a thing. And then she, too, was running.

Turing looked down at the man in her arms. He was dead; she could see that now. He wasn't coughing or struggling, his body was stiff, and his skin had a loose feeling to it, as though it wasn't quite sticking to him anymore. She sighed. She had seen a dead body from time to time, usually someone who had fallen into the river while drunk. This was different, though. Those girls had killed this man.

She dragged him a little ways away from the bank, and looked at him in the early morning light. He wore dark blue pants and a button-up shirt of the same color, and shiny shoes. He had badges and patches on his clothes, insignia. He was a police officer, she realized. She saw them sometimes, breaking up homeless encampments on the island. But they never came to the castle. She'd never seen one this close. She studied him for a moment, wondering how he had come to be dead.

He was stiff enough that she couldn't bend his arms across his chest, but she could pull up his shirt a little, to cover his face. She didn't like the idea of leaving him there, but the sky was lightening. Soon there would be more people, the early morning runners. And then they'd go get the police. More police, she corrected.

She slipped away, back into the water, and watched. She wanted to flee, but she didn't like the idea of leaving the dead man alone. She wanted to be sure he was found.

And after a little while, someone came along.

At first, she thought it was a man, in a leather jacket and faded jeans. All she could see in the dark was the silhouette and the glowing tip of a cigarette. The figure noticed the body lying on the trail and broke into a sprint.

It was a woman, she realized—a woman with stubbly light hair and a small hard body. She knelt beside the dead man, pulled the shirt down from his face, slapped his cheek once or twice, listened at his chest for a heartbeat. Turing watched her realize that the man was a corpse. She gritted her teeth but did not flinch or look away.

The woman stood up, looking around to see if anyone else had seen. And then she dragged the man a little bit off the path, into a stand of blackberry bushes. She came out, dusting her hands off on her jeans, and glanced toward the river.

Turing ducked underwater, uncertain whether she'd been seen. She went deeper, clinging to a rock near the bottom until she was sure the woman would be gone. She didn't bother to check, just swam for her island as fast as she could, her mind racing.

It had all happened so fast. The fairies, with their story of the king. The body in the river. Had the king killed that man? Is that what they'd meant, when they said that they had felt the pull of magic?

And now, that woman. Turing had never seen anyone like her before.

When she reached the island, she pulled herself from the water and went dripping into her hut, where she rummaged in her crate of books, to pull out her oldest and most battered volume, her book of fairy tales. She flipped through it, looking for an illustration she remembered: a knight in white armor on the back of a white horse. She was certain that she'd recognize his features in the woman on the shore.

But the book fell open onto a different illustration, one she had never cared for. A different horse, the red of hot metal or a setting sun. Its rider held a flaming sword. His face, she could see. His teeth were gritted together in rage. His whole body tilted forward to bring his weight into the force of his blow.

She shut the book harder than she meant to, tearing the worn binding. She ran her hands over the cover, as though to soothe it, and put it back into the crate.

She'd have to find out where this king was. That would be the first step. She would find him, and then she would—talk to him. Reason with him. Tell him to be careful with magic, that he would hurt himself and everyone else if he used it too fiercely. The thought of leaving the island filled her with dread. On the island, she was safe.

She usually slept in the day, particularly in the summer, to escape the heat. But as she lay down on her old mattress, she could not stop her mind from circling. The fairies. The dead man. The woman on the riverbank, her sharp efficiency, the tip of her cigarette the color of a burning setting sun.

SEVEN

Jack Marley, a white woman with a man's name and a man's chiseled face, local boxing legend and occasional murderer, usually worked all night for her employer and then went home and slept into the late afternoon. Today, though, she was going to be up all day, and it was her own damn fault. Take a walk along the riverbank, she'd thought. Wind down before bed. And of course, her being her, she'd stumbled upon a body.

Well, it hadn't been quite that simple. Hannah had shared some additional thoughts about their relationship, and Jack had left the club before she had the chance to say something she'd regret. She'd decided to stay off the street and take the riverside walking trail back to her place in London Hill, all steep hill and brambles on one side and the river on the other. And then, in the dark, a large man had suddenly blocked her way.

She'd seen the guy around once or twice. He was impossible to miss: a huge hobo with a white beard and one blind eye. He looked like a cartoon of a wizard. He'd been surprisingly silent, so that when he was suddenly in front of her, she found herself startled.

"The policeman," he announced.

"Excuse me?" she said. But he was already pushing past her on the narrow trail beside the river. She had to catch herself on a tree to avoid falling into the water.

"Shit!" she said, righting herself and swiveling around to see if

he was going to come at her again. But when she did, he was—
gone.

She loosened her stance, unfocused her eyes, and listened. He shouldn't be out of sight already, so if he was still here . . . but after a few moments, she realized she couldn't hear him, either. No rustle in the bushes, no breathing. She turned in a slow circle, making sure, one hand inside her jacket. Nothing.

She breathed out. Okay, weird. But he was gone.

Jack kept going up the trail. When her heart stopped pounding, she pulled out a cigarette and cupped it with her palm while she lit it. She breathed deliberately until she felt calm again, but kept her ears open. That was enough weirdness for one night.

As she got closer to London Hill, the riverbank flattened out into a wider plane. Soon she'd be at the steep steps that led up past the underside of the highway overpass, and she could climb those and be home in a few minutes. Then, rest. No more drama tonight. Not now that Hannah was done with her.

When she first saw the crumpled heap in the middle of the path, she thought it was a sleeping bag. A few more steps and she saw a pair of shoes. That was when she started to run.

He was dead. She knew that immediately, but she had to be sure. She dug in her back pocket for her black bandanna, and used it to pull the shirt down from his face.

He had been in the river, but not for long. There might be duckweed tangled in his hair, but this man's face was instantly recognizable. It was Pete McNair, one of Sir's paid cops. A local man in late middle age. She'd seen him just last week at the bar downtown where Sir kept his headquarters. It was weird that he was dead. She hadn't heard anything about him being in trouble, and it unsettled her to think that there'd been something she hadn't known about.

No marks on his neck, so he hadn't been strangled. She wrapped her hand in the bandanna and pressed down hard on his ribs. Nothing came out of his mouth other than a little stale breath. So he probably hadn't drowned, either, if his lungs weren't full of water.

She looked around for any other signs of what might have happened to him. He certainly hadn't washed out of the water. Which meant someone had pulled him out. Dragged him into a little bit of cover, but not so much cover that he wouldn't be found eventually. Folded his arms. Pulled his shirt up over his head like a shroud.

She started making a list in her head. She needed to call Sir. He needed to call the police. She thought, for a moment, about just shoving the body back into the water. It was choppy today, gray and fast-moving. But no. A missing cop was more trouble than a dead one. A missing cop could be alive, and that would be a more urgent and brutal investigation.

She grabbed hold of the body by the arms and dragged it off of the path and behind a bush. It wasn't much of a hiding place, but it would probably work long enough for her to call this in.

As she stepped out of the bushes, she looked left and right to see if anyone had spotted her. Her eyes skimmed over the water. And for just a moment, she thought she saw something. A face. She squinted. No, maybe not. It had looked a little like a seal, or a mermaid, and there were neither in the Otiotan River.

Still, it unsettled her as she made her way up the steep steps set into the hillside, up past the piling of the highway overpass. She kept thinking about the dead man's face.

Pete had looked surprised. Which she'd seen before on a corpse. Something about the eyes, the jaw muscles. Nothing that couldn't be explained. But it still chilled her. No amount of rationalization could tell her it wasn't creepy. She felt like he was watching her, and that made her want to get this settled as soon as possible.

She went past her apartment to the pay phone on the corner and dialed. "It's me, Sir," Jack said. "I've got some bad news."

Sir was predictably furious when she told him. She waited patiently while he put the phone down; she could dimly hear him growling and swearing. Then he was back on the line.

"Tell me you've got a lead, Jack," he said.

"Not yet," she said. "You're gonna want to call the chief."

"Are you my boss?"

"I'm sorry," she said, cradling the phone against her shoulder. "But I think it'll be better if they hear it from you than somebody else. You can tell them they can interview me if they want. I'll tell them whatever they want to know."

"I hope you're right."

"So, off the record, did we have anything to do with this?"

"None of my people," he said. "No marks on the body, you said? That sounds like magic."

"With all due respect, Sir," Jack said, "if there was still enough magic left to kill someone, don't you think the witches would be using it for something? Like, I don't know, anything else?"

Sir made a high-pitched sound in the back of his throat. Jack knew what that meant. Sir was deeply old-school superstitious. He didn't like talking to witches face-to-face, he wouldn't walk outside between midnight and three a.m., and he liked to have all business involving death resolved or on hold for the week surrounding the city's annual fall Carnival. For fear of making kings, he said. Still, Sir had more reason than most to be wary of magic, even if general consensus said that magic was dead. Jack sighed.

"Well, I'll check in with Astrid," she said. A concession. "If it had anything to do with magic, she'll know."

"Good girl."

"And if she's got a lead?"

"Chase it. But don't engage until you talk to me. We're too close to Carnival."

Always with Carnival. Jack was glad he couldn't hear her rolling her eyes.

"Who else do we have over at the PD?" she asked.

"Walsh."

"Got his extension?"

"You're my liaison, you find out." And he hung up on her. Great.

She called in to the PD nonemergency line, spent some time chatting with Angie the dispatcher, and ended up on the phone with Walsh. He sounded anxious, like a second-stringer unexpectedly on the field, and he said he could get her the details of McNair's beat, but that it might take him a while to get back to her.

"Have you all heard from Mannering?" Walsh asked.

"Who's Mannering?"

"Matthew Mannering. McNair's partner," he said. "He's new, just left school. We were supposed to get coffee after he got off shift this morning but he never showed."

Well, that was interesting. "Who else knows you two were getting coffee?"

"Nobody."

"Keep it that way. No reason to attract attention to yourself. But I'll look into it. Call into the club when you've got their beat, have them take a message."

"But it wasn't . . . you?" he asked.

He was like a baby bird. Jack sighed. "If I did it, I'd already know his beat."

"Oh," he said. "Okay."

"Be discreet," Jack said. "I'd rather you take longer and not get yourself in trouble, okay? You're gonna do great."

"Sorry. This is getting to me."

"Everything's fine, Walsh," Jack said. "Nobody wants this to escalate. We'll figure it out together."

She hung up. No wonder he was nervous. One cop dead, one missing. The PD was going to throw a fit about this. The sooner she found out who did it, the better it would be for everyone else.

As she walked back to her apartment, Jack found her shoulders tensing up as though she were bracing for impact. It was going to be a rough couple of weeks. She should catch a quick nap, while the rest of the town was still sleeping. She looked at the sky. It was five, maybe six. She could set an alarm for nine. Then: coffee. Then: answers. Certainly not now. Not with her body aching from exhaustion.

Jack's apartment was on the third floor of an old storefront, accessed via a rickety set of stairs from the alley in back. She trudged up, using the railing to heave herself over the broken stair, fumbled for her keys, slipped inside, and shut her door behind her. Took off her jacket, unbuttoned her pants and stepped out of them on her way to her bedroom and the bare mattress on the floor that awaited her. Hung up her shoulder holster on the back of the wooden kitchen chair she used for a bedside table. Set her alarm. Turned on the box fan. Lay down.

The next thing she knew, someone was pounding on the back door.

She sat up, dazed. Her clock said eight. Shit, who did she even know who woke up that early?

Jack slipped her jeans back on and tucked her gun into the back waistband. She was careful to shuffle as she left her room; no sense in seeming like she was on edge, even if she was.

Through the window in the door, she saw who it was, and her shoulders relaxed. She set the gun down on the kitchen counter as she passed by it. Astrid flattened out one eyebrow and raised the other. Jack curled her lip a little in response. Astrid didn't like guns. That was fine with Jack. A witch with a gun would be too much trouble.

Jack unlocked the dead bolt and the safety latch, and stuck her head out. She realized Astrid wasn't alone; there was a kid lurking there, sitting a few steps down. He looked up when he heard the door open.

"Hi, your step is broken," he said.

"It's my security step," Jack said. "Astrid, what's going on?"

"I need to talk to you."

"So talk?"

"Inside. Jesse, stay put."

Jack shrugged. "Sure, come on in. Sit down."

Astrid eased herself down into Jack's only chair, a huge leather monstrosity, and looked around the apartment. When other people came here, they always felt the need to say things like *Why don't you have any furniture* or *When are you going to do the dishes.* But Astrid knew better than that. She clicked her tongue on her teeth once, and faced Jack.

"How's your arm doing, Miss Marley?" she asked.

Jack glanced down at her new scar, puffy and pink and wrapping almost all the way around her right bicep. "It's still on," she said. "I guess that means you're here to collect?"

"I need a favor," Astrid said. "I think it's about equivalent."

Jack sucked in a breath. Astrid almost never liked to cash in a favor on one request. She'd let Jack stay at her house once a few years ago while some legal trouble was clearing up, and she was still calling that in, in bits and pieces.

"Tell me," Jack said.

"The boy out there. Did you notice anything about him?"

Jack glanced at the window and saw the small, worried face pressed against the glass. When he saw her, he ducked down, as though she wouldn't realize he'd been spying.

"Not very bright," Jack said. "What is he, like, a nephew or something?"

"He's not a he," Astrid said. "Nathan found him. He's the Maiden."

Usually, Jack tried not to laugh in Astrid's face, but she was tired and cranky enough that it came out. "What?" she said. "So all those times you were like *Magic is dying, Jack, you have to be more careful* and *Once this was a great city but never again*? And now you're telling me you found the Maiden?"

Astrid pursed her lips.

"I know you don't believe me," she said. "It must be hard to. You were just a baby when we killed magic here. You've grown up with it dying around you. But I wasn't lying when I said that there used to be more of it. More than you can possibly imagine. Things that would make putting your arm back on look like child's play."

Jack didn't really like when Astrid got like this. It was hard to tell, in those moments, if she was talking to a woman in the early stages of dementia, or someone who knew the secrets of the universe.

"So this kid is, what, the big magic battery?"

"More like a spark that starts a fire, if it makes you feel better."

"And he's gonna bring back magic."

"When he meets the Hero."

"Okay. And the Hero is . . ."

Astrid's face momentarily lit up, and then closed like a vise. Jack knew that look; she wasn't going to tell her shit about that.

"And you want me to . . ."

"Watch him."

Jack recoiled. "Watch him? Like a babysitter?"

"You certainly don't mind spending time with young women generally."

"He's not a woman, he's a teenage boy. Do you know how much they eat?"

"You're not hard up for money."

"I really don't have time for this," Jack said. She needed to wake up, she realized. Caffeine. She went to her fridge. "Iced tea, Astrid?"

"Do you have unsweet? The doctor said I need to watch my sugar." She said it with such disdain that Jack almost laughed.

"Oh my god, how the mighty have fallen," Jack said. "So if magic comes back, you'll be young and spry again?"

"This isn't about my vanity," Astrid said. "This is about restoring a world of power and beauty the likes of which you cannot possibly imagine."

"Then why'd you kill it in the first place?"

"We didn't mean to," Astrid said. "We were trying to . . . do something else."

"Like what?"

"Free ourselves from a curse."

Jack nodded. "But you broke . . . all of magic. And now you think you can fix it."

"I think I can see that world again before I die."

Jack looked at Astrid's face. She was a really . . . admirable woman, Jack thought. She liked her. They were both lifelong professional problem solvers, although Jack got paid better. Who cared if magic was real in the way Astrid remembered? The woman never seemed to get what she wanted. And Jack Marley always wanted admirable women to get what they wanted.

"All right," Jack said. "I'll take the kid. But he's got to get a job and pay bills. Not because of the money, but because otherwise he'll be here bothering me all day."

"All right," Astrid said. "Just keep him away from that club."

Jack shrugged to avoid making a promise she wouldn't keep. Sir's club was a great place to find work. "There's one other thing, though."

"What's that?"

"I was meaning to come see you later," Jack said. "But now that you're here, I might as well ask you. You told me you guys know when someone does big magic. Did you . . . feel anything last night?"

"Like what?"

Jack sighed. Astrid would know before the day was done anyway. She might as well be the one to tell her.

"I found a body this morning," Jack said. "Down by the river. Pete McNair."

Astrid sucked in a breath.

"Oh, Pete," she said. "I just spoke to him yesterday. He didn't say anything about being in trouble. Where'd you find him?"

"Down by the river."

"Right by the river?"

Jack nodded.

"I was worried about that," Astrid said. "No, I don't think that was magic, then. Have you heard about the Otiotan River Monster?"

Jack thought of the face she'd seen—or thought she'd seen—in the river that morning. It certainly hadn't looked like a mythological creature, though. "I thought that was just a story."

"You work for monsters. Surely you're not skeptical."

Jack sighed. "First off, that's rude. Second, I've been hearing stories about this river snake since I was a little kid. Swallowing boats or whatever. I've never seen it. Nobody's ever—"

Astrid's eyes went cold. "I've seen it."

"Oh-kay? So . . . what is it?"

"It's a *monster*, Jack. I don't know what you want me to say."

"Okay, maybe you saw something," Jack said. "But how do you know it's not just some guy?"

Astrid wrinkled her nose. "I once saw it go after a child. It tried to eat him. It had sharp teeth and a body like an octopus."

"And you've seen it since? I thought a lot of the really weird ones died when magic went down the drain."

"Not this one. It's only gotten bigger."

"Huh, maybe it's radioactive."

"What?"

"Don't worry about it." Older citizens were wild; Jack had to constantly remind herself that the city had only started teaching science in school when she was ten. "So I guess I've got to go question him."

Astrid frowned at her, tilting her head from side to side.

"I wouldn't," she said. "It's almost Carnival. It's too risky to chase down a monster about a murder."

"Oh, not you, too."

"You should listen to Sir. He knows better than most the power of real magic." She started easing herself up out of the chair.

Jack offered her arm to Astrid, and helped get her back on her feet. "You know," Jack said. "You could get a cane."

Astrid gave her a withering look.

"I don't want the kid to stay forever," Jack said.

"He won't," Astrid said. "Carnival's almost here. He'll be here for a month."

Jack shook her head. "If you say so."

Astrid crossed to the back door, and opened it. "Jesse," she said. "Come meet Jack Marley."

Jesse slunk in over the threshold. He had a big baggy sweat-shirt on, and jeans stained with dirt and ripped at one knee, and a backpack bigger around than he was. He came in, did the usual look-around-in-awe that people did in Jack's apartment: at the vast open space with a kitchen at one end and a bricked-up fireplace at the other, the bare floors, the single chair, the record cabinet and turntable, the nothing-at-all-else. And then at Jack.

"Hi," he said, and stuck out his hand.

She reached her hand out to shake. When they did, she felt a strange jolt, almost like static, but not quite. And the boy holding her hand was . . . different. No longer a boy, but a girl in baggy clothes with a bad haircut.

"Huh," Jack said. She glanced at Astrid. "You're right, this is going to be trouble."

"I'll work really hard," the girl said.

Jack glanced back at her. She recognized that look of panic. Jesse was calculating.

"I can cook real well," Jesse said. "I worked at a diner for two years in high school. I can get this place cleaned up. I'll make it worth your time. I just need somewhere to stay. I won't be any trouble, I swear."

Jack shrugged. "All right," she said. "Who am I to argue with you? Clean up the place, and we'll see."

She glanced over at Astrid who smirked back. She was glad the witch wasn't angry at her for messing with the kid. If Jack was getting stuck with . . . her? . . . she might as well have a little fun.

"I'm leaving now," Astrid said. "I'll see you soon, Jesse."

She started to bustle out. Jesse chased after her. "Wait! I still have so many ques—" Astrid shut the door behind her, and was down the steps pretty quickly, Jack thought, for an old woman with a bad leg. She must be real eager to get rid of the kid.

Jesse turned to Jack. She still looked scared, Jack thought. Like Jack was going to lunge and bite her any second.

"I'm sorry," Jesse said. "I asked her if I could stay with her, if I could help in the shop, and she—"

Jack sighed.

"Look," she said. "Please believe me when I say that you are actually my smallest problem today. I'd usually be asleep right now, but instead I'm going to go deal with a crisis. Okay?"

Jesse nodded. "Uh. Okay."

"So, like . . . stay here, try not to break anything, and I'll see you later."

Jesse nodded. "Sure." She'd spotted the gun on the counter and was eyeing it. Jack picked it up, and Jesse flinched.

"I work security at a nightclub," Jack said. "Actually, I'll take you down there when we get a chance. They might need a dishwasher or something."

"I can wash dishes," Jesse said.

"Great. Wash mine."

Jack retreated into her room. Jesse was still watching her, until finally she shut the door on the kid. She slid her shoulder holster back on, stored the gun, put her jacket on over it. It was going to be another hot one today, but she was used to that. Better to be too hot than underdressed for a fight. Especially since the cops were likely to be riled up by now.

She tried to think what she'd known of Pete McNair. She wished she'd asked Astrid more questions about him. She'd seen him around at the club now and then. Since he already worked for Sir, and therefore wasn't a problem, she'd had no reason to talk to him. Had he known her father? What were his vices? She was embarrassed she didn't know. He wasn't an employee in their organization, at least not in the way that counted, and he wasn't a cop she was supposed to keep an eye on, so now he was the center of a big blank space in her knowledge of the city.

When she emerged in boots and a jacket, Jesse had turned back into a boy. He was staring at the mound of dishes. Well, Jack had never been much of a housewife. "Do you, uh," Jesse said. "Do you have dish soap?"

"Probably not," Jack said. She dug around in her pocket for some money and slapped it into the kid's hand. "Corner store. I'll see you later."

She shut the door behind her and took the back stairs two at a time. At the bottom she unchained her bike. An old Triumph that whined at a pitch everyone in the city recognized. She didn't always like to take it out, but she had a lot of ground to cover today. A lot of questions that needed answers.

She thought about what Astrid had said about the Otiotan River Monster. A stupid story with lots of iterations. Some people called it Bloody Marla and said it was the ghost of the last queen, who still wandered the halls of the old summer palace, a blood-red ghoul with sharp teeth. Some people said it was a big octopus that ate boats. Some people said it was a man with a set of bat wings growing from his back. Jack had always laughed this stuff off before. If someone like that lived so close to home, surely Sir would have hired him by now to scare debtors and guard doors. Sir had an eye for talent.

But still. Jack couldn't stop thinking about the face she'd maybe, maybe-not seen in the water. She'd been about to write it off as being tired. But Astrid had seemed so sure.

Well, she'd do all the routine stuff first. Go downtown and make sure Sir had actually called the chief of police like he'd said. Ask the people who stood on street corners all day if they'd seen anything. But if that didn't work . . . well. She started thinking about where she could get a boat.

EIGHT

Alone in Jack's apartment, Jesse turned in a slow circle. Being in this city had felt so . . . fast, somehow. Like she'd just gotten here and suddenly everything was happening all at once. She stretched, and felt her body stretching out, back to the shape he was more used to. He felt a little sheepish that Jack had touched him and he'd . . . popped, like that. Like he had the sense she'd like him better if he was a girl. It was embarrassing.

Still, Jack had been nicer than she needed to be, letting him stay here. So had Astrid, even if she didn't seem to like Jesse very much. Even if she'd doped him up the night before, when he'd woken up in the morning she'd given him breakfast, told him she was going to find him a place to stay. Astrid even tried to find him some old men's clothes in a drawer, but when she'd pulled them out, they were way too big for him, like something a giant might wear. It was weird, being so . . . helped. Back home in Chicasaw, nobody had done anything for him unless he'd worked for it.

And now here he was in this strange woman's huge, empty apartment. He opened some doors: a bathroom, a utility closet with a hot water heater, a second bedroom that was full of plants but no furniture. He wondered where he was supposed to sleep. Maybe Jack had a blow-up mattress or something.

He opened Jack's bedroom door to peek inside. Just a bare mattress on the floor, a rickety chair, and—he froze. That poster he'd seen downtown, tacked up. Just the four words, RISE UP OLD CITY, stacked on top of one another in a narrow column on plain brown paper. There was no name attached, no date or time, no message except those words. It made him nervous; he felt like it meant something dangerous. He didn't want to be involved with this. He didn't want any of this. Right now, he wished he could just go home.

He remembered what Astrid had said the other night about the hospital. If it was true, he had to stay as far away from there as he could. But he didn't want it to be true. He didn't want the doctors to be murderers. He wanted them to fix him. If they could fix him, he could get away from these crazy women. Jack seemed dangerous.

Jesse glanced behind him at the door. He wondered how far he could get on foot; maybe he could go home and try to convince his mom to let him stay in the shed for a few days, just until he could get a job and a hotel room. Maybe Paul wouldn't have to know he was even there.

No, he thought. That wasn't how this was going to go.

Ever since he was little, Jesse had had—feelings, he supposed, about how things should be. They were what had sustained him through his childhood, and right now, every nerve in Jesse's body said that going home was a mistake. Going home would be running away. He'd have to stay here for now. And if he wanted to keep a roof over his head, Jack had to think he was useful.

He went around the apartment, making a list of what needed cleaning. The bathroom was horrifying, the sink full of bits of hair, the clippers lying gummed-up in their open case on top of the toilet tank. The toilet and the tub were both vaguely gray on the inside. The floor—well, he didn't like looking at the floor.

He went down the back stairs, careful of the security step now that he knew which one it was. She should get that fixed. She was going to break her leg. Or Jesse was.

He'd spotted a corner store on the walk over with Astrid. Retracing his steps, he found it again on the next block over. The guy behind the counter looked up vaguely.

"Never seen you before," he said.

"I'm new in town," said Jesse. "Do you have cleaning supplies? I just moved in and my place is filthy."

"First aisle," the old man said. He was perched on a stool behind a counter crammed with tchotchkes for sale: little ceramic turtles, lighters, key chains, and a rack of postcards. Jesse scanned the postcards, looking for any that matched his own.

"You like those?" the shopkeeper asked. "They're a dollar."

"I was looking to see if you had one . . ." Jesse fumbled in his pocket. "One that looks like this."

He unfolded the card and placed it on the counter, careful to keep a hand on it. The old man peered down at it.

"Well," he said. "The front's the palace. But this is real old. See, there's no chain-link fence around the outside."

"Chain-link fence?"

"It's the police headquarters now," he said. "They put the fence around it, probably in Kingless Year 10, I wanna say?"

"But where do you think the postcard came from?" Jesse asked. "Is there a shop that sells them?"

"Everyone's got postcards," he said. "Don't sell very many of them, but they're cheap and they last forever. I've probably got some on the rack as old as that one."

"But where do you buy them?"

"Used to buy them from the printer on 4th," he said. "But they shut down a few years ago. Sold all their stuff to Belle Marley. She runs a shop with some girls out of the old Bodwell School."

"Belle Marley? Any relation of Jack Marley?"

The man blinked. "Her sister, I think. You sure you're new here?"

Jack had a sister, then. Interesting. "Do you think Belle would know how to get in touch with the old printer?"

"Not sure," he said. "What you trying to find?"

"Uh," Jesse said. "This postcard belonged to my best friend when we were kids. I haven't seen him in like seven years. It's the only thing I have of his, and I'm trying to figure out where he got it, because maybe if I know that, I can figure out how he got it, and maybe . . ." Jesse shook his head. "Maybe I can find him? I know it seems like a long shot. I mean, they probably sell hundreds of these cards . . ."

It took Jesse a moment to realize that the old man had started to cry a little. He swiped at his eyes with two fingers, and handed the postcard back to Jesse.

"You'll find him," he said. "Carnival will help. It's when everything that was lost turns back up."

"Carnival?" Jesse asked. Had Astrid mentioned it to him?

"Yep, coming up. I'll have to stock costumes soon."

"What is it?"

The old man shook his head. "I could tell you," he said. "But to really understand it, you have to see it." He saw the look of disappointment on Jesse's face. "But if you want to find Belle Marley, I can help with that."

The shopkeeper got a map out of a rack behind him and spread it out on the counter. With a ballpoint pen, he made a mark on a block of the Old City, right in the middle of the sprawling tangle of streets.

"This is the old Bodwell School," he said. "Used to be for training housekeepers. Little Belle moved in a few years ago. Think they're all squatting there. But they print things for people. Store signs, flyers. Postcards."

"Posters?" Jesse asked, thinking of the RISE UP OLD CITY poster.

"Probably," he said, pushing the map into Jesse's hands. "Fastest way to get there from here is to turn left on Rue and just keep walking. That's the hypotenuse."

"Thank you so much," Jesse said. He started to leave, but the shopkeeper called him back. "Wait! Didn't you want to clean your apartment?"

"Oh," Jesse said. "Yeah, thanks."

He bought cleaning spray and dish soap and a scrub brush, a little disappointed at being brought back down to earth. The money Jack had given him wasn't quite enough, but the old man waved him off. "Don't worry about it," he said. "Just come back and tell me if you find your friend. I don't hear enough good news anymore."

Jesse smiled. "Will do."

Wow. It wasn't just his imagination; everyone here was really, really helpful. Back home they'd always said cities were dangerous, that no one cared about their neighbors. But in Chicasaw, nobody would've been that excited to talk to a stranger. And certainly no single women back home would've let a strange kid sleep in their guest room. Here, he'd somehow found two already.

Jesse wondered if it was related to that thing Astrid had said. She'd told him about what Nathan thought he was. A Maiden, she'd said. A magical girl. That was why Jesse could . . . do what he did. Because he was full of power. But Astrid had said people would hate him for it, try to kill him. So far, all anyone had been was nice.

Jack's apartment looked even worse after being outside. The dishes were piled high enough in the sink to block the faucet. He sighed. Well, it wasn't like he hadn't cleaned before.

It took him about four hours to get the place from the state his mother would have called *disastrous* down to *sorry about the mess*. He still hadn't really dealt with the cobwebs up top on the ceiling, but he'd swept and wiped down the floors, scrubbed up most of the mysterious stains on the stove and the fridge, wiped out the bathtub with a towel and hung it outside on the stair railing to dry. But now he was exhausted. He checked behind the other doors in the apartment, and found a utility closet and a bedroom that was entirely empty except for a large potted date palm and the faint smell of cigarettes. He finally sat down in the one chair, thinking he would just sit for a minute, and that if he thought he needed to sleep, he could roll himself onto the floor—

He was sleeping when he heard the back door open. He was on his feet before Jack stumbled in. She saw him and flinched, and so did he, mirroring her. She relaxed. He let himself exhale.

"Ah, Jesus," she said, scratching at her scalp. Her hair was shorter than his. "I was hoping you weren't real."

"I cleaned the house," he said.

"Huh." She skirted past him and leaned into the open bath-room door. "Where's my towel?"

Panic was growing in his throat. "I used it to clean up, so I hung it on the railing."

She ducked past him again, opened the door to the stairs. She turned back to him, looking—annoyed? He couldn't tell how annoyed, and that thought tied his stomach into knots; annoyed bordered on angry, and he had no idea how quickly she would go from angry to furious. She was shorter than him, but she looked stronger.

"Well, it's on the ground now," she said.

"I'll—I'll get it," he said. He tried to duck around her but she caught him with one arm. He tried to wriggle free of her and felt his body contract, shrinking to girl-size.

"Sorry!" she squeaked out. "I won't mess up again, I promise, I'm sorry—"

Hearing the change in her voice, Jack let go of her arm.

As she tore off through the door, she thought she heard Jack mutter something—sorry, maybe. Jesse took the steps two at a time, heart pounding. She scooped the damp grassy towel off the dirt and started back up the stairs. Halfway up she stopped—Jack stood on the landing, arms folded across her chest.

"Why'd you run away from me?" Jack asked.

"You were angry."

"I was confused," Jack said. "Subtle difference."

Jesse ducked her head. "Sorry."

"Enough with the fucking sorry," Jack said. "Get up here."

Jesse climbed the stairs slowly, one at a time. She watched the expression on Jack's face change from angry to—something hard to read. She felt the panic again. And then she realized Jack looked worried. She held out her arms as Jesse reached the landing, and Jesse tentatively handed the towel to her.

"Wow, kid," she said. "Someone did a number on you, huh?"

Jesse looked down and away, her face burning.

"Hey," she said.

"Yes?"

"Look at me."

Jesse looked up. Jack was smiling tentatively, like someone who had forgotten how. Jesse felt a rush of relief. She wasn't mad. She couldn't stay mad.

"I'm not an asshole, okay?" she said. "I'm not gonna hurt you."

Jesse swallowed, and nodded. Jesse gave her the brightest smile she could manage.

She punched Jesse lightly on the arm. "Goddamn, you looked scared."

"Was not," Jesse said.

She laughed, and Jesse felt the fear drain away a little, her body returning to its familiar shape. As soon as he relaxed, his stomach rumbled.

"You hungry, kid?" Jack asked.

"Yeah."

"Let's go get—" She glanced at the kitchen. "Wait, did you do dishes?" She sounded so incredulous Jesse almost thought she was angry again.

"You told me to?"

She shrugged. "I'll make pancakes."

He sat down on the floor and watched her work in the kitchen. She made the pancakes in a wok, which kind of impressed him. He liked the way she moved, too. Smoothly and efficiently.

"Did you used to be a line cook?" he asked.

"Nah," she said. "Pancakes is the only dish in my repertoire."

"You just look really . . . graceful."

She glanced over her shoulder. "I'm gay, Jesse."

She sounded so matter of fact that Jesse blushed. "No, I don't mean it like that. I mean, like . . . you look like a dancer."

"I was a dancer." She flipped a pancake out of the pan with a little backhand, and poured more batter from the measuring cup she'd mixed it in. "And now I'm a boxer."

"Like . . . fighting?"

"Yeah, like fighting. Semiprofessionally."

Jesse sat quietly while Jack finished the pancakes. When she brought the plate down to the floor, he blurted out, "I'm gay, too."

She cocked her head to one side. "Okay. You want butter syrup?"

"What's butter syrup?"

"It's syrup that tastes like butter."

That had been the fastest he'd ever told anyone. Not that he had much practice; the only other people he'd told were a few at the restaurant. Everyone else had just sort of figured it out on their own.

"Yeah," he said. "Butter syrup sounds good."

When the pancakes were gone, Jack stood up, dusted the crumbs from her lap onto the floor, and tossed the plate into the sink so carelessly that Jesse thought she'd break it for sure. He suddenly understood why her place was such a mess. He felt tired just thinking about having to do something about it. Jack, though, looked wide awake.

"You'll need somewhere to sleep," she said. "You should look for a mattress."

"What do you mean, look for?"

"College students from the New City live around here, and they throw a lot of shit away. And it hasn't rained in a while."

Jesse wrinkled his nose. "Are you serious?"

"Do you wanna sleep on the floor?"

He sighed. "Okay, where do I look?"

"Check the alleys," Jack said. She fiddled with her key ring and tossed Jesse a single key. "That's for the house. Don't lose it. I've got an errand to run, so you're on your own."

"What do you do?"

Jack sighed. "You really don't want to know."

That immediately got Jesse's attention. "What, like if you told me you'd have to kill me?"

Jack glared at him, and Jesse realized suddenly that asking if someone killed people probably wasn't very polite. "Sorry," he said. "I really don't know anything."

"Keep it that way," Jack said.

"But Astrid said it was dangerous for me to—walk around by myself," he said. When he said it, it sounded impossibly pathetic.

"You're a big kid, you'll be fine." Jack was pulling on her boots now. "See you later tonight. Good luck."

Jesse sat down on the back steps for a while to fret. He didn't know the city, so how was he supposed to find a mattress? Maybe he could just sleep in Jack's bed while she was working, and be up before she got home. But the thought of Jack catching him sleeping in her bed filled him with fear for his life. So eventually he stood up and started walking.

The alleys had a life of their own, overgrown with pokeweed and piled high with everything from kitchen trash to discarded paintings. Some of the stuff he passed, he couldn't understand why anyone would throw away: a coffee maker that seemed fine, a living room couch with a floral print. He sat down on it experimentally, gave it a few test bounces. Yeah, he'd watch TV on that. He thought about grabbing the cushions and just using those as a bed, when up ahead he spotted a mattress.

It was saggy, but it didn't have any big mysterious stains on it. It was propped up against the crumbling brick wall of an old carriage house. Jesse looked around to see if anyone was watching. There was a plain panel van parked a little further down the alley, its back doors facing his way, but he couldn't see anyone from this angle. And anyway, it wasn't stealing if someone had thrown it out, right?

He tried to lift it, and it flopped all around, threatening to topple him over. His body was the wrong shape for carrying something like this, too tall and skinny. As he tried to brace the mattress, he felt his body shift under him, getting shorter and wider, his hips spreading out, and she realized that without thinking, she'd turned into a girl again. Damn. But the weight of the mattress did feel better balanced like this. Convenient. She started walking slowly back the way she'd come. And then, Jesse heard the doors to the van open.

"Well, hi, there," someone said behind him. "Do you need help with that, miss?"

"No thanks," Jesse called, hearing how high and uncertain her own voice sounded. "I got this."

Footsteps behind her. Jesse put down the mattress and looked.

There were two men back there, dressed in slacks and polo shirts. Behind them the van doors were open, and Jesse could see a tangle of video monitoring equipment, and further back something that looked like a live animal trap, like the kind Paul used to put out for coyotes.

"Hey, are you guys, like . . . city maintenance or something?" Jesse asked.

"We're scientists," said one of them, a guy with a buzz cut. He didn't look like a scientist; he looked like an off-duty cop if Jesse had ever seen one. "We're studying the wildlife here."

The other one nudged him. He looked a little older, and wore horn-rimmed glasses. "We were about to call it quits for the day," he said. "You look like you could use some help with that. We've got the van here already. My name's Marty, and this is Kyle. Can we give you a ride?"

"I'm good," Jesse said. "I don't really have very far to go."

"Oh? Where do you live?" said Buzz Cut. Glasses gave him another nudge, harder this time. Buzz Cut took a step forward. Jesse took a step back.

"Hey, don't be silly," Glasses said. "We're not trying to intrude."

"Then leave me alone!" Jesse said.

Buzz Cut looked at Glasses, and Glasses gave him a little nod. And then they both charged toward Jesse.

She left the mattress behind. As she ran, she felt her legs elongate underneath her as he turned back into a boy, stretching his steps. He heard both men behind him shouting, but didn't hear them running after. And then he heard the van start up.

He vaulted over a fence and into an overgrown backyard, and hunkered down low. After a few minutes, he heard the van speed past. Through a crack in the fenceboards, he watched it disappear from the alley and out of sight.

He sat there in the grass for a few minutes, shivering. He thought about what Astrid had said, that the scientists in the New City didn't care who you were, they'd take you apart just to see how you worked. He thought about how certain they'd been that he was stupid, that they could do whatever they wanted with him. With her, he thought, and he felt a rush of sympathy for that girl they'd thought he was. The girl he . . . kind of was.

Eventually, he climbed back over the fence. He thought about going straight home, but he still needed that mattress.

He went back to where he'd left it. No cars around this time, no men in polo shirts. Jesse tried to get his body to shift, but it refused, the transformation hiding inside of him like a scared animal. He sighed, bent his knees and picked up the stupid, heavy thing, and started trudging home with it.

NINE

The police boats had been trolling up and down the river all day, making it impossible for the nameless girl to leave the island to fish. Hungry and irritable, she lay on her stomach in her house, reading to pass the time and slip out of herself. Eventually, they sent men onto the island, where they searched up and down in the ruined castle but didn't think to investigate the jumbled pile of logs at the far end. She put down her book when they started stomping up and down on the flagstones outside. Inches from them, she could see flashes of their uniforms through gaps in the logs.

They were talking about the man who'd died. Pete, they called him. And there was another one missing. Matthew. She didn't like that. She hadn't liked the look of those girls at all. Especially their leader, the witch. She hadn't seen her face, but she'd sensed her. She didn't seem afraid the way people usually were when they looked at her. That witch had looked like she was studying her, picking her apart. She couldn't imagine what the witch would do to someone who she'd kidnapped.

Those men outside didn't seem to know about the witch. They were looking around, clomping up and down stone staircases inside and outside the summer palace, knocking over boxes and looking for homeless people. No homeless people lived in the castle, although some had tents elsewhere on the island. The nameless girl shut her eyes and hoped they'd had the sense to clear out before the police showed up. But they couldn't swim like she could.

Eventually the police got back in their boats and left, and she breathed out. She could go back to reading, even if she was jolted out of it sometimes by the whine of the engines and the shouts as they trolled up and down the river. They were looking, she realized, for a second body. She felt certain they wouldn't find one.

Turing pushed aside the branches she'd stacked in front of her doorway and rolled up the dark green tarp to let the setting sunlight in. She stretched out all her arms as wide as they would go, rolling out her back and letting it crack. There was still some light left; she should shave her head.

She'd been doing it for as long as she could remember, scraping her scalp with a half-scissor she'd fished out of the Otiotan. It made her sad to do it, but it was a habit she had picked up from the scientists who'd found her. They'd said that things got caught in her hair, that it was dirty, that it got in the way of the sticky pads they sometimes stuck to her head to measure her brain waves. Living on an island as she did now, she had found that they were right: When it grew out, things got stuck in it, twigs and leaves and the smell of the river. And so now whenever the little crop of auburn stubble started to curl back on itself, she took her half-scissor to it, trying to make it as neat as she could, at least the parts she could see in her cracked compact mirror. The light really was fading fast, so she hurried, scraping the hair away down to the scalp, and finally pouring a little water from a jug over her head to wash away all the stray hairs. When it was done, she stood dripping in the courtyard, feeling relieved and sad.

The police boat noises had died down as they moved around to the other side of the city. Leaving behind only the sounds of the birds and the hushing over the river. Except now there was splashing. Irregular at first, although it quickly found its rhythm. Turing knew that sound: a kayak. But usually there would be several all at once: a rowing class or an afternoon picnic trip to the sunny southern tip of the Isle of Bells. This was at the wrong time of day, and she could only hear one paddle.

She hoisted herself up onto the parapet of the old courtyard and looked over. The river had washed piles of logs and debris up against this upper wall until they formed a long, sloping heap down to the river. Beyond the logs, far away now but getting closer, was a small red boat. And in it, a person. She held very still and watched the boat get closer until, when she at last saw who was in it, she drew in a sharp breath.

It was the woman from that morning on the riverbank. Not the one who had left the body, but the one who had found it. She'd taken off her jacket now and was wearing a white undershirt and a gun in a shoulder holster, the muscles of her shoulders straining hard against the weight of the water as she pushed it away behind her. She was rowing badly, but it didn't matter, because she was stronger than the river. Bending it to her will. Turing thought, once again, of the picture of the knight she'd gone looking for. But a different image came to mind as the woman got close enough for her face to be visible. She looked like a statue of a young Apollo, with a sloping nose and soft lips.

At last, the boat reached the heap of logs piled around the fortress wall. The woman jumped out, slipped, caught herself, grabbed the boat, and dragged it with one mighty heave up out of the water. The nameless girl found herself riveted to the spot. The woman had a thick scar wrapped around her arm and smaller ones crosshatching her shoulders, a dog's head tattooed on her collarbone, a chipped lower front tooth. She looked ferocious. The nameless girl found herself wanting to smooth her hand down the woman's back like she would calm a cat. But she shrank away and slid backward down the wall as quietly as she could, away from the woman, and crept to the door of her hut. She needed to hide. Nobody could know she was here. Nobody—

"Hello? Hey!"

The woman was already at the top of the wall, sitting on it. How had she moved so quickly? Turing stood silhouetted in the open doorway, as visible as she had ever been.

"Go away," the nameless girl said. "You're not welcome here."

"Hey, I just want to talk."

The nameless girl stepped through the doorway, all her long arms spilling out around her in a halo. She'd read a book about bears once, about how you had to make yourself look bigger than them. It worked on people, too, she'd discovered, over the years that she'd spent here. They always gave up and ran when they saw her.

This woman just studied her. The daughter of the river was suddenly conscious of how she looked, in the faded and tattered swim trunks she wore, shoeless, hairless. It almost hurt to be looked at by this woman, who studied her without fear, who seemed to be searching her for something.

"I saw you this morning," the woman said at last.

She hesitated. That was not what she'd expected.

"My name's Jack," the woman said. "Jack Marley. What's yours?"

"The scientists called me Turing," she said. "I don't have a last name."

She was annoyed. Alone on the island, she didn't usually refer to herself by a name. She was just a part of the landscape. And so the name that came to mind, when she opened her mouth, was the one she'd used before. Now it was stuck to her.

"The scientists?" Jack asked.

"They kidnapped me, for a while."

"And so now you live out here?" Jack asked. "What do you eat?"

Turing bared her long, slender teeth. "Fish."

"All by yourself?"

"I like being alone."

"Huh, me too," Jack said.

Turing narrowed her eyes. Was the woman purposely not understanding her? "What do you want?"

"I just want to ask about what you saw this morning," Jack said. "Somebody killed that man, and I think you might know who it is."

That took her aback. She'd been expecting an accusation.

"Maybe it was me," she said.

Jack snorted. "I doubt it."

In spite of herself, Turing relaxed.

"Come down from there," she said to Jack. She nodded toward the door of her hut. "Come inside."

"Thanks," Jack said.

Jack took her gun out of her shoulder holster and set it down. Then she slid down from the wall, her shirt catching on the stones and riding up at the back. She landed with knees bent. Everything she did seemed easy, like she had jumped off that same wall a hundred times. Jack straightened up. She was much shorter than Turing, which made Turing feel gangly, like the herons that sometimes waded into the river among the ducks.

"This way," Turing said, and led her to the hut.

When they stepped inside, she folded herself up onto the mattress at the far end and let Jack look around. She watched her take in the camp stove, the glitter of flattened tin cans tucked into the ceiling in rows. Jack's eyes lit on the crate of books.

"I've read that one," she said. She pulled out a spy novel. "What'd you think of it?"

"You didn't come here to ask me what I thought of *Dark Passenger*."

Jack ran a hand over her scalp. "I read a lot," she said. "The guys I work with, not so much. Which is fine, I don't really rely on them for their literary analysis."

"It was like I'd read it before," Turing said. "Once you've read enough of these, unless there's something new in them, it's like chewing gum that's lost its taste." She had never chewed gum; she hoped she'd read enough about it that it wouldn't show.

Jack nodded. "I can see that," she said. "Yeah, I mean, he writes the same book every couple of years. Guy has to stop a war in some backwater place where he doesn't understand the customs . . ."

Turing smiled a little. "And then he meets a beautiful woman who tells him it's not what he thought it was."

"And then he realizes his bosses lied to him."

"And then he has to choose—will he finish his mission?"

Jack laughed, and looked at the ground. "I've read probably ten of these. God help me, I love them."

Turing realized that she had lost any desire to protect herself, to not say the wrong thing. Jack might work for the police, for all she knew, but suddenly she felt she could tell her anything. She wondered if Jack did it on purpose, that self-effacing laugh.

"You were there before I was this morning," Jack said. "Can you tell me what you saw? Who was there?"

"A woman," Turing said. "Well, a group of them. They had their faces covered. But I could see that one of them had blond hair." Jack reached up to rub her own head. "No, not like yours. Long."

Jack nodded. "Okay," she said. "Did they say anything? Or do anything?"

And so she told Jack about it. About the body. The girls. Staying and watching, waiting for him to be found. She watched Jack's face flicker with emotion as she spoke.

"You didn't even know the guy," Jack said.

"I don't know what he did, or why they killed him," Turing said. "But I didn't like the idea that nobody would know what happened to him."

Jack was silent for a long moment, regarding her. The nameless girl felt again that sensation she had outside, of being read.

"How long have you been out here all alone?" Jack asked.

The question caught her off guard. She wrapped her long arms around her body, but it had already struck her in the chest.

"That's different," she said. "I choose to live out here."

"Why, because it's safe?" Jack asked. "Look, I work for this guy who runs a few businesses in town. He could find something for you to do. He's always looking to hire people with special talents, and they'll take care of you."

Turing folded her human arms. "You mean you work for a criminal who hires monsters." Jack looked so stunned that she had to stifle a laugh. "I'm not naive. I read books where people talk like that. And that man who died was a cop, but you don't seem like one."

Jack shrugged. "Okay, yes, you're not completely wrong," she said. "But it's not as bad as it sounds. If you want to see the city up close, and you want to be protected from scientists, you could do a lot worse than to work for Sir."

"Do you like working for him?" Turing asked.

Jack went silent for a minute, studying the ceiling while she thought.

"It's complicated," she said. "But he's loyal to his people. He's a good boss."

"Let me think about it," Turing said. "Can you come back and see me in a week? I can have an answer by then."

Jack bristled a little. "What, exactly a week from now? I don't really have a fixed schedule."

"All right, then my answer is no. I need time to think."

"Okay, a week. Jesus. Same time, same place?"

"Just come to the riverbank," Turing said. "I'll find you."

"Fine," Jack muttered. She seemed upset. Was it so much to

ask that she take a week to consider? Was that enough to rip the bottom out of the conversation?

"I don't understand you, Jack." Turing tipped her head to one side. "I feel as though you like me, but everything you say sounds like you're angry with me."

Jack's head tipped up. "Really?"

"Are you upset about your friend?"

"He's not exactly my friend. And no, I think that's just how I talk." Jack shrugged. "We've just met, and I've said more to you than I usually say in a week. God, we talked about books. So yeah, I do like you."

The daughter of the river had to resist the urge to cover her face in embarrassment and joy. Instead, she just smiled.

"I like you, too," she said. "I'm glad I'll see you again."

"Well, great," Jack said. She stood up, stooping under the low ceiling. "I'll let Sir know you're thinking about it. I'll talk you up."

"Tell him—" Turing hesitated. "Tell him I'm not going to be any good at killing people."

"That's okay," Jack said. "Most of the time, that's not how it goes. It's all about intimidation."

"And I'm intimidating." She realized as she said it that she wasn't concealing the sorrow in her voice. Jack stopped halfway through pushing open the tarp over the doorway.

"That bother you?" she asked.

The daughter of the river had no answer.

"You're an interesting guy, Turing," Jack said. "I hope you go for it. I'd like to know you better. And I can't remember the last time I said that about anyone."

The daughter of the river thought about a story she read once where a creature from the sea was made into a woman, her tail ripped in half to make legs, so that dancing with her beloved on land felt like being cut with knives. She almost had to laugh at herself for feeling cut in half by Jack Marley calling her an *interesting guy*.

And then, Jack held out a hand. And Turing, not sure at first what the gesture was, took it and held it. Jack's hand was hot in hers, slippery with sweat. They looked at each other.

"I'm sorry," Jack said. "I was trying to help you up."

"Oh," Turing said. "I've never done that before."

"Well, it goes like this," Jack said. She leaned back on her heels, and the daughter of the river felt herself pulled up to standing.

"How was that?" Jack asked.

"Different," she said.

In the silence that followed, they both became aware of the low buzzing. Two sets of ears pricked to the sound, growing higher pitched as it got closer.

"Police boat?" Jack asked.

"They were here earlier," Turing said. "They left."

"They must have seen the kayak."

The daughter of the river followed Jack out into the courtyard. Jack reached overhead to grab the wall, boosted herself up onto it, and turned back to look at her.

"One week," Jack said. "Don't be late."

"You won't outrun them," Turing said.

"So they catch me," Jack said. "They know me. You stay low, okay?"

Jack flashed a grin so big that the nameless girl felt it tugging on the corners of her own mouth, and then she was running down the wobbly heap of logs and debris to her boat. And then she was shoving away.

She climbed onto the wall, staying low, hugging it for support while she watched Jack go. Jack was really a terrible kayaker. But that didn't matter; she wore her clothes like they were armor, and moved as though she were on horseback. Even her name was like a hero in a children's story. The girl had never heard of a woman named Jack. That was a mystery, that someone could be a woman and a prince at the same time. She liked the feeling of wholeness that the idea gave her.

She saw the police boat peel off of its trajectory, turning from the island toward Jack's little boat. It was big and clumsy, slicing up the water.

She shrank back against the logs. She wrapped her long arms around her body, shielding herself from sight, and waited.

A wave from the police boat struck the kayak sidelong, and while she sat aghast, it rolled over. All at once, the boat shot into the air and then skidded across the water, light as a leaf, Jack gone.

Jack would be killed, thrown against the rapids further down. The police boat was turning and shouting, aiming for the little craft. The nameless girl scrambled down the logs and slipped herself between the ribs of white water.

Under the river, the nameless girl was fast. Under the river, her arms didn't feel heavy; they jetted her through the water in steady bursts, curling and uncurling. She'd long ago recovered from the injury she'd done herself when she'd first returned to the island,

and now her seven remaining arms did the work of eight. They propelled her through layers of dark water until she saw a tumbling bright shape. Jack was still struggling, but with slowing movements. Soon she would drown.

She scooped Jack up in her arms. But as she tried to pull her toward the air, something heavy settled over her, and somehow the surface seemed further away than it had a moment ago.

It was like falling in place, and the more she fought it, the weaker she felt. Jack was going to die, and all she could do was fall.

INTERLUDE

The Witches

Minutes of Emergency Meeting of River City's Board of Witches, 1st September, Kingless Year 21, 8 p.m.

In attendance:

Chair: Astrid Epps

Secretary: Deirdre Riviere

Members: Marlena Golding, Artemis Anderson, Mrs. Pickett, Lacrimosa "Lacey" Stackpoole, Belle Marley, Paris Nguyen, Asha Hampton

Also Present: Wendy McNair

Not in attendance: Betty Odina (scheduling conflict)

Agenda:

- A. Hampton presents list of Betty Odina's written opinions and votes, collected in advance for this special session. Secretary Riviere reminds the board that only present members may vote, according to agreed-upon rules of order. Motion by Chair Epps to suspend this rule because it's "not fair to Betty." Seconded by A. Anderson. Motion passes 8–1. ~~This is a clear violation of our charter.~~
- Reading of minutes from last meeting, 31st August. Corrections made to several line items (see previous minutes).
- Chair reopens a discussion of the incidents of the previous

night: the large discharge of magic at approximately 10 p.m. and the death of P. McNair and disappearance of M. Mannering at an unknown time.

- Discussion focuses on magical discharge first. Chair Epps asks "We can't do this all night, ladies. Which one of you was it?" No one present claims responsibility. B. Marley notes that the scientists in the New City are experimenting with magic, saying that she saw a professor summon a negligible amount of magic using a machine. Marley tasked by the Board with "finding out if they were messing around last night."

- Discussion of alleged influx of magic at appx. midday previous day; issue raised by B. Marley. After heated debate, membership is split on whether there was measurable fluctuation or whether it "felt normal enough." Brief discussion of what to do if Maiden appears; many suggestions made, no motions carried.

- Discussion of continued missing-person status of Matthew Mannering. Motion by W. McNair to propose using magic to locate missing officer of the law. Secretary Riviere reminds the board that our bylaws state that only board members can bring motions. Chair Epps reminds attendees that the board's bylaws further state that magic cannot be used in matters pertaining to law enforcement. After sustained discussion, W. McNair motions for the board to suspend the bylaws. No seconds.

- W. McNair walks out, along with L. Stackpoole, who says that she's going to "just follow along and keep an eye on her."

- Motion by Mrs. Pickett to request a tea break. Motion carried unanimously. Discussion of whether it is appropriate for the witches to cooperate with law enforcement in any form, magical or otherwise. Discussion of whether Pete McNair's death and Matthew Mannering's disappearance constitute a "possible magical event" given the circumstances, and whether the university could potentially be involved. Return of L. Stackpoole and W. McNair. A. Epps calls meeting to order again.

- Proposed motion by L. Stackpoole that "we all ask around" and bring any information found to Chair Epps as quickly as possible before making a decision about police involvement, with the chair to call a follow-up emergency session if necessary. Motion passes 5–4 with no previously recorded opinion from B. Odina, ~~which is why we don't let people who aren't present vote, their votes aren't informed by the discussion, it's just common sense.~~

- W. McNair leaves meeting, citing a headache. Table talk speculating on the fate of M. Mannering, the cause of death of P. McNair, and what this must be like for W.

- Time check made. Rapid resolution of several matters unrelated to special session, including: use of magic in case of Mrs. Dowser's left ankle (rejected unanimously), approval of weeklong vacations and appropriate coverage for Secretary Riviere and Mrs. Pickett (approved unanimously), and nomination of Carnival Committee members M. Golding, A. Anderson, B. Odina, B. Marley, and A. Hampton. B. Marley declines nomination, stating that she has other plans on Carnival Night; all others accept and are voted in.

- Meeting adjourns at 10:20 p.m. Next meeting set for 8 Sept. at 5 p.m.

TEN

Time moved differently below the river. The nameless girl and Jack fell down and down for what seemed like forever, through layers of debris, until they weren't in water at all. Some other medium, a thicker liquid. The nameless girl looked up and couldn't see the lights that usually danced on the surface of the river. They were under something—had they been washed under the island's shelf of bedrock?

Jack kicked and flailed in panic, her head lolling forward. Her mouth slipped open and she breathed in the water. Turing gasped, and her own mouth filled with the stuff, but once she stopped panicking she realized that she could breathe it through her lungs as easily as through her gills. And when she looked down at Jack, she realized that she too was breathing now, the strange half-liquid stuff drifting in and out of her mouth in currents. She gathered Jack tightly to her side and dared, at last, to look around.

They were in a graveyard of ships: broken masts and split hulls. But when she reached out to touch one, her fingers slid through it and into it. It was no more solid than the stuff they swam in. And when she touched it, it changed into something else. Turing recoiled as she saw the ships change to a village of log houses with smoke curling out of their chimneys, no more substantial than the ships. It was like standing in the pages of a storybook, like a ghost, like a reflection in the water.

The image rippled, and then it formed her own shape. A tall tapered body with a cluster of tentacles erupting from its back. It turned this way and that, as though trying to get a look at itself.

Turing clutched Jack closer to her. She suddenly had the sense that she was not immersed in a medium, but in a creature. A thing, or a person, but impossibly large and very old.

The weight of it pressed Turing down further. She got the sense that it was sizing her up, trying her on somehow. She didn't like that, and she didn't like the way the shadow-her was looking at Jack. The ghostly shape crouched down, made its long tentacles bristle, opened its mouth, and bared its teeth. It made no sound, but Turing was frightened looking at it, even though it was just her. It looked like a monster. And then it lunged for her—no, for Jack.

She wouldn't have that. Not today. Today she'd met a prince. With all her arms she shoved the water down and away, jetting as hard as she could toward the surface, trying to leave this terrible, watching thing behind them. She struggled upward against some tough membrane, until at last, with a cry of frustration, she broke through it.

The white water churned all around them as she brought Jack's head up to the surface. She heard the other girl gasp and choke, taking in air and water in equal measure.

Turing dragged Jack along toward the shore, slithered up the riverbank, and set her down on the grass on her side. Jack coughed up water from her lungs, and rolled over onto her knees, and hung onto the grass with both hands, like she was afraid she might fall off the earth.

"The boat," Jack said, when at last she could speak. "We have to get out of sight."

Turing felt a stab of doubt about that. And when she looked up at the sky, she understood why.

"Jack," she said. "It's midnight."

Jack looked up at the sky, gone somehow instantly from twilight to black. There were no boats on the river now, just empty flat black water all the way to the Isle of Bells.

"How long was I out?" Jack said.

Turing shook her head. "I don't know. We were underwater. No, not . . ."

"I know," Jack said. "I remember being able to breathe the water. And . . . that's it."

"There was something down there," Turing said. "I don't know what it was."

Jack wiped mud from her forehead, spat out a mouthful of grit that dribbled down her chin. "Magic?"

"I don't know. I can't describe it." She didn't want to. She didn't want to tell Jack that it had turned into her, how frightened she'd been of its imitation of her.

"You saved my life," Jack said.

"You were trying to save mine."

"I owe you one."

Turing smiled, and Jack shook her head. "No, I'm serious," Jack said. "Let me know as soon as you think of something you want."

Turing knew instantly what she wanted. A kiss. But she knew at the same moment that she wouldn't ask. It wouldn't be the same if she asked. She would never know, if she asked now, what it would feel like for Jack to kiss her because she wanted to.

"You don't owe me anything," she said. "I'm glad you're alive."

"Yeah, well." Jack looked away. She was embarrassed, Turing realized, and almost blushed with pride.

"I want to work with you," Turing said. "I've decided."

"Oh," Jack said. "Okay. I'll do that. I'll set you up an interview." She shook her head, wiping her hand off on the grass before offering it to Turing to shake. "Pleasure—doing business with you."

Over Jack's shoulder, she spotted someone. A big man trudging along the riverbank.

The creature who called herself Turing sometimes, but who really had no name at all, wanted to stay there with Jack forever. She wanted to make sure she was safe, follow her home, put her to bed. The creature who lived among the rocks did not like to be seen, was afraid of people, hated the way they stared at her, the way they yelled. So she inclined her head, and as Jack turned to look, she slid backward into the water until just her eyes were visible. She watched Jack gather herself up onto her feet and then turn to look for her. Their eyes met from the water, and Jack gave her a little nod. She understood.

The man came closer. He reminded Turing of a bear on two legs, his head shaggy with red hair, his red beard peppered with white.

"Hey," Jack said. Turing could hear the warning in her voice, almost a growl.

"Here's a history lesson," the man said. Jack watched him warily and said nothing. "On this day in 1587, a group of Englishmen left the city, then nothing more than a ring of huts surrounded by a stakewall. They said they were going to England and promised to bring back more supplies. When they returned to it after a delay of many years overseas, they could not find the city again."

"Hey, back off," Jack said. But the man took a step closer.

"This is important," the man said. "They searched the surrounding woods and fields, captured and tortured the native men, asking over and over again how an entire town could vanish from sight. None of them saw the wooden bridge that led across the river to a more defensible island, an island so safe that the people who now lived on it had wondered why they didn't choose it sooner, why they hadn't seen it before, why they would ever want to leave. Since then, it has remained missing but not missing, there but not there, periodically discovered and lost again. Do you understand, son?"

"I'm not your son. How'd you know about the cop? Did you kill him?"

But the man wasn't looking at Jack. Something about his eyes frightened the creature who lived on the Isle of Bells. He looked too familiar somehow, like the vision of herself as a monster, like all the worst parts of her own face. She held still, hoping she was wrong and that he hadn't seen her.

He turned to Jack, seeming to notice the gun in her hand for the first time. He sighed.

"Kids never listen," he said. "I didn't listen, either."

He stumbled off into the night, scratching himself as he went.

As soon as he was gone, Jack sagged. Turing was out of the

water before she could stop herself. She caught Jack, who glanced up at her in surprise.

"What do you need?" Turing asked.

"I'm fine," Jack said. "I just need to get home."

"Where do you live?"

Jack pointed up the hill with a shaky hand. "Not too far."

Turing glanced around. It was midnight. Nobody here had seen her. She had plenty of time before dawn to slip out of sight.

"I'll help you," she said. "Here."

Jack nodded, and the girl from the river draped one of Jack's arms over her shoulders, and wrapped a hand around her waist. Together they started up the slope. Halfway up, they came to a set of concrete switchback stairs built into the hillside. And beyond that, narrow streets of row houses, silent in the hours before the sun came up. Walking down the street, as though she were a person like anyone else, filled Turing with unspeakable terror. But Jack was here beside her.

At last they came to an alley, and the backside of a brick building with a set of rickety wooden stairs leading up to a high distant door. And there, Jack stopped.

"This is my place," she said. "I . . . I really owe you now."

"Don't worry about it," Turing said.

Jack ran a hand over her hair, dislodging mud that crumbled into dust. "I'm gonna sleep until someone wakes me up," she said. She seemed about to say something else when she turned suddenly, looking up her own staircase. And Turing saw it, too: Someone was sitting huddled halfway up the stairs, her face hidden in shadows. Waiting for Jack.

Of course a girl like Jack had a girlfriend. Of course she was up waiting for her. And she, Turing, might save her life, but never be anything more than an *interesting guy*.

"I'm going to go," Turing said.

Jack gave her a look that was hard to describe, and then she was trudging for her staircase, and Turing was fading into the shadows.

"Jackie," the girl called softly. "I need you."

Turing did not stay to hear Jack's reply. She snuck back out of the neighborhood, down the hill, her bare feet sliding on the rough stones of the slope until she got to the river, where she could fling herself in and douse her humiliation.

She had come to the island to be away from people, to live isolated in her fantasies, after her escape from the laboratory. However, she found that certain things about the laboratory persisted in her: shaving her head, wearing that old name. Until today, she had never had a visitor.

And now she'd had one. And she'd saved her life. And she'd almost—almost!—followed her home.

When she got back to her hut in the courtyard, she flung herself down on the mattress, letting her toes drag cool circles on the flagstones.

She touched her own face with her hands, trying to remember that it was still her face, that she was still the same person. Everything felt different now. Everything and nothing.

"Are you going to do it?" came a small, chittering voice close to her head.

She lifted her hands from her face. From the stuffing in the mattress to the cans glittering in the rafters, her hut was once again full of fairies.

"You went to the city," they said. "You will kill the king."

"I don't know," Turing said. "I don't know. I don't know."

"You must," said the little shriveled one. "They have seen you. They know you. His sword is aimed at your heart. He will spill your blood on the stone if you do not fight."

She closed her eyes. They continued to chatter at her, but she let exhaustion turn their words into a liquid that washed over her, emptied of meaning.

She didn't know how she could do what they asked. But what they had offered was now worth more than ever.

She lay on her mattress, stared up into the rafters of her house, and tried to imagine it. What it would be like to put on a summer dress and walk the path that wound along the river. What it would be like to climb London Hill without fear, to sit on Jack Marley's stoop, waiting for her to get home.

Alone in her hut, the nameless girl sighed. She had no idea how she could stop the king, but for a moment, she imagined herself different, transformed. She imagined a face, a body that a girl who was a prince could love.

ELEVEN

Covered in bruises, half-drowned, Jack stared at the girl sitting in the shadows. Her blond braid was flipped forward over her shoulder so she could fiddle with the ends. She looked skinnier than usual, all corners. She was looking thoughtfully into the shadows where Turing had disappeared.

"Belle," Jack said. "What's going on?"

Belle gazed up at her. She seemed scared. But then, she almost always seemed scared when she was talking to Jack.

"I need help," she said. "Can we talk inside?"

"I have a roommate now."

Belle's brow furrowed. "I thought you lived alone."

"I'm doing someone a favor."

"Is it a girl?"

"No," Jack said, turning away. "Some teenage boy. Astrid asked me to put him up."

Belle started to say something, but then she shook her head.

"You've heard by now," she said. "About the cop."

Jack nearly fell down. "Oh, Jesus, Belle."

"I didn't mean to!" Belle's eyes darted around anxiously. "I just . . . He was going after Tanya."

A handful of girls lived with Belle in the old Bodwell School and worked at the print shop they ran out of the place. Some of them had guys they slept with for money to keep the lights on, and since it was a bunch of girls living alone, the cops hassled them sometimes, for money or sex. That's what Pete had been doing, Belle said: bothering Tanya when she'd gone out to smoke in the alley. It had gotten physical; she'd yelled for Belle. And Belle had, she said, put a tiny bit of magic into Pete. Just a little. In his brain.

"It didn't even use that much," Belle said. Her eyes had a weird glint. "I wouldn't have thought of it, except one of the scientists talked about how you probably could do surgery with magic."

Jack shook her head. "Okay, well, you were right to tell me. We can explain this. What happened to his partner?"

Belle's brow furrowed in gentle confusion. "What partner?"

"You haven't heard? Matthew Mannering? He's missing, too."

She shook her head. "I don't know him. Sorry, Jackie."

"Okay, well," she said. "Who else knows?"

"Just me and the girls."

"Nobody saw you?"

Belle hesitated.

"When we went to the river," she said, "this . . . creature came out of the water. We ran."

Turing. Jack shook her head. "Well, I talked to him," she said. "If I tell him what happened, he'll understand. He won't say anything."

Belle seemed to be considering something, weighing it in her mind. "We can't tell anyone," she said. "I don't know your friend but I don't trust him."

Jack sighed. "We're gonna have to tell Sir," she said. "He'll help us get this straightened out. He did last time."

"This is different," Belle said. "This was one of his cops, wasn't it? He'll kill me." Her lip trembled. "I'm scared, Jackie."

"Don't be," Jack said. She was too tired to think straight. "I won't tell anyone for now. But even the cops will figure this out eventually."

"Please," Belle said. "It's not just me. If I get in trouble, the girls won't have anywhere to live."

Jack felt old. She reached out to steady herself on the porch railing, and Belle flinched away from her. That stung.

"I just—I need sleep," Jack said. "We'll talk soon. We'll figure this out. It's you and me. Right?"

Belle eased herself up, out of Jack's way. "Right."

She walked backward away from Jack, as though afraid to turn her back on her. Jack squeezed her eyes shut and breathed. She tried to remind herself that Belle had been through a lot. It must have been shocking to kill Pete. Jack, at least, had planned the first time she'd killed someone. It had been a decision, not an accident.

The stairs lay in front of Jack. She dragged herself up them and fumbled in her wet pocket for her keys. The apartment was cleaner than she'd ever seen it. The light was on under the kid's door. What was he still doing up?

She knocked on his door. "Hey. Cinderella."

He answered, looking triumphant. "I found a mattress," he said. "Some guys from the university tried to stick me in their van, but I lost 'em."

"Good work," she said. "Listen. You need to get a job. You can't just be hanging out here by yourself all the time."

"Sure, I'm not afraid of hard work."

"Tomorrow I'll take you downtown and introduce you to my boss."

"Wait a sec. Why are you wet?"

She shut her eyes. "It's a long story."

"Is something wrong?"

The kid was looking at her like he pitied her. Fuck that. She was Jack Marley. She'd figure it out.

"I just need a shower," she said. "Don't stay up too late. You're interviewing for a job tomorrow."

Jack staggered into the bathroom and stripped off her wet clothes while she ran the faucet. She climbed under the hot water, feeling it sting in a dozen little scrapes and cuts, blood and mud pooling in the tub. Something was wrong. She knew to listen to that feeling. It had saved her life before.

What had Belle said? That some scientist was talking about using magic to do surgeries? As if they didn't have enough ways to cut people up. Those rich pricks. Rumor had it they sometimes bailed people out of jail if they were scientifically interesting, on the condition that they come back with them. Jack believed it. If one of them could do what Belle had just done, that was a problem—

Later. Her dad would have told her that worrying instead of sleeping was a waste of time. She turned off the spray, wrapped herself in a towel, and staggered to bed half-washed and still smelling like the river. Jack forced the thoughts out of her head and made a little blank space, and put herself in the middle of that space, and dreamed of nothing at all.

TWELVE

Lying on his back in the spare bedroom of Jack's house on Charity Street, Jesse opened his book to a poem he never finished reading on the bus. His body was heavy with exhaustion and sweat as he lay on the beat-up mattress he'd finally hauled up the stairs. His eyes fell shut over and over again as he struggled to finish a stanza:

> *Merged, you and I, my love, seal the silence*
> *while the sea destroys its continual forms,*
> *collapses its turrets of wildness and whiteness,*
> *because in the weft of those unseen garments*
> *of headlong water, and perpetual sand,*
> *we bear the sole, relentless tenderness—*

And the next morning, across town in an extra-long twin bed, David woke up, thinking briefly that he was drowning under a wall of water. He sat up, gasping, breathing heavily in the pool of concentrated sunlight that filtered through the plexiglass of his dormitory window. The weak plywood bed creaked under his sudden movement. He glanced at the clock. He had a meeting with his adviser in ten minutes.

He'd stayed up way too late puzzling over *Planned Magic*. He'd gotten most of the basics down, hadn't started any more fires, although he had put a pretty upsetting crack in his plate glass window. He'd been up half the night trying to work up a spell to fix it, but putting things back together was harder than taking them apart. Which made sense; making order out of disorder always had a higher energetic cost. He'd probably have to sacrifice something pretty big to get a plate glass window back into shape. He'd gotten an unsettling feeling when working on some of the more complicated spells, like the power was fluctuating.

David realized that he'd stopped moving, sleepiness and rumination taking over his body. He scrambled into some wrinkled pants, stooped in the mirror to frown at his hair, then slipped on the fronts of his shoes and took off at a shuffle down the hallway, checking the contents of his backpack as he ran. Pencils, he needed pencils. He ducked into his neighbor's door (always half-open) and grabbed a handful off Seth's desk. Seth, buried somewhere under the layers of duvets, didn't move at all. David shut the door as quietly as he could, and hustled down the hall until he hit the bank of elevators and stopped there, waiting in the gentle wash of the fluorescent lights and the hallway music while the numbers counted up toward his floor on the overhead display.

He sighed. The song was the one he called "The [x] from Ipanema," which he'd always liked because it had two sets of lyrics, one for girls and one for boys:

Tall and tan and young and [lovely/handsome]
The [girl/boy] from Ipanema goes walking

He found himself nodding along. He felt good. He'd slept in, but he was also working on the greatest breakthrough his field had made in some time. So really, it all balanced out. Nobody would look back on this time in his life and say *David Blank really slacked off.*

A white girl wandered over, groggy in sweatpants, and stared up at him, up and up and up until she found his face, and then her eyes darted away and she stared directly in front of her without blinking, shifting her weight away from him. He tried not to let it get to him—*Just ignore them*, he thought, in his foster mom's voice. The girl was probably an undergrad, fresh from some shitty little southern hometown. And he was enormous. He apologized for it with every muscle in his body. He looked the other way and heard her sigh and relax.

The elevator dinged. He stepped toward the door at the same time as her; she balked, and let him get into the elevator alone, where he hunched a little under the low ceiling. She continued to watch him with open worry until the elevator doors slid shut on him. Jesus. When they closed on her entirely, he shook himself and stomped up and down a little, and then growled like a monster ravaging Tokyo for the next six floors. "Argh! Gar!"

He thought for a moment that he could hear a faint voice laughing at him, but then it was gone, and the elevator doors dinged open with him still in a monster-pose, arms held close to his sides like a T-rex. The undergraduates on this floor, mostly boys, stared at him for a moment before he ducked out, and then they poured into the vacant elevator, jostling him and each other in the process. The doors dinged shut, and he sighed, finally feeling alone again—

"Hey!"

A hand slapped him on the back, and then Seth was beside him, a lanky Asian kid in pajama pants, whose hair had somehow fallen into a perfect boy band swoop fresh off the pillow. Seth was older than David, but still an undergraduate. But then again, lots of undergrads were older than David.

"I thought you were sleeping," David said.

"I'm like the law," Seth said. "I never sleep."

"Then why do you always dress for it?"

Seth ducked and wove like a boxer, looking very awake for someone who had been facedown and drooling only a few minutes before. "This is a matter of pride. A man cannot be robbed in his own room."

"I've got a meeting, and then I'll satisfy your pride. Buy you a hoagie?"

"Fine." Seth grinned. "You would not believe the night I had . . ." He counted on his fingers. "Three nights ago. Maybe four."

"Crazy night?" David asked.

"Insane," Seth said. "I woke up next to this gorgeous woman, right? And then I look over, and on her far side is"—his eyes darted around the hallway to make sure no one was listening—"this other *guy*, and he opens one eye and I swear to god he winked at me. David, I have never found my pants so fast in my *life* . . ." He squinted. "Hey, you look exhausted. When did you go to bed?"

"Eventually," David said.

"Don't be coy, d'ja get laid?"

David rolled his eyes.

"I'm fat and I'm poor," he said. "And this morning when I was waiting for the elevator a girl stared at me like I was fucking King Ghidorah. So yes, absolutely. That's why I'm tired. All the sex I've been having."

"Hey, hey," Seth said. "It's not you, man. That is their problem, and they are missing *out*."

David scowled. "Don't patronize me."

"Hey."

Seth planted himself in front of David, one hand up in the "Stop! In the Name of Love" position. David found himself smiling, looking down at him. Seth was . . . handsome, he supposed. He didn't like thinking it.

"You're a fine young man," Seth said. "Becky from the suburbs isn't going to be into you, but that's her loss."

David snorted. "I'm not worried about Becky," he said.

"Well then," Seth said, and began doing a backward samba down the hallway, "let me take you out this weekend and introduce you to Hannah, who is . . ." He cha-cha-ed around a group of girls, who started giggling. "Double jointed. And also works at the skeeziest club I have ever seen. I'm pretty sure they were betting on costumed knife fights. There was a stripper with a vestigial tail. It was some dark shit, man. You'd fit right in."

David sighed. "I'm not dark. *I'm* from the suburbs. I'm practically Becky."

Seth shook his head.

"Davey boy," he said. "We both know that's not true . . ." His eyes glazed over for a second, and he glanced at his watch and then began running backward. "I've gotta go, though, Lang's failing me if I'm late again and I'm on probation and—"

David laughed and watched Seth sprint off. He realized he felt better, his whole body relaxing into his clothes, from his head to his shoes. Goddammit. He liked Seth, wished he could stop dodging his offers to go out and do something stupid. But David had too much work to do if he wanted to keep his job. Seth had all the time in the world to coast through undergrad; David was one mistake away from losing his stipend and having to go—home. Good god.

When he got to his adviser's office, Haughan was half asleep, hunched over a cup of coffee. "Oh, David. Are we meeting today?"

So much for busting ass getting down here. David sank into the guest chair. "Yes, sir." David could put up with Haughan; he was one of the few people around here who didn't treat David like he must somehow be stupid. Haughan was bearable, as long as you weren't a young woman, in which case he assumed you were useless and would tell you so to your face. It was the kind of shit David had come to expect; as soon as you met someone here who was in your corner, it turned out they were a bastard to somebody else.

"I'm swamped with lectures," Haughan said. "Do you think you could finish the grant proposal?"

"Already done," David said, producing a manila envelope. "You just have to look over it, make sure I'm not leaving anything out."

Haughan put it into his desk tray without opening it. "Wonderful. You're better at those than me anyway. I've never had a talent like yours for bullshitting."

"Please be sure to file it on time," David said. "That grant covers my pay for the spring."

"Always worrying," Haughan said. "You should relax more.

Meet some girls. Surely one of them wants to have a half-genius baby with you."

David flicked his eyes down to study his hands and tried to keep his voice breezy. "I don't know when I'd find the time."

"You're not gay, are you?"

David glanced back up. "Sorry, what?"

"No, excuse me," Haughan said. "Oh, would you mind grading these?" He passed David a folder stuffed with papers. "From 101. It'll be good practice for when you have a hundred little nuisances of your own."

"Of course."

"And can you recalibrate the particle generator when you get a chance?"

David wanted to tell him that they'd never need the particle generator again, that he was the damn particle generator, that he had the crack in his window to show it. But he smiled. "Absolutely."

"You've been skipping that recently." *Because it doesn't do anything useful; it's a toy to show students.* "It's important to me that you stay on task with that."

Sure, David thought. Right after he relaxed more, met a girl, had a baby, and graded all these papers from 101. "I hear you. I'll get that done today."

"Good. I've got some tests I need to run." Haughan smiled. "I really am impressed with you, David. When you first showed up, I didn't think you'd make it this far."

David gathered up his things, ducking to get through Haughan's doorway. He could always switch advisers. But Evelyn Lang was the only other person of any caliber, and she made it her policy to never let students touch the equipment unsupervised. With Haughan, David could probably write and publish a whole paper without him caring, as long as Haughan's name appeared first in the byline.

The fastest route between Haughan's office and his was to cut directly across the towers, and that meant taking the skybridges. This one was a great tunnel of cloudy glass that allowed no view of the world below. He often wondered what architect had thought it up: It was brilliant, made the University Hospital feel like a citadel in the sky.

And then, running down the hall toward him came two little girls, balancing precariously on one set of legs. They wore hospital pajamas and had their arms slung around each other's shoulders. David recognized them from the bus loop the day before yesterday. A nurse with a wheelchair trotted after them at a safe distance. The girls flung themselves at one of the frosted glass walls of the skybridge, hitting it with a decidedly heavy smack, four small hands pressed to the wonder of a seemingly endless expanse of cloud. The nurse gave him an apologetic grimace. David smiled in spite of himself, and thought about a friend he'd had growing up—what was that guy's name?—who would've loved seeing those kids. He would have said that they were proof of miracles. David couldn't quite agree. Proof, certainly, of biodiversity. Of the immense innovation of random chance. One of the girls ignored him as he passed, but the other turned on their shared hips and gawked up at him, like he was some specimen in the aquarium. He smiled as gently as he could manage.

He realized, walking onward through the ortho wing of the hospital, that he was sad. He didn't like to think about that friend he'd had as a kid. He couldn't even remember the kid's name, as unsolvable as the [x] in "Ipanema." That time in his life had been . . . well, Seth would probably say *dark*. David had taken a literature class in undergrad where the professor said that calling bad things dark was a manifestation of racism. He bought her argument and yet he still did it, and didn't really think about it, except when the idea surfaced in his mind in association with some other thing. Anyway. He didn't like to think about what had happened back then with . . . goddammit, it was on the tip of his tongue. *That Time in Chicasaw*, as his foster parents called it when they mentioned it at all, had only cemented in his mind that being a kid was bullshit. The best decision he'd ever made was to stop being one as soon as possible.

He hoped the two girls in the skywalk were enjoying it, though. He wished he could be that excited about a window.

But he could do magic, he reminded himself, to stop from circling down even deeper. A miracle you could control. What more could he want?

THIRTEEN

Jack slept so long that Jesse was starting to worry about her. He'd already cleaned the muddy footprints off the floor and thumbed through her spy paperbacks, and was just about to work up the courage to knock on her door when she emerged in midafternoon with pillow lines on her face. She looked better than the night before, at least, but her arms were covered in little nicks and bruises, like she'd been rolled down a hill.

"What happened?" Jesse asked. "You look . . . rough."

"I've had worse," she said. She opened the fridge, the puffy pink scar on her arm flexing, and popped a can of soda. Jesse wondered if that was the *worse* she meant. "I've got to go downtown and check in with my boss. And you're coming with me."

"Right this second?"

"Listen," she said. "Astrid told me to look out for you, and I like you just fine. The house looks great. But I can't pay for things for you. You can stay here, but you'll need money for food and clothes. And the longer you wait, the harder it's going to be."

Jesse folded his arms over his chest. "Do you think I don't know how to work? I've been working since I was fifteen."

"Good. Then you know what I'm talking about."

Jack chugged the can of soda and threw it in the sink, and sat down on the floor to tug on her mud-spattered boots. Jesse was annoyed about the can—why not the recycling bin?—and he realized she'd dodged his question handily. But he knew she was right about the job. He pulled his shoes on, and Jack stood up and waved him through the door.

"Oh, just so you know," she said over her shoulder, "this job is really more for a girl. But you've got magic powers, so you can swing that, right?"

Jesse stopped. "Wait. What?"

She turned to face him.

"You know," she said. "Magic powers. You turn into a girl. That'll be useful, because the place I work always has a job opening for a pretty girl."

"I've been a server," Jesse said. "I'm good at it."

"This is more of a cocktail waitress position."

Jesse thought about saying no. He didn't, in fact, have magic powers; he had a medical condition. "Can't I just do what you do?"

Jack crossed her arms and grinned in a way that made Jesse's blood run cold. "You cannot do what I do."

"I can't control it, though."

Jack nodded thoughtfully and squinted at Jesse a little.

"Okay," she said. "Well, you're cute. If you say you want to be a waitress, I doubt Sir will say no. You'll probably need to buy a wig."

Jesse felt a twinge. This was embarrassing, a bad dead-end job. So why did he feel elated?

"What color?" he asked.

"What?"

"What color wig?"

"Um . . . blond, purple, I don't know. Come on."

Jesse followed her down the rickety wooden steps to the back-yard. Jack went around under the stairs and dragged a tarp off of a small motorcycle that looked like it was cobbled together out of spare parts. She swung a leg over it and started it.

Riding on Jack's bike was nothing like being in a car. Jesse could feel the speed under him, and the closeness of the asphalt, and the hot breath of cars all around. It was exhilarating, like flying without wings, especially when they crossed the Boulevard of Bells and began the descent into downtown.

The University Hospital loomed, but they turned right down a side street and were soon lost in a neighborhood that looked more Old City than New. Overhead a railroad bridge rumbled with freight cars, and underneath that bridge was a narrow three-story brick building illuminated with a neon sign that said GIRLS! GIRLS! GIRLS!

"You sure it'll be okay?" Jesse asked.

"What?" Jack turned off the bike and turned around. "Wow, you look sick."

She led him around to a side entrance, where a broad-shouldered man covered in a head-to-toe pelt of dark gray fur worked a tooth-pick around and around in his mouth. Jack walked up to him and said, "I'm here to speak to Sir."

"Get in line," the man said. "The whole city's on the phone asking him if he knows what happened to Pete McNair."

"Tell him Jack's here with some ideas, then."

He sighed and unclipped a walkie-talkie from under his blazer.

"Sir, Marley's here to see you. Says she's got news. Has a kid with her for some reason."

The walkie-talkie chirped. "Send her in. This better be good, Jack."

The man nodded them through. Jesse couldn't stop looking at his big, hairy hands tipped with long sharp claws.

They were in a hallway. To the left, Jesse could see a cluster of tables and couches, empty now, and a stage where a woman in a halter top was spray-cleaning a brass pole. Jack steered him right, past several closed doors with plaques on them, to a set of double doors at the far end guarded by another large hairy man. He looked like the one outside, except bigger and brindled instead of dark gray. When he saw Jack, he bristled and glared daggers.

"Hey," Jack said, apparently ignoring the look. "Sir wanted to see me."

"Who's the kid?"

"Looking for a job."

"What are you, kid?" the guy asked.

Jesse shrank. He never knew what to do or say in moments like this, other than get very small and—

"Oh, hey," the guy said, looking suddenly concerned. "It's not like that. Hey, look at me. I didn't mean to be disrespectful."

Jesse glanced over the bouncer's shoulder at Jack, who was staring back, perplexed.

"Okay," Jack said. "Rex, I'm gonna—"

"Yeah, he's waiting for you," Rex said. Jesse started to follow, and Rex stopped him. "You can wait here with me," he said.

Jack stepped into the office and was gone. Jesse was alone in the hall with Rex.

"Sorry," Jesse said. "I just assumed you were getting ready to kick my ass."

"Hey, lots of people who work here aren't like regular folks," Rex said. "You want me to show you around?"

This was weird, Jesse thought. The guy was two hundred pounds of fangs and muscle, and more than that, the look he'd given Jack when they'd walked up was pure murder. And now here he was, showing Jesse the bar, introducing Jesse to Agnolo the bartender and to Hannah the barback. He helped Jesse up onto the stage in the middle of the room with one large clawed hand, and Jesse did an experimental twirl on the pole while Rex laughed.

"You'd start out on the floor, if you get the job," Rex said, helping Jesse back down. "Serving drinks, shit like that. Pardon my language." *Pardon my language?* Nobody talked to Jesse like that. Rex was talking to him like he was a girl. *Or a Maiden.* The thought came unbidden.

"Sounds great," Jesse said. "I used to bus tables in Chicasaw."

"Never heard of it."

"It's just a real little town, a few states south of here."

Rex shrugged. "I don't leave River City."

"I can see why," Jesse said. "It's a great place."

"The best place in the world. Want a drink?" Rex went behind the bar, elbowed Agnolo out of the way. "What you like?"

"I'm not twenty-one. I don't drink."

"I can work with that."

Rex rolled up his sleeves, exposing arms as hairy as his face. He made Jesse something with syrup and soda, put it in a fancy glass, and garnished it with a cherry. He slid it across the empty bar to Jesse, who caught it, splashing a little on the wood.

"Look, I feel bad about asking this," Rex said. "But there's . . . something really special about you. I guess I wanna know if I should be asking you out. So are you a girl or . . . what?"

Jesse thought about it.

"I don't really know," he said. "Yesterday I would've told you no. Today I guess . . . I don't really have a clear answer. I hope that . . . answers your question."

"Yeah." Rex looked a little vague. "Sure. Well, if you ever get sure about that . . ." And he smiled, as nicely as someone could, Jesse thought, with a mouthful of sharp yellowed teeth.

"Jesse?"

Jack was striding across the floor toward the bar. She looked at the drink, and then at Rex. "What are you doing?"

Rex snorted. "Making him a drink. What?"

"It's just soda," Jesse said quickly. Out of the corner of his eye, he saw that girl, Hannah, frown at Jack, throw down her dish towel, and leave the room. Jesse made a note to ask Jack about that later.

"Well, I just got my ass handed to me, so make me something," Jack said to Rex.

"Make your own drink," Rex said. "C'mon, Jesse. We're gonna talk to Dad."

Jesse started to get up but Jack grabbed him by the collar.

"Don't be weird in there," she said. "That's my boss you're talking to."

"Uh, I won't," Jesse said.

Jack let him go, and he staggered back a little bit. And then Rex was ushering Jesse down the hall and through the doors into the nicest office Jesse had ever seen.

It was like a temple: white stone floors, potted palm trees, a skylight that shone down directly onto a desk, where a woman with backward knees and horse hooves was bending over in a tight skirt to pour coffee into a shallow bowl in front of a large, elderly-looking German shepherd mix with a pair of reading glasses balanced on his nose.

"Yes?" the dog said as Jesse and Rex came in. Jesse took a deep breath, wishing Jack had given him any idea of what he shouldn't be weird *about*. If he'd known he could've . . . well, he would've known.

"Dad," Rex said. "This is Jesse. He . . . they . . . wanna work in the bar."

"Are you a dancer?"

Jesse didn't hesitate—that would've been weird, right? "I'm a quick learner."

"So you don't know how to dance."

"Dad," Rex said. "Give Jesse a chance."

The dog yawned. "What do you look like in women's clothes?"

"Like a girl. Sir."

"Why'd you show up in a dirty sweatshirt, then?"

"It's the only clothes I have."

The dog blinked once, slowly.

"I like you, kid," he said. "You're honest, and that takes guts. I'm fronting you your first paycheck, which means you owe me two weeks, during which you will be on your best behavior. You'll work weeknights till you show me I can trust you with weekends. With this money, you will buy a tight dress before your first shift tomorrow night, and you will buy yourself a decent wig, because your haircut is shit. No unnatural colors, they look cheap. Mandy, write the kid a check." The secretary clopped over to a smaller desk in a corner and took out a checkbook. While she wrote, Sir tilted his head from side to side, eyeing Jesse.

"You living with Jack?" Sir asked at last.

"For now."

"Are the two of you together?"

"Oh gosh, no. Sir."

"Good. Don't get mixed up with Jack, I don't want her distracted."

"Yes, Sir." It was unlikely to be a problem. Not that he wouldn't, Jesse thought, if it came up. Jack seemed like she might kill him, and he had to admit he liked that. But why didn't Sir want her distracted? What was she even doing at her weird job where she went out late at night and came back soaking wet and covered in scratches?

"You look bothered, kid."

"No, Sir," Jesse said quickly. "Just thinking about what wig I'm gonna get, Sir."

"Who do we make the check out to?" Mandy asked.

Jesse hesitated. "Uh, I just remembered I don't have a bank account."

Sir flicked his ears. "Pay the kid in cash. Get a bank account. You live here now."

When Jesse staggered back out into the bar, Jack nearly knocked her chair over standing up.

"Hey," she said. "You get the job?"

Jesse held up a handful of cash. "Yep."

"Shit, don't flash that around. Getting paid under the table is a privilege."

"Sorry."

"You got it, though?"

"I got two weeks and I have to buy a wig."

"That's fine. Let's get out of here."

"You go ahead. I'll be right out."

Once she was gone, Jesse turned to Rex.

"Thanks for sticking up for me," Jesse said. "You didn't have to do that."

"Hey, no problem." Rex looked uncomfortable with the praise. "I mean, there's just something about you. I knew Dad would see it."

"Can I ask—has he always been . . ."

"Oh, what? Hell no. Cursed by a witch, back in the day. Whoever it was, they got us, too. But he's always been good to anyone who's sorta made wrong. He likes to say we're 'gifted.'"

"Cool, gifted," Jesse said. "I guess that's me."

"Like how?"

Jesse looked around to see if anyone else was watching. Nope; the bar was empty. He swallowed, and breathed out, and let himself change shape. She blinked up at Rex a few times.

Rex slapped his forehead. "Aw, wow, you're cute," he said. "And you can't just stay like that? I thought you were something before, but—wow!"

"It doesn't stick," Jesse said, bouncing back.

"That's . . . whoa," Rex said. "Don't tell my dad, he'll want you to make it into a whole act!"

Jesse was whistling when he met Jack by the bike. It was early evening, the sky growing light in that way it did as the sun was just beginning to dip. Jack was not as pleased.

"What did you do to Rex?" Jack asked.

"What?"

"He was being nice. Rex is never nice."

"He was just being friendly."

"Okay, that is a straight-up lie," Jack said. "He normally only goes for girls. And he was all over you."

"I think he was intrigued."

"Intrigued my ass. Get on."

"I got paid!"

"I heard."

"I have a job!"

"Just get on already."

Jesse grinned the whole way back to the apartment.

"So," he said as Jack turned off the motorcycle. "What's this big investigation you're doing?"

Jack shook her head.

"I know you don't know any better," she said. "But that's really not a question you can ask me. It's better for you if you don't know."

Jesse bristled a little at that.

"I live with you," he said as they climbed the rickety back staircase. "What if you don't come home? What do I do next?"

Jack stopped at the top landing and turned toward him with one hand on her hip, her mouth open like she was about to say something. She scoffed once, then laughed.

"You're worried about me," she said.

"Is there, like, someone I should call?"

"Call Sir," she said. "I'll give you his number. Tell him how long I've been gone and he'll know what to do."

"Okay," Jesse said. "Well, then, you should tell me when you expect to be back, usually."

Jack rolled her eyes. "All right. If I'm staying out all night, I'll tell you."

Jack turned to unlock the door, shaking her head. She was warming up to him, Jesse could tell. Which was a relief. A Jack who didn't like him was a scary proposition.

"I am going out tonight," Jack said. "And I won't be back till morning. I'm bringing a new guy to meet Sir. It'll take some time."

"I guess I won't wait up," Jesse said.

"You should do something fun," Jack said. "Go get acquainted with the town or something. I'll see you later."

As Jack retreated down the stairs, Jesse knew exactly where he was going. He went to his room and dug around under the old mattress until he pulled out David's postcard and the map the shopkeeper had drawn for him with directions to the Bodwell School.

Jesse followed the map into the tangled streets of the Old City. He remembered some of this from his walk from Astrid's house; he recognized the long street lined with statues, which Astrid had said were the city's former kings. He started to head in that direction, since that street was the hypotenuse the shopkeeper had mentioned. But when he got a little closer, he stopped.

He didn't like the look of the statue facing him down, a bronze rider on the back of a rearing horse. The man was turning back in the saddle to look at him, and something about his posture made it seem as though at any second he might wheel the horse around to run Jesse down. There was something wild in his eyes that seemed too . . . alive.

No, the side streets were more scenic anyway. Screw the hypotenuse, even if it took a little longer. He had a map, didn't he?

So he picked his way down statue-free avenues lined with trees, streets where the houses slumped against one another or tilted forward drunkenly into the road, past city parks where kids chased each other with sticks. Eventually he came to the crumbling brick building marked on his map as the Bodwell School. It had a brick wall around most of the schoolyard, and a chain-link fence stretched across the place where there had once been a gate. A sign on the fence in the shape of a pointing finger read ENTRANCE THIS WAY. Jesse followed the point around to the front of the building.

It looked like every school built at a certain time: a concrete and blacade with concrete steps leading up to metal double doors. Except that where the name of the school would usually be, there was instead a printed banner stretched taut over the bricks that read SENSIBLE GIRLS COLLECTIVE, and in smaller letters underneath, PRINTING AND BINDING. Jesse mounted the steps. The door had a sign in the window in red ink that said REGULAR HOURS 9–5 M–S,

CARNIVAL HOURS: CLOSED FRIDAY AND SATURDAY. Jesse grabbed the door by the handle and pulled.

He found himself in a school's front hallway. It was lined with posters from various events, some framed, some taped up. A teacher's desk stood in the middle of the hall in front of stairs leading up to second-floor classrooms. Nobody was at the desk, but there was a bell, so Jesse rang it.

Eventually, a woman emerged from a corridor near the back. She had long blond hair in a braid and wore a faded black jumpsuit, stained darker in places as though splashed with ink. She looked startlingly like Jack. This must be the sister the shopkeeper had mentioned. This girl was definitely the older of the two, although smaller and thinner. She had a kind of concentrated intensity to her, like a lamp with no shade.

"What can I do for you?"

"Hi," Jesse said. "Are you Belle?"

"I am! Who am I speaking to?"

"Jesse Archer," he said.

Belle Marley reached out and took Jesse's hand. "It's nice to meet you, too," Belle said. "What brings you here today?"

"Um," Jesse said. "So I have this postcard. Did you make it?"

He pulled it out and showed Belle, who turned it over, to his surprise, and read the message on the back. Jesse stood there feeling a little uncomfortable, and Belle noticed quickly.

"Oh, that was rude of me," she said. "That was private. I didn't realize; I was looking for the date. Can you forgive me?"

"Of course," Jesse said.

"We've never made this one," she said. "We have the print plate for it, but we don't really like to print images of the palace. It's the police station now, and people think of it that way." She shrugged. "Honestly, it was never a very good symbol of our city. A monument to the tyranny of men."

"Hm," Jesse said, shrinking down in his sweatshirt a little.

"You're new in town, right?" Belle said. "People were saying they saw Astrid talking to a strange boy. Is that you?"

"Yeah," Jesse said. "I just moved to town this summer. To get away from my parents."

Belle smiled. "You're not the only one," she said. "I hope this is a place you can feel safe."

"Thanks," Jesse said. "So . . . do you have any idea where someone might have gotten this? Or, like . . ."

Belle shook her head.

"I'm sorry," she said. "The most I can tell you is that it's old. If your friend is your age, it was probably given to them by someone else, back before the city changed. You know about that part, right?"

"Not really," Jesse said.

"I was very young then," she said. "The city used to be a place of wonder and magic. There was a museum where all the exhibits talked. There was a footbridge that floated in the air that led to that island in the middle of the river." She smiled faintly. "It feels like everyone forgot about it. But I was maybe . . . five? Six? And I can remember it all so clearly." She tilted her head to one side. "Actually, do you want to see?"

Jesse nodded, not really sure of what else to say.

Belle motioned for him to follow. She led him down the hallway, past classrooms with open doors where young women were talking, laughing, hanging up wet printed sheets of paper on clotheslines. Jesse caught a glimpse of one of those RISE UP OLD CITY posters he'd seen before—so this was where they'd come from.

She took him to a room at the end of the corridor. It was empty, except for pots of paint and drop cloths on the floor, a stack of big books and postcards in the middle of the room, and in one corner, a stepladder. But the walls were painted with a mural.

"I've been working on this for a while," she said. "It takes time to find the reference images."

It was a picture of the city from above, as though in the center of the room they were standing on top of a hill. People walked the streets, or rode in glittering contraptions that had no wheels and didn't touch the ground. Witches were everywhere: women in dark dresses bending over baby carriages and tending gardens, or flying while sitting in buckets or perched on tandem bicycles. The streets were paved in flowers.

"This is what I remember," Belle said. "How safe it felt to know that there was always a powerful woman you could go to when things went wrong."

"This is beautiful," Jesse said. And then she heard her own voice. Shit.

Belle turned slowly to look at her.

"I'm sorry," Jesse said. "I didn't—I mean—"

"Jesse," she said. "That's amazing."

"I don't want you to think—" Jesse stammered. "I mean, I know you keep saying all this stuff about women, and I know what this looks like, but I'm not—"

Belle put her hands on Jesse's arms.

"Jesse," she said. "Do you think of yourself as a woman?"

"Uh," Jesse said. "Sometimes?"

"That's a really special gift you have," Belle said. "And if you feel like a woman, you are."

"Oh," Jesse said. That was nice to hear, sort of. But at the same time, she felt a little uncertain. Like she was still lying to Belle, somehow.

"You're always welcome here if you need a place to stay," Belle said.

"I've got a place, actually," Jesse said. "Um, it's weird—I think I might be living with your sister. Jack?"

Belle smiled, but her brow was furrowed. Jesse found herself waiting to be yelled at. That was silly, though, right?

"Oh, yes," Belle said. "Astrid and my sister are great friends. It makes sense that she'd ask her to put you up. How's that going?"

"Great, actually," Jesse said. "Jack's been really cool."

Belle pursed her lips. "Mm," she said. "I'd be careful around Jack if I were you."

"How do you mean?"

Belle sighed.

"I'm glad if she's been a good friend to you," Belle said. "But Jack is . . . well, she identifies really strongly with men. And she acts like a man a lot of the time, because she likes the power that comes from being like a man. And sometimes she treats women badly because of that. She's obsessed with sex, because sex is conquest. Do you know what I mean?"

Jesse blushed. "I mean, she hasn't tried anything with me,"she said.

"Well, that's good, at least," Belle said. She put a hand on Jesse's shoulder. "Listen. If you ever feel unsafe, you should come and stay with us. We've got lots of space here."

Belle had that same undercurrent of power that Jack did, the one that made Jesse excited and a little scared at the same time. Jesse nodded. "I mean, I'd love to be a part of what you're doing here, either way," she said. "Maybe I could learn how to print things?"

"We always need more people," Belle said. "We've got a lot of experienced printers, but we need people to hang up posters, feed people, expand our operations. There's a lot to do. And you've got something really special, I can tell. Have you ever done any magic?"

"Uh," Jesse said. "I don't think so? Astrid says I can't."

"Astrid says a lot of things. And she likes to put people down."

"Yeah, she basically said I was stupid," Jesse said.

"Well, I don't think you're stupid." She smiled, almost seeming shy. "Actually, I think you're pretty great."

Jesse beamed. "So, like . . . do you do magic?"

"Not much," Belle said. "We try to be careful. There's not much magic right now. Has Astrid told you that?"

Jesse nodded. "Yeah. She said it's running out."

Belle started to open her mouth. Jesse found herself waiting for what Belle was going to say. But then Belle shook her head.

"Jesse," she said. "Can you change your gender whenever you want?"

"No," Jesse said. "I really . . . can't control it."

"You should practice," Belle said. "I think Astrid's wrong about you. I think you can do a lot more than you think. And if you ever want help, come ask me."

Jesse nodded. "Cool," she said. "Um . . . I actually have to get going now, though."

Belle put a hand on Jesse's arm. "Stop by whenever you like," she said. "And I'll ask around about this card, if you want. Maybe there's more to this story."

"Oh my god, thank you," Jesse said. "You don't have to do that."

"It's no trouble at all!"

She walked Jesse to the door, and twiddled her braid when she said goodbye, filling Jesse with the uncanny certainty that Belle liked her.

"Oh, can I ask you something?" Belle asked.

"Sure."

"Do you mind not telling Jackie that we talked?" Belle looked worried. "I'm glad she's been good to you, but in the past, she's sometimes been . . . very angry with me, and I don't always know why."

"Oh god," Jesse said. "Yeah, I totally understand."

"Thanks," Belle said. "I really appreciate it."

Jesse felt weird as she left, still thinking about what Belle had said. Did she mean that Jack had hurt her? Was Jack dangerous? She did . . . maybe kill people? And Jesse knew that just because someone was nice to you didn't mean they were nice to everyone.

She headed home through the twilight, digesting what Belle had said, wondering who'd given David this postcard. Maybe if Jesse found that person, somehow, she'd find David. She said the name to herself a few times in her head. The name of the only person who'd ever really understood. She'd find him no matter what.

He, she reminded herself, trying to straighten her posture. His body reluctantly oozed back into its usual shape. This place was getting to him. He couldn't forget who he was, or—

Or what? He thought about what Astrid had said, the first time she'd seen him change. Not cursed, not blessed, either. Just . . . what he was. He didn't know what to make of that, not yet. But it felt like some new truth was coming, just out of sight. What had Astrid said after? Plain as the nose on your face. Visible, he guessed, to everyone but him.

FOURTEEN

On her island, the daughter of the river scrabbled through her clothes, trying to figure out what to wear to meet Jack.

She didn't have much: By the time most clothes made it into her collection, they were sun-bleached and battered from the water. And even if she'd had so much as a matching pair of flip-flops, her feet were too long for most shoes. She'd found one once that looked like her foot, but it was a swim flipper, meant to turn a regular foot into one of hers. She'd kept it and hung it up as a kind of talisman over her clothes heap, which was mostly lost swim trunks and bikini tops, T-shirts advertising beer, baseball caps with fishhooks stuck in their brims. She knew from her books that when you went to see someone you liked, you wore your best clothes. What was best here? The old yellow slicker? The mildewed sweater? She held up various things, and at last sighed and gave up. Anything she wore would be soaked from the river anyway. She settled for a pair of aquamarine running shorts. No shirt; she had never quite figured out how to get one on. She wished she had a sliver of mirror so that she could make sure there was no dirt or grit on her face. But even the river was too choppy today for her to be able to say for certain what she looked like.

The sun was starting to go down as she left her hut and swam across the river, in through a hole in the foundation of the boathouse, and into the musty, spidery dark. She pushed on the floorboards until she found a loose one, eased it up and slid herself into the hot wooden shed. She hid there among the jumbled boats to wait.

The door rattled, and after a moment, the bolt slid back. The daughter of the river tensed and crouched low, and then sighed when she saw Jack Marley step through the door carrying a backpack. Her breath caught when she saw Jack. The nameless girl hadn't entirely let herself believe Jack would come, but here she was, wearing a battered leather jacket. Of course she was. The daughter of the river wanted to die of bliss.

"Hey, you in here?"

"Hi," Turing said, standing up a little too quickly. She'd practiced the *hi*, trying to replace her usual *hello*. It sounded strange and tinny, but Jack didn't seem to notice.

"Hey." Jack set the backpack down and unzipped it. She pulled out a long coat, unfurled it with a *whump*. "This is for you."

Turing took the coat and draped it over her back. Her arms twitched under its touch, trying to scramble out. Settle down, she willed, and they settled, but slowly. The coat was heavy and itchy.

"I got something with some, uh, pleats in the back," Jack said. "I think it's a lady coat, but I thought it'd have the most room."

"I don't mind," Turing said quickly. "Do you have any more clothes?"

"No, I didn't really think you . . . wore clothes."

"No, but people do."

"Huh. Right." Jack stuck her hands in her pockets. "Sorry, I didn't really think of that."

Turing put her hands through the sleeves of the coat and buttoned it around her. It was blue and long, and took her instantly from shivering to too hot. She had no shoes; her feet, red and webbed, stuck out from under the coat and looked ridiculous. She laughed a little.

"What?" Jack asked.

"I look a little like a duck."

Jack looked down and laughed, too. "Shit, I should've gotten you shoes. I don't know what size you wear."

"Neither do I."

"Let's go to Sir's. There's usually some clothes lying around for guys coming in off the street."

"How will we get there?"

Jack grinned. "Step outside."

Turing followed Jack out of the shed. The sun had gone down now and the night air was cool on her face. She was glad for the warmth of the coat. Jack waved a hand, and Turing, following her gesture, saw a motorcycle parked just off the road. She smiled a little to herself. Of course Jack had a motorcycle.

"What are you grinning about?" Jack asked.

"It's very . . . you."

Jack blushed, and ran a hand over her scalp—a nervous gesture, Turing realized. "I didn't know I was such a type."

"That's not what I meant," Turing said. "I love it."

"Well, get on."

Jack swung a leg over the bike. Turing arranged herself carefully behind her. "I'm a little nervous," Turing said, gripping the seat.

"What, about the job?"

"About the bike. Does it go fast?"

"It doesn't have to," Jack said. "Here."

She reached back and took Turing's hands, and wrapped them around her waist. Turing heard the leather jacket squeak, felt Jack's body, warm and hard with muscle.

"Hang on," Jack said. She started the bike, and kicked off.

It wasn't as bad as Turing had thought. Then again, she kept her eyes shut most of the time. The one time she did open them, they were rolling down a hill, picking up speed as they went, as much as Jack tried to let them coast. Turing just held on, tucking her face in against the leather jacket. It was warm in that little pocket between her face and Jack's body, and it smelled good, although Turing hoped Jack didn't notice that she was sniffing. Finally, they came to a stop, and Jack leaned toward her and said, "Hey, you okay?"

"I'm fine." Turing scrambled to her feet and off the bike.

"Was that too fast?"

"No," Turing said. "You were perfect."

They were outside of an old brick building. Jack nodded to the man standing guard, a creature with a thick pelt like a wolf. He gave Turing a long look, and waved her inside, too. She hurried after Jack.

Jack had warned her that the place was a nightclub. Turing wasn't sure she knew what a nightclub was; she'd only ever read about them in books. She looked around, trying to figure it out.

"What's up?" Jack asked, leaning in close and putting a hand on her shoulder. "You're not scared, are you?"

"I thought there would be music. And more people." The only people milling around looked like they worked there. A fat man wiping down the bar. Another wolf-looking man standing by a door.

"It's early in the evening. People tend to come out later."

A brown-skinned woman in a short dress came out from behind the bar. She had straight black hair down to her waist, with perfectly straight bangs, and candy-red lipstick. Turing felt instantly envious. The woman spotted Jack and frowned, but came over anyway.

"Hannah," Jack said. "This is Turing."

Hannah looked from Turing to Jack. Turing saw her get a little flicker of recognition, and then Hannah smirked.

"Wow, Jack," she said. "That was fast, even for you."

"He's interviewing for a job," Jack said.

"Sure he is."

"Excuse me," Turing said. "Did I do something wrong?"

Hannah tilted her chin, barely, to look at Turing.

"I don't know what you know about Jack," she said. "And I don't know why the flavor of the week is boy, but I really shouldn't be surprised by anything Jack does anymore. Honestly, I feel sorry for you." Her eyes flicked back to Jack. "You're ridiculous," she said.

She turned on her heel and walked away. Turing watched her long hair swish behind her as she went.

"Come on," Jack said. "Let's go talk to Sir."

"Who was that?"

Jack sighed. "Nobody." She pulled Turing by the arm down a hallway. "We should—"

"Jack," Turing said. "What did she mean when she said she felt sorry for me? Did she mean because of how I look?"

Jack looked furious for a moment, and then sad. Turing loved watching the way Jack's face changed sometimes when she talked to her. It was like watching your own feeling dawning on her face instead of yours.

"No, she's not making fun of you," Jack said. "You look fine. She's just mad at me."

"Why?"

Jack seemed embarrassed. "I'll tell you later."

The man guarding the door to the office wasn't one of the wolf-like men; he was skinny, with little growths of horn protruding from his face and hands. He gave her a friendly wink. "Who's the lady friend, Jack?"

"*His* name's Turing," Jack said, and Turing felt both touched by Jack's gallantry and disappointed at the correction.

"Oh," the guard said. "Sorry, man."

"It's the coat," said Jack, pulling Turing through the door. But Turing beamed anyway. She felt different, then, for just a moment. Like magic had touched her.

Sir liked her the second she took the coat off. "Wow. Jack, you've always had an eye for talent. Can you pick stuff up with those things?"

She reached out and curled the ends of her arms around the legs of his desk. It was a strain, but she could lift it and hold it over her head. As she lowered the desk back down, Sir's face came into view wearing a big, open-mouthed grin.

"You're a natural," he said. "Now that's going to scare people."

"I've been scaring people since I was a child," she said.

"And doing it for free? More fool you," Sir said. His sleek-haired secretary teetered over on her delicate cloven hooves and perched

on the lip of his desk. The daughter of the river couldn't stop looking at her skirt, a tight column of fabric with a glossy sheen. "I'd
want you to work as an enforcer, primarily. Show up to places,
stand behind the man doing the talking. Or go out with Jack when
she needs backup. We'd need to get you a pager."

"And a waterproof bag," Jack said. "He can swim underwater,
too. Canals and shit."

"Ohhhh," Sir said. It was amazing, Turing thought, how much
emotion his eyes showed, how his brows furrowed and lifted. You
could see the man superimposed over the dog. She looked over at
Jack, and learned something else she hadn't expected. Jack's eyes
were darting back and forth between her and Sir with a kind of
hopeful worry. Jack wanted this to go well.

"I think you're going to be an asset," Sir said. "We'll pay you
hourly, plus expenses. Is there anything else you want? Anything
that would seal the deal?"

The daughter of the river, without thinking, said, "I'd like some
clothes."

Sir laughed. "Jack, where do you find all these lost souls without clothes? Get him kitted out, okay?"

Jack smiled. "Thanks, Sir," she said. They ducked out of the
room, into that dimly lit back hallway. When she door shut, Jack
grinned at her. "That went great," she said. "He likes you."

"You like him a lot."

"He's all right," Jack said. "This way."

Jack led Turing down the hall to a storage room with a long
shelf of neatly stacked piles of white T-shirts and black pants, and
rows of plain black canvas shoes with rubber soles.

"Why?" Turing asked.

Jack shrugged. "Sometimes we get dirty."

Turing turned her back on Jack, and shrugged off the long coat. She took down a pair of pants from the shelf, held it up to her waist. "These are too big."

"Here. They have numbers in them." Jack rummaged around on the shelf. "Try these."

Turing glanced back at Jack. "Don't look."

"What? Oh." Jack turned around. "Go ahead."

Turing slipped off the running shorts and stepped into the pants. They fit fine. She got a shirt down from one of the shelves. Hmm, shirts were trickier. She'd need some time to figure it out. "How did you start working for Sir?" she asked.

"Uh," Jack said. "I was in some trouble, and he helped me out. He said he liked my guts, and I could pay him back by working for him for a year and a day. Once I'd done that, I just sort of stayed on."

"And what do you do? What am *I* going to do?"

"I threaten people," Jack said. "Mostly. Sometimes we need to escalate the situation, if the threats don't work. But by then they've usually got it coming."

"How do you decide?"

"What?"

"How do you decide if they have it coming?"

"I don't. Sir does." Jack turned around. "Oh, jeez?"

Turing was stuck with the shirt half on. "It doesn't fit. With my back."

Jack reached into her pocket and pulled out a knife. Turing

flinched. Jack glanced down. "For the shirt! Why do people always assume I'm gonna hurt them?"

Jack looked so pained that Turing wanted to pet her. "Because you pull a knife the way other people take out a pen," Turing said.

"Hey now," Jack said. "When was the last time you saw someone take out a pen?"

"It has been a while."

"It can be very menacing," Jack said. "Now. Turn around. God, you're tall. Can you kneel down?"

The blush rose up Turing's body from her feet to her scalp. She knelt in front of Jack, and felt Jack put a hand on her shoulder and then grab the shirt. Jack used the knife to slit it up the back, untangling it.

"Okay," Jack said. "Put your arms through the sleeves."

The daughter of the river pulled the cut shirt on over her front. She noted how careful Jack was with her. Jack tied the two cut halves of the shirt together at the small of her back.

"When I was a teenager, I used to cut my shirts up and tie them all different ways," Jack said, so close that Turing could feel her breath on her ear. "I thought I was so cool. That feel okay?"

"That's fine."

"All right," Jack said. She gave Turing a clap on the shoulder that felt a little too hard, too jovial. "Nothing too difficult tonight," Jack said. "I'll show you the ropes. We won't be doing anything public-facing."

"Will it be dangerous?"

"Not with me," Jack said. "Stay close."

They left the club together, and Turing followed Jack up the block, heading uphill. Turing willed her arms to stay put under the coat, to not wriggle or bulge. After a few blocks, the shoes had already started to chafe on her feet.

Jack motioned down a narrow alley edged with trash cans and laced overhead with power lines. "This way. Come on."

Turing followed her. Jack dragged a trash can under a fire escape. "Hold this still, okay?" Turing held it while Jack clambered on top, grabbed the metal rungs of the fire escape, and boosted herself up. It lowered to the ground with a long, loud groan. Turing glanced around, worried that someone might hear. "What are we doing?" she asked.

"We're going to rob a guy," Jack said. "Don't worry, his girlfriend's home and she knows what's up."

"What? Why?"

"He has it coming." Jack held out a hand. "Let's go."

Turing followed her up the ladder to the window. There was a woman inside washing dishes. When she saw Jack at the window, she stepped back from the sink. Jack took out a short baton from the lining of her leather jacket and smashed the window in two quick hits. Turing winced as the glass shattered, and again as Jack stuck her arm in through the jagged hole and turned the latch to pull the window open.

"Careful of the glass," Jack said, scrambling through. Turing followed carefully. Her coat snagged on the window frame and pulled back from her shoulders a little, but she managed to get it inside. The woman who'd been washing dishes raised her eyebrows as she saw Turing's other arms, but said nothing.

Turing hadn't been in an apartment before. There were

houseplants up on high shelves. A kitchen table. A recycling bin. Turing looked around in awe.

"Hey, Alice," Jack said. "Where's Jeff keep the money?"

"He went out and bought a TV," Alice said. Her hair was like spun gold, Turing thought, but she looked as sad as the woman at the nightclub.

"Okay, but that's not two grand," Jack said. "What about the rest?"

"Under the floorboards. And he bought me this." She tugged a ring off her finger and held it out to Jack. Turing saw a strange wistful look come over Alice when Jack reached out her palm and the ring dropped into it. Jack held the ring up to the light.

"This is worth a lot," Jack said. "Tell him I stole it, and hang onto it."

"I can't do that," Alice said. "I can't lie to him."

"Then give it to me," Jack said. "Or, I don't know. I'm threatening you."

The woman smiled a little.

"You can come get this whenever," Jack said.

"Sure. Who's your friend?"

"Turing. He's gonna help me carry the TV out."

"Like you need help with that."

"He's new, I'm showing him the ropes. This is, uh, what's that thing? Human resources."

"A training exercise?" Alice was all but laughing now. Turing noticed purple fingerprints on Alice's arm, right where the sleeve of her dress ended. Alice saw her looking, and tugged at her sleeve. "I tried to tell him this was going to happen."

"Well, if he gives you any shit about it, you come to me," Jack said. She strode into the adjoining room, and Turing followed. A small living room with a couch, a rickety glass-topped table, and the TV. Jack started unplugging the TV from the wall. "What's he even watching on this? We get one channel."

"Mainland DVDs."

"We'll take those, and the player. Doesn't need them without a TV, right?" Jack went over to a cabinet and opened it. "Alice, can you get us a bag?"

"Sure," Alice said, and she darted out of the room.

"This is wrong," Turing said.

"Nah, Jeff is seriously in arrears."

"I mean Alice. I think he's hurting her."

"Yeah, well." Jack glanced up, and Turing saw that her eyes had gone carefully blank. "She says she loves him, so my hands are tied."

"You could do something about this," Turing said. "You're strong."

"What, I'm going to kill every man in the city? You think I don't have enough women mad at me?"

"Why was that girl at the club mad at you?" Turing asked. "You said you'd tell me."

Alice came back in with a trash bag. "Later," Jack said. "All right, you two get this. Alice, uh, do it or I'll hurt you, I guess? Does that help?"

Alice laughed. "Mm, say it slower."

Jack shot Alice a grin that crushed Turing's heart. She started helping Alice stuff plastic cases into the garbage bag while Jack unplugged the DVD player.

"Can you . . . not take the money under the floor?" Alice asked. "I'll get him to give it to you, I promise, but if he thinks I told you where it is, he's going to be . . . very angry."

"Oh, hey, sure," Jack said. "Just get it to us in the next couple weeks." She glanced at the coffee table. "You like this? Hate it?"

Alice smiled. "It's so ugly."

Jack handed her the baton. "You wanna do something about it?"

Alice smiled a little, hefted the baton. She brought it down on the glass of the coffee table again and again. When the glass was broken, Jack brought down a foot on the wooden frame and smashed it in.

"We gotta get going," she said. "Thanks, Al. Come see me if you need anything."

Alice smiled. "Yeah. Be careful out there." And she leaned forward and whispered something that Turing couldn't hear.

They left through the door, went down a flight of stairs to a back door that locked from the inside, which opened onto a different alley. There was a van waiting there idling, its back doors open. Jack put the TV and DVDs inside, then shut the doors. She knocked twice on the back window, and the van drove off.

"All right, next," Jack said.

"Jack."

Jack stopped moving. "What?"

"You said you'd tell me."

"It's really none of your business."

Turing stood still. She didn't know what to do. She felt like something was missing, some piece she needed to understand what was happening to her, to both of them. To know what she was going to do next.

Jack sighed.

"God, you're gonna make me say it? We had sex. And now she's mad at me."

"Why is she mad at you?"

"Because she thinks I didn't treat her well." Jack looked away.

"Is she right?" Turing wondered if Hannah had been the woman on the steps that night that she'd taken Jack home.

"Look, I don't . . . really fall in love with people," Jack said. "It's like that part of me is used up. And that makes people really angry, because even when I tell them, they think they can fix it."

Turing stood very still for a moment.

"Hey," Jack said softly. "Hey, you okay?"

"I'm sad for you," Turing said.

Jack laughed bitterly. "That sure makes me feel better about it."

The daughter of the river wanted Jack Marley to have whatever she needed. She wanted her to be happy.

"I'm sorry," she said. "You're right, why worry about it?"

Jack nodded. "That's the spirit. Actually, maybe this is enough for one night. Let's get you home, okay?"

The daughter of the river let Jack take her back to the boathouse, where she hid her new clothes under an old canoe. She kept expecting to hear the motorcycle take off, but when she stepped back out, Jack was still there, waiting for her.

"Well," Jack said. "Good night."

The daughter of the river had read books where people went on dates. This was the part at the end where the two people wondered whether they would kiss. Except she knew she was the only person wondering that, because Jack was already looking away, across the water. The moment was just her imagination.

"See you tomorrow?" Turing asked.

"Yeah," Jack said. "See you."

The nameless girl flung herself into the river as quickly as she could. She only glanced back when she was halfway across, and was surprised to see Jack still standing on the riverbank, but in the dark, it was hard to tell whether she was smiling.

FIFTEEN

Jack stared into the river after Turing had gone. She'd been hoping for a nice, easy night with no new complications. She'd even thought maybe afterward she could take Turing to—well, it didn't matter. Because when they were leaving Alice's place, Al had leaned in and said, *The cops are talking about your friend.*

Of course they were. Jack wondered if Astrid had told them the same thing she'd told Jack, that song and dance about a monster who lived in the river and ate babies. Well, wherever it had started, Jack needed to know if it was just a rumor or a whole new line of inquiry.

Jack headed uptown, past the first precinct's headquarters, a big, squat fortress in the middle of the city that had apparently been a palace when Jack was a baby. She was heading for the Brass Tax, a shitty little bar a few blocks away where cops liked to drink when they went off shift. She was marginally welcome there. Certainly more so than anyone else who worked for Sir.

Jack had been to the mainland exactly once in her life, and her chief memory of it was a restaurant that had a bunch of junk nailed to the walls: old musical instruments and front ends of cars and such. The Brass Tax was like that place, but more stuff and less space. Low girders overhead were strung with pennants from long-gone soccer matches. Group photos of training corps cohorts were tacked up on every available surface. She couldn't hear herself over the sound of the mainland music they liked to blast, and had been blasting since the dawn of time. Whoever Eileen was, Jack wished she'd just hurry up and come already so they could stop singing about it.

At least the place was empty for now, with the early guys gone home and the late guys not here yet. She ordered a beer and sat down in a corner, pretending to drink it while she waited.

Eventually, a guy she recognized came in. An older beat cop, Carter. She lifted her beer to him and he nodded back at her.

"Want a beer?" she said. "On me."

He nodded, grabbed one from the bartender, and wandered over to her. It was one of those messy on-tap beers, the kind with foam taller than the rim of the glass. She gestured at the other chair, and he sat down.

"You know your boss is a real shithead, right?" he said. "Acting all sorry."

"He didn't do it. We are, I swear to you, as baffled as y'all are."

He didn't say he believed her, but he did settle more firmly into the chair. Kyle Carter was the right guy to be having this chat with. He'd never become brass, but he was an old hand and everyone listened to him—if he believed her, they'd believe him. He'd taught a whole generation of cops how to be assholes. Some old friend of Pete's, apparently, from before the revolution.

"Has Matthew turned up yet?" Jack asked. Kyle scowled and shook his head.

"You know, you'd have been a good cop, Jack," Kyle said. "Maybe a detective. Why you still work for that fucking dog?"

Jack could never figure out why guys like this always seemed to like her. They had enough shit to say about women and queers, depending on who was in the room and how much they'd had to drink. But they talked to her like she wasn't either of those things. They talked to her like she was some cool young guy they wanted to impress. Maybe because she talked to all of them like they were her dad.

"Look," Jack said. "Whatever you think about Sir, what problem would he have with Matthew Mannering? I don't know shit about the guy. I didn't even know the *name* Mannering this time last week. And you've known Sir for a long time. You know how he is about Carnival. You think he'd be looking to start trouble right now?"

Kyle looked uncomfortable. Maybe it was just gas, Jack thought. But then he looked around theatrically to see if anyone was listening.

"Look," he said. "I know you're soft about monsters. But you don't know how it used to be. I can't just forget that shit. And anyway, we know it was a monster who killed Pete."

Jack flinched. "What?"

"They found him down by the river, all covered in marks."

Jack held her tongue. The rumor really had migrated. "What kind of marks?"

"Like he was choked out," he said. "By some huge snake."

"Who told you that?" Jack asked.

He grimaced. "We've all heard about that thing that lives in the river. Fucking Bloody Marla."

So they were sure it was Turing. Well, that sucked. "And you think, what? Sir has a giant snake on payroll? You've seen our guys."

"You think he's telling you everything?"

"He doesn't have to tell me shit. I've lived here my whole life. There are no giant snakes in River City."

He leaned forward in his chair. "You know, I was there the night Queen Marla died," he said.

Oh, this shit. Everyone was there the night Queen Marla died. Jack tried not to roll her eyes. "Yeah?"

"It rained that night," he said. "It rained for thirty days from that night on. Wouldn't stop. The whole city flooded. We couldn't get around, we had to make rafts. People were living on their roofs. Starving." He shook his head. "This shit? This reminds me of how it used to be. We've got a nice, peaceful city going now. I don't want any of that shit starting up again."

Nice, peaceful city. Sure. "And you think that . . ."

"This is how it starts. Monsters killing people. Chaos."

"And then it'll rain for thirty days straight?"

He glowered at her. "Don't get smart with me. You don't know."

"Hey, I'm sorry," Jack said. "I'm just trying to understand."

"Okay, well," he said. "If y'all hand over whoever did it, maybe this doesn't have to be trouble."

"That the PD's official position?" Jack asked.

"It's my position," Kyle said. "And I'm not the only one. Silent majority." He stood up. "Thanks for the beer. I'm gonna get home before some monster kills me, too."

When he was gone, she got out her notebook and made some notes. She waited to see if anyone else would come in, but it was just her and some song about a lowrider that wouldn't end, so Jack paid for the beers and closed out.

Well, this was fucked. She'd literally just gotten Turing a job, and now he was in trouble. The smart thing would be to cut him loose before anything got more complicated. That's what she should advise Sir to do.

She got on her bike and headed downtown. Stopped at the light at the Boulevard of Bells, she saw flashing lights off to her right. She walked her bike forward to the corner so she could see properly.

There were a handful of cop cars parked in front of the bridge that led off-island. Floodlights. They were setting up barricades on the bridge.

She turned right instead of waiting for the light, parked on the street a little ways away, and ambled up as casually as she could. "Hey," she said. "What's all this?"

A cop looked up. "Official business. We're closing the bridge."

"'Scuse me, closing the bridge? It unsafe or something?"

"We believe that there's a risk of flight from a criminal," he said.

Uh-huh. So it was a snake who lived in the river, and they were going to barricade off the bridge to stop it. "How long will it be up?" she asked.

"Till we catch our suspect," he said.

"Thanks, officer," she said. "You've been very helpful."

He shrugged and went back to watching younger men move barricades into place. They had some big armored car full of them—the university had bought them all these expensive toys when they'd moved in on the island, and now they dragged them out any excuse they got. She went back to her bike, seething a little. This wasn't about stopping Turing from leaving; this was about making everyone else miserable until someone told them what was going on.

Well, fuck that. Jack kicked off and headed downtown.

"Bad news, boss," she said, pushing her way into Sir's office past his door guy. "Cops are shutting down the bridge. They think Turing did it, but they're not likely to find him without help."

Sir cocked his head to one side. "What do you think?"

"He didn't do shit. I'd like to request we don't hand him in."

"You don't know him that well," Sir said. "Let's say he did kill Pete. You still think he's worth it?"

"Was I worth it?" Jack asked.

Sir's mouth dropped open into a grin.

"I haven't made up my mind," he said. "All right, we won't say anything. But don't bring him here for a while. We've got enough problems right now."

Jack breathed a sigh of relief. That wasn't perfect, but it was about as good as she was likely to get.

"What do I tell him in the meantime?" Jack asked.

"Nothing," Sir said. "You've got work to do. I want you to find out who actually did this."

"Big job."

"It's what I pay you for. And I want this done before Carnival. This smells bad to me."

Jack nodded. "Glad you trust me."

Not that he should, of course, considering what she knew.

Belle couldn't take the fall for this, she thought, striding double-time past the bar so Hannah wouldn't have a chance to say anything. Belle had just been defending herself and her girls. Jack would've done the same. But Sir wouldn't see it that way—he'd hang Belle out to dry.

She tried to quiet the voice in her head that asked what had happened to Matthew Mannering. If he'd seen what happened, he'd have run and told his bosses. If he'd skipped that shift, he'd have turned up for work the next day, clueless that Pete was dead. And if what Belle had done was an accident, Jack thought, then why was Matthew still missing?

SIXTEEN

Within a few days, David had worked his way through *Planned Magic*, done every spell you could safely do in a broom closet and a few that you probably shouldn't, and he'd run over the other ones again and again in his head. For example, he'd skipped the spell called Clean that actually destroyed all matter in the radius of the circle, which he'd concluded could cause a nuclear explosion, depending on what they meant by "destroyed." Until he had a big empty stretch of desert to practice that in, he needed new spells.

Back in his office, he checked his answering machine, looking for a message from Astrid. He'd called her pager number a dozen times as he ran through the last safe-ish spells in *Planned Magic*. Nothing. How was he going to make any progress if she wouldn't sell him a second book?

A little impulse caught him then, like the muse. And he realized that he could just . . . go visit her. He knew she lived in the Old City somewhere. He knew she was friends with the DVD stall lady. He could go ask her. He had to teach Physics 205 in the evening, but that was hours away.

It felt a little dangerous. There was a real risk of him losing his funding over this. It sounded like quackery, like if someone in biology was wasting department time and resources studying chakras or something. But this was different. They just didn't know it yet.

He tossed his wallet into his backpack, along with *Planned*

Magic, on the off chance that it was useful. *Hey, I've already got one book of magic, you might as well sell me another, right?*

And so he went: down the elevators, through the lobby of Tower 4, and out into the traffic circle to try to catch a bus to the Old City.

He had only a general idea of where he was going. The bootleg DVD lady had her stall in a vacant lot in a part of town he'd only been to once, with Seth. He knew you caught the 22 and then rode it for what felt like an ungodly amount of time as it stopped on every block once it hit the Old City. He sat tight, waiting for something outside the window to look familiar as the bus picked up more and more people. Ragged women with plastic shopping bags full of plastic shopping bags, kids in torn jeans—but not like the pre-torn jeans of the university students, torn like used-up. Which made David think of that friend he'd had when he was a kid, the one whose name had been on the tip of his tongue lately. That kid never had a pair of jeans that wasn't ripped at both knees, or knees that weren't dirty. Tangled hair. Big shirts. David's parents would never have let him leave the house like that, and so that kind of anarchy had seemed to him like the ultimate freedom. Looking at these kids now, though, David found himself realizing that his friend had probably just been poor.

A man got on who was almost as tall as David, but bent over with great age, his huge white beard as big as his face, his body hunched over a heavy cane. He hobbled stiffly to a seat at the back and almost immediately began snoring so loudly that the bus rattled with it. David rolled his eyes and hunched smaller in his own seat. He wished he had a Walkman, but they were expensive as hell here. He could probably have asked his foster parents for one for Christmas, but he didn't like to ask them for anything. And anyway, this year he didn't really plan on going home for Christmas at all.

There was nothing wrong with them, not really. They were nice enough, and loved him approximately—buying him stuff he'd liked when he was twelve, asking him about people he hadn't spoken to in years, nodding and saying they were proud of him, all the right things. But it was obvious to him that they'd gotten hold of him just a little too late to really latch on. It was something about the way they were always polite to him, like he was a guest at dinner. Watching him nervously while he complimented the peas. At least here, it made sense that he was a stranger to everyone he met.

The bus jolted over a pothole, and the old man let out a cluster of grunts. Sleep apnea, David thought, based on the one premed class he'd audited. Should really get that checked out. An old guy like that could die in his sleep, especially if he slept alone.

As though thinking about him had summoned him, the man was lurching up the aisle of the moving bus. He turned to look at David, and David had a sudden horror that the guy had stumbled up to see him, somehow—but then another jerk of the bus carried the guy forward a few more rows, and David saw him stick his hand in someone else's face, a pretty obvious call for loose change. David relaxed. Could be worse.

The route must have been cleaned up since the last time David took it; pretty quickly they came to a stop where everyone seemed to be pouring off at the same time, and David deduced that this was either the place he was trying to get to or the end of the line. So he joined the throng and descended the bus steps right in front of a big wooden sign that said GOD STREET MARKET. Well, okay, then. First try and everything.

The market was in an open square in the middle of an otherwise-narrow street lined with vacant shops. There was a central fountain that looked like it hadn't run in years, with a big slab of rough-hewn rock in the middle. Around it, people had set up cheap pop-up tents selling all kinds of stuff: knockoff bags, plant cuttings, moonshine in unmarked brown bottles. David wondered for a moment why there were so many tents if there were so many empty storefronts. It seemed weird, too, that so many people were selling shit that was clearly illegal, and there was a cop sitting on the lip of the empty fountain smoking a cigarette. What was the guy there to look for, or to stop? It made David nervous. Better get this over with as quickly as possible.

It didn't take him long to find the DVD lady. Her sign said DIDI'S DVDs in an extremely no-nonsense sans serif font, and the lady herself sat at her card table with her bootlegs in filing boxes. She looked like a grandma who was also a CPA, with her permed gray hair and her half-moon spectacles on a beaded chain around her neck. When he sidled up to the table, she folded her hands.

"Hi," he said.

"Anime's on your left."

He blushed. "No, I'm just—you told me about, uh, Astrid."

She squinted at him. "You from here?"

"No. No, ma'am."

"You look like someone I know," she said. "Is your father white?"

David felt his blood run cold. He hated that question, it and all its possibly-white relatives. "We've met before. I'm really just looking for Astrid. I bought this—"

He started to reach for his backpack, but she held up a hand.

"Don't show me," she said. "I don't want to know."

"But will you tell me where I can find her?"

"You have her pager number."

"Yeah, well, she's not calling me back."

"It sounds like she could find you if she wanted to."

David felt a pit in his stomach. He was starting to think this had been a bad idea. How had he done it last time? She seemed wary of him in a way that she hadn't been before.

"Look," he said, straightening up to his full height, his forehead brushing the top of the stall's awning. "She sold me a book. And I've read it all, cover to cover."

She raised an eyebrow. "Are you threatening me, young man?"

"I'm guessing that she sold me the book either because she wanted me to use it, or because she didn't think I'd be able to use it. So either way, I bet Astrid will want to know how this went. I don't know why she's not answering me. But you'll tell her I stopped by?"

He expected her to reluctantly agree or, more likely, snap at him and send him on his way. But her face had furrowed into an expression of intense concentration.

"I know what you are," she said. "I was at the Battle of the Boulevard."

What was she talking about? David realized that blue had

seeped into the whites of her eyes. Deep and concentrated, like he'd seen before. She was casting a spell.

"I really don't recommend that," David said. "You're not supposed to cast in front of people, right?"

"Only if they notice."

David racked his brain; as it always did when he was panicked, it slowed down and took an interest in the situation writ large. The woman seemed to be about to cast a spell. But all the spells he'd done had taken forever to prep. Surely she couldn't just make magic appear out of the air. Where was her chalk, her pencils, her object of equivalent exchange?

Someone bumped into him from behind, sending him stumbling forward. David had to plant his hands on the card table to keep from falling, and his weight made it rattle, sending a stack of DVDs sliding to the ground. Didi let out a startled cry, distracted, and David whipped around, hoping to see who had bumped him. There, retreating through the crowd, leaving a wake behind him, was that huge old man from the bus.

David pushed away from the card table, back onto his feet. Fumbling in his pocket, he pulled out a bill—he wasn't sure if it was a five or a twenty—dropped it on the table, and booked it. People stared at him. He squared his shoulders. Suddenly everyone was scattering before him as he plowed through the crowd after the big man with the Santa Claus beard. He could feel their eyes on his back, but he didn't care. He'd been right. That guy had been eyeing him on the bus. Who the hell was he?

David caught up to the guy at the edge of the market. The man wasn't running, just ambling toward a brick-paved alley. David followed him into it, and then said, "Hey." It came out more quietly than he'd expected, and he felt embarrassed. He wasn't cut out for this sort of thing, chasing old men into alleys. Who did he think he was?

The man turned slowly. He was bigger than David had remembered. Or maybe he was just standing up straighter. The walking stick was gone—what had he done with it?—and the man's beard wasn't white but gray, streaked with red. The man laughed at him.

"I don't often face off against someone as tall as I," the old man said.

"Why were you following me?" David asked. "You looked at me on the bus. Why?"

This man scared the shit out of him. He was so calm, with his one good eye fixed on David, one milky blue eye roaming wildly around in its socket, his mouth a smile of broken, rotting teeth.

"Here's a history lesson for you," the old man said. "On the road to Thebes, two men quarreled in their chariots over who had the right to pass first. They drew swords and the older man died."

David shook his head. "What is that supposed to mean?"

"Kids," the old man said. "You can't tell kids anything. They have to do it for themselves. Even if I could tell you, could I stop you?"

"Stop me from what?"

The man smiled ironically.

"Listen, son," he said. "You should leave. Stop doing magic. Stop looking for answers. On Carnival Night, go to bed early. When they open the bridge, take the first bus out of town and never come back."

"Or what?" David said. "What's your problem?"

"See?" the old man said. "Can't tell you anything. I told Astrid. I said, 'They'll just do it again'—"

"Wait," David said. "You know Astrid? Do you know where I can find her?"

The man turned around and started shuffling away toward the distant opening of the alley. Without thinking, David lunged for the man and grabbed him by the back of his dirty black raincoat.

As soon as his hands gripped the old man, David knew he'd fucked up. He'd never laid hands on another person, not that he could remember in his lifetime. And as the man turned, David's eyes widened in terror. The man grabbed him back, by the arms, so that they were locked together. The guy looked so angry, like Zeus, like a storm cloud.

And then, the man disappeared.

David staggered forward, into the space where the other man had just been. Gone. No trace of him. Not even his smell lingered, that odd smell of rotten teeth. David was alone.

What did it take, to do the kind of magic that could make someone pop out of existence like that? It felt like more magic than should exist in the whole city, based on what he'd seen so far. Was that the spell that was sucking up all the power? Was that old guy doing it all the time, just vanishing and reappearing?

David had to find him again. The guy was powerful, and he knew Astrid. But the thought made David's hands shake with fear.

He left the alley, blinking as he emerged back into the sun-lit square. The crowd seemed to have mostly forgotten about him, except for over at Didi's DVDs, where the cop had joined Didi. Their heads were close together in whispered conversation. David ducked down, hoping they hadn't seen him. What a stupid thought.

Fuck the Old City, with all its weird superstitious bullshit. He hoped the whole dry-rotted place caught fire. David started purposefully for the bus stop, aware that they were watching him, that they could see him. Fuck this whole rotten day—

And then, suddenly, Astrid was coming down the street toward him. She had a basket over one arm and hadn't spotted him yet. He stopped, blocking her path, and she gasped a little when she saw him.

"You haven't answered my page," he said. "I need another book."

She stared at him, slack-jawed. God, more staring. Really?

"You don't need another book," she said, when she finally mastered herself. "If you understand everything in that book, you can write your own spells. And soon, you won't need to write them down at all. You'll hold them in other ways. In clay, or hair, or the wave of your hands."

It was like a cloud had parted. David felt his whole body relaxing, expanding. The possibilities were endless.

"I want to talk," David said. "Ride with me back to the university?"

She glanced up at the bus, as though just seeing it for the first time.

"Thank you, no," she said. "I can tell you more very soon. Just . . . not yet."

She darted away and was gone in a moment. He got on the bus in a kind of daze. Found a seat, slumped down on it, not even bothering to make himself small.

He'd nearly dueled a witch with magic. He'd nearly punched an old man. He'd very nearly gotten a straight answer from Astrid. He felt like he was pushing up against the skin of something that would soon burst.

The bus slowly emptied of its Old City residents, until it was just David and a middle-aged woman gnawing on the corner of a handkerchief. She had a plastic shopping bag crammed with toys and picture books, with a pink stuffed unicorn's head sticking out through a handle. She saw David watching her and smiled nervously.

"Is somebody having a birthday?" David asked.

The woman looked startled. "Um. She's getting surgery."

"Wow, I'm sorry," David said. "I hope she feels better."

The woman offered him a shaky smile. ". . . yeah. Thank you."

The magic wasn't in the books. Spells could be crafted. They didn't have to be written down. The knowledge swirled around and around in David's mind. He could write his own spell. He could show it to the department. He could publish on this. And if he did that, he'd never have to worry about funding ever again.

When the bus disgorged him, David went up to his office, locked the door behind him, and opened *Planned Magic* again. With Astrid's words in mind, the book looked completely different to him. It wasn't a 101 primer. It was the Rosetta Stone for a whole language. If he was going to show Seth some magic, he should write something good, something original.

David used a piece of string to draw a perfect circle with the chalk, stopping just short of closing it. He thought again about that kid he'd known back when his family lived in Chicasaw. It bugged him that he could remember the name of the shitty little town but not the kid who'd given him the book of poetry, and told him that in order to understand it, you had to read between the lines. If he were here now, David was sure he would've figured out the secret of *Planned Magic* weeks ago.

As he crouched down on his office floor, he felt a breeze on the back of his neck and jumped. But when he looked behind him, nothing was there—just a gust from the window he'd cracked in an earlier attempt at a spell. He settled down, realizing that he'd thought, for a moment, that it was the old man from before, appearing suddenly in his room.

The guy's advice came back to him as he worked. Stop doing magic, get on a bus, and leave. And something about Carnival, not like David ever went to that weird fake Mardi Gras anyway. The old man's speech was the kind of bullshit that people love to say to people they don't like. You're meddling with things beyond your ken. You should heed my warning. But how often did someone's life just go magically great when they gave up stuff they cared about because someone told them no? He'd never heard of it happening.

Still. The guy had spotted him on the bus. What was that about? How did he know him? He'd said something about two men meeting on a road. But David was sure he'd never seen the guy before in his life.

SEVENTEEN

Jesse tried not to look at the clock. It was harder to concentrate when she did. She lay on the mattress on the floor, now thankfully with sheets, practicing being a girl on purpose.

Her face, her body, everything felt different this way, like she was the exact same person but not quite. Like a full-body sensation of one of those magic pictures. Right now it was easy to see the girl. When she went there, she tried to remember how she felt when she switched by accident—when she was talking to Jack, or to Belle in the school. Or when she'd been so overjoyed by the sight of the city. There. She found the feeling and held onto it.

She took off her shorts so that she could feel the way the fat of her thighs stuck together in the heat. The ceiling fan turned lazily overhead. She shut her eyes, half dreaming, reveling in the new feeling. Dimly, she heard Jack come in, throw down her stuff, turn on the record player. It was a cheesy song, one she remembered from David's parents, who'd had a lot of jazz and bossa nova tapes they played in their house, where they never fully unpacked their moving boxes:

> *Tall and tan and young and lovely*
> *The girl from Ipanema goes walking . . .*

(Across town, David glanced up from his computer and shut his eyes, overwhelmed by a sudden nostalgia for a friend whose name he could not remember—)

She tried to move slowly. If she surprised herself, she always changed abruptly back. She shut her eyes and slid her hand up to the place where her legs met.

And when she passes, each boy she passes
Goes—ahhh.

There. She had to fight the urge to look. She told herself this wasn't dirty, this was for science. Or . . . whatever.

It felt so odd that she looked down, and as soon as she did, she changed. Jesse sat up, crossing his legs. He decided that this counted as a success; he'd never gotten that far without looking before, without breaking the moment. He sighed, and then he caught sight of the clock on the milk crate by his mattress. 7:50.

"Shit!" He sprang up and pulled on his shorts and stuck his head out into the living room. Jack was sitting in her chair, leaning back, motorcycle helmet and boots strewn around her on the floor. The record player was still going.

Jack glanced up. "Yeah?"

Jesse fumbled with the hem of his shirt. "Nothing," he said. His shoes were by the door; maybe he could get out before she realized what time it was.

"Are you late for work again?" she asked.

Jack had a knife on the table beside her, and as Jesse watched, she picked it up and began cleaning under her fingernails. She was wearing one of those undershirts she wore the way other people wore regular shirts, and he could see her nipples through it, something he could never get used to.

"No," he lied.

"What time do you work?" she asked.

"Eight."

She pinched the bridge of her nose. "Fuck me."

"I'm sorry," he said. "I just—"

"Get your shoes on. I gotta go down there anyway."

Jesse pulled on his sneakers while Jack bent down and hunted for her socks, which she'd thrown on the floor. She turned around suddenly and Jesse realized that he'd been frozen in the act of tying a shoe, watching her.

"This is the last time I drive you," she said. "And I said that last time."

"I know."

Jesse stood up, and Jack shoved him out the door in front of her, marching behind him down the stairs.

"If you hate it so much, get a different job," she said.

"It's not that," Jesse said. "It's just, I get nervous. And when I get nervous, I change. I spent half of last night hiding in the bathroom. If I could just stick with one or the other, I could work with it, but . . ."

Jack took Jesse by the shoulders. Jesse found himself staring right into Jack's eyes. Jack was studying him in a way that reminded him of Astrid.

"Honestly?" Jack said. "In good light, I can see when you switch. In makeup? In a dark bar? With naked girls onstage? Nobody's going to look at you long enough to notice."

"What if they do see? What if they see me change and they know I'm magic and—"

"Then you get to a phone and page me. I'll come get you."

Jesse grinned. "Thanks, Dad."

Jack cuffed Jesse on the side of the head, but not hard. "Just get on."

Jesse sat astride the bike with her arms around Jack's waist, perhaps tighter than was really necessary, as they headed downtown. Night had already fallen, and the streetlights stained the road orange in front of them.

They stopped at a light, and a cop car pulled up alongside them. The window rolled down, and Jesse was sure that they were looking right at them. Jesse felt Jack twitch, but her face remained forward, her hands steady. Jesse held her breath, hoping nothing would come of it. When the light turned green, the police car sped on. Jack let it take off before she got going again.

"Lots of cops out lately," Jack said. "Don't want to give them an excuse."

"Because that guy's missing?"

"Don't talk to anyone about that," Jack said. "You don't want anyone thinking you know anything."

"But I don't know anything!"

"That's good. You should keep it that way."

They drove down the long, steep slope into downtown and stopped outside the club. The neon sign on the roof flashed GIRLS!

GIRLS! GIRLS! Jesse hopped off the bike and stood looking at Jack while she dismounted and pulled off her helmet.

"Well," Jesse said, scratching the back of her head, "thanks for the ride."

"Don't do anything stupid tonight," Jack said. "I'm talking to Sir and then I'm heading back out." Jack nodded briefly at Rex, who growled a little as she slipped past him and into the club.

"Hey," Jesse said, stopping by Rex. "How's it going tonight?"

He glowered. "Not good," he said. "You seen this new guy Jack brought in yet?"

"No, what's he supposed to do?"

"Not stuff you should know about."

"Hey," Jesse said. "You've told me you don't like that end of things anyway, right?"

"Yeah," Rex said. "But I heard Dad talking about him. He's some kind of octopus guy. How you get like that? Your mom has sex with an octopus or something?"

Jesse frowned. "Hey, that's really rude."

"Sorry. But you know they say some kind of river monster killed that cop?"

"Wait, what?" Jesse asked.

"Don't you know? Jack found the body. She didn't tell you? Right by the river. And then this guy shows up right after." Rex shook his head. "And now we're hiring the guy the cops say they're looking for? I don't like it."

"But Jack likes him?"

"Yeah."

"I dunno," Jesse said. "I feel like Jack wouldn't vouch for

someone unless she was pretty sure. I mean, she's mean to everyone. Why would she be nice to this guy?"

Rex looked like he wanted to say something, but stopped himself. "I guess."

"Are you sure it's not just that you don't like Jack?"

He shrugged. "I mean. Doesn't help." He grinned. "You know, Hannah's pissed she's letting you shack up with her. They used to fight about that all the time."

"Yeah, I talked to her about it," Jesse said. "I told her nothing's happening."

Rex's eyes went wide.

"Really?" he said. "And she believed it?"

"Why wouldn't she?" Jesse said. "It's true."

"Yeah, whatever. You know, no girl I've ever known's lived with Jack. And not for lack of trying, you know what I mean?"

"Rex!" Jesse punched him in the arm. "We're seriously not together, I swear to you. Scout's honor."

"If you say so."

"Hannah's a good dancer," Jesse said. "You think I could dance?"

"You? You can't even walk in heels."

"Well, that's just because I don't have a pole to hold me up!"

Rex laughed.

"You know something?" he said. "I think you can be anything you want to be. Like if you told me you were gonna run for mayor, I don't think I'd be surprised if you won."

Jesse smiled, and scurried away toward the dressing room. It was such a relief, being here where people liked her. No one had ever been this nice to her in Chicasaw.

Jack came out from the back room with a look of grim determination on her face.

"I've got errands to run," Jack said. "Don't do anything dumb while I'm gone."

"I won't," Jesse said, and, surprising herself, darted out her arms to give Jack a hug. Jack shook her off and headed for the door. Jesse ducked into the dressing room.

Hannah was in there, freshening up her makeup after a set. She had a stack of ones and another of fives on the dressing table in front of her, and her dress lay in her lap. Jesse tried not to stare. Hannah was gorgeous. Jesse made eye contact in the mirror and waved.

"You want stage time tonight?" Hannah asked, using her little finger to clean up a stray swipe of lipstick. "Laura's out tonight, we could use you."

"I dunno," Jesse said. "I don't look like you."

Hannah looked surprised. "Whatever," she said. "It doesn't actually matter what you look like. Someone's into it. It matters if you can dance."

"I'm fine serving drinks," Jesse said. "I really don't mind."

"You know you can't serve drinks forever, right? Sooner or later you'll need to dance or get another job."

"Jack didn't tell me that."

"Jack doesn't know shit about stripping," Hannah said. Her face tensed, then, like she was expecting a fight. Like she was worried about how Jesse would respond.

"Okay, well, thanks for telling me," Jesse said.

Hannah squinted. "Thanks for telling you?"

"Yeah. I would've just served drinks till they fired me. So thanks."

Hannah smiled, shaking her head. "You're a weird one, Jesse," she said. "Is this about, you know . . . being . . ."

"Uh," Jesse said. "I mean, is it obvious?"

"Not really," Hannah said. "You just never take your clothes off in front of anyone."

"Oh."

Hannah's face softened a little bit.

"Sir wouldn't have hired you if he didn't think you could make money here," she said. "Try the practice stage. You can get used to it. I'll put you on the schedule for next week."

"Thank you," Jesse said. "I'll get it together, I promise."

Hannah rolled her eyes, turning back to the mirror. "We'll see," she said, but the corners of her mouth were still tugging upward. Jesse could see why she and Jack had gotten together. They were both hard on the outside to stop people from seeing how kind they were. Too bad they had never figured it out with each other.

Out on the floor, Jesse studied the practice stage. It was shrouded in shadow. Same pole as the big stage, but way less space. Nobody seemed like they were watching, and Jesse didn't see any drink trays on deck. Well, okay. If not now, then when?

Jesse took the two quick steps up onto the platform and nearly slipped. She reached out and gripped the pole, and clung onto it while she regained her balance. She let out a huge breath; she hadn't gone plummeting out onto the concrete floor below. She straightened up, using the pole to hold her body upright on her shoes. Her arms were strong, although her legs felt flimsy like a baby deer's. She could use that. She found herself testing the weight of her body against the pole, leaning back, seeing how far she could push the limits of her hips and arms.

She gave an experimental wiggle. She practiced leaning her weight back against the pole.

And then she realized an odd hush had fallen over the bar. It started as a beat or two between songs, then went on longer than it should have. Even when the music picked back up, the conversation had died. And people were watching her. They were waiting to see what she would do.

She set her jaw. Goddammit, they'd be entertained if she had anything to say about it.

She popped her hips and arched her back, leaned forward and ran her arms up and down the pole like it was a long-lost lover, then shoved it away with a slap, heel-turned, caught it behind her back and swung around in a long parabola. This felt easy and natural now that she was doing it; shoving her ass back into the pole so that everyone in the room could imagine it was their body she was stroking, and then skirting away, letting her legs stumble over themselves in the shoes, letting that vulnerability seep back in, the same frightened-deer look that made them all love her so much, made them all want to shelter her and never let her go. She suddenly knew what she was doing. She was telling a story.

Jesse danced, and thought about two lovers. A meeting in secret, peering at each other from behind the pole—which was an oak tree, a mighty one that sheltered their love. His departure. Her wasting disease. The lover she took in his absence. The heat of battle that threatened to drive the heat of her love from his mind. At some point her dress came off, but it made sense, like, narratively, and she felt pretty good about the hush that fell over the room. It felt like reverence.

She was a little disappointed that her powers didn't seem to include big tits. Even Jack's were bigger. Still, the ones she had seemed to work well enough. She couldn't hear it over the sound of her own heart pounding in her ears, but she could see a few bills touching down onto the edge of the stage, and she could imagine that it would sound like gentle rain.

She knelt down and let the rain fall on the face of the man she had been a second ago. She stroked her own face and held the ghost of him in her own arms—his own heroine, her own warrior love. And then Jesse knew what she had to do next to really bring it home: She had to die, dramatically, tragically.

She died.

She wished she didn't have to die, she thought, as she lay spread-eagled on the stage with her legs folded under her, her hips thrusting upward to pull her body toward heaven on a string, her head snapped back, while bills fluttered down upon her, thrown by hands that didn't understand why they were compelled, that had never felt like this before in their lives. She knew what she was doing, and she relished it. But she didn't understand why she'd had to die. She was crying a little, silently. It didn't seem fair that they should die. Not after all they'd been through.

"That was crazy!" Jesse heard someone saying in her ear, although it sounded muffled and distant. She realized that Hannah was half carrying her away from the stage and that she was clutching a handful of small bills and that her shoes were wobbly under her. "Okay, you lied to me. You've been practicing."

"Yeah," Jesse pretended to admit. It wasn't right, she thought hazily. She *shouldn't* have been that good. She should have fallen on her ass and hurt herself. She should be nursing a bruise with a handful of ice wrapped in a dish towel in the back right now. She shouldn't be—holy shit, that was a lot of money.

"How did you do that?" Agnolo the bartender said, suddenly looming in front of Jesse.

"Huh?" Jesse said, feeling wounded, wondering if this was when she was going to get caught, found out as a shape-shifter, banished from the club, taken to the hospital, dissected—

"That was good," he said. "You taking lessons or something?"

Jesse nodded silently, feeling like a liar.

"Well," Agnolo said. "You can have stage time if you wanna. Some of that shit was weird, though. Tone down the manly stuff, you hear? This isn't theater school."

"Sure," Jesse said, and let Hannah help her stumble back-stage.

"Jesus," Hannah said. "How did you do that?"

Jesse realized she was sweating profusely. Her hair, under her wig, was plastered to her scalp.

"I dunno," she said. "It was really . . . fun."

She realized Hannah was staring at her, and she felt so awkward, she tried to turn away and fell off her shoe again. It always hurt, that sudden buckling of the ankle. She grabbed a dressing table to steady herself, and she and Hannah both laughed.

When Hannah left, Jesse stared at her reflection in the mirror for a long time. She pulled her clothes back into place, adjusted the wig, steadied her breath. Drinks service for the rest of the night.

No more risks for a minute. But now she had a handful of cash, which would go a long way toward getting a mattress that didn't smell like mildew.

The bar stayed open until two, and by the time they closed, Jesse was exhausted and her calves ached. She changed back into her jeans and T-shirt. They were starting to look threadbare from constant wear; maybe she could get something new, now that she had some money coming in. The other girls hung around the dressing room, taking their time swabbing off their makeup, some waiting for rides.

"You walking back to the Old City?" Hannah asked.

"Yeah," Jesse said.

"Let's go most of the way together. Last night I got hassled by myself. Cops."

"Shit. Really?"

"Yeah. Went through my bag. Felt me up. I think they would've put me in the car if someone hadn't come by."

"Jesus. Yeah, let me walk you to your door, okay?"

"Me? What about you?"

Jesse shrugged. She couldn't explain why, but she was sure that nothing in this city could hurt her.

Jesse pulled on her sweatshirt and waited while Hannah bundled all her stuff into a gym bag. They waved goodbye to Agnolo, left through the side door, and headed up Canal Street toward London Hill.

"So," Jesse said awkwardly. "Are you and Jack still, you know, a thing?"

Hannah shook her head. "I want to let that go."

"I'm sorry to hear that," Jesse said. "I was just thinking tonight how alike you two are."

Hannah looked like she was about to say something, thought better of it, and tried again.

"Jesse," she said. "I know you two are friends, but she jerked me around for a year. Have you met her sister?"

"No?" Jesse said, feeling bad about the lie.

"Whenever I thought we were getting close, her sister would ask her for something, and I was always the first thing to go," she said. "I don't know what's going on with the two of them, but I do know it can't be my problem anymore."

"I'm sorry," Jesse said. "You deserve better."

"I know," Hannah said. "I'm choosing myself."

Jesse nodded. "I like that. You should."

"Still sucks that two days after we break up, she shows up with a fucking boyfriend."

Jesse was surprised. "Is this that monster guy Rex was talking about?"

"Yeah, I'd never seen him before."

"Maybe they're just friends."

Hannah snorted.

"I know Jack," she said. "You and her are friends. She's—" She stopped, shutting her eyes and taking a deep breath, as though to steady herself.

"She's not your problem," Jesse said.

Hannah let the breath out. "Exactly," she said.

"You deserve someone who's going to treat you well," Jesse said. "She just doesn't get how cool you are."

"Are you asking me out?"

"Oh, me? Gosh, no," Jesse said. "I just—"

There was a chirp of sirens behind them, and the sidewalk in front of them lit up red and blue. They both stopped. Hannah glanced at Jesse, her face pure fear.

"Turn around," a man said.

Jesse turned. A cop had gotten out of his car. He had his hand on his holster. When he saw Jesse's face, he slipped his thumb back and hooked it into his belt instead.

"Hi, officer," Jesse said. She reached out and took Hannah's hand, and squeezed it hard. "What can we do for you?"

"Where are you going?" he asked.

"We just got off work," Jesse said. "We're heading home."

The man looked at Hannah, then back at Jesse. "You two work together?"

"Yessir," Jesse said in his best hometown accent, realizing as he said it how deep his voice was. He'd changed over seamlessly, without even noticing

The man relaxed.

"All right, hurry on home, then," he said. "It's not safe for good people out here anymore."

He got back in his car and drove off. Hannah and Jesse stood together, shaking, until he was gone.

"You okay?" Jesse asked.

Hannah nodded. "Thanks," she said.

"No way," Jesse said. "It was my pleasure."

They stood there breathless for a minute, and then Hannah shook her head. "Ugh," she said. "No more white girls. Even chivalrous ones."

"Oh, no," Jesse said. "I'm sorry, I'm not trying anything. I don't do anything with anyone."

"Not interested?"

"I mean, I am. It's just that I'm actually, uh, in love, sort of."

"What?" Hannah asked.

And it all came rushing out.

"I had this friend when I was a kid in Chicasaw," Jesse said. "He was, like, the only Black kid in town, and I was the only gay kid, and so we hung out together a lot this one summer, and he was just so smart. We kissed this one time, and my stepdad found out and went over to their house. I don't know what he did, but the kid and his parents moved away. But he sent me this postcard." He fished around in his pocket. "He said to meet him here when we grew up. I carry it everywhere I go."

Hannah shook her head. "You moved here to try and find this kid you grew up with?"

"Yeah," Jesse said. "I don't know, is that weird?"

"It's a little weird," she said. "But it's also kind of sweet. I hope you find him."

"Thanks," Jesse said. He realized he was still holding her hand. "Let's get you home, okay?"

Jesse walked Hannah to her place on the edge of the Boulevard of Bells. At her door, Hannah leaned in and gave Jesse a peck on the cheek.

"Don't wait around for this guy forever," she said. "You should choose yourself, too."

Jesse walked the last several blocks to his place with his hands in his pockets. When Jesse finally got back to the apartment, it was easily three in the morning, and the whole house was dark. He flung down his backpack and stripped off his shirt. He scratched at his back urgently. Everything he'd worn that night had been itchy.

"Long night?"

Jesse glanced up. Jack was sitting in the wingback chair in the dark. She had a tumbler on the table beside her, half full of cigarette butts, and a bottle of whiskey on the floor beside the chair. The apartment smelled of smoke.

"Yeah," Jesse said. "They asked me to stay late and help close up. Where were you going in such a hurry?"

"Interviewing people," Jack said.

"Rex said something about your new friend," Jesse said. "Do you think he might be the one who killed those cops?"

"They're not supposed to talk about that with front of house."

"What did you find out about him?"

"Oh, that he's the ghost of the dead queen, come back to get her revenge on us all," Jack said. "You know, sane, sensible shit. Nobody has anything good to say, but none of it's real."

"But you don't think he did it."

"No." She brushed her hand over her hair. "You know, the bar closes at like two. It didn't take you all that time to get home."

Jesse blushed. What would Jack think about the kiss? Hannah was Jack's . . . well, not girlfriend. That much was clear.

"I . . . walked Hannah home. With all the police around, she's scared to be out by herself."

Jack smirked out of one side of her mouth.

"Why, Jesse," she said, in a long-syllabled Southern drawl. "That's practically responsible of you."

Jesse tried to scoff and roll his eyes, his imitation of Jack, but he was beaming and he was sure she could see it. Better not tell her about the pole dancing. Or the kiss.

"She's a good person," Jesse said. "Why were you such a dick to her?"

Jack turned on the lamp next to the chair. The sudden illumination made her squint, or maybe she was just tired.

"I dunno," Jack said. "I didn't love her, I guess."

"Why not?"

"I've only ever loved two things," Jack said. "My sister, and the river."

Jesse smiled. "Why the river?"

Jack sighed and stretched.

"Oh, y'know," she said. "It's big, and it doesn't need anything from me."

Jesse knew he was playing with fire, but he couldn't resist. "And what about your sister?"

"Psh. She wishes I didn't exist."

"That's so sad."

"And we're done with this conversation."

"I'm glad you exist," Jesse said.

Jack stood up, holding on to the chair for balance. She waved her hand back and forth, as though pointing at two Jesses. Jesse was aware suddenly of his shirtlessness, not quite sure whether he should feel naked or not.

"Y'all are cute," she said. "But I'm going to bed." She stumbled to her door and disappeared inside. Jesse heard her hit the mattress.

I'm cute, Jesse thought as he went and flopped down on his own filthy mattress. Cute, cute, cute. He was cute. She was cute. They, together, were cute.

Jesse wondered if he could get people to call him *they*. It sounded disjointed, like there were two of them at the same time. But there was really only one. And they were cute. Jack Marley had said so, and she ought to know.

INTERLUDE

River City Romance

The morning after she kissed Jesse Archer, Hannah woke up to the smell of crushed violets. She rolled over and opened one eye and saw the bright red-orange of poppies. She sat up and ran her fingers over her bed, blossomed in the night like a seed bomb, soft and fragrant and a little itchy. When she stood up and walked to the bathroom, her feet left patches of forget-me-nots blooming where she'd stepped. She closed her eyes and breathed in the smell that still clung to her skin. By the time she brushed her teeth it had worn off, and her tread and her touch no longer sprouted, but her bed was still a useless garden of wild carrot and black-eyed Susans and milk thistle and basil bloom.

A few days later, Seth put on a Hawaiian shirt he thought was kind of funny and went to a bar in the distant corners of the Old City where the music was loud and the lights were low and sometimes guys got with guys. He danced bachata with a white boy in tattered jeans, and then dragged him by the waist to the wall across from the bathroom, where he covered the boy's lips in bruises and ground up against him through their two layers of pants. It didn't last long before they got shooed away by the club manager, and the kid in the jeans said he wasn't really ready for anything else and then kissed Seth on the forehead and told him he was so—a long suck of air that made Seth's blood run cold and then hot—*wonderful*, the boy said, and then turned and darted away. Seth lost him in the crowd, but when he stood on tiptoe to look for him, his feet left the ground and he floated there, scared to move, to make himself fall, to break the feeling of exhilaration at his own weightlessness.

On Sunday, at the market where the city's rooftop and backyard farmers traded each other their vegetables, Alice, a blond-haired vegetable vendor, gave a cute girl the last box of cherry tomatoes from the summer, and after a long look, the two of them retreated to an alley a block away, where, along an ivy-covered wall, they ran their fingers through each other's hair and smelled each other's necks until they were dizzy. When Alice went home that night and washed her hair under the sink, the water that ran out glittered. She looked down to see that the sink strainer had filled up with glimmering flakes, which when held up to the light turned out to be slivers of gold leaf. She scraped them into an envelope, which she taped under her mattress before her boyfriend got home.

On Monday, Mike, the mechanic for all of Sir's people, met Jack Marley's new roommate when he brought Jack's bike by for a tune-up. The boy sat on the hood of a dismantled car, kicking his heels and talking about nothing. Mike gave him a discount and got a squeeze of the knuckles that made his scarred hands glow with a warm, radiating light.

At the club on Monday night, Rex came in with a fresh bruise where a few cops had roughed him up, asking when they were going to get answers. After Rex got drunk on his ever-growing tab, Jesse, coming off a shift, asked what had happened, opened up his big concerned eyes, and asked if Rex wanted consolation—with a caveat. I'll only be a boy, Jesse said, I really don't feel like a girl today, not even for you. And the line is *here* and no further. And if you can live with that . . .

Rex agreed hastily, took Jesse to a supply closet, kicked the mop bucket out of the door, and in the dark, learned that he could, after all, be very happy with ambiguity.

When he stepped out again, his bruises were healed, and on the way home that night, he said something nice to Agnolito—who looked startled, like he expected a kick—and Rex realized that he had never been very kind to his little brother.

And all across the city, those who could feel it sensed the magic growing, in little spatters, the way rain falls at first before the deluge. The magic fed by the Maiden and the dozen little love stories that sprang up around her. Astrid felt it, uptown in her little house, and fretted over it. The fairies felt it, and rejoiced that the river of light was rising around them, no matter how little.

David felt it, too. It filled him with joy and nervous energy as he experimented with spells late into the night. One morning after an all-nighter, he left the high towers of the University Hospital at dawn to go for a walk downtown to clear his head. He was leaving a coffee shop when, across the busy street, he saw someone he thought he knew. A face that reminded him of a name he'd lost. But no, it couldn't be. Just a girl in a blue dress with a pair of high-heeled shoes in one hand, picking her way around the broken glass on the sidewalk across the street. She'd looked so familiar. But the person he'd thought he'd seen had been a boy. He looked away, missing the moment when recognition lit her from within, the moment when she raised her right arm as though she were flagging down a cab, stood on her toes, and stretched as though she might fly into the air before the traffic separated him from her view. But magic doesn't work that way for the Maiden; it exists only to give away, never to keep.

EIGHTEEN

A week blurred past for David, in a wash of students and lab reports and endless hours recalibrating the stupid particle generator. The police came by and posted up big flyers saying that students should avoid unnecessary trips off campus, but David didn't have much reason to leave the towers. And then it was Friday and his students were streaming out of the lecture hall, muttering *thanks* and *have a good weekend*. He found himself whistling as he packed up his bag in the empty lecture hall, thinking about how none of them knew he was about to go take the math they'd slept through and write spells with it. Real spells, his own spells, not recipes out of a book.

Of course, he should probably be grading—he had his own growing pile of papers on top of what was left of Haughan's. But what would he be remembered for in twenty years: sweeping innovations, or his commitment to paperwork?

He hurried back to his office and unlocked his desk drawer. He was still using the book, but knowing it was a reference material, he felt a little freer to experiment. He still didn't know what Astrid had meant by casting with a wave of your hands, or with your hair—was it that you encoded a spell into a pattern, like a computer program? If so, what read the program? What performed the function? He worked for hours, tracing and retracing, practicing balancing equivalent forces until a pounding at his door distracted him.

"David! Open up! It's the fun police!"

David hastily scraped some desk trash over the diagram on the floor. He opened the door. Seth stood there in a velvet shirt and a long scarf.

"Oh, thank god, officer," David said. "I'm being harassed by a man who wants me to go clubbing. Can you talk to him about that?"

"If you're going to hide up here, at least let me see what you're up to," Seth said. He stepped over the threshold. "Oof, what the hell?"

Shit, he'd—no, he'd just spotted a wrapper from a honey bun. How long had that been on David's desk? Seth picked it up between his thumb and forefinger, like you might hold a dead mouse. "You know these things are gonna kill you, right?"

David sighed. "I've been working late."

"This building has two takeout salad places." Seth sighed. "You can't spend your whole life working. Come out with me."

"Yeah, because what's missing from my diet is beer. And anyway, the cops said not to leave campus."

"They're bluffing. There's, like, no way to actually enforce that." Seth glowered. "I hardly see you anymore, man."

David softened. Seth had been trying to graduate for longer than David had been here, and he'd always been friendly. It had stunned David at first; he was used to being bullied by good-looking slackers. The first time Seth had asked him to come chill and play video games, David had assumed it was a joke. But no, he'd gone to the guy's room, ready to bolt if there was anyone else in there, and Seth was already blowing into a cartridge, trying to get it to load.

It was kind of touching that Seth was doing all this work,

David thought. He should really try to make some time. And more importantly, if Seth kept stomping around in here, he was going to spot something he shouldn't.

"Okay, fine," David said. "If you really want me to come out, I will."

"Yus!" Seth jumped into the air and clicked his heels together. "All right, let's get you dressed."

"I'm not changing my clothes," David said.

"Trust me," Seth said. "You're not going to want to take a shirt that nice into a bar this bad."

Seth had slightly undersold the risks of leaving campus; there was, in fact, a pair of cops stationed at the bus loop, watching the doors of the towers. Seth nodded confidently at them and one of them nodded back. He had a little gadget in his hand, and he clicked it as they went by. A people counter, David thought. Tracking people going out.

"Is it hard to get back in?" he asked. "Will they ask us where we've been?"

Seth rolled his eyes. "If they really wanted us to stay put, they'd issue a curfew. They're just trying to look good for the investors. Some cop fell into the river and drowned and now they're worried we think they're incompetent."

David thought briefly of the cops he'd met the other day, the guy who'd rifled through his bag while his partner jeered from the sidewalk. "Fell in?" David asked. "What was he doing?"

"I dunno, drinking?" Seth meandered through a little maze of barricades that the cops had set up around the usual traffic pattern in the bus loop. "Have you ever talked to the cops here? They're unhinged. They talk like they're fighting the forces of darkness or something."

The streets outside campus seemed oddly deserted. David was used to more of a bustle on Friday nights as students and townies all headed out to bars. He'd seen it from his window dozens of times.

"What's the forces of darkness?"

"You know how there's like all these weird mutations here? Claws and tumors and stuff?"

The history class David had taken had explained that the townies had bad genes from centuries of inbreeding. David had always privately suspected it was more to do with the island's ambient radiation. "Sure."

"Yeah, the cops think those guys are, like, the orc army or something."

"Jesus."

"Right?"

A surprisingly short walk later, Seth and David stood outside of a crumbling brick edifice with an enormous neon sign strapped to its roof that flashed GIRLS! GIRLS! GIRLS! in blue and pink. David hadn't realized they'd be so close to campus. Seth grinned up at him, looking pleased with himself.

"This?" David said. "Dude, is this a strip club?"

Seth bumped against his shoulder, releasing a whiff of strong cologne. David breathed in deeply without realizing at first what he was doing.

"You're twenty-one, right?" Seth asked.

"Not till the spring," David said.

"Well. Somehow I doubt they'll ask."

They went up to the door. The bouncer, David realized, either had that hairy-face disorder or was wearing a werewolf mask on the job. He glanced down at the man's hands. He was wearing black leather gloves, so that didn't help.

"Two please," Seth said, handing the man a bill. The bouncer shrugged, and gestured toward the door.

Inside the light was murky and red, and the music thudded. They had a platform stage with a stripper pole in the middle, but a man was unscrewing the pole from the ceiling while two women in short dresses and staggeringly tall heels set up what looked like a cordon around the edge. One of the women glanced over at Seth and winked.

"Friend of yours?" David said.

Seth laughed. "Jealous?"

Seth led them to one of a few empty café tables—the room had perhaps a dozen, and burly men sat at them in pairs and threes, and a few scattered women, too. The men—well, they were ugly, David thought. Monstrous, even. Frog-faced and warty, sickly green even in the red light, faces like red putty or unspeakably hairy, like the guy outside. The med students from the university would kill to know about this place and its array of test subjects. How had Seth found out about it?

A fat bartender wandered up, and Seth threw his arms up. "Agnolo, you bastard! Bottle of wine?"

"Two glasses?" The man had a tonsure like Friar Tuck and a pair of tusks. A gut covered in thick dark hair jutted out from his too-small shirt.

"Yeah, thanks," Seth said. "Quiet for a Friday."

Agnolo scowled. "All this cop shit is bad for business. Nobody wants to leave the house."

"What, the whole stay-off-the-streets thing? C'mon," Seth said. David wanted to kick him. How could he be so stupid? But Agnolo smacked Seth on the back of the head hard enough that Seth lurched forward.

"You think they're cracking down on pretty college boys like you?" he said.

Seth rubbed his head. "Nooooo," he said, grinning, a little petulant. Agnolo seemed satisfied and grunted.

"That's right," he said. "Talk shit, get hit, right, big guy?"

"Uh," David said.

"Speaking of," Seth said. "When's the fight starting?"

"Challenger's having second thoughts." Agnolo stared grimly at the ring. "No one likes to fight Jack when she's like this."

Seth tapped David's hand and pointed across the room to a corner table where a white woman with a buzz cut sat hunched under a leather jacket. She had a half-empty bottle in front of her and a small spiral notepad. A guy with a third eye in the middle of his cheek sat across from her waving his hands, and Jack was taking notes on what he said. She did look irritated, David thought.

"That's Jack Marley," Seth said to David. "She's a legend."

"She's like five nothing."

"Five four, actually. Technically welterweight, but she'll fight anything when she's been drinking."

"Is that responsible?" David asked.

"Not really. I saw her mess a dude *up*."

The two women finished setting up the ring and clambered down. Agnolo came back with the wine, and then sighed.

"All right, I'm bringing in the boys," he said. "Gotta give people something."

Agnolo scrambled onto the stage, and someone passed him a microphone. David heard a sudden thunder, and realized it was every man in the room stomping their feet all at once. He took a swig from the glass Seth had poured him. He didn't know what good wine was supposed to taste like, but he guessed this wasn't it. Sugar and vinegar. He took another gulp.

"All right, we know what you're here for," Agnolo said. "But there's no Marley fight tonight"—a sudden swell of grumbling— "not unless one of you sons of bitches wants a go."

A lull.

"Okay, so we've got a few of Sir's boys for you. You know sibling rivalry's a cornerstone of this operation. On the left: two hundred five pounds, double-jointed knees, it's Reeeeex!" A low rumble of approbation from the crowd as a hairy guy stepped in, on knees that were, in fact, backward. *Costumed fights*, Seth had said. These were no costumes. Seth was an idiot. An idiot who was now bouncing up and down in the chair next to him with childlike excitement.

"And on my right, the prince of darkness, a hundred and sixty pounds, two rows of teeth, it's Agnolito! My godson and dare I say it, the one I've got my money on tonight." A creature covered from head to toe in black fur, peltlike, gleaming red where the light hit him, stepped in on the other side and snarled. They circled each other warily, and when a girl rang a bell, they launched as though spring-loaded.

They fought, but David could barely see it. His vision had narrowed to a tunnel that faced the stage, but he was more preoccupied by the warm darkness all around him, the roar of the crowd, the perpetual stamping. The thunder of horses' hooves, it sounded like. Of an army behind him. He drank more wine. He sat up straighter, lifted his head and shoulders until they were perpendicular with the floor. He felt heat rising inside of him, and he expanded until for once, he filled his body.

The fight ended with Agnolito pinned and wriggling under Rex's left knee. Agnolo counted ten, and it was over. Seth reached across the table to shake David by the shoulder, and David had the sudden impulse to flash a smile back, a big one. Seth's face opened up like a flower.

"Hey, kid," Agnolo yelled from the stage. It took David a minute to realize the man meant him.

David blinked in surprise. "Who, me?"

"Yeah, you." Agnolo was talking into the microphone now. "You're a big guy, how big are you?"

"Uh. Six ten?"

"Six ten, he says. Hell, if I were six ten I'd just go ahead and say I was seven feet fucking tall! You wanna fight Jack Marley? Come on, six ten!"

David could feel the whole room shifting to look at him. He felt his legs moving on their own, carrying him out of the chair and onto his feet.

"What are you doing?" Seth asked.

"Sure," David said to Agnolo. "Why not?"

The crowd roared. He stepped up alongside the stage. David

was surprised when Agnolo squeezed his arm and muttered, "Kid, now I look at you closer, I'm not so sure. You've got muscles like veal. What do you do for a living, sit on your ass?"

"I'm twice her weight. I'll be fine."

Agnolo shrugged. "Your funeral." He took up his microphone again. "Folks, he's serious. I'm not sure I was serious, but he is. What's your name, kid?"

"David Blank." Embarrassing last name. It was, however, what was written on his birth certificate. His adoptive parents had asked him if he'd wanted to change it, and he never had. By the time they'd gotten him, he'd been Blank for three years. He couldn't imagine himself as a Richards.

"David Blank. Blank slate here, folks. Big guy, though. Maybe he can fight, maybe he can't. You wanna bet on him? You wanna bet on Jack? You've got five minutes."

People started shuffling toward the bar, cash in hand. David glanced over at the table where Jack had been sitting. She'd taken off her jacket. Even in the dim light of the bar he could see that her arms were corded with muscle, and she had a big tattoo of a dog's head on her collarbone. She was stretching like a dancer, gently manipulating one joint at a time, her motions a little deliberate in a way that made David think maybe she was drunk.

"David," Seth said, running up and tugging on his sleeve. "She's gonna kill you, David. I saw her tear off a guy's ear once."

David felt a twinge of annoyance. Hadn't Seth asked him to come out and have a good time? Hadn't he brought him to this place where everyone was fucking crazy?

"Look," David said. "You don't know me that well. Maybe I'll surprise you." God, Seth was right, he was going to get killed. The woman was small and about his age, but she looked mean. She slipped into the ring and continued her stretching there. In the harsher light, her shoulders and arms glittered with scars. One big scar wrapped all the way around her bicep, like someone had tried to saw her arm off.

He felt a hand thud into his back, and he jumped.

"Not a good sign," Agnolo said. "All right, time's up. Get in there."

David nodded. He tried to hop onto the platform, but he overshot and got his foot caught in a rope, and ended up stumbling into the ring, squinting in the bright light. He realized he still had his glasses on. He took them off, glanced at the blur he thought might be Seth, and tossed them toward him. The crowd *oooh*ed dramatically.

Fine, he thought. He pushed his head up and his shoulders back, even though they ached a little at the unusual request. He flexed. He tilted his chin up. He could be imperious. Maybe it would even be kinda funny to watch him get pummeled by a woman half his size. Maybe that would be something Seth would comment on later, tell him he had guts, if nothing else. He held his palms upward and turned, left and right, beckoning the crowd to cheer. Some laughed, but he could also hear the low drumbeat of stomping feet start again. They liked him. There was that warm rush again, that little thrill of invincibility. God, he wasn't this guy. So why did it feel so easy?

He looked over at Jack—he half expected her to tell him to walk away. She didn't. She looked . . . not bored. Calibrating.

Figuring out what he was going to do. Probably a lot of beginners rushed her, he thought. But cowards probably feinted and dodged a lot—

The bell went off.

She didn't wait to see what he would do. She moved in quick and socked him twice in the stomach. It hurt more than he was expecting; he doubled over a little, breathing hard. He had to get her away. He brought up his knee as sharply as he could, and wonder of wonders, he got it in between them and shoved her off. She tried to get in again, and again he used his leg, this time adding a little kick. He knew physics; he had the leverage on her. He was starting to feel good about this.

She came in again. He put up his knee, but suddenly he found himself arcing backward, through the air, looking sideways at Jack, who had knocked his other leg out from under him somehow while he wasn't looking. He hit like fallen timber, and she leaped in on top of him. He threw up his hands while she rained punches down on him.

"That's enough! Jack, that's enough!"

Agnolo was between them, pushing Jack back toward her corner. She went mechanically, and turned to watch him as Agnolo helped him to his feet. David tried to read her. What was she thinking?

This time he put his hands up, and they circled each other warily. David was distantly aware that the crowd seemed kind of quiet. He had to bend a little to be on eye level with her, but he didn't want to look away from the girl's eyes. She scared him. But at the same time, he felt calm, alert. His legs moved without him having to tell them how. Or rather, he and his legs were the same creature. Or rather, he didn't have to think things like "his legs"; his body was all one smoothly operating piece instead of a jumble of too-big parts. He was calibrating, too.

And then Jack stepped quickly, trying the same tactic to get in where she could pummel him, and David shifted his weight backward on his heels, and without really thinking about it, he spoke the words he'd been practicing in his head all day and traced the diagram he'd been composing in the air with his forefinger.

Fire sprang from his palms. The flame was fragile, only lasting a few seconds. But Jack sprang back as though bitten as the gout of flame rushed past her head. He knew without looking that back at his café table, his thimbleful of cheap wine had crumbled to ash in his glass.

The crowd fell silent. David was alone again, in a square of light with a woman who wanted to beat the shit out of him, and all around him was the watching dark, teeming with warm bodies shifting in their seats.

Agnolo broke the silence. "Hey!" he said. "You wanna get us all in trouble? Fists. Kicks. No fire. Get it?"

David nodded. Agnolo pushed his comb-over back over his bald head, and brought his arm down between David and Jack, and jerked it back like a gate. "Fight!"

Jack sprang at him more fiercely than he expected. David wasn't ready, and he realized it as he saw her whole body arcing up toward him, one leg extended. How was she so light, he thought, a ball of muscle who floated like a feather, and he felt a kind of detached awe as the toe of her boot struck him in the temple.

He knew he was going to fall over, and he tried to put his arms out to stop it, but he realized he couldn't quite reach his arms, that they felt like jelly, and so did his legs, and so did the ring and the lights and the waiting dark. His head slammed into the mat, and he felt a kind of lightning strike him, and the dark swallowed him up.

When he sat up again, it was to a roar.

He got shakily to his feet and stood in the center of the ring. The roar went on and on, a thunder of stamping feet and voices going hoarse. He lifted his arms. Why did he do that? The cheers climbed, though, into whistles and shouts.

Jack stood at the edge of the ring. As he turned to look at her, she hopped from the platform and disappeared into the dark, but the roar went on and on. Why were they cheering? For him? he thought. She'd clearly won. The girl called Jack had kicked him so hard, he'd thought he died. Jack the giant killer, he thought. And they were cheering for the giant.

"Why?" David said to Agnolo, who it seemed was holding his arm now.

Agnolo shrugged. "You took it better than anyone ever has."

David climbed down from the ring, temporarily blinded by the light, and into the warm embrace of strangers. People rushed to thump his back. He spotted Seth and waded toward him. Seth flung his arms around David's belly.

"I thought you were a goner, man," Seth said. "Let me buy you a drink."

"I don't think we're buying any drinks tonight," David said. In the sparse crowd, it was easy to see that Jack was gone. It was wrong, it was so wrong. She was the one who had knocked out a guy the size of a cab. He also thought he probably shouldn't be drinking right after passing out, but men with heavy hands were urging him toward the bar, sliding him beers down the counter, pouring him shots, raising their bottles and yelling whenever he or Seth took a drink.

By the end of the night, David was almost too drunk to remember that he'd gotten beaten up, especially when they left and it was raining and they had to stagger-run from overhang to overhang with their jackets over their heads. He didn't remember until they were back in the high white walls of the University Hospital, when, alone in the elevator, Seth reached up and touched the bruise on David's temple, and it throbbed.

"Ah, Jesus," David said.

"Your students are gonna ask about that." Seth stepped a little closer.

"I'll just tell them I joined a fight club," David said.

"You could tell them it's a hickey."

David felt a gentle weight. When he looked down, Seth was hanging off the front of his shirt.

"You're drunk," David said, shoving him lightly. Then he realized that Seth was tipping over and grabbed him again before he fell. "Oop."

"Hey," Seth said, his face half-muffled in David's shirt. "You were great out there. You were like . . . a god."

David knew if he looked down, Seth's handsome face would be

right there, breath reeking of liquor, eyes glazed and starry. David wanted to look into those eyes, but then he remembered: *I swear he winked at me. I've never found my pants so fast . . .*

"You're a weird drunk," David said, as the elevator door dinged open on their floor. He half carried Seth down the hall to his room, held him up while he fumbled in Seth's pocket for the keys. As the door opened, he let Seth go and watched him stumble in.

"Davey, buddy," Seth said, gripping his doorway for support with one arm, leaning out to grab at David's shoulder with the other. "Don't leave me like this."

"Night, Seth," David said.

Back in his room, David sat down hard on his own bed and looked down at his hands. Gray ash clung to his palms. From the fireball, he supposed. When he clapped them together, crumbs of the stuff fell to the floor like chalk dust.

He'd done magic without the book, in the air. He'd fought a woman who kicked him in the head so hard he'd passed out. He'd drank until he could barely walk. And Seth . . .

He didn't want to think about that. Seth was a drunk idiot who'd forget all this in the morning. David tried to tell himself that it didn't matter, that he wasn't really upset. Logically, he shouldn't be. It had been a great night, all things considered.

But still, he stood up and studied his reflection in the mirror. He turned his head back and forth, watching his own perplexed expression as he tried to get a glimpse of a god.

NINETEEN

Leaving David alone in his room and Seth sleeping with his body curled around a pillow, we swerve upward into a sky thick with rain. Tomorrow, people will get up hungover or still drunk, look out at the rain that still comes streaking down, and ask themselves why they stayed so late drinking with yet another loser in the long line of men overthrown by Jack Marley.

Jack wasn't interested in that question. She stood outside under the eave of Sir's nightclub. She took out her silver lighter and lit a cigarette under the eave of her hand, and cupped the cherry with her palm, smoking the way her dad had taught her because it hid the glow. As the heat of the embers warmed her palm, she thought about the guy she'd fought that night, the way he'd cupped fire and thrown it. She'd never seen anyone do magic like that. Astrid was going to notice that big ticket piece of magic for sure. Jack had almost been scared. Thank god the guy had no discipline. Most big men didn't. They thought they were invincible, but all it took was one swift kick to the head.

She stepped out from under the roofline. As the rain began to fall on the back of her neck and her fresh crew cut, she turned up her jacket collar. She was on foot tonight. The whiskey had long since worn off, but she was walking because she was thinking, just like she'd been drinking and fighting because she was thinking. It always took her a while to get to the core of a problem. The important thing was to keep her body moving steadily until her mind caught up.

She felt like she hadn't stopped moving since they found Pete McNair. Since the night she'd gone to the island and met Turing. Since the night her sister had come to visit her at home. Told her she'd killed Pete, said it was an accident, said she'd never even heard of Matthew Mannering. But here he was, still missing.

Belle thought Jack was stupid, and that was a problem. Jack wished she knew how to convince her that it'd be easier if she just told Jack the truth. They could work with the truth. And just from a sanity perspective, Jack would feel a whole lot better if she knew where the second body was. Because the police were definitely looking for it. They wouldn't dare come down to Sir's club, not yet. But they'd harassed a dozen of Sir's employees in the last week: home visits to security people and dancers alike. Barging in on them during their day jobs if they had them, or stopping them in the street.

Matthew was missing. He'd been seen last with Pete. Belle had said *what partner*. The cops thought it was Turing, but none of them had gotten a good enough look at him to even know who or what he was, which meant someone had started that rumor. And Sir had told her to leave him swinging.

She thought of Turing, alone on that stupid rock, reading the same shitty paperbacks over and over again. Well, maybe it didn't have to be forever. Maybe just till this was all over. Whenever it was over. The bridge had been closed for weeks now, shops running out of sodas and paper towels, but the police wouldn't budge. To keep the killer from escaping, the cops said, as if they hadn't had days to run if they were going to. In that time Jack could've gone to the mainland, bought a big snake off of someone, and set it loose. The idea almost made her laugh.

This felt like a joke. Like someone, somewhere, had devised the perfect dilemma for Jack Marley specifically. And sooner or later, she was going to have to pick. Irritated, she turned her body toward the old city.

It took Jack an hour to reach the old Bodwell School for Sensible Girls, and by the time she did, her jeans were soaked with rain. She could feel the way her body radiated heat out into the chill, could see the steam of her own breath. She went around to the back of the school and let herself in through the hole in the old chain-link fence into the schoolyard. The schoolyard-facing door had been off its hinges for years, but someone had recently reinstalled it. She tried to open it and found it locked. So she knocked and waited.

The girl who answered the door was tall and had her head shaved to the scalp, with big earrings in the shape of dragonflies. She wore a quilt thrown across her shoulders like a cape. But one hand, tucked away under the quilt, clearly held something. Jack relaxed her shoulders and tried not to look like a threat. Behind her, she could see an old teacher's desk dragged into the hallway to serve as a front desk, and a darkened stairwell beyond. The whole place smelled like paper pulp and chemicals.

"We're closed," the girl said.

"I'm here to see Belle," Jack said. "Is she home?"

"See her about what?"

"I just want to talk to her. I know she's around. She runs this place now, right?"

"You're gonna have to leave."

"I'm her sister," Jack said.

The girl tilted her head and sized Jack up. It didn't take long.

"I can see it," the girl said, and straightened up. Jack saw a gun hanging from her hand as she turned and disappeared into the stairwell behind them. Bad security, Jack thought. You really needed a door guard *and* a runner. Jack let herself into the hall to get out of the rain.

A girl came out of one of the rooms, laughing and talking, leading a man by the hand to the exit. When she saw Jack, she quieted down. After a minute, the first girl came down.

"She says you can go up."

Jack climbed the stairs. She felt acutely aware of the possibility of ambush, here in the dark, and kept her ears pricked. Up here, none of the rooms were lit, except for one at the far end of the hall. She walked down the long corridor, acutely aware of the sound of her shoes on the cracked tiles, until she came to the last door at the end. She knocked. "Belle?" she said. "It's me."

"Jackie, I'm not feeling well," Belle said through the door. "I can talk, but you can't come in."

And then a low thump, and a sound like chair legs scraping slightly against the floor. And Jack knew, without a shadow of a doubt, that behind that door, alive or dead, was Matthew Mannering.

Jack sighed and slumped down with her back to the door. She took out her lighter again and turned it over and over in her fingers, feeling the engraved letters on it. It was warm where it had pressed against her leg through her pocket. She flipped it open and clicked it, just to make the little jet of flame. The motion steadied her.

"Belle," Jack said. "Your story isn't holding up. I'm not sure why you killed McNair, but I don't think it was an accident. I think you planned it. And I think I know why you won't let me in right now."

A long silence.

"So what happens now?" Belle asked. "Are you gonna hand me over to the cops? Will that make things easier for your little friend?"

"What are you talking about?"

"I saw you with him the other night," Belle said. "Sometimes I think you collect people like that to feel better about yourself. Jackie and all her dogs."

"Sir took care of us," Jack said. "Show some respect."

"He made you get a tattoo of his head."

"It's—you're not listening," Jack said. "What are you doing here? What's your plan? It can't just be killing two cops." Maybe she'd slip up. Maybe she'd say Matthew was alive, and Jack could feel justified breaking down the door. And then what? she wondered. Fight her sister, and then fight her way out, dragging some wounded asshole who'd seen her sister's face? She doubted the Bodwell girls would be any good at violence, but there were a lot of them. Although fewer than there'd been a year ago. Belle's schemes were getting increasingly . . . risky.

"We can't keep letting them treat us like this," Belle said. "You know it, too. The university—"

"Nobody likes the New City," Jack said. "Look, if you want to do something about it other than print posters, you should talk to some people who've fought cops before. Sir and Astrid both hate 'em, too."

"Your dog friend has no reason to hate the New City. He loves their money. And Astrid is weak. You should hear her talk about it. She won't even say she refuses to work with the police."

"There are no perfect coalitions. You killed one cop? Two? Do you think that'll make the rest of them mind their manners? They've only gotten worse. They shut down the bridge, Belle. If you think it's bad for you and your girls, you can't imagine what it's like for us downtown."

"Good," Belle said. "The people have been asleep for too long. It's time they rose up."

"Rose up? You've got, what, twenty girls? That's not a violent uprising, that's an afternoon's work for the cops and jail time for all of you."

"I can't tell you what I'm doing. You're compromised."

"Compromised? Why, because I work for Sir?" Jack flicked up the lid on the lighter, lit it, snapped it shut, flicked it open. "Because I actually know what I'm doing? If you'd come to me, they wouldn't have found the body!"

There was a long silence.

"I can hear it when you click that lighter, you know," Belle said. For a moment, her voice wasn't so hard. "I'd know that sound anywhere."

Jack looked down at it, shoved it into her pocket. "Sorry."

"And you wonder why I don't tell you things."

Jack snorted. "I killed him. What more do I have to do to make you trust me?"

"Is that how you think this works?" Belle's voice climbed upward, mocking. "What do you want me to say? 'Thanks, Jackie, that must have been so hard for you'?"

"I don't mean it like that!" Jack slammed her hand on the chipped tile floor so hard it went numb. "It wasn't a favor. I didn't do it to make myself feel better." She realized she was all but crying. "If you won't tell me what's going on, I can't keep you safe."

Belle's voice, when it came again, was hard. "If you want to keep me safe," she said, "keep your mouth shut, and don't get in the way. You don't know anything about what's going on here."

Jack stood up.

"I'm gonna get you some money," she said. "In case you need to lie low for a while. Okay?"

Silence from behind the door.

"All right," Jack said. "I'm going. Bye, Belle."

She went down the echoing industrial staircase of the Bodwell School. Belle wasn't going to do a good job of hiding this. Fuck, she wasn't even trying to hide this. It was only a matter of time before Sir found out. Or Astrid. And either of them would turn Belle over to the cops before they took the hit themselves. Jack would do the same damn thing if it were anyone but Belle.

In the entryway, a cluster of girls huddled around the desk. One of them was keeping a furtive eye on the front door, but from Jack's vantage point she could see that they were looking at a map of the city. There were lines in red, and arrows pointing toward downtown. The girl wearing the quilt raised her bald head to look at Jack as she descended. Jack thought suddenly of Turing, although she didn't quite know why. She'd promised she'd come get him weeks ago, and she hadn't because Sir had told her to leave him. He must be wondering where she was. She should go talk to him tonight. Tell him that he shouldn't come to the city right now, that it wasn't safe for him here. He was too gentle to withstand the cops if they really pressed him.

It had been raining for hours by the time Jack reached the water's edge. The ground around the boathouse was soaked and spongy. Jack made short work of the lock and took out a yellow boat. From here, the island was just a darker shape; she wondered if the lantern that hung from the rafters of Turing's shack was lit. The water was high, sloshing up onto the banks and making the grass stream as though it were blowing in the wind.

She was carrying the boat through ankle-deep mud on the riverbank when she saw a shape break the surface like a seal and look at her with wet eyes. Turing spotted her and scrambled onto the shore, crouching warily, looking left and right. Tentacles curling around arms and legs, huddling against the chill in the air.

"It's not safe out here for you, Jack," Turing said.

Jack glanced down at the boat she was carrying; it suddenly seemed flimsy compared to the white torrent of water.

"Did something happen?" Turing asked. "I waited for you. I thought you'd forgotten."

"I . . . Do you want to come inside?" Jack asked, pointing toward the shed. She laughed bitterly. "We're getting wet out here."

They went in together. The roof was corrugated metal, and the rain hitting it sounded like pebbles. Jack set the boat down keel-up, and Turing settled onto it, and after a minute, Jack sat down, too, shivering in her wet clothes. Turing's body seemed to radiate coolness. Jack glanced at him out of the corner of her eye. She couldn't see him well in the dark, just the outline of a body, the rise and fall of breathing.

She didn't know what to say. She didn't know why she'd come here to the water's edge and stolen a boat and gotten ready to throw herself into the river, hoping there would be a light on when she reached the far shore.

"Things are really bad right now," Jack said.

"They haven't stopped searching the river."

"No."

"And nobody crosses the bridge," Turing said. "I saw someone try to cross the river in a boat. Someone else tried to swim. The police got them."

"They're guarding the bridge," Jack said. "They think whoever did this is gonna try to leave."

"Do you think that?" Turing asked.

Jack shook her head. "No," she said. "This is personal. I don't think they're done."

Turing nodded. "I didn't think so."

"But it's not like they don't have a point," Jack said. "The cops suck. They don't actually . . . you know. Protect anyone."

"Would killing one change that?"

"I dunno," Jack said. "I mean. There's hundreds of cops. It's like kicking a beehive. They just made them mad."

"What if it did work that way, though?" Turing asked. "Would you be all right with them killing one person if it meant that everything would be better for everyone else?"

Jack tilted her head to one side.

"Yeah," she said. "I think I would be okay with that."

"What if it wasn't a cop?" Turing asked.

"Depends on what they did, I guess." Jack shook her head. "Look, I wanted to talk to you. They're cracking down really hard right now on—on people like you."

"Monsters."

"Sure," Jack said. "So it's dangerous out here right now. I talked to a cop who says they're looking for a big snake. I think they might mean you."

"And you want me to stay away from your friends," Turing said. "So they don't get dragged into this."

If he stayed out here, Belle was going to get him killed. She wouldn't mean to, of course; she'd think of him as an innocent casualty, she'd get real angry about it, she'd point to it as proof that everyone in this damn town just needed to *rise up* already. And by the time they did, Turing would be gone. Jack thought about what Turing had asked. Would she be all right with them killing just one person if everything went great from then out? But it didn't work like that.

Jack took a deep breath.

"No, actually," she said. It was one of those times she realized what she was thinking and feeling as she listened to herself say it. "I think that means you should come in with me."

Turing's body went still.

"Look," Jack said. "Sir likes you. We can find you somewhere to stay. You shouldn't be out here right now. There's a second cop still missing. The people who dumped that first body—they're proba-bly going to have a second one sooner or later. And I don't think you should be out here when that happens."

Turing drew in a deep breath.

"I can't do this," Turing said. "It's a beautiful thought. But the last time I lived on land, I was a prisoner. I can't do that again. What if your friends turn me in to the police?"

"They won't," Jack said.

"Why not?" Turing asked. "Wouldn't that be easier?"

Jack shook her head. "You don't understand," she said. "That's not who we are." In the long silence, she realized that if she wanted to protect him, she was going to have to tell him something. Maybe not all of it, but enough.

"I . . . killed someone once," Jack said. "A cop, actually. I wasn't even working for Sir then, and I went to him for help, because I was a kid and I had no idea what to do. And he took over." She shrugged. "It was bad for a year. Really bad. And you're right. It would have been easier if he'd handed me in. But he didn't. We . . ." Well. She wouldn't say *We're good people.* "We stick together."

Turing nodded. "Okay."

"What do you mean, *okay?*"

"I mean I'll come with you."

He wasn't even going to ask. He was too credulous. Someone should really talk him out of that.

"Don't you even want to know why?" she asked. "I just tell you I killed someone and your whole reaction is *okay, that's fine?*"

"If you wanted to tell me, you'd have told me."

"And that doesn't bother you?"

"I don't think you'd kill someone if you didn't have a reason," he said. "You're a bit of a knight, Jack."

He leaned toward her. It broke the sphere of his curled body, changed his shape. He placed a cool long-fingered hand on hers. Jack flinched. Girls did this sometimes, right before they told Jack that she was good after all, that she couldn't see how beautiful she was, that she was kind and strong and generous. Jack hated it all. Hated how much she wanted to hear it, and how she ate it up, and how in the light of day it always made her feel worse. She got ready to scoff, to turn away. She couldn't hear it now, not after just having come from talking to Belle. That was all the proof Jack needed to know she was rotten.

"You read too many fairy tales, dude," Jack said. "You don't think they're unrealistic?"

"And books about spies and detectives aren't?"

Jack rubbed the back of her neck. "I guess it depends on where you're standing."

"It's nice to imagine that good things will happen to good people," Turing said. "And that who you really are will be revealed in the end."

It was dark in the shed, and warmer now. The rain rattled outside. Jack could feel the nearness of Turing, the strangeness of that lanky body, bent in on itself like an apology, or like an embrace. Jack felt a sudden stab of panic, the way she often did when someone liked her too much. It made her feel like she couldn't breathe.

"Well, let's skip to the end," Jack said. "I'll tell you right now that I'm not a good person."

"You don't have to be good," Turing said. "Good things haven't happened to you."

Jack was startled. "What makes you think that?"

"It's obvious," Turing said. "I can see it on your face."

It was like being hit in the chest, or the moment of relief after a dish breaks. Jack felt exposed, a pain blooming in her lungs that she'd been holding in since she'd met him. She'd been waiting, she realized, for him to know who she was, and he'd known all along.

"This is a first for me," Jack said.

"What's that?"

"I think we might be friends." That was what this was. It was good that she'd said it; *friends* was what you called it when you wanted to just be around someone. It had to happen sometimes, even to someone like her.

"Friends," Turing said, with that sad smile that could mean anything. "I've been alone for a long time. I'm not sure who I'd be with other people."

"Let me show you something," Jack said.

TWENTY

Jack waited while the nameless girl wrapped herself back up in her big coat. Together, they walked through rainy night streets until they came to a diner on a corner. The closed sign was up and the blinds drawn, but the nameless girl could see little slivers of light between the slats. Jack opened the door without hesitation and waved Turing inside.

It was filled to the gills with monsters. The daughter of the river knew no other word to describe them. A woman with a hat pulled down tightly over a lumpy head was tending the grill. A man covered in warts, wearing a bus driver's uniform, sat on a barstool drinking a cup of coffee and reading a paperback book. Packed into the red-vinyl booths were feathers and skins like raw meat and horns and scales and such a proliferation of eyes that it made the daughter of the river dizzy.

The waitress was young and pregnant, and when she saw Jack she lit up as though she knew a good secret.

"Counter or table?" she asked.

"We'll be eating," Jack said. "Can we get a booth?'

"Sure, Jack."

Turing had to force herself to sit down. There were so many people in here, and not one of them like her, but none of them like anyone else, either. She scanned the room, smiling whenever anyone met her eyes. Some grimaced, but some smiled back. When she finally faced front again, Jack was grinning at her.

"What do you think?" Jack asked.

"They're beautiful."

Jack nodded. "The cops don't know about it, not even the paid ones. It's a good place to hole up on a rough night."

Turing felt a tightness in her throat. She wanted to reach across the table and grab Jack's hand from where it rested on the vinyl. But she was getting the impression that to love Jack would mean to not do things like this, not if they would only frighten her or make her sad. So instead, she said, "How did you find out about this place?"

"It was the first place Sir put me to work," Jack said. "It's one of his businesses. That and the bar downtown. But I told him I didn't want to wait tables, I wanted to learn the trade. He thought that was pretty funny."

"Why?"

"'You weigh a hundred pounds soaking wet, Jack,'" she said, in imitation of Sir's gravelly voice. "He didn't see how I was going to be an enforcer. I told him I'd put on weight."

The waitress reappeared. "What can I get for you?"

"Waffles," Jack said. "Coffee, too."

Turing had only read about diners. She grabbed a menu and skimmed it for the first words she liked. "Um . . . salted herring. And water."

"Your eggs?"

"Um." Turing looked at the pictures on the menu; they all looked horrible. "Can you just bring them to me without doing anything to them?"

The waitress laughed. "You got it, hon." She balanced her note-pad on her belly as she wrote. "Be right back," she said, and winked.

Jack leaned forward, steepling her hands in front of her. "So, when do I get to ask about your life?"

Turing thought about it. "What do you want to know?"

Jack raised her eyebrows and waited. The daughter of the river felt her face grow hot.

"I don't have much of a life to talk about," she said. "I read. I watch the joggers along the riverbank in the morning. I catch fish."

"What do you read? Not crime novels. You made fun of me for that."

"No, I read them," Turing said. "I just know how they're all going to end. When you've read enough, you start to see the patterns." She felt like she was rambling, but Jack propped her chin on one fist and waited. "A book is like a spiderweb, all interlacing strands. After a while, you start to understand how they work."

"You ever read anything you didn't know how it worked?"

"Fairy tales," Turing said.

"You said you liked those. Is that why?"

"Those are the stories that bend the most. Where people turn out to be birds. Or they cut off the horse's head and it learns how to talk. They have patterns, too, but . . . sometimes they surprise me."

"You said they always end the same."

"I said that by the end, all is revealed." She stared down at the table, at the little black triangles on the white Formica. "I feel like I've spent years waiting for that to happen for me. For something that tells me it's time to change my life. Do you know what I mean?"

Jack looked thoughtful.

"No, that makes sense," she said. "I mean. I don't feel that way. I feel like it already happened to me, the thing that changed my life."

"And what was that?"

"Well," Jack said. "I told you about . . . the guy. He was messing with my sister. And I didn't want to do it, but at some point, I had to make a decision."

"Oh," Turing said. "Wow."

"Hey, I told you I'm not a good person."

Turing studied Jack, who was picking at the edge of the table. "Did he deserve it?"

"Oh, yeah," Jack said. "No question."

"And you did it to protect your sister."

"Yeah," she said. "I'm still protecting her."

"How?"

"Oh, you know. In general," Jack said. But Turing got the sense that Jack had said more than she'd planned to.

"What's going on, Jack?" Turing asked.

Jack looked away, ran a hand over her short hair. "Trust me. You don't want to be involved."

"What if I do?"

Jack looked at her and sighed.

"Listen," Jack said. "She's mixed up in something dangerous, and if I don't help her, and she gets hurt, I don't know if I'll be able to forgive myself." Jack looked strained, as though each word took effort to dredge up. "But if I do help her, I'm not sure that's great, either. There's no good choice here."

Turing thought of the fairies. Of what they'd offered her: Murder the king, and you can have anything you want. Or you can watch him burn the world down.

"Maybe there's some third way," she said. "Maybe there's something you haven't thought of yet." In fairy tales, there always was. Some trick to put the needle through the egg without piercing its shell. Some way to speak the name of the queen without saying it out loud.

Jack laughed. "I'm thinking about it," she said. "That's why I haven't done anything yet, you know?"

Their food came. Jack laughed when Turing popped a whole egg into her mouth and crunched.

"I'm sorry," Turing said, when she'd swallowed. "Is that not right?"

"You know, you're like what a mermaid would actually be, instead of what people expect."

"When I was a child, I'd pretend to be a mermaid," Turing said. "The scientists thought it was funny."

For a moment she thought she'd gone too far, tipped her hand. But Jack nodded like that made perfect sense.

"When I was a kid, I'd pretend to be my dad," Jack said. "Stepdad, I guess. But you know. I'd put soda in a whiskey glass and swish it around. Roll up a piece of brown paper and make a cigar."

Turing smiled. "Are there pictures?"

Jack looked away. "Not really."

"I don't really have pictures, either," Turing said quickly. "I mean, the scientists took lots of pictures. But they didn't let me keep any of them."

"That must have been in the early days," Jack said. "People at the club told me how they used to kidnap people and study them, and now they just want to see if they can make 'em normal."

"I think some of the scientists knew that was coming," Turing said. "Because they started forgetting to lock my . . . enclosure." She didn't like the word. "Even with that, it took me a few days before I was brave enough to just leave."

"And you've been on your own since?"

"Mostly, yes."

"You had kind of a hard time, huh?"

"I don't know," Turing said. "I feel like in some ways I was very lucky. Compared to other people I've heard about, or things I've read. Even if I wasn't always happy, I've almost always been safe."

Jack raised her coffee mug in agreement. Turing picked up her plastic cup, and they clinked them together, then sat and sipped quietly for a while. As the night turned into morning, Turing imagined what it would be like to sit here with Jack the way she wanted to: with their feet touching under the table, or their hands intertwined across the Formica. But she felt as though they were touching without touching.

Too soon, the waitress returned with the bill. Too soon, Jack fished cash from her pocket and folded it up in the receipt. And like that, the night was over.

On the way out of the diner, Turing spotted someone watching them from a street corner. That old man she'd seen before on the riverbank. He huddled under a streetlamp in his huge black raincoat.

"Hey, girls," he called when he saw them. "You want to know a history lesson?"

Jack took Turing by the arm and yelled "Fuck off!" hustling her away down the street. Turing let herself be moved, liking the feeling of Jack guiding her, protecting her. Still, a part of her felt anxious, like she'd just missed something important.

"So," Jack said. "Let's take you back to Sir's place. You can probably crash there for tonight, until we can find you somewhere to stay."

"Wait," Turing said. The force of her own refusal astonished her. "I have to go get my books."

"I dunno," Jack said. "You could have new books. How will you even get them across?"

"I'll figure it out." The idea of being without them pained her. With her gone, they'd be waterlogged and rotten in a season. And she needed to say goodbye to the island if she was leaving it for good.

"Okay, okay," Jack said. "If that's what you want. I'll wait for you, though, and we'll come straight back here."

"Okay," Turing said.

They picked up Jack's motorcycle, and Jack took her back to the river's edge.

"I'll be right back," Turing said.

In the river, her body did not feel strange to her. In the river, she was fast and graceful. Schools of fish split in half to let her pass. She tumbled and rolled with the current, letting the pressure of the water soothe her, rub the ache out of the small of her back from stooping.

She could keep this up, she thought. Work with Jack, sleep in that mildewy bar. She might make friends, working for Sir. She could be the kind of man they expected her to be, and when she went to bed, she could use the little bits she learned about the world to embroider her dreams of sneakers, diners, dates. It wasn't much of a life, but it would do. And maybe it would keep her from killing the king, which seemed both more urgent and more wrong after the day she'd had. The gift from the fairies was all the more appealing now, but the nagging doubts grew as she met person after person and tried to imagine what it would be like to have to kill them. Every one of them had a world in them. Would she kill that old man on the street corner? The waitress at the diner? Jack?

After all, she thought as she swam, who was the king? Just some boy, probably, as lost and confused as anyone else. She could almost picture him, some thin gawky youth with jug ears, pulling a sword from a stone. And anyway, she thought, weren't kings made by monsters? Maybe the best thing she could do for the both of them was to stay away from him.

She kept that thought up as she used her long arms to ease herself over the edge of the old castle wall. Until she saw, on the ground on the far side, the dead man.

He looked worse off than the one she'd pulled from the river. That first man had looked frightened. This man didn't look like a man. He looked like a pile.

She slid down the wall and took a slow step toward the man. His body jittered and released a tide of flies into the air. His blood had pooled on the flagstones beneath him. The daughter of the river felt sick, thinking of how easily blood could desert a body like that. He had not much face left.

She took a few steps back, then ran for a far corner of the

courtyard, where she pressed her hands and face to the cool stones, still in shadow in the early morning. She sobbed so hard that her stomach hurt. Someone had come into her home and killed a man. Who was he? Who had done this? And why here?

She wondered what Jack would say about this. And then she thought about what it would look like. She'd told Jack the truth about the first body, and somehow, miracle beyond miracles, Jack had believed her. Who would believe her now, with a body in her home? She thought about Sir looking at her, admiring her strength. She thought about the ghost under the river, mocking her by copying her body like a trick mirror. Nobody would doubt it was her, not for a second.

She forced herself to push away from the wall, to walk back to the body, scattering flies away as she got closer. He looked like someone had bashed his head in. He had on the same kind of blue uniform as the man she'd found in the river before. This must be the second one, the one who had been missing, who Jack had mentioned. A second policeman. And they wanted it to look like it was her. That hadn't been clear before. But why else would they leave him here in the ruined castle?

And her jaw hardened as she realized that it wasn't just that she would look like a monster if she told. Someone, somewhere, *wanted* to make it seem like it was her. She thought about detective stories. *I was framed*, they always said. She could feel the edges of the frame around her when she moved, bouncing off of things.

She wished she could speak to the fairies. But they were small and quick, and only came out at night, and unless they sought her out, she was unlikely to find them. She wanted to ask them about this. But then she realized she already knew what they would say.

It is the king, son of the river. He's doing this to you now so that he can kill you later. To claim his power. To claim his throne. If he is to have the city, first he must have you.

She couldn't go back to Jack. Not like this. She had to hide.

She tried not to run, but to crawl down the far side of the castle courtyard and into the water. She eased herself down, down, looking for some deep crevice to ooze into where she could hide until this was all over. Beneath her, some place in the river opened up, and there was darkness deeper than she'd seen before. Had the rains last night washed out the bottom here? No, it could not have been made so deep so quickly. She didn't know where this place was. But it was deep. So she dove.

And then suddenly, she was in the ghostly place she'd been in before. The forest of broken ships. It had opened for her, as it had opened the night she'd pulled Jack from the water.

And she felt it again. The presence of that strange creature, something between a spirit and a worm. Felt it ripple past her, brushing her skin with its ghostly body, wrapping around her like a ribbon. She wanted to shriek. She had the sense that it was drinking from her, like a leech as big as an island, the water around it saturated with a dark blue fluid that burned cold against her skin. Shuddering, she tore herself loose from it and kicked for the surface as hard as she could.

When she broke the surface of the river, she felt the choppy current and knew that a boat was heading for the island. She hid instead among the submerged logs, where nobody would be able to find her, listening overhead to the rumble of boat engines and those shouts loud enough to get beneath the surface. They were searching the island. Soon, they'd find the body. It could be worse, though. They could have found her.

She'd been wrong, she realized, when she'd told Jack she'd always been safe. What she'd been was alive. It had always been like this, hadn't it? Always running, hiding, worrying? She couldn't keep living like this. She was tired, so tired.

So that was where the daughter of the river eventually drifted to sleep that day: suspended just under the surface of the water, her long arms wrapped around her like a cocoon, her tired mind full of circular thoughts. Stop the king, save herself, free the city, get the boon, if she could, that might make her unrecognizable, and therefore, for the first time in her life, safe.

TWENTY-ONE

Walking to his adviser's office along the glass sky-bridge, David was lost in his thoughts when he realized that two undergrad girls had stopped several feet ahead, staring at him. Usually this would be his cue to hunch over or walk away. Instead, he found himself slowing his pace and raising his eyebrows. They clung to each other a little for balance; the glass corridor had a tendency to sway when David walked along it.

"'Scuse me," said one of them shyly. The other one blushed hard and looked away. "We were wondering, uh, how tall you are?"

David thought about Agnolo losing his shit over "six ten," so he shrugged and said "Five eight, five nine?"

They giggled and got out of his way. He wondered what exactly had changed from the week before. Was he smiling at people without realizing it? He didn't look any different, really; he hadn't gone on some fitness kick, hadn't cut his hair, hadn't changed anything. Except that wasn't quite true. Ever since the night he'd fought that girl Jack, David had felt different. For a few days, he wondered if he'd had another growth spurt and nearly panicked, because everyone around him suddenly seemed a little shorter, and then he realized he had just stopped slouching.

Drawn up to his full height, he attracted more attention than ever. But it had a different quality to it than before. Less sidling away, less clutching at bags or railings. Fewer of those tight smiles he hated. And women—it was so weird to have women looking at him the way they did. Like they wanted him to overhead press them. Which was weird in its own way, but it beat suspicion and horror any day, he'd say that much. Some dudes still seemed scared of him, but he got a lot more little nods of acknowledgment than he used to. Like he'd been inducted into a club he hadn't known existed.

Seth, on the other hand, hadn't been around much. David was trying not to read too much into it. Seth had always sort of faded in and out based on his busy partying schedule. It probably didn't have anything to do with the fireball. Or the—whatever that had been in the elevator.

Coming down the hall toward Haughan's office, he noticed a girl sitting outside, her books in her arms, her head down. As he got closer he realized she was crying.

"Oh, hey," he said. "It's none of my business, but . . . are you okay?"

She glanced up at him. It was worse than he'd thought; the tears were running so fast that they'd looped around and were beading off the bottom of her chin. It was the girl who'd asked him in lecture about why the course was so hard—Nina? Nita.

"I'm fine," she said.

"That's not true."

She jerked her head toward the door.

"I . . . asked him if I could drop . . . ," she said. "Exobiology. To focus on physics."

"And he said no?"

She nodded.

"Why?"

"H . . . he said I should quit."

David closed his eyes and sighed.

"Did he say why?"

She nodded.

"Did he say anything explicit? Anything you can take to the Dean of Students? Sometimes he slips up."

She shook her head. He sighed.

"Would you like me to deal with it?"

She nodded.

"All right, let me see what I can do." He girded himself. He was good at this, he was realizing. If people wanted intimidation, he could deliver that. He ran a hand over his hair and stepped into his adviser's office.

The man looked up from his desk and smiled. "David!"

"There's a girl crying outside your office," David said.

Dr. Haughan shrugged.

"Too emotional," he said. "She won't be able to cut it in the long run."

"Oh yeah? I'm feeling a little emotional myself right now."

Dr. Haughan looked David up and down appraisingly. The upward look took a while.

"I don't want to have to talk to the Chair," David said.

"You've got nothing."

"Oh, I didn't mean about the girl," David said. "I meant about bringing her on as my adviser instead. I know how much you love teaching your own classes."

That got him. Haughan gave David a long glower.

"Lang won't give you half the freedom you're getting with me,"

Haughan said. "She'll have you typing up her notes a hundred feet away from any real work. What's your problem? You sleeping with that girl?"

David surprised himself by slamming his hand down on Haughan's desk. He felt a glimmer of satisfaction at watching the man jump. Some small interior part of him made a note of that satisfaction, but the rest of him was at the surface, hard and looming over Haughan's desk, chin jutting at an accusing angle.

"I know you're a piece of shit," David said, "but the one thing I swore when I agreed to work with you was that you wouldn't rub off on me. Unlike you, I've never slept with an undergrad." Which was technically true, since he'd never slept with anyone. "Now. You're going to go out into the hall and tell her you've changed your mind."

Haughan tried to hold his gaze, but his eyes shifted downward, and he seemed suddenly very interested in the state of his cuticles.

"You know," Haughan said, "I haven't filed that grant yet. We might not be able to have a research assistant without that money. But I'm sure you'd find some other way into a lab, hm?"

David's blood ran cold. He thought about that little creature on the operating table upstairs. "And I'm sure you'll find some other way to pay off your condo," David said. "Here, allow me."

It was bold of him, he knew, to reach across the desk to where his blue file folder still sat in Haughan's paper tray. Haughan's hand shot out and caught his wrist—or tried to; his hand was too small to wrap all the way around.

Haughan flinched as though David had hit him. "If you ever put your hands on my desk again, I'm calling security."

"Have a nice day," David said.

As he stepped out of Haughan's office, he realized his hands were shaking. Nita looked up at him, but he couldn't meet her eyes.

"He'll be right out," he said.

"I heard everything," she said. She was frowning at him as though she were trying to figure something out. "Thank you."

"When he's done apologizing, go to your adviser, re-enroll, and just . . . stay out of Haughan's way. Don't take any of his classes till your senior year. By then, he will have either forgotten about you, or he'll be patting himself on the back for having taught you perseverance or whatever."

"I don't understand," she said. "After that first class I thought . . ."

She'd thought he was an asshole like Haughan. When actually, he'd just been a coward. Why had he thought picking on Nita would make him any safer?

"I was wrong," he said. "That's on me."

Her eyes widened until he thought they'd fall out.

"See you in class," he said.

He could feel her staring after him as he stalked off down the hall toward his office. When he was out of sight, he realized how tense he'd gotten and shook himself out. Holy shit. He felt good, like he'd fought something big. He felt like an idiot, too. As his anger started to burn off, he wondered if maybe he'd been a little too hasty. It dawned on him slowly that Haughan had threatened to call security. He tried to let it go. Haughan needed him. His own research was falling apart, and David's was keeping their lab afloat.

He looked at the grant application in his hands. Better go over it again before he filed it, just to be sure the guy hadn't struck him from it. Actually, maybe he should just try to get an appointment with Lang for later in the day, just to be safe. Talk about how he really admired her last paper. He should go to her office now, he thought, as his feet carried him in the opposite direction toward the residential floors. He found himself outside Seth's door. It was shut for once. He knocked.

"Who is it?" Seth called out blearily.

"It's me," David said. "Do you have a minute?"

There was rustling from within the room, and Seth came to the door, opening it just a crack. He was wearing boxers. His hair, of course, was perfect. His eyes were full of concern.

"What's up?" he asked.

There was a girl in there, David was sure. That's why he wouldn't open the door. He could hear someone turning over in the bed. David sighed.

"Look, you're busy," David said.

"Nah, man. You okay?"

Ugh, any minute now the girl in Seth's bed would pad into sight, wrapped in a sheet, and he'd be standing there looking like a big weirdo.

"I . . . was thinking about transferring to Lang," David said. "Do you know what her schedule's like today?"

"Oh," Seth said. "Sure, she's got office hours at three. What's going on? I can put some clothes on and—"

"No, I'll tell you later. Sorry to bother you."

He speed walked away before Seth could say anything else. He heard the door click shut behind him. Dammit. The file folder in his hands was getting clammy with sweat. Now he really felt like an idiot. He'd come here all prepared to tell Seth this story about what a big hero he'd been for standing up for the student he'd discouraged in the first place. He'd wanted Seth to look at him again like he had the other night. He'd wanted him to call him a god again.

Distracted, David got into an elevator without realizing it was full of med students in scrubs. They barely scooted over for him, wrapped up in conversation.

"I mean, it's like Christmas, right? New cryptid just dropped."

"Dude, we should go get it before the cops find it."

"Are you kidding? It ate that second cop's face. You really think you can fight it?"

"This guy could. Hey, man, you want to help us bag a specimen?"

David looked down at the little white guy who'd just addressed him. *Jackal*, he thought. *Through and through.*

"Sorry, man," he said. "But I'm kind of hoping it eats your face."

The guy looked like he was trying to decide whether he was being threatened. And then the guy's friends started laughing. One of them clapped David on the back. "I'd pay to see that," he said. Consensus was reached quickly that everyone in the elevator would like to see the little twerp get eaten by a sea monster, and that David was a funny, funny guy.

The elevator dinged. David slipped off, not a hundred percent sure it was the right floor. Behind him, the guys still roasted away. He was reminded of the feeling he'd had at the nightclub, of not being entirely sure why he was suddenly the guy everyone wanted to impress. He didn't like it; it felt precarious, liable to change at any second. He was sure that the little guy in the elevator had been the big man until David had cut him down.

TWENTY-TWO

Later on, if people had asked an old and grizzled Jack Marley when she thought things had gotten really bad, when violence was certain, she would have said that it wasn't when the cops found Matthew on the Isle of Bells, but a few days after that. That was the day Jack found herself down at the precinct in her only suit, trying to get Rex out of jail.

She hadn't seen Turing since the night she'd taken him to the diner. Then he'd gone to the island to *get his stuff*, and like an asshole she'd waited on the shore for him for an hour before she realized he wasn't coming back. And then that morning Walsh, their second-string paid cop, told her the cops had found the body after someone had tipped them off that the corpse was in the ruined palace. What a mess. Why the fuck had he run from her? She'd told him she knew he didn't kill McNair. Of course, she should have known better than to expect anyone would trust her.

Jack still instinctively relaxed when she stepped into the precinct. The place smelled like her dad, even if now she knew that the smell was just stale air and lingering cigarette smoke. She'd put her feet up on some of those desks as a kid: leaned back in an old swivel chair, read an arrest report, imagined her future. That was probably part of why she was so effective here—that familiarity didn't go away. Most of Sir's people got panicky in the precinct, and it made them freeze up or get aggressive. Sir had told her on day one that the key to this business was finding a way to stay calm. Of course, right now he was hardly taking his own advice. He'd been near frothing rage on the phone.

The big main hall, crammed full of desks, always had a low hum to it. When she stepped inside and took off her sunglasses, that hum dropped an octave. They shouldn't have been surprised that Sir would send her. She went up to the front desk and planted both hands on the wood. The uniform behind the desk sat up straighter. She could feel his shoulders tensing.

"I'm here to pick up Reginald Sahwet," she said.

"You mean, post bail?" the guy asked.

"Is he being held on bond?"

"Uh." The guy looked down at a big ledger in front of him. Jack didn't even try to read it; she was sure there was nothing in it. And sure enough, he looked up abruptly.

"Are you sure he's here, ma'am?" he said.

The room had gone almost completely silent. They were all watching her.

"I think you should go get your boss," Jack said. "You should tell him who's here, and who I'm here to get."

"Ma'am," the guy said. Whose kid was he? He looked like a Blithe, but he might be a Curtis. Especially with that red nose. She studied him dispassionately while he struggled to figure out what to say next.

"Officer," she said. "I understand that it's your job to keep out the riffraff. But this is above your paygrade."

Jack could feel the currents in the room around her. There were the guys who had known her since she was a kid, who were laughing into their sleeves about Jack Marley making some young uni nearly piss himself. And then there were the younger guys, probably this guy's friends, who were sizing her up, thinking about how she was the lackey of their enemy, and certainly an arrogant bitch, and certainly breathing their air a little too calmly for their comfort. It was the little noises that told her: The creak and pop of swivel chairs changing position. The scuff of polished shoes on the worn tile floor. The current of breathing that changed from soft to harsh.

The guy swallowed and stood up at. He was taller than her, but not by much. She imagined grabbing him by his epaulets and slamming his face into the desk. It wouldn't be hard.

"Ma'am," he said. Third time. "I don't see any record of some guy named Reginald being in here. I'm gonna have to ask you to leave."

"Definitely a Curtis," Jack said.

"Excuse me?"

"You're a Curtis, right? Like, William Curtis?"

He flushed red from the nose out. Okay, she was right.

"I don't know if you know this," Jack said. "But if your dad's William Curtis, he's pretty well known to our organization. He owes Sir—excuse me for putting it this way—a fuckton of money. And he has for a long time. But he's a nice guy, respectful, good tipper down at the club. We all like William Curtis a lot."

"Are you threatening me?" he asked.

"I'm just making conversation," she said. "This town's always smaller than you think. We should all act like neighbors. My employer tries to be a good neighbor to y'all. And now he just wants to know if you're holding his son, and if so, for how long, and for what reason. You know, fathers like to look out for their sons. I know if your father were here, he'd probably say the same thing—"

The man lunged across the desk at her. It was a stupid move; all she had to do was step back, and he lost his balance, sticking half-sprawled across the tall front desk. He knocked a clipboard and pen off the ledge and onto the floor with a clatter. More dramatic than what she'd had in mind, but that was fine.

The uni devolved into swearing at her, calling her all kinds of names. It was loud enough to draw out some detectives from their offices upstairs, and she waved at them and pointed to her watch. One of them gave her the finger, but one of them started for the chief's office. It was good Sir had sent her. She'd do this right.

Eventually, a detective she knew came downstairs, an old guy, Van-something. She vaguely remembered him. He clearly remembered her.

"Miss Marley," he said. "Upstairs?"

"I'd rather not be alone, if that's all right," she said. "I'm just here to get my friend."

"Listen, maybe we can talk privately."

"I don't think that's a good idea," she said. "Because when I came in here to pick up my friend, who several people saw arrested, Officer Curtis here told me there's no record of his arrest. Until I know where my friend is, I don't really feel comfortable being alone in a room with any policeman."

His eyes flashed. He was the guy they'd sent to try to get her to leave quietly. Well, that wasn't happening.

"Look," he said. "The chief isn't gonna come talk to you out here."

"I don't need him to," Jack said. "I just want to know a simple yes or no. Is Reginald Sahwet here? Can you tell me?"

His face closed like a gate. "I don't have that information."

"Well, can you please check?"

"Miss Marley, why don't you leave, and we can give you a call?"

"I'm happy to wait. I just need to know if my friend, Reginald Sahwet, is being held, so that I can bail him out. It seems weird to me that you can't tell me that. If you tell me he's not here, I could leave."

She let the offer hang in the air for a moment, waiting to see if he spoke. He didn't. Okay, it was her turn.

"Of course, if you told me he wasn't here, and I left," she said, "and I found out later that he was here, and you lied to me, well— that would be pretty fucked. That would be less like arresting someone and more like kidnapping."

The problem with her sister, Jack thought, was that she said all this stuff without having any way to back it up. Jack had heard stories about Belle coming down here by herself, without even telling the witches, to bail some girl out of jail, and ending up getting booked herself after she'd made a scene. And she seemed proud of that, like getting thrown in a holding cell automatically made her a martyr. What Belle didn't understand was that if you were going to walk up to a bunch of shaved-head assholes with guns and say *that's illegal*, it was a lot easier if the implicit message was *and if we're gonna get illegal, I'm gonna win*.

Van-something sighed.

270 • ROSE SZABO

"I will check for you, Miss Marley," he said. "Are you sure you wouldn't want to wait somewhere more comfortable?"

"Thank you," Jack said, waited for him to relax, and then added, "but I'm comfortable right here."

A girl at the far end of the room, being fingerprinted by some beat cop, raised her eyes to look at Jack. She had a single horn growing from one side of her forehead, mostly covered by her long, dark hair. Her eyes were pleading. Jack met them but shook her head. She was here for one person. She couldn't get everyone out. They were pushing it, even here. If this had been someone lower on the org chart, Sir would've probably expected them to stew for another day or two while he took a subtler approach.

Eventually, the detective came back downstairs. He motioned her to one side of the room. She let him. It was mostly over now, just down to details.

"We found his paperwork," he said. "Booked last night when walking home with tools that could be used in a burglary or robbery."

"Such as?" Jack asked.

The guy pinched his nose. "Look, Miss Marley, I'm tired. You're tired."

"Not really."

"Okay. Fine. You want to know the truth? The unis did a sweep. Picked up everyone on the street who fit a description."

"What description? Can you be more specific?"

"Oh, fuck me, Jack. You know what this is about."

"Yeah," Jack said. "You found a body on an island and now you're rounding up—what? Hairy people? Find a lot of hair at that scene? That girl out there being booked, she happen to fit the description?"

He looked like he was about to cry, or punch her. Probably double overtime on this. It was so stupid, the way they were working so hard and doing so little. So stupid that they were thinking about monsters and not about little Belle Marley, who they'd all known when she was a kid, who they'd all seen down here a dozen times. Since she was little, the cops had joked about how much Belle Marley hated them, how the sight of their uniforms made her spitting mad. It would never occur to them that she'd killed two cops, no matter how much she'd screamed at them in the past. She was—well, not innocent, they knew that. But weak. They didn't ever seem to learn that weak could boil over.

"Well, Sir would like him back, please," Jack said. "If you're not gonna charge him with anything."

"Will he cooperate with our investigation in the future?"

"Sir has always been a strong supporter of the RCPD," Jack said. "I'm sure we want this resolved as much as you do."

"Well," Van-something said. "The chief said, tell you what: He's heard you've been making inquiries. He wants to make a gentleman's agreement. You say what you've got, we can let Mr. Sahwet go."

And Jack briefly wondered if she was wrong. Sure, she knew Belle had killed the first cop. Sure, she'd lied to her. But this had Jack on edge. She had a hard time imagining her sister doing what they said had been done to that body. And he'd asked her that weird question about what if you could kill one person and save everyone else. But she realized none of that was why she was questioning him now.

Turing had run from her. *Why* had he run from her? Hadn't he known she'd help?

Van-something had seen her hesitate. He nodded. "So you've got a candidate."

"Yeah," she said. "I do. There's this kid I saw at Sir's nightclub the other night. Huge guy. Six foot ten, he said. I saw him do something weird with his hands, and then something caught on fire."

The words slid out so easily that Jack wondered what had given her the idea. She'd barely thought of the kid since she'd kicked him in the head. But now that her mind had caught up to her mouth, she realized he was perfect.

"You're joking," Van-something said. "That shit doesn't happen anymore."

"Wish I was joking," Jack said. "I talked to a few witnesses who said McNair's body didn't have a mark on it. I'm not a magic expert, but that sounds like magic to me."

He was nodding, his brow furrowed. Oh, thank god he was buying this. Jack felt sick thinking that Turing's name had been on the tip of her tongue. Not that she'd said it. Not that she would have. But it had been right there, ready for her to say.

No, that weird, huge kid was better. Some university student, Agnolo had told her later. Came in with the skinny college boy who always made a fool of himself with the dancers. College boys had money, and the university took their side in fights with townies. He'd be fine in the end.

Jack told the detective everything she could remember about the man who'd thrown fire.

"He even said his name," she said. "David Blank. Sounded fake to me, but maybe you'll get lucky."

"Sure." Van-something snapped his notebook shut. "I'll have Mr. Sahwet cleaned up and sent down."

"Just send him down. We'll clean him up ourselves."

"You take care of your own," he said. "You'd have made a good cop, Miss Marley."

"Yeah," Jack said. "I worry about that, too."

He frowned but retreated. She went back to the middle of the bullpen and leaned against the front desk until some unis brought Rex down. Even in the bad light, he looked like shit.

"Hey," she said. "Let's get you home."

She'd borrowed a car from Sir; it was parked a block away. Rex could walk, but he was favoring one leg. When they got to the car, Jack opened the door for him, and he all but fell into the passenger's seat. She shut the door, careful that no part of him was still in the way. Only when she started the car did she look over at him and ask what happened.

"Rough ride," he said. His voice was hoarse. "They were just shoving people in the wagon. By the time I got in, there wasn't even a seat, so I tried to just stay standing up, but we took a bad corner and I fell down. I think I swallowed a tooth."

"Open your mouth," she said. He stared at her, but eventually, he did. She looked. "I can see which one you mean. It's broken, and really swollen, but you've still got some of it. Someone can put a crown on that."

He relaxed his mouth. "Thanks."

"Don't touch anything. We'll take photos first in case Sir wants to push the issue. We've already got a medic downstairs. An anesthesiology intern from the hospital, so you know he's got the good stuff."

He was silent again as Jack drove. She went slowly, cautiously. It still felt like they were passing a cop car every few blocks.

"You remember it being this bad after my dad died?" Jack asked.

Rex snorted. "Yeah, almost."

"You remember how we got through it then?"

"*We* got through it. *You* laid low."

They stopped at a red light, and Jack glanced sideways at Rex. "Well. Sorry about that. This sucks."

He closed his eyes and leaned back in his seat. "Yeah," he said. "It does."

Agnolito was waiting for them back at the club, along with their sister Juno. They eased Rex out of the car and in through the back entrance. Jack tossed the car key to the back door guy and went inside to find a drink.

Jesse was working, and Jack waved. The little shit gave her a head toss and a dramatic, over-the-shoulder wink. Well, at least someone was having fun tonight. Jack went to the bar and eased herself into a seat. Agnolo silently mixed her an old-fashioned.

"Hannah's off tonight," Agnolo said when he handed her the glass. "You could stick around."

"Agnolo," Jack said. "If we could stop this by just giving them the asshole, would we do it?"

"Yeah, probably," Agnolo said.

"But they suck."

"Yeah, but they've got guns and money."

"But nobody likes them. The witches sure as hell don't like them."

"Yeah," he said. "But the witches don't really like us, either."

Jack thought about that. "No, not really."

"What happened to that friend of yours?" Agnolo asked.

Jack shook her head. "Everyone's looking for the big snake," she said. "Guess that's him. You seen him?"

"Not since the first night," Agnolo said. "Guys saying maybe he did it."

"Not a chance," Jack said. "He's not a killer. I'm not even sure he'd kill someone to save his own life."

"Why you so interested?" Agnolo said.

Jack had been halfway off her barstool when the question caught her by surprise. She turned back to Agnolo.

"How do you mean?" she said.

"You don't usually give a shit what happens to men," he said.

"That's not true. I like y'all just fine, you know, as colleagues."

He snorted. "Yeah. Colleagues. This guy, you've known him a few weeks and you're wondering where he is and what he's up to. He some long-lost brother or something?"

"I dunno. We talked. He reads books. We're friends." She waved in the vague direction of Jesse, who was telling a long and involved joke to a group of enraptured men in dirty overalls. "Sometimes I just like people. It's not unheard of."

"Sure," Agnolo said. "I just thought it was interesting. So he's a reader?"

"Fucking prolific," she said. "Shit I haven't heard of."

"Huh, a friend of the mind. Who'd have guessed?" Agnolo shrugged. "Well, if you want to save his ass, get him to come explain himself before Sir writes him off. It'd be better if we know where he is when the next body hits."

"Why do you think there's gonna be another one?" Jack asked.

Agnolo looked askance. "Someone's on a cop-killing bender. Why wouldn't there be another one?"

"Maybe it's not a bender," Jack said. "Maybe it's part of a plan. Maybe the plan is just two guys."

Agnolo shook his head. "The only way there's not a third body is if someone catches this guy."

That wasn't true, Jack told herself. Belle wasn't just killing at random—she had a plan, even if it was a bad one. Jack wished she knew what it was. She'd stopped Belle from getting in over her head before; she could do it again, if only she knew what was happening.

"Hey, Agnolo," she said. "We still have a spare floodlight in the back?"

He shrugged. "Your guess is as good as mine."

She found the portable floodlight and strapped it to her bike. She also brought the big coat from the first night she'd taken Turing to see Sir. She rode down to the riverbank, far from the boathouse, and pointed the light at the island. She didn't know Morse code, but she figured turning on the light and flashing it a bunch would get the job done. She did it until she saw a police boat on the water turn and flash its own lights. She'd figured that would happen, but it was still a tense moment, dousing the floodlight, strapping it to her bike, and taking off. She wound through a number of side streets to get to the boathouse downstream. From there, she could see the police boat scanning the river upstream, trying to figure out who'd signaled them, and why. She waited in the shadow of the boathouse. Eventually, she heard a splash.

"You stood me up," Jack said.

Turing's sleek head appeared above the water. She realized he had hair now; it suited him. "They're looking for me," he said.

"No, they're looking for anyone they can make it stick to."

"Because they can't find me. And they're not going to." He looked away. "They destroyed my house, Jack."

Jack felt a bolt of white-hot anger. "My god," she said. "Okay, well, fuck that. Come with me, right now."

"Where are we going?"

"We're going to Sir's. We're gonna talk to him, find you a new place to stay. Somewhere to hide out until this is all over."

Turing shook his head. "No. I can't get him in trouble. Or you. If they find out you're hiding me . . ."

"They're looking into someone else," Jack said. "Don't worry about me. And don't worry about Sir, either."

"He'll get in trouble too."

"So what?" Jack said. "He's got a business, three terrifying kids, plenty of money. He can afford to help you. And he should, because you signed a contract. And if he won't do it for you, he'll do it for me. So get out right now, and I'll take you straight there."

Turing eased himself out of the water. He looked frail in a way she hadn't expected, like he hadn't been sleeping.

"You don't have to do this," he said.

"Yeah, I do," Jack said. "They did this for me, and I can do it for you. And unlike me, you haven't done anything wrong."

Turing laughed and lowered his eyes. "What if I did do something wrong? Would you help me, then?"

"We can talk hypotheticals when we're inside." She unfurled the coat she'd given him the first night. "Put this on."

Turing hesitated. Jack could feel him straining, like any second he was going to make a break for the river.

"You don't need to hide anymore," she said. "We've got you."

"I hope that's true," he said. "I want it to be true."

"Well," Jack said. "Get on and come find out."

She stuck to alleys with the headlight off all the way back to Sir's place, stopping and turning off the bike whenever she spotted a cop car, hiding in shadows. She went in the back door and rushed Turing straight to Sir's office. Sir glanced up from his desk, his reading glasses sliding down his nose.

"I told you not to bring him here," he said. He turned to Turing. "You kill those two cops?"

"No," Turing said.

Sir studied him for a long moment. Then he glanced back down at his paperwork.

"So find him somewhere to hide out," he said. "If anyone has anything to say about it, send them to me. I won't have us fighting this close to Carnival Night. And Turing, don't you ever run like that again. It looks bad."

"Thank you, Sir," Jack said, and hustled Turing out of his office. She took him into the storage room across the hall, with its shelves of black shirts and black shoes, boxes of paper napkins and disinfecting wipes and bleach bottles.

"See?" Jack said. "I told you it'd be fine." She grinned breathlessly at Turing, and realized that he was crying silently. His shoulders shook a little.

"What's wrong?" she said. "You okay?"

"I know that went well," Turing said. He fell silent for a long time. Just as Jack was about to say something, he said, "I know I should be grateful he believed me. I just hate that he had to ask. I wish there was someone who wouldn't have to."

Jack almost said, *Hey now, I never asked.* But then she thought about earlier that night, when Turing's name had come to her mind without being bidden.

"Well," she said. "They're looking at someone else now, so hopefully they'll ease up on us for a few days. We'll probably just keep you on leave until after Carnival. Things will probably settle down then." Because after that, Belle's stupid plan would fail, just like every other stupid plan she'd ever had. And hopefully she'd take the money Jack had given her and leave town. And then, if Jack was lucky, things could get back to normal.

Turing nodded and wiped his eyes on his wrist.

"Thank you," he said. "For believing me."

"Hey," Jack said. "You're right. You shouldn't have had to say it."

"You said they're looking into someone else," Turing said.

"Yeah, this weird guy from the university," Jack said. "I'd been looking into him after I saw him use magic here once."

"Magic?" Turing asked. "Are you sure?"

"Yeah, it was wild. Anyway, they're onto him now, so hopefully things'll quiet down. Let the university and the cops fight it out and leave us alone."

"Do you think he's a witch?"

"I dunno," she said. This room was too small; they weren't touching, but Jack felt like she was crowding him. So she clapped him on both arms and looked up at him briskly. "Let's figure out where you're staying the night."

"Not with you?"

"You should be so lucky," she said. "We've got a few apartments. We'll get a key from Agnolo." She pivoted past him to the door. "Maybe after Carnival, you can stay over. We'll build a blanket fort or something."

"You know, Jack," Turing said. "I think you would actually like that."

She turned back to him, one eyebrow up.

"We'll talk about it when you're not a wanted man," she said. "Come on. Let's get you home."

She was laughing to herself as she brought him back to the bar, to Agnolo, who gave her a wry smile when she told him to grab the key to 44 D Leigh—the basement apartment under the bar. She felt a little bit like she'd lost a fight, that breathless feeling of having the wind knocked out of you, but more than that, of being actually surprised.

A friend of the mind, Agnolo had said. Well, she certainly hadn't been looking for one. But maybe it was good to have one. He couldn't have come at a worse time. But she was glad, as she left, that in the moment when she could've screwed him over, she hadn't. That had to be good for something.

TWENTY-THREE

The daughter of the river was having some trouble getting used to the basement apartment under the nightclub. After Jack left her there, she wandered from room to room, trying to feel out the limitations of the place. There was no breeze, unless you turned on the loud air-conditioning unit. All the overhead lights were too close and too bright, and when the lights were off, the darkness was darker than anything on the island, which was always lit by the moon, the stars, the lights from the city. The main room with its double bed and dining table was twice as big as her house had been, to say nothing of the kitchen or the bathroom.

She settled down into the bed, which was soft and sagged in the middle, and willed herself to try to sleep. She'd been awake for too long, hiding from the police in the river. She was tired, so very tired. But she was restless. She slipped on her long coat that Jack had found for her and eased her way out the basement door, leaving it unlocked behind her because she wasn't entirely sure she trusted her ability to use the key Jack had given her. The street was dark and quiet in this pre-dawn hour. The club patrons had all gone home.

This part of the town was familiar to her, at least a little; in the old days, it had been a nest of mostly abandoned warehouses. Scientists ran labs out of them. The buildings were different now, but the layout was the same. She crept along alleys, clinging to shadows, until she could see the towers up close.

They glowed like mushrooms. One of them had a large display where the lights changed color in a continuous wave, painting the street below with undulating bands of red and blue and purple. Almost nobody came and went at this hour; there were two cops posted at the end of one block, counting college students coming in and out and stopping anyone else who tried to enter that way.

This was where the king lived. Somewhere in there he'd written the spells that had sucked life out of the river, that had angered the fairies, that had killed two men. Did he know he was the king, as she knew she was the monster? Or was he unaware that destiny was driving him toward her? Had he planted the body on her island, or were those girls helping him?

She wanted to see him. Foolishly, perhaps—there must be hundreds, if not thousands, of people living in the towers. Or maybe she just wanted to see how he lived. She wished she could walk in, roam the halls, feel out the facets of his life.

A large shadow lumbered past her hiding place, and she flinched back, thinking at first that it was the old man who had frightened her twice before. But no, it was a boy about her own age, light brown–skinned, holding a cup of something that fogged his glasses. He leaned against the brick wall to drink it, looking up at the night sky. He had a university ID clipped to the hem of his faded sweater.

She held still for a long time, clinging to the wall and trying not to breathe too loudly, watching him. He seemed tired, she thought. She wondered if he knew any of the scientists who had kidnapped her all those years ago. She wondered if he knew the king, if he'd taken classes with him, if he'd passed him in the halls, if he liked him, or hated him, or found him unremarkable.

And then, from somewhere near her feet, she heard a creak. Set into the wall was a small iron door. And from it protruded a tiny clawlike hand.

They clambered over her in near-silence, too quickly for her to fight back, the only sound the rustling of their tiny wings as they scrambled up her legs, onto her shoulders, into her hair until she was tangled in them. One of them wrapped its legs around her neck and leaned in to hiss in her ear.

"You have found him."

She shook her head, trying to back up quietly. No.

"Do not kill him here," the fairy whispered. She felt other fairies forcing her hand open, placing something cold and hard into it. She risked a glance down. It was carved from a single piece of stone, the blade a series of rough chips forming a jagged edge. It would hurt a lot to be cut with this. It would leave a ragged wound. She felt sick thinking about it.

"Get to the altar in God Street Market," it whispered. "Wait for magic to be reborn. He will see you, and when he does, he will try to slaughter you on the stone. If you stick him with this, he will not be able to cast magic while it is in his body."

She stared at the boy. He was no older than her. He was staring up at the night sky like he wanted to fall into it. She could warn him. She could tell him everything. It wasn't Carnival Night yet. She surged forward, trying to make herself seen, but the fairies held her back, dug their heels into the ground, pinned her in place with surprising strength.

The fairy holding her neck tightened its grip. "Ungrateful!" it hissed. "You will not betray us to him."

At last, the king eased himself up from the wall with a grunt and rubbed the back of his head with one hand. He wandered back across the street and through the sliding doors of the hospital.

"Remember," the fairy whispered. "Once he is dead, you can have anything you desire."

The fairies poured off of her, siphoning back into the small door.

When they had gone, she sagged against the wall. She wanted to gasp for air, but she was still hiding. She waited in silence. Alone, she stared at the dagger in her hand. It was dull and gray and seemed to kill any light that hit it.

Jack had said that the cops were looking for a boy who'd thrown fire. That must be him. She knew it. Sneaking back to the basement beneath the club, she prayed the police would find him before Carnival. She felt like a doll in the hands of something large and terrible. The best thing she could hope for was to stay far away from him. If they came that close again, she was sure, one of them would end up dead.

TWENTY-FOUR

David was teaching class when the police came.

David turned around from changing out a slide and saw them in the back of the room. For a moment, they looked sheepish, like late students. Then they came down one of the aisles, and squinting, David noticed their uniforms for the first time.

"David Blank?"

"That's me?"

"We're going to need you to come with us."

"Why?" he asked. This couldn't be about Haughan, could it? The man wasn't that petty.

"Because you're under arrest."

He wasn't frightened, not at first. It was humiliating, in the moment, all those watching eyes as four officers wound their way up to the podium. He heard his students start whispering and shifting around in their seats, heard someone say "Anyone got a phone?" which was stupid; they wouldn't be able to send that video until they were home on break. He felt his mind ducking outside to observe the whole procedure from a distance: offering his hands behind his back, and then the fumbling with the handcuffs, and then one of the cops telling him to hold still.

"They're just too small," David said. A ripple of nervous laughter swept the room, and he felt a sudden relief at the sheer number of witnesses, followed immediately by anger: Why wasn't someone doing something? Why were they all just sitting there watching?

Finally, one of the officers gave up on handcuffs and instead twisted David's arms behind his back, holding his wrists in his hands. "Walk," he said.

David walked.

He'd had this nightmare his whole life. His foster parents hadn't been very helpful about it; they'd told him to be polite, taught him to bend his body in, and maybe they'd been right, he thought as he was led out past his students and through the double doors of the lecture hall, taken down the elevator with the cops clustered around him and that damn "[x] from Ipanema" playing again, unsolvable for *x* without its lyrics. Maybe they'd been right, because only a week ago he'd fought some woman in a nightclub and started standing with his shoulders squared, started smiling and meeting people's eyes. He'd gotten too big. It hadn't been the long hours and the endless coffee that was going to kill him, he thought deliriously, as the elevator door dinged:

> *Oh, but I watch him so sadly*
> *How can I tell him I love him?*

(Jesse, cooking spaghetti in Jack's apartment across town, started crying and didn't know why.)

They squeezed him into the back of a patrol car, and he noticed they'd brought two cars. For all four officers, he supposed, although it seemed like a lot for a grad student TA. They still hadn't handcuffed him, so he sat with his hands folded in his lap.

"What am I being charged with?" he asked.

"Just sit quietly till we get to the station," said the man in the driver's seat.

David ducked his head as other cars went by, realizing that he was embarrassed, although he doubted anyone could get a good look at him through the dirty window. It was covered in nose prints. When did they wash these things? The station loomed ahead, a building that looked like an old palace or cathedral. He'd walked past it half a dozen times, wondering what it used to be. It had a high wall around it with a gate that the police car drove through into a flagstone courtyard overgrown with ivy. They made him climb out, and then two officers trained their guns on him while a third held his arms and a fourth ran inside. He tried not to move or even blink.

"Stop flexing," said the man holding his arms.

"Sorry."

"Don't talk."

David ran through proofs in his head and thought about the fireball. He imagined, for a moment, reaching down into that river of light and flicking a whip of flame, knocking both gunmen off their feet, shrugging this man off his arms like a bad coat, and striding off into the day. Who would stop him? Who could stop him?

"His eyes are changing," said one officer. "Hey, stop that!"

"Don't be an idiot, Kowalski," said the officer next to him, a guy with a big gut.

"My grandma—"

"Your grandma is superstitious as hell."

"Look at his eyes! Look at that blue!"

"Don't be weird."

David realized he was full of magic, that he'd saturated himself with it, ready to strike without even really meaning to. No, that was how he'd get killed. He let it all go and felt it ebb out of him, and when he did, he felt so frail he could barely keep his feet.

"Hey, no pushing," said the cop holding his arms. "Where's Cassidy gone?"

"Bigger cuffs."

"He'd better hurry. This guy's a beast."

David went cold. He had to get out of here before these guys talked each other into murdering him. But how? He had the fire, but that wouldn't save him if he got shot. He was drenched in sweat. He felt like he might pass out. Stay on your feet, he told himself.

Cassidy came back, carrying a pack of extra-long zip ties. "Mainland thing," he said. "Check it out." He tightened one around David's wrists until it cut into his skin.

"Will that hold?"

"It'll have to," Cassidy said ominously. "Let's go."

They marched him into the police station. The high vaulted ceiling overhead was painted with a mural of a brown man in a tricorn hat killing a serpent with a flaming sword. Its body was severed in two, the head half still striking at him with poisonous fangs, the coils of its tail unclenching in death from the waist of a busty pilgrim maiden with golden hair spilling out from under her colonial cap. One of the panels had been water damaged, and a bucket was set up under a perpetual drip. The tile mosaic of fish on the floor under his feet was broken in several places and had been repaired with black and white bathroom tiles. The atrium was divided into cubicles, crammed with desks overflowing with papers.

After they took his stuff, they put him into one of those little rooms he'd seen a hundred times on television, except that it was made of huge slabs of gray stone instead of cinder blocks. They sat him down at the table, which was bolted to the floor. They shut the door, and it was dim in there, a dim that hurt David's eyes by being neither light nor dark.

Eventually, the door opened and two men came in, plainclothes. They sat down opposite him. They were both white, middle-aged— one hard and one pouchy-looking. They watched him. He felt cold in the pit of his stomach.

"You wanna tell us how you got here?" asked the hard-looking one. He had a tight crew cut. The buttons of his white shirt strained against the muscles of his chest.

David shook his head. "I want a lawyer."

"City's a sovereign principality," said Pouchy. He leaned forward and steepled his fingers. "Has been since 1650. You're not under the Constitution. So start talking."

They were bluffing, weren't they? David tried to think back three years, before his quick tour through undergrad, his rise through the department. They'd mentioned something like that in orientation, in a talk meant to scare undergraduates. That the police in this town were a little unwieldy, and it was better just to stay out of their way.

"I don't know anything," David said. "I don't even know why I'm here."

"That's funny," said Pouchy. "Since you had a run-in with the police earlier this month."

The stop on the hill. He'd been covered in mud. What did they think that was about?

"We just had a conversation," David said. "He asked me where I was going. I said I was going back to the university. That's all I can remember."

"Where were you coming from?"

"I'd gone for a walk."

"Awfully dirty for a walk."

"I fell. I'm clumsy."

"That's funny, because we heard you're something of a physical marvel. Some kind of prizefighter. Want to tell us about that?"

"I went to a bar. One night. They had some legendary boxing champion or something. No one would fight her, so I said I would to impress my friend. And then she beat me up, because I'm not actually very strong. She knocked me out cold. What does that have to do with anything?"

"You sound angry, son," said Hard. "Angry at who? Getting beat up by a girl make you angry?"

"What? No!"

"Settle down," said Pouchy.

"Angry at cops, maybe?" Hard said.

"Think we should show him?"

"Oh, I think he's already seen, but maybe he wants another look."

Hard reached down and pulled out an eight by ten photograph. He slid it across the table, and David nearly choked. It was a dead man, bloated, lying on green, green grass. And then another photo of a crumpled uniform and a pulpy purple melon where a head should be.

"Recognize him?" Hard's voice got very low. "I had a hard time with it."

"I don't know why you're showing me this," David said. Did they think he'd killed this man?

"I think you do. You're a smart guy, right? I hear you graduated college in two years, and now you're teaching classes."

"I had a lot of credits from high school."

"*I had a lot of*—do you hear this guy? We show him a murder victim, and he's talking about his fucking credits."

"I'm sorry about your friend," David said. "But I had nothing to do with this. I've never met him. I've never killed anyone."

"You met 'em both—they talked to you the day before Pete died," Hard said. "And you knew Matthew Mannering. You two were in a class together freshman year. Before you rose to the top and he dropped out to join the force. And now here he is with his face beaten in."

"Those are big classes," David said.

"You mean to tell me it's just a coincidence that your classmate goes missing, his partner gets killed, and they both talked to you the day before? On your way up the hill from where they were found? Covered in mud? What are you hiding, David?"

"I swear," David said. "I don't know anything about this. I don't even know who this guy is." And as he said it, he had a terrible thought. The day on the hillside. The guy who'd said *Good for you, man*, and patted him on the arm after digging through his backpack. Had the cop known him? Was that why he'd been so familiar with him? He glanced down at the picture, wondering if there were any clues, but the thing in the picture didn't look like a person. His throat closed up.

Pouchy sighed.

"Let's go," he said to Hard. "Give him some time to think."

They left him and shut the door, and as they left they turned off the light in the interrogation room.

"Hey," David said. "Hey, you turned the light off." As he said it, he realized how stupid he sounded. They'd done it on purpose. The only light he had now was what came through the narrow window in the door. He realized he was shivering. He tried to tell himself he was being ridiculous. But the walls felt like they were getting tighter, and in the hall outside, he could see the flickering shadows of people passing by his room, none of them stopping or even looking at him. He banged his restrained hands on the tabletop. "Hey!" he yelled. "Hey! Someone!"

He wasn't sure how long he yelled for or when he gave up. After a while, he started to feel tired, but the dread of falling asleep in a place like this kept him awake. He wondered if any of the hundred students who'd seen him get arrested had told anyone. They'd surely talked about it. He wondered what the university policy on coming to collect arrested grad students was.

The two cops came in again. He asked them for water, or something to eat, or a chance to stretch his legs and use the bathroom.

"Tell us where you were that day," said Pouchy. "What were you doing by the river?"

"I was buying something," he said. "I bought a book from an old lady."

"What were you buying? Drugs?"

"A *book*," David said. "It's in the bag I had with me when I was teaching. You can go find it, it's probably still there. I have nothing to hide."

"Why were you covered in mud if you were buying a book?"

"She wanted to meet me on the hill. I don't know why."

"This sounds like bullshit," Pouchy said. "Doesn't it sound like bullshit?"

Hard nodded.

"I need some water," David said. "I need to take a piss. Please."

"Which is it?" Pouchy said. "Water or piss?"

Without waiting for an answer, the two men stood up and left him in darkness again.

"You can't do this!" David yelled. "You can't do this!"

He reached for the river of light. He tried to bring it up through his hands, to smash something. Blue fire bloomed in his hands. He couldn't move his arms very far, but he launched the fire as hard as he could at the door. It dissipated before it even got close, leaving behind only a faint smell of ozone.

It was the room, he realized. It was made of local bedrock, like the slab they kept on casters in their department to dispel theta radiation. Of course. Just his luck he'd get thrown in a cell meant for holding wizards in jail, or something. He should never have bought that book. He should never have gone to that bar. He should never have come to this island. And then, he realized he was thinking too small, and that he should never have tried to do anything, in his entire fucking life. It was all leading up to this. It was always leading up to this. His fucking foster parents had known. They'd told him to keep his head down, and he'd tried, but he was just too big and too strange for that.

Eventually, he fell asleep slumped over the table. He woke up when someone opened the door. A man in a suit. David sat up quickly, and the man drew back his hand, toward his hip. "Stop," David said, reflexively, holding out his hands. Still tied together. The man withdrew his hand and sat down in the chair opposite David's.

"Just tell me what happened," the man said.

David suddenly felt cold. It was as though something in him had turned over.

"I'm only going to say this one more time," David said. He was surprised by his own voice; it didn't quite sound like him—chilly and deep and hollow. "I didn't do anything, and I don't know anything."

"What were you doing down by the river?"

He said nothing. He shifted his weight in the chair, sitting up a little taller.

"What about the class you had with Matthew?" the man asked.

David stared at him, radiating contempt. The anger was a barrier between him and the man, him and the room. Inside of it, he felt a little safer.

"Fine," the man said. "We've got time."

He got up and left, shut the door behind him.

TWENTY-FIVE

The Maiden! We've almost forgotten about the Maiden! What has our little catalyst been up to? Reader, I am embarrassed to report that they have done little of interest. New jobs are new jobs the world over: You learn where they keep the cleaning supplies, you chat with your coworkers, you find out what parts of your body are sore at the end of a shift. Jesse's life didn't get interesting again until the day after David's arrest, when they find themselves with an afternoon to kill. Jack had promised they could cruise alleys and look for a second chair for the living room, but she'd come in at nine in the morning and promptly passed out. Jesse was bummed. But then again, Jesse thought, it was rare to have a completely free day. No work, no Jack. That meant they could do anything they wanted. But what?

They thought about the Sensible Girls Collective. About the painting of the witches. All this stuff with the club had them thinking about the city, about politics. Jesse realized they wanted to talk to Belle again. She was the one who'd told Jesse to try magic, to try seeing what their body could do. But still, Jesse felt a little apprehension at the idea of going back to talk to her, but also excitement. Belle was full of energy. And maybe she'd be willing to tell Jesse what was going on with all these police, and the monsters, and the witches, and everything else. Everyone else that Jesse tried to talk to either talked nonsense, or told Jesse, kindly or cruelly, that it was none of their business. Belle wouldn't do that. She thought Jesse was smart. She'd said so.

Jesse set out right away. The city was getting ready for Carnival. Jesse passed men on ladders stringing lights across streets; girls on balconies hanging out moth-eaten banners in black, red, and gold; businesses with signs in their windows advertising specials on king cakes and rubber monster masks. Jesse had asked Jack about Carnival, whether it was like Halloween, and Jack, bless her, had said, "Like what now?" It was incredible, Jesse thought, that a place like this existed in the world, and that they'd found their way here. The big party was in a few days, and Jesse had expected to have to ask for the time off to go see it, only to be delighted to learn that Sir was closing the club. Everyone was going.

Jesse stopped outside the corner store—the same one they had visited the other week. Someone had spiffed up the place with red and black pennants and a rack of costumes outside. There were one or two things they might have seen back at a grocery store in Chicasaw: an old Spiderman costume with no mask in sight, a child's princess dress made of crunchy polyester. But the rest of the things on the rack looked much older: dusty velvet gowns, hats sewn all over with buttons and small bells. They stepped into the shop to ask how much for a pair of patchwork pants that laced up the front.

"Hm," the shopkeeper said, not quite glancing up. "You sure you want to go as a patchwork man?"

"Uh," Jesse said. "I just thought they looked cool?"

"Patchwork man gets free food. But he has to eat or drink anything offered," the man said.

"That doesn't sound so bad," Jesse said.

"Huh. Suit yourself," the man said, in a tone that suggested that it was Jesse's funeral.

"Maybe not," Jesse said. "I'll just put these back?"

"Good choice," the man said.

"Do all the costumes come with, like, an obligation?" Jesse asked.

The man squinted over his newspaper at Jesse. "Oh, it's you! Didn't recognize you. You get a haircut?"

"It's growing out," Jesse said.

"It looks good. Just don't be a patchwork man or a skeleton," the old man said. "Not a young thing like you. If you want to have a fun time, go as a Maiden. Maidens just run from monsters and chase Heroes. That's easy."

"Is the patchwork man a monster?"

"You could go as a monster," the old man said, not understanding. "You chase Maidens and run from Heroes. Or a Hero, and you chase monsters and run from Maidens. Easy."

"What about witches?" Jesse asked. "Could I go as a witch?"

The man shook his head. "What?" he said. "What kind of costume is that?"

"You know, with the black clothes and the pointy hat?"

"Never seen a witch dress like that," he said. "How pointy we talking?"

"Where I come from, witches are a kind of costume. You dress up like them for Hallow—uh, for holidays?"

The man shook his head in wonder. "Huh."

"Anyway," Jesse said. "Thanks for telling me about the costumes. It was really nice of you to be patient with me."

The man's face softened. "Hey, no problem," he said. "You gonna be a Maiden?"

"I think I'll skip the costume this year," Jesse said. "This is my first time, and I'm really excited, and I just want to see everything. I don't want to be busy running away from anyone."

"A nice kid like you, you'll have plenty of people chasing you anyway," the shopkeeper said. "Hey, did you ever find your friend?"

Jesse shook their head. "No," they said. "I thought I saw him once. But I waved, and the guy didn't recognize me. I feel like this guy . . . if he was the way I remember him, he would've known me anywhere. He wouldn't have forgotten. It was kind of sad, actually. Like, what if it was him, but he did forget, and that means it didn't matter to him the way it mattered to me, you know?" They realized they were rambling. "I'm sorry, you don't need to hear all this."

"You're right," the man said. "If he could forget you, he's not who you thought he was. But I have a hard time imagining anyone could forget you."

"Um," Jesse said. "Thanks?"

The man leaned over the counter. This was, Jesse realized, the only downside of the place being so friendly. Often these days, Jesse found themself in conversations with strangers who wanted them. Not . . . like, to have sex with. Like, wanted to be close to them, wanted to give them things, wanted to tell Jesse all about their day in this way that felt like what they really wanted was to take a big bite out of Jesse like a slice of cake.

"You'll find him," the shopkeeper said. "Carnival will help. It's when everything that was lost turns back up."

"Really?" Jesse said.

The man nodded. "I believe it."

"Thank you so much," Jesse said. They cast about for something to buy, and saw a basket of oranges on the counter. They picked one up, and started to reach for their wallet, but the old man held up a hand and shook his head.

"Go ahead," he said. "Some guy stole an orange from me on Carnival Night thirty years ago, and then it turned out he was the king. I had good luck for a year after. Since then, around Carnival I give 'em away."

"Wow, thank you," Jesse said. They reached across the counter and shook the old man's hand. "Seriously, I can't thank you enough."

"Just bring me some luck," the old man said, and winked.

Jesse stepped out into the street with the orange, feeling a sense of expanded possibility. Carnival Night. Astrid had said it was a big deal, the night that everything was supposed to happen, but Jesse had kind of thought she'd exaggerated it.

Their route into the heart of the Old City was scattered with familiar faces. Jesse passed that girl Alice, who they'd met at the market, and waved cheerfully, and Alice shifted her basket of red peppers to her other hip to brush her long golden hair out of her eyes, and Jesse blushed and grinned at the ground and kept moving. How, in so little time, had this place come to feel so much like home?

When they got to the old Bodwell School, Belle was outside smoking a cigarette on the steps. Her blond braid was coiled on top of her head, and she wore a moth-eaten velvet gown—a Maiden costume, Jesse realized. She smiled down at Jesse.

"You're back!" she said. She took Jesse's hand. A little jolt passed between them, although whether it was real or in their mind, Jesse couldn't tell.

"Yeah," Jesse said. "I had some questions."

"Questions about what we do?" Belle asked.

"Yeah, sort of."

"Well, come on in." Belle put out her cigarette in a tin can; she did it just the way Jack did, swiping the ash off on the rim before throwing the butt away. Jesse felt a little guilty, being here without telling Jack. But who even knew what Jack did, most of the time? It wasn't like they told each other everything.

Belle waved them inside, through an archway into the print room. "I have to do a few things while we talk," she said. In the room, girls were pulling fresh RISE UP OLD CITY posters off the printing blocks and pinning them on a clothesline. "Looks good in here, girls."

"What does that mean?" Jesse asked, pointing at the poster.

Belle gave them a wise look. "What do you think it means?"

"Um." Jesse fumbled. They'd never been good at being put on the spot. "Is it about the cops? I know they harass people. Especially where I work."

Belle nodded. "You're smart. You've only been here a little while, and you already know how it works. We've been trying to use our art to help people develop some awareness of their situation. But people have a hard time opening their eyes to what's going on around them."

"Yeah," Jesse said. "People don't want to do anything that's gonna get them in trouble."

"Exactly!" She clapped her hands together. "Come on, this way."

Another door, a hallway, and they were in the school's cafeteria. Girls were patching up Maiden costumes like the one Belle was wearing. At a table in a distant corner, some girls were doing something different—they had a heap of antique jewelry in front of them, and they were scraping little bits of dried-up blue powder out of the jewelry's crevices and into a little pile on the table. An empty brass tube lay on the table near them.

"Eventually," Belle said, "I want to start a program where we feed people every day. Anyone who wants it. But right now, we just don't have the women or the resources to do it." She sighed. "Things would be really different if we still had magic. I wouldn't have to do everything by hand."

"Yeah, Astrid told me a little about that," Jesse said. "She said it's dying out?"

"She doesn't understand how it really works," Belle said. "The old witches have it all wrong. They think there's this mystical cycle, and that it requires a king, and that as long as we don't have a king, we can't have any more magic. And they think a king is a very specific kind of person."

"But they're wrong?"

"They are," Belle said. "I've studied it—the king is just the name for whoever wins the Maiden. Whoever wins the Maiden can make magic appear again. It's not about who you are, it's—a kind of invocation. Completing the pattern." Belle flashed a smile. "It always struck me as so strange that the witches couldn't believe that the most powerful person in the city is a young girl."

"But someone still has to . . . win the heart of the Maiden?"

"That's what I suspect," Belle said. "That's what the old books say. But they never say anything about a king. It could be anyone." She winked. "It could be a woman."

Jesse blushed a little. "I mean, maybe."

"Well, Jesse," Belle said. "What do you think of my vision?"

Belle had that same undercurrent of power Jack did, the one that made Jesse excited and a little scared at the same time. Jesse nodded. "It's great," they said.

"Oh, I meant to ask," Belle said. "Have you practiced with your special skill any since we last talked?"

Jesse realized that all day, they hadn't really been thinking about themself as one thing or another. They shut their eyes, and willed themself more feminine. When Belle squealed in delight, they opened their eyes.

"Oh, that's incredible!" Belle said. "You know, it's amazing how you manage to do that with magic so low. How do you do it?"

Jesse hesitated, not entirely sure they wanted to tell Belle they were the Maiden. She seemed nice, but . . . "I'm not sure. I think I should go ask Astrid about it. I want to be sure I'm not using any up, you know?"

"No, that makes perfect sense," Belle said.

"So, I'm gonna go do that," said Jesse. "But I'd love to come back here soon. Maybe after Carnival?"

"Jesse," Belle said. "Before you go, I wanted to say: I really like you. And . . ." She took a deep breath. "There's something I want to ask you."

"Yeah?" Jesse said.

"Would you like to meet me at Carnival?" Belle asked. "I think it might be nice to go on a date."

Jesse blushed. A date! Incredible. They hadn't been on a date since they'd come to the city. Well, not really. They'd made out with a lot of people, but that wasn't really the same thing.

"Um," Jesse said. "Yes? Yes."

Belle grabbed Jesse's hands. "I'm so excited," she said. "I'm really looking forward to it. Why don't you meet me by the fountain in God Street Market at nine tomorrow night? Does that work for you?"

"Yeah," Jesse said. "That's perfect."

Belle beamed brightly. "This is so great. Oh my gosh."

Jesse stumbled out into the sun, feeling as though they'd just stepped off a carousel. The ground felt heavy underfoot, the world trying to spin even as they stood still in the bright morning. They'd been asked out on a date by Jack's sister. They'd met a bunch of radical women who made posters. Maybe this was the beginning of something special. Jesse briefly pictured their life as a revolutionary leader, distributing pamphlets, feeding people. Maybe, Jesse thought, they shouldn't tell Jack just yet that they were going to go on a date with her sister. That seemed like it could go over badly. And anyway, who knew how the date would even go?

Jesse headed in the general direction of Astrid's shop in the crisp bright sunlight that had just a little bit of a chilly nip to it. Maybe, they thought, they'd stop and buy some new clothes. Not a costume, just something that wasn't torn jeans or the dress they wore to work. They stopped in a little shop that sold old clothes and bought a blue Hawaiian shirt that reminded them of a guy they'd made out with at a bar a few weeks back, a faded sundress, and a pair of jeans that weren't ripped at the knees. The girl behind the counter volunteered to turn Jesse's old jeans into cutoffs. Jesse tried to pay her, and she shook her head.

"Carnival season," she said. "It's good luck to do boons for cute boys. They might turn out to be Heroes."

"Nah," Jesse said. "I'm definitely a Maiden."

She laughed Jesse off and got a pair of cheap sunglasses from a bin. She put them on Jesse's face. "There. Now you look really cool."

Jesse wandered out of the shop a few minutes later in their new jeans, their old pants now shorts in a bag. They realized they were closer to Astrid's bakery than they'd thought. There it was, between the two empty storefronts on God Street. Jesse wondered how they'd broach the subject of magic. Maybe they'd buy a scone first or something.

Jesse pushed open the door. The bell clanked against the glass in the jarring way that always made them think it had cracked, and Astrid looked up from ringing up an old lady with a perm. Her eyes narrowed, and she seemed to be trying to communicate something to Jesse with just her eyebrows, but Jesse couldn't figure out whether it was *Stay put* or *Get out*, so they stood awkwardly in the corner until the customer turned around. She, too, gave Jesse a strange, quizzical look, and turned back to Astrid.

"Ah, Jesse," Astrid said. "Miss Riviere, this is Jesse. Jesse, my good friend Miss Deirdre Riviere."

"Pleased to meet you, ma'am," Jesse said.

"And you, young man," Miss Riviere said. "How do you know Astrid?"

"Uh," Jesse said.

"He's the son of an old friend who moved to the mainland," Astrid said. "You remember Stephanie, Josephine's daughter?"

"Oh, yes," Miss Riviere said. "Is your mother well, Jesse?"

"Yeah, she's doing great," Jesse said, hoping the woman in question was someone you'd expect to be doing great. "I'll tell her you asked after her when I write."

"I see. Well, have a good afternoon, both of you."

She left. Astrid motioned for Jesse to get behind the counter, and once Jesse was back there, grabbed a low stool and had them sit down out of sight.

"Why are you doing this?" Jesse asked. "Is it really so bad if someone knows I'm here? What are you worried about?"

"Surely you've noticed that most people treat you differently by now," Astrid said. "Some people are smart enough to notice, and they'll put the pieces together. Deirdre would jump at the chance to end your life before you can assume your power."

Jesse shook their head. "Why didn't you tell me this?"

"I told you that you were in danger, and that you needed to keep to yourself. Why didn't you listen to me? How many people know about you now?"

"Know . . . what exactly?"

"What you can do. That you're the Maiden. Anything."

Jesse thought. "Um."

Astrid pinched her nose. "Help us. All right, how did you get here? What are you even doing out? Where's Jack?"

"She's at work," Jesse said. "I have the day off."

"What? Where are you working?"

"Um."

"Oh god. You're working in that club."

"Well, what was I supposed to do?" Jesse asked. "Sit around waiting for something to happen? You said you'd tell me what was happening next."

"I've been trying to keep you away from the worst of it. I don't know if you're aware of this, but two cops are dead," Astrid said.

Jesse crossed their arms.

"Yeah, and the rest of them are harassing my friends while you just sit there," they said. "Aren't witches supposed to help people? Isn't that what you said? Why aren't you doing anything about it?"

"Sir's people are *his* business."

Jesse rolled their eyes. "Uh-huh," they said. "And it has nothing to do with the fact that they're mostly monsters?"

"Who's been telling you all this?"

"Nobody had to tell me," Jesse said. "I'm not stupid, you know. And even if I were, it's not that hard to figure out when someone's being treated differently for no damn reason."

"They take care of their own. They don't need my help."

"They do, though," Jesse said. "The cops think they had something to do with those murders. But it wasn't them! It was some college student experimenting with magic."

Astrid's face went rigid. But then the bell jingled, and Astrid faced front. At waist height, she gave a sharp gesture with her hand—*shut up*. Jesse sat quietly while she rang up the customer, wished them a good day. As soon as they left, Astrid dropped to her knees and put her hands on Jesse's shoulder.

"Say that again," she said. "About the college student. What have you heard?"

Jesse shrugged her off. "Look, I don't know anything, right?" they said. "Because nobody will tell me anything. Even Jack won't tell me shit. If I'm so important, why are you treating me like a child?"

Even as Jesse spoke, the look of pure desperation on Astrid's face stunned them. Both of them stood silent for a moment, aware of the impasse.

"Jesse," Astrid said. "I'm sorry. But this is important. I need you to tell me what Jack told you. I know that boy. Please."

Jesse eyed her suspiciously. "What are you gonna do?" they asked.

Astrid looked so upset that Jesse almost felt bad about tearing into her like that. She looked suddenly very old.

"I'm going to try to help him," she said. "Now. Tell me everything."

TWENTY-SIX

Astrid sent Jesse back uptown with a story about how the boy in question was the son of her best friend, who had died tragically young, who she missed every day. She was surprised at how well it worked. But then, Maidens were always too trusting. The boy said he was so sorry. She told him it wasn't his fault. It was important he not get involved now. He and David should meet at Carnival, and not a moment before. Astrid was taking no chances about knocking anything loose.

"Are you going to try to get him out of jail?" Jesse asked.

"I just want to make sure he's all right," Astrid said. "I'd appreciate if you didn't tell anyone I'm looking into it. We're not supposed to have favorites. I'd . . . It'd be very generous of you."

A Maiden was always generous. "Of course," Jesse said.

As soon as she got rid of him, she went to her telephone in the back and dialed the police. After winding her way through a number of them, she was transferred to someone she knew, Vandenberg. He agreed to meet her a few blocks away from her shop in a discreet car.

"The man we arrested," he said when she climbed into the passenger's seat. "Astrid, he looks familiar."

She sat silently, waiting for him to say more.

"I know you were . . . a revolutionary," he said. "But, I mean, even you must have noticed that *way* King Nathan had. Like he was made of metal and everything else would have to bend around him." He shook his head in disbelief as he drove. "Astrid—this man is the same. I think he's . . ."

"It's almost Carnival Night," Astrid said quietly.

He glanced at her at a red light. "Do you think everything could be as it was?" he asked.

"I think things could be different than they are now," Astrid said.

His face flooded with relief. Hearing her say it made it more possible.

"Why did you bring him in?" she asked.

"Honestly," he said. "We were grasping at straws. Nothing made sense. We heard Jack was investigating, so we put some pressure on her, and she gave us his name."

Astrid's pulse raced. Jack, of all people? She was hardly likely to turn anyone over to the police.

"When did she give you that name?"

"A few days ago. We'd heard she'd been making inquiries, so we asked her if she knew where we could find . . ." He looked embarrassed. "Bloody Marla."

Astrid shook her head. "That thing is nothing like Marla."

"So it's real?"

"You asked her where you could find something you didn't think was real?"

"None of this is my idea, all right? The university's expressed interest in the creature, the boys in the bullpen think it killed Pete and Matthew—I'm under a lot of pressure."

Hah. Astrid had known Vandenberg since he was a child.

He'd always been like this: always on the right side, and yet somehow always surrounded by wrongdoers.

Jack had turned David in. This knowledge was still settling into place for Astrid, altering her sense of Jack, and in turn, of the cosmology of the city. Any good witch understood that everything was connected to everything else. Jack didn't help the police; that was a rule Astrid had come to rely on, the reason she'd been able to trust Jack at all. And Jack only broke her own rules when she was protecting her sister.

Astrid skimmed back over her last few encounters with Belle Marley. She'd said something about being busy on Carnival Night, hadn't she, at their last board meeting? She was always talking about revolution in the abstract way young people did when they'd never actually led one. A picture was developing. So Belle Marley had killed those men. And her sister had covered it up by throwing David under the bus. *Disgusting.*

"Had Jack even met him?" Astrid asked Vandenberg.

"Apparently there was an altercation at her boss's place," he said. "She said he used magic. We've talked to the university, and they're going through their equipment, trying to figure out if he smuggled something off-premises."

"Of course they are," Astrid said.

"They never believed us," Vandenberg said. "About what we used to be."

"What we are, and what we *will* be," Astrid corrected him, knowing he'd like being corrected in that way. She needed him on her side through this.

"What are we going to do?" he asked her.

"We're going to tell your bosses who really did this," Astrid said. Throwing Belle Marley to the cops wasn't her idea of a good time. But something about this situation seemed large and unwieldy, and she'd feel a lot better if Belle Marley spent the days surrounding Carnival cooling her heels in jail.

It was strange to be driven through the gates of the palace, only to emerge into a parking lot full of squad cars. They'd paved over what used to be an ornamental garden. Vandenberg helped her out of the passenger's side, and they went in through the former grand front entrance. He led her through the bullpen, in what had once been the throne room. The throne and the long table had been hauled away, presumably to a museum, since neither one would have fit comfortably in a private home, no matter how extravagant. Oh, the mural was doing badly. Astrid sighed. That was one of Nathan's, and she'd always thought it was pretty good. Now it had a spreading dark stain over the face of the serpent, which gave it a pathetic look. The tile mosaic on the floor, of the fish of the Saint James, had seen better days.

Police looked up as she came in. She knew a lot of them. Some disliked her; some were the children of women she'd known her whole life, which wasn't the same as liking her, but made her feel a little safer.

"This way," Vandenberg said, and led her through the maze of desks toward a door at the far end. It used to lead into a corridor, Astrid knew, and off the corridor were the guts of the palace, rooms where servants folded linen, kitchens where they cooked in ovens as tall as a man. Astrid had cooked here, once. Nathan had requested her pastries for his coronation. He'd known better, at least, than to ask her to cook for his wedding.

They ushered her into another corridor, the ceiling lowered with new acoustic tiling, and into an office that used to be a butler's pantry. A man sat slumped behind the desk there. He was New City, from off-island, a white man with fleshy fingers. He squinted at her when she came in.

"I know who killed your policemen," she said. "It wasn't that boy in lockup."

"Uh-huh," he said.

"Her name is Belle Marley," Astrid said. "She thinks of herself as a revolutionary. She lives in an abandoned school building with several of her followers. She prints those 'Rise Up Old City' posters. She's alluded many times to wanting to kill police. She's been arrested multiple times over the years for various petty crimes, including vandalizing this building and physically assaulting police. I am sure there are records."

He squinted. "Huh."

"You liaise with the university," Astrid said. "How do they feel about the claim that one of their students killed two policemen with magic?"

"That's not for me to speculate," he said. But Astrid could see in his face that her theory looked a lot better to him.

"What's your interest?" the man asked. "What's the nature of your relationship with this boy?"

"I sold him a book about spells," Astrid said. "This is against the rules of my community. Because I knew they wouldn't approve,

I asked him to meet me outside the city, near the river. When I heard later that he'd been arrested because he supposedly killed someone, I felt responsible."

"You sold him a book about magic?" the man asked. "Wouldn't that lend more credence to the idea that he killed someone with it?"

Astrid raised her eyebrows.

"Sir," she said. "I realize other citizens might have given you the wrong impression, but we're not all stupid. Magic isn't real. It's a religion, a metaphor. You cannot commit a crime with a weapon that doesn't exist."

The man relaxed into his seat. The world made sense to him again.

"Just give me something I can use," he said.

Astrid smiled and folded her hands in her lap. "Of course."

TWENTY-SEVEN

When the door opened again, the man in the trench coat was holding it for a small woman. David blinked in the light, and after a moment of confusion, recognized Astrid. She was wearing a black dress and had her hair pulled back into a serious bun. She ran over to him and clutched his hands. When she met his eyes, hers flared with that familiar dark blue for just a moment and she gave him a small nod before turning back to the officer.

"Get these off of him," she said.

David sat quietly while a uniformed officer undid the zip ties. When they were gone, he felt the magic surge through his body and into his hands, and it was all he could do to keep it still, to not burn the whole building to the ground just so he could be sure it would never hold him again. Astrid helped him to his feet. He could smell himself; he stank of fear sweat.

"Let's go," Astrid said. David tried to take a step forward and stumbled; his legs had fallen asleep. She braced her whole body against his side and helped him limp out the door of the cell.

In the bullpen, under that strange painted ceiling, a cop handed Astrid a bag with David's effects. They walked out of the police station together into afternoon sunlight. He'd been there all night? It somehow felt like longer and like no time at all. His legs were stiff, but as he walked, they came grudgingly back to life.

"We should go to my house," Astrid said. "We have much to discuss."

He eyed her warily. "Why'd you come for me? How did you know I was there?"

"One of the detectives told me," she said.

"And who are you, really? You said you'd tell me."

"A friend."

"Whose friend?" he asked.

"I got you out of prison, didn't I? Does that get me a conversation?"

"What do you want to talk about?"

"Let's catch a ride," she said. "It's a long walk."

He shook his head. "I can't be somewhere that small right now."

They walked uptown. She seemed to be keeping them to deserted streets, and it took a while with her slow, uneven gait. At last they came to a street buckled by thick tree roots, and to a little row house with herb bushes growing in the front yard.

"Come in," she said. She led him into her living room and sat him down on a scratchy couch with a striped afghan draped over the back. He moved mechanically. Astrid seemed nervous. She was digging her hands into the folds of her skirt.

"Do you want something to eat?" she said. "Some tea?"

"Water, please."

She brought him a glass. He finished it, and she brought him another, and a plate of cookies. He ignored them. He planted his hands on his knees.

"Why am I here?" David asked. "Tell me what's going on."

"You need to rest," she said.

"I need to know. Or I'm leaving."

He started to stand up, his knees protesting loudly. But she put out a hand. "No," she said. "I'll tell you. Just . . . sit down."

He settled into the couch, and she took the seat opposite him.

"So," she said. "What do you know about your parents?"

"Nothing," he said. "I was a ward of the state until I got adopted when I was three. You know. Sad orphan kid. No backstory. Someone wrote Blank on my birth certificate where my last name should have gone."

"How did you find this place, then?" she asked. "How did you know to come here? Did you have the postcard?"

He blinked, and his eyes went wide. He found himself looking over her, trying to line up features. Was she—

"Stop that, I'm not your mother," she snapped. He sat back, and she looked a little remorseful. "I knew your father. He was . . ." She swallowed. "You know the history of this place?"

"It was some kind of independent state?"

"A principality," she said. "And your father was king here, when he was younger. King Nathan."

"There must be a mistake," he said.

Astrid clicked her tongue. She crossed to a bookcase and got down a photo album. She opened it to a page that showed an enormously tall white man with pale freckled skin, a head of wild auburn hair. He wore a circlet of gold around his head and a white jacket with military epaulets. The man did look like him. The same high forehead, the same slope of the cheeks. And all at once, David realized that he'd seen him before.

David reached out and touched the picture with his fingertips. He dug his teeth into his lower lip. Then he looked up at her.

"Is this a joke?" he asked. "I've met this guy. He's like a hundred years old, and he's homeless. He told me to leave town."

Astrid nodded. "He's not well. He doesn't always know where or when he is. But when Nathan was your age, he was doing magic that no one had ever seen before. He built the bridge that leads to the mainland. He bent the steel with his bare hands. But all that's gone now. I wish you could have seen it, the way things used to be."

She told him about the great things they'd done in the city when magic had flowed freely. Healthy babies, full gardens, improbable architectures, works of art that had all relied on magic. He listened, trying to absorb as much as he could. When she paused for a moment, he said, "And my mother?"

Astrid blinked. "Yes. Of course."

She flipped quickly through the album, past portraits of women dressed in black in somber poses, and picnics in upside-down gardens, and a Polaroid of Nathan in blue jeans, posing with a young Astrid looking like a punk-rock Eartha Kitt perched on the arm of his chair. Near the back was a wedding photograph of a whole group of people standing on the flagstones in front of a castle. And in the middle, his mother. He knew her immediately.

"Her name was Marla," Astrid said.

She was short but built wide like him, with ebony skin and cropped hair. She wore a coronet of freshwater pearls and a cream colored dress that flowed from her shoulders to the ground. She seemed more real, more saturated than everyone else in the picture; they looked washed out, like a background. Her eyes seemed to stare out of the picture and into David, and he realized that she was where his ears came from, his mouth, his eyes. On any other day, this picture would have made him weep. But he could only feel it dimly, the ache of longing, faint under the layer of stone that had formed over his heart.

"What happened to her?" he asked.

"Some people who thought they were doing the right thing asked Nathan to abdicate. The people of River City didn't want him to, they hadn't asked him to, so he said he would still serve. And so a mob attacked his palace. Your mother escaped to the Isle of Bells. She died having you. And I . . ." Astrid paused. "I was your midwife. And I took you off the island."

"And you got me out of jail. How?"

"I know who actually killed those men," she said. "I wasn't going to let you sit in jail for it. Not you."

"So," he said. "What do you want me for?"

She looked up from the album. "What do you mean?"

"Nobody talks to me unless they want something," he said. "They want me to do their work, or kick someone's ass, or be a murderer, and now I guess . . . you want me to be a king?"

"I want you to have your birthright," she said. "Magic, and power, and your throne."

"Why?"

"Because it was taken from you."

"I don't know how to be a king," he said. "That's a . . . job. Like being a politician. I'm a physicist, I don't know anything about the law." He knew he was making sense, but it sounded ridiculous, as though this were not something that could be argued with using logic.

"Magic can't survive without a king," she said. "And we are running dangerously low."

"What do you mean, low?"

"Let me show you."

She took his hand, and they were suddenly plummeting.

David knew they were still in Astrid's living room. But at the same time, they were falling deep below the earth, past worms and roots of trees until they hit the bedrock and slipped beneath it, and under them was a huge and empty cave, and far below, almost invisible, a glimmer. A trickle of iridescent light.

"This should be full," Astrid said. "But there's almost none left."

David thought about his research, the feeling he'd had of pulling from something, how difficult it had been. How wan and pale the beams of blue light. Now he understood why. He felt sick.

"Get us out of here," he said, and Astrid let go of his hand, and all at once they were back in her living room. He clung to the couch, trying to steady himself.

"Oh god," he said. "I didn't know. I used so much."

"We all make mistakes."

"What happens when it's gone?"

"That won't happen," Astrid said.

"How do you know?"

"Tomorrow is Carnival Night," Astrid said. "That's when you are destined to become king. You'll come into your powers then, and you'll be able to restore magic."

"How?" he asked. "What do I have to do?"

"Nothing," she said. "You'll show up, and it will happen. That's how it happened for your father. He went to Carnival Night and was king by the next morning. It's a little different every time, but it cannot be stopped."

David felt impossibly tired. His bones hurt. He couldn't fathom what was in front of him.

"I need to sleep," he said.

"You'll stay here tonight," said Astrid.

He nodded, too tired to argue. He let her lead him up the narrow stairs, bumping his head on their low sloping ceiling. There was an old scuff mark there. Had his father bumped his head climbing these same stairs? The floorboards groaned under his weight. Had his mother ever been in this house? Somehow he doubted it.

The bed was too short for him, but he was used to that. Astrid fussed around with pillows, got out a new blanket. Some familiar smell lingered in the room, something David recognized but couldn't place, something that made him think of his friend—*what was his name?* But as soon as Astrid left, shutting the door behind her, all thoughts were swept from his mind in an obliterating wave of sleep. He would have been frightened by it if he weren't so tired.

TWENTY-EIGHT

Across town, the nameless girl woke up to someone pounding on the door.

She sat up in bed, still clutching the stone dagger. She must have fallen asleep holding it. She almost dropped it; she hated the look of the thing in her hand. "Who is it?" she called.

"Who do you think?" Jack answered. "Can you get the door?"

She tucked the dagger hastily under the pillow and pulled the covers up over the bed. She went to the door and opened it.

The basement apartment was down a little set of brick stairs outside the club's back entrance. Looking out the door, she could see a scrap of darkening sky. Late afternoon already; she'd slept most of the day. The little bit of breeze told her it had finally rolled over, truly, from summer into autumn. Jack stood at the bottom, holding a huge box and surrounded by paper bags. She had traded her undershirt for a flannel under her leather jacket. The daughter of the river tried to stifle her delight.

"I thought you might be hungry," Jack said. "Those bags are groceries. I had to guess what you'd eat."

"What's in the box?" Turing asked.

Jack grinned. "Here, take it."

She half tossed it to Turing, who caught it in four arms and let out an oof—it was heavy. She set it down on the floor and gasped. It was packed with books. All paperbacks, some with ripped covers.

"I tried to get a few complete series in there," Jack said. "I'm guessing you've never finished a series."

"How did you know?" Turing asked.

"You know. Because you probably get whatever people leave behind. Nobody brings volumes one through ten on a picnic."

It was such a pleasure to watch Jack strut and preen over her good gift. She wanted to reach out and put her arms around Jack's neck and sway back and forth. But instead, she just told her how much she loved the books. How she was going to read them in the right order, cover to cover.

"If you have them in order, you should skip the part at the end where they ruin the next book," Jack said.

"That part always made me so angry. I'd get to the end of it and be upset. So I usually skipped them anyway." She got to the next grocery bag: She could smell fresh fish. "My favorite part is where the writer talks about who they are and what they do."

"I never read those. They always try to be clever."

"They *are* clever! They wrote a book! Let them be funny."

"But how can they have written a book and still sound so terrible?" Then Jack read a few of them to her, in voices, until the daughter of the river laughed so hard she had to ask Jack to stop.

"It's not fair," the nameless girl said when she could speak again. "It's harder to talk about yourself than to make things up. You know that."

Jack shrugged. "I wouldn't say anything. Who am I? Just some asshole who wrote a book."

"'Jack Marley is an asshole who wrote a book. When she isn't writing, she enjoys riding her motorcycle and wearing a very nice jacket.'"

"Maybe it's just that if you describe anyone, they sound like an asshole."

The daughter of the river smiled and bit her lip. It was a habit she'd picked up, she realized, from watching Jack.

"Are you working tonight?" she asked Jack.

"Yeah, but it should be pretty quiet. Cops arrested that guy yesterday."

The nameless girl was flooded with relief and guilt. She hoped he was all right, but if he wasn't at Carnival, he couldn't kill her, and she couldn't kill him. She'd bury that stone dagger when all this was over. "That's good," she said.

"Yeah, maybe now they'll stop rounding up random people."

She shook her head, frowning. "They're not rounding up random people. They're rounding up monsters."

Jack flinched at the word. It was strange, the daughter of the river thought, how Jack, who she was sure had killed men before, seemed so nervous sometimes.

"Why don't you like that word?" Turing asked.

"I dunno," Jack said. "It sounds like dyke. Like I know what it means, but people say it to mean something worse than what it is."

"I don't like it, either," she said. "I don't like that you're always trying not to say it. It feels like you're lying to me."

Jack looked askance.

"I'm not trying to lie to you," she said. "I just . . . like. When I see you, I don't see a . . . monster. You're my friend."

"But if I weren't your friend, you'd see a monster?"

"What? No, that's not what I mean. I mean, like, Agnolo's not a monster. He's just a guy. I can't fucking stand Rex, but is he a monster? No, he's just an asshole. And you're . . ." Jack shrugged. "You're a person. A really good person. I don't get why I can't just say person."

"Because that's not what other people see. You can't pretend that you can't tell the difference."

Jack shook her head.

"Okay, you're above my philosophical pay grade," she said. "But. You should talk to Agnolo. He's got a whole thing about it."

"Are you done having this conversation with me, Jack?"

Oh, how she loved watching Jack go soft in the face.

"No, of course not," Jack said. "Look. I need some time to think about what you said. I'd never thought about it that way before. If I say something right now, it's going to be stupid."

"You're never stupid," she said.

"You just don't know me that well yet."

Turing laughed. "Okay. Maybe you're a little stupid. But don't be stupid tonight, all right?"

"Hah." Jack shrugged back into her very nice jacket, the one that the daughter of the river could smell from halfway across the room: worn leather, sweat, cologne. "How about this: I'll meet you at the bar for a drink after I get done, okay? I'll have some better thoughts by then."

"I'd like that," she said.

And then Jack was heading out the door, stopping at the threshold. If they were in love, Turing thought, this was the moment where she would take her in her arms and kiss her goodbye. Even so, she couldn't help but stare.

"Well," Jack said. "See you."

Turing wanted to know what Agnolo had to say about monsters, but at the same time, the thought of going outside chilled her, especially after seeing the king. She thought about distracting herself by reading, or eating the groceries Jack had left, but nothing interested her.

She took a deep breath. She had spent her whole life reading books and never talking to people. She'd never know what Agnolo had to say unless she asked him herself.

She put on her coat, and slipped out through the basement door and up the little flight of steps. She peered around the corner of the building to make sure there were no cops or fairies or kings.

There was nobody, not even the usual guard on the back door, which was propped open with a brick. She slid inside, and she could hear the guard in the bathroom. Poor man.

She passed the doorway to the dressing room, and for a moment, caught a glimpse of the gorgeous mess inside—flimsy dresses and bras flung over the backs of chairs, glowing mirrors like portals to other worlds. Some of the girls were keeping their costumes for Carnival Night here, on coat hangers or dressmakers' dummies. But then she spotted a few girls in there chatting, and slipped by the door as quietly as she could before they saw her staring in.

The inside of the nightclub made her think of caves underwater, the ceiling low and given a sort of round shape by the pattern of the shadows. She'd read books about strip clubs, and she'd read books about cabarets, and it was a delight to her to find a place that didn't match a description she'd already read. And there was Agnolo, moving from table to table, lighting the tiny candles in jars.

When she'd first seen Agnolo, she'd hardly thought of him as a monster. Not like her, not like Rex or Agnolito, his godson. But if he had a theory, she wanted to hear it.

She wasted no time. She went over to him, waved.

"Oh, hey," he said. "You get settled in?"

"Yes," she said. "Jack brought me some books."

He grinned at her. Aside from his tusks, his other teeth were also large and flat, and he seemed to have fewer than most people. "She did, huh? You know, I don't think I've ever seen her hung up on a boy before."

"We're just friends," Turing said.

"Oh. I see all kinds of friends in here," Agnolo said. "That little shit over there? In the purple shirt? Came in here a week ago, getting all handsy with some guy he's *just friends* with. Just friends is only just friends till you get drunk." He looked Turing up and down. "You want a drink?"

Turing smiled and glanced at the floor. "I've never had one before."

"I'll make you something. Put some hair on your chest."

"I hope not."

Agnolo grunted at her and stepped behind the bar. He motioned to a barstool.

"Jack said you have a theory about monsters," Turing said.

"Hah, I didn't think she was listening." Agnolo put a big ice cube in a glass and tapped it with a spoon until it cracked. "You know where the word monster comes from? So, in Italian, you'd say *mostro*. And in Italian, to teach, to demonstrate, is *dimostrare*." He poured something blood red into the glass, topped it with something from a dark green bottle, uncorked a bottle of wine and added a little splash. Rubbed a bit of orange peel on the rim of the glass before tossing it in. "All right, there you go. This drink's called the fuckup. It's an *aperitivo*, for before dinner. Some guys will say cocktails are for women, but they're just scared of a little liquor. I like one with a nice cigar."

"Thank you," Turing said. She took a sip, and her lips puckered. It was sweeter and more bitter all at once than anything she'd ever drank before. Of course, until that very moment, she'd only drank water. As soon as she swallowed, her throat felt warm, and soon the warmth spread to her whole body.

"What were you saying?" she asked. "*Dimostrare?*"

"*Monster* means *teacher*," Agnolo said. "The Greeks believed that monsters were prophesies. Signs from the gods. If a two-headed calf was born, it meant a king had committed a grave sin with his mother."

"With his mother?"

"Or, you know, done something," Agnolo said. "I don't think they were too specific. But their point was that a monster wasn't wrong by itself, it was a sign something else was wrong. And that's why people hate monsters. They don't want to think about their own sins."

"You think we're signs someone else committed a sin?"

"Sure. We're instruments of fate. We get to just be ugly on the outside. They have to be ugly on the inside."

Turing winced a little. "You think we're ugly?" she said. "Then why don't you change? You could. It wouldn't be hard. Not for you."

Agnolo's doughy face melted in sympathy.

"I saw you," he said. "That first night you came in. You're

missing one of your, uh, things, aren't you? You tried to cut 'em off?"

Turing looked down at the bar. It was covered in layers of varnish, chipped off and varnished over again, so that it had a texture like a rotting log.

"When I was little, I was kidnapped by scientists," she said. "I escaped to the Isle of Bells. I was going to get rid of them, and then I would go be a normal—child. I'd go find a family to adopt me." She ran her fingers over the grooves and ridges of the wood. "I only made it through one—there was so much blood. I was sick for a month after. I was lucky I survived."

Agnolo nodded, thoughtfully stroking one of his tusks.

"I never wanted to get rid of these," he said. "They made me different from my brothers and sisters. I knew what I was."

"What about the people who hate you?" she asked. "Doesn't that bother you?"

"Well, I'm just a little bit of a monster," he said. "Just a little lesson, you know. Probably my dad was a cheating bastard or something. He didn't like me very much. But you!" He shook his head and smiled. "You make people think about big sins. Treasonous shit. And that's not your fault. You're not the criminal there. They're scared of your persecution."

She shook her head. "I don't want to persecute anyone."

"You don't have to," he said. "They look at you, and they persecute themselves. Because you're just too big and too strange for them not to think about sin when they look at you." He scratched the back of his head. "I bet that's why Jack likes you. Deep down, Jack isn't afraid of sin."

"I don't want to be that," Turing said. "I just want to be a person."

She realized that she was on the verge of crying again. The drink was making her feel sloshy, full of tears that kept threatening to tip out. Agnolo spotted her and shook his head.

"Hey," he said. "Stop that. You've gotta toughen up. You don't get to change it. So you gotta live with it."

"That's easy for you to say. You could change whenever you want."

"It's a fucking test, okay? You have a face like this," he said, running the back of his hand down his cheek in mock sensuousness, "you know if someone loves you, they love you. You never have to wonder if it's just your stunning good looks. Best to think of it as an asshole detector."

Turing had to smile a little at that. "It's an expensive one."

"Hey, now," Agnolo said. "You've got the love of a good woman." Turing opened her mouth, and Agnolo waved her off. "Don't tell me you're friends again. Jack Marley doesn't have friends. Well, other than that one kid over there." He pointed at a skinny girl who Turing had seen a few times before. She was laughing with that girl Hannah, the one with the long hair who was angry at Jack. "But look at 'em, they could make friends with a wolverine. My point is: You're gonna have to be a man and say something to her."

"I can't."

"Well," Agnolo said. "Maybe you'll get lucky and Jack will be the man."

"I'd like that," Turing said without thinking, and Agnolo

laughed and leaned over the bar and slapped her hard on the shoulder.

"You're funny," he said. "Well, that's—"

The daughter of the river was aware of the color draining from the moment. A kind of slowness as Agnolo's affable face turned hard. As the sound in the room faded from loud to quiet. As the only sound that was audible was a growing hiss coming from that back hallway where the dressing rooms were, where Sir's office was. Turing swiveled on her barstool and saw what Agnolo saw: a cloud of smoke, filling the room, something thick and dark. And from the front of the bar, she heard shouts and breaking glass.

"Gas," Agnolo said. He was already wetting a dishrag. He tossed it to her. "Cover your face. Fucking pigs."

She tied it over her nose and mouth as quickly as she could. Agnolo sprinted from behind the bar. He had a bat in one hand and a gun in the other, his own face covered. She recoiled. "Come on. Back door, now. Take a deep breath and hold it."

She followed him into the smoke. Almost immediately, she was blinded. It stung in her eyes, her gills. It was like being underwater, except she couldn't breathe. She used her arms to find the edges of the corridor and moved down it as quickly as she could, one step behind Agnolo, until they hit the back door. Agnolo was pounding on it, unable to open it. Someone must have wedged it shut. Agnolo was grunting in frustration. He was going to run out of air. She pushed him aside, as gently as she could manage, and rammed her whole body into the door.

It gave under her weight. Another shove and she heard something grinding across the pavement. There was something heavy behind the door. She shoved as hard as she could and went stumbling out into the cool night air. She could barely see around the tears streaming down her face. But she could hear, and what she heard were voices. Cursing her. And then there were hands on her. She shoved them away, they grabbed her again, and without knowing what else to do, she wrapped her long arms around his wrists and yanked him into the air. A startled yelp. She still couldn't see. The man kicked at her, wrenching in midair as he tried to free himself.

"Get on the fucking ground!" she heard, and then a dozen hard clicking sounds. Were those guns? She couldn't see—

Something hissed past her, over her head, and the cops around her screamed, and she felt them moving back from her. She tossed the man in her arms, praying for his soft landing. And then people were grabbing her from behind, dragging her backward into the bar, and someone had turned on the sprinkler system, and cool water streamed down her face and arms, and it didn't help with the burning all over her skin, but at least the air she breathed was clear.

Someone untied the wet towel around her face. Hands touched her all over, pouring water onto her, and then someone said "milk," and they pressed her shoulders until she knelt down so that they could pour it over her face and bathe her body in it. Someone pressed a new cool wet towel into her hands. She held it to her eyes, and let them lead her to a chair, where she sat down. All around her was chatter, and the sensation of the pain and fear catching up to her, her body trembling, her skin and lungs on fire. She sat, dripping milk, while she waited for her eyes to stop burning.

When at last she opened her eyes, she was surrounded on all sides by monsters.

Some of them were ones she'd seen here before. Some of them were new to her. They weren't exactly standing around waiting for her, but when she opened her eyes, she could feel the monsters in the room taking notice. Hannah came over, her black hair swishing from side to side, and offered her a glass of water. She took it and drank. The cool water burned a little in her throat, but she finished the glass and held it back up. She tried to say *thank you*, but it came out as barely a whisper.

And then the crowd was parting, and Sir was padding across the sticky bar floor toward her. He stopped in front of her.

"I was in my office," he said. "I saw the smoke come in under the door. I'm getting older, it could've killed me." He held up a paw. "You might have saved my life tonight."

She gingerly took Sir's paw and shook. She was glad her throat hurt too much to laugh. She was touched, and she wouldn't have wanted to ruin it.

"You ever need anything," Sir said, "you let me know. You let us know. You're our man."

She nodded, feeling dizzy with joy and heartbreak as everyone nodded along. She wished she could be theirs without being their man. It was almost as bad as being Jack's *interesting guy*.

The story got told around her as she sat in the hard wooden chair, people bringing her water and salted peanuts. The cops had come, dressed in black with their faces covered, and had thrown the gas into the bar. No one was sure why just yet; everyone had thought the matter was resolved with the arrest of the college boy the day before, and no one's theories made much sense.

Rex and Agnolito had handled the guys who tried to throw a can in the front door, but the guard on the back door had been missing from his post because, as they said, he had the shits. Then Turing had burst out through the back door and the cops had panicked, not expecting anyone to be able to move the cinderblocks the cops had stacked.

"If they were smart, they would've backed up a car," Agnolo said, and she shuddered at the idea of it. She wasn't sure if she could have moved a car. "And then of course they've all got eyes on *him*, flinging one of the cops around like a rag doll, right up until I throw what's left of the can at them. They didn't have much to say after that."

"Is anyone hurt?" Turing asked.

"You," Agnolo said. "And the guy you threw hit another guy. And one of them took a can to the face when I threw it back. So mostly them."

Sir inclined his head. "Agnolo. You know I'm grateful to you for this."

"And for plenty else. Let the kid have the moment," Agnolo said, and then continued talking.

She let the conversation go on without her. At the edge of the crowd stood the skinny girl that Agnolo had pointed out, the one who was friends with Jack. The girl was watching her differently than everyone else. Not with admiration, or grudging respect, but like she was trying to read a sign from far away. Agnolo turned and told her to go back to work. She saw Turing watching her, and gave her a shy smile and a little gesture: pointing to her own eyes and then to Turing's. Turing nodded, not sure exactly what it meant, but knowing it was meant kindly.

The place turned into a party—more and more people showed up and got the story, and stayed to get angry and drink and complain about the cops and talk about how one of these days someone should do something about it. The conversation sometimes came to her, but mostly it moved around her. She didn't mind it. She had been many things to people over the years, but she had never been comfortably ignored.

All she could think about was what Agnolo had said. *Mostro.* And just as he'd said it, those cops had come to emphasize the point. Here to punish them for being, as Agnolo had said, *so big and so strange.* The fairies were wrong. People didn't need a king to give them an excuse to persecute monsters.

And yet, here they all were, alive for the moment, and happy. Rex and Agnolito getting along for once, congratulating themselves for their work on the cops out front. The girls talking proudly about how they had rushed from their dressing room and through the smoke to grab Turing and pull her back, the hairspray they'd sprayed in the cops' faces. The story accumulated mass as more people added where they'd been, what they'd seen from their angle, what they knew about the investigation. It wasn't the story of how she had done something brave. It was the story of those dozens of hands that had carried her when she was sure she was about to be killed.

"You'd better lay a little lower, T," Agnolo said. "They're gonna be looking to single you out after that. Better give them time to forget."

They wouldn't forget, she thought. Now they'd seen her. Now that she'd attacked them, they'd never believe she hadn't killed their friends. As long as she was alive, the cops of River City would be after her. And they'd hurt anyone who got in their way.

She realized she might drift off to sleep if she stayed here, so she said she wanted to go to bed. Rex and Agnolito insisted on walking out on either side of her, which she didn't protest. It was nice. She would have wanted to cry if she weren't so tired. She stumbled down the stairs, locked the dead bolt on the basement apartment, and crawled into the bathroom. She turned the water on and slithered into the tub. It wasn't home, but it was familiar, at least.

A few minutes later, there was a knock at the door. "It's me," Jack called.

She wrapped herself in a towel and stumbled to the door. Jack looked her over. "Are you hurt?" she asked.

"No."

Jack stepped forward and took both of her arms. Her hands were warm and rough, and she reflexively ran her thumb over the soft skin on the inside of the nameless girl's elbow.

"This is my fault," Jack said. "I was wrong about the guy. The cops let him go and now they're mad at me for lying to them. I'm sorry."

The nameless girl shook her head. "That's not your fault."

"You need to lay low, okay? No matter what, don't let them see you again."

She'd never seen Jack like this. She looked panicked.

"I'm fine, Jack," she said. "Really."

"I'll fix this," Jack said.

The nameless girl was sad, then. "There are some things you can't fix," she said. "Some things just are."

"Fuck no," Jack said. "They can't have you. I've never met anyone like you."

They stared at each other in silence for a moment. Jack looked startled, like she had just realized something previously unthinkable.

"I've got to go," she said. She turned away, starting for the door, but then turned back. "I'm serious. Lay low. We'll protect you."

Jack slipped out through the door, and it shut behind her with a click. The nameless girl sank to the bed, touching her thumbs to the creases in her elbows where Jack's hands had been.

She loved her. Somehow, incredibly, she loved her.

She wished she could do what Jack said. Stay safe, wait here beneath the earth for Carnival to be over, for other people to solve these problems. But she knew now that she had to go, and she had to stop the king, or be stopped by him. Because if she didn't go, it would be someone else. Now that she'd met others like her, she couldn't imagine leaving it to any of them. *They can't have you,* she thought about all of them: Agnolo, Rex, Sir. The people at the diner. She loved them without even knowing them.

The king was out of jail. He'd be at Carnival tomorrow night. She found the stone dagger from under her pillow. She had to get used to the way it felt in her hand.

TWENTY-NINE

Jack left the bar with fear coagulating in her chest. The guy was out of jail, and the cops knew she'd lied. But if they hadn't showed up ready to fight, that must mean the bosses had a new suspect.

She hopped on her bike and raced uptown into the Old City. She parked it in an alley a block away from the Bodwell School and climbed onto an old shed to see into the fenced yard.

Someone had knocked down part of the chain-link fence, and the back lot was filled with cop cars, their lights flashing red and blue. From here, she couldn't hear what anyone was saying, but people were moving fast. Cops shoved girls out the side door, handcuffed and barefoot.

No Belle as far as she could see. Two of the brass stood next to an empty cop car. One of them was waving his arms. Jack thought *Maybe they shot her.* She imagined her sister lying facedown somewhere in the empty corridors of the Bodwell School, her long gold braid trailing out around her.

She thought about who she could call now for help, for backup. Not Sir; she'd have to tell him what she'd done. Not Astrid; some growing tingle in the back of her head told her that Astrid wasn't telling her the whole truth. And wide-eyed Jesse would be no help.

She thought briefly of Turing. He'd help her.

And then it hit her, like waking up from a dream. She couldn't ask Turing for help, because Belle had been framing him.

Maybe not at the beginning; maybe, that first day, she'd just rolled a body into the river. Maybe she'd been shocked when someone had emerged from the river with the body, laid it back on the shore. Maybe. But the second time had been no mistake. Not with cops trolling the river every day. It had been work, Jack realized, to take a dead man—or maybe a live one—out to the Isle of Bells and leave him in the courtyard in front of Turing's house.

Why him? Why some random guy she didn't know? Why not pin it on Sir, who at least had some protection? Goddammit, why not pin it on Jack, who'd found the first body? It wasn't as if Belle liked Jack any, and at least Jack would've been able to stand up for herself. She couldn't believe that Belle would be so—

They were leading someone out of the school now, someone in handcuffs, with long blond hair. Jack flattened herself to the roof and watched closely. She saw the woman talk to the cops. Belle? No, she was moving wrong; Belle didn't walk, or stand, quite like that. The officers put a hand on her head and shoved her into a cop car. And then that cop car drove away. The cops calmed down; Jack saw two of them shake hands. What did they think had happened?

Jack looked closer at the girls sitting on the ground. There weren't very many of them, she realized, less than half the girls who lived at the school. And they were all shaking now—with tears? She realized they were laughing. All of them laughing at the same thing. The cops yelled at them and they quieted down, but only just. They were smiling and looking at each other conspiratorially as the police loaded them into squad cars. Jack counted as the girls disappeared into cars, one by one.

Those girls loved Belle. If they were laughing, Jack thought, that meant Belle was somewhere else, with the rest of them.

Jack realized her mistake had been pinning the crime on David. University kid, too much power, friends in high places. Friends with Astrid, for that matter, even if she hadn't known that. She should've picked someone it would've stuck to.

Which, of course, was what Belle had tried to do.

She felt empty. What the fuck was she supposed to do now? If Belle was going to start shit on Carnival Night, the best person to help Jack catch her was . . . shit. It was Astrid.

It was dawn when she got to Astrid's door. Astrid answered fully dressed. Jack could see a steaming cup of coffee on the end table behind her. So she wasn't sleeping.

"Astrid," Jack said. "I need to tell you something."

"Do you?" Astrid said. "Let me guess—Belle killed Pete and Matthew?"

"When did you know?"

Astrid pursed her lips. "Not as soon as you did."

"Look, you've got to understand," Jack said. "She's my sister. I—"

"No," Astrid said. "You don't understand. What were you thinking, blaming it on David?"

Jack's mind raced. "What, the college kid?"

"You set him up for murder, and you can't even remember his name?"

"So what? He's New City. Nothing bad was going to happen to him. Those assholes can do whatever they want."

The whites of Astrid's eyes deepened, for just a moment, to dark blue. Jack took a step back.

"You know nothing," Astrid said.

"Astrid, I—"

"Don't you ever," Astrid said. "Ever, ever ask me for anything again. And you had better find Belle before I do."

Jack shook her head. "Please," she said. "If you know anything, please tell me."

"I don't know anything, apparently," Astrid said. "I didn't know you at all."

She shut the door in Jack's face. Jack could feel Astrid watching her through the window as she went down the porch steps and got back on her bike to ride off.

It was morning now. She was bone tired. She'd been up all night, and now this. Belle could be anywhere; this town was full of abandoned buildings, garages, basements. She could look all day and not find her. She needed something—coffee, food. A quick nap, just an hour, and she'd start looking for Belle.

She trudged up the back stairs. Her dingy apartment was warm and full of light. Her roommate was a girl today, a tea towel tucked into the front of her dress while she bustled around the kitchen like a little fairy godmother.

"I'm making pancakes," she said as Jack came in.

"They're kinda flat," Jack said. Things were normal here. Nothing bad was happening. Jesse exuded a state of it'll-be-okay.

"They're crepes. You roll fruit up in them. Like a taco."

Jack shrugged and picked one up, tore off a bite. Jesse swatted at her with the plastic spatula. "Hey, no!"

"What? Can't I eat my creep in peace?"

"*Crepe*. Plate, fruit, powdered sugar."

"All right, all right . . ." Jack grinned and took a plate out of the cupboard. She followed Jesse's instructions on rolling up the strawberries and sprinkling the powdered sugar. When she bit into it, she shut her eyes.

"God, I haven't had a crepe in years," Jack said.

"I thought you said you didn't know what they were!"

"I never said that. You inferred it."

"'Oh, I'm Jack, and I'm just a big dumb himbo who's never seen a crepe . . .'"

"These are really good," Jack said. "You make a lot of those at a diner in Chicasaw?"

"Sunday brunch special," Jesse said. "And if you put butter syrup on them, I will kill you."

Jack hopped up on the counter and watched Jesse pour the batter, swirling the pan to spread it into a thin, even layer. It was kind of beautiful to watch. Meditative.

"You ever thought about being a chef?" Jack asked.

Jesse frowned. "I never really thought about it," she said. "I didn't really plan to like . . . grow up and have a job."

"Not a kid with a lot of forethought?"

Jesse looked thoughtful. "I mean, I used to think I was just lazy," she said. "But being here, I realize I kind of thought I'd be dead too young for it to matter."

That knocked Jack back a little.

"What, you never felt that way?" Jesse asked.

"Not when I was a kid," Jack said. "I mean, I know my job is dangerous, but even now, if I die, I'll be surprised."

"You must have had good parents."

"Not good all around," Jack said. "My mom was a piece of work. But my stepdad really got me. He said he'd always wanted a son."

"That make you mad?"

"Nah," Jack said. "I knew what he meant."

Jack wanted to end the conversation, so she rolled a strawberry onto her tongue and spat it at Jesse, who ducked too slowly and ended up with a smear of pink on her cheek. "Eeeew!"

"You kept your form just then," Jack said. "That's new."

"I spent so long fighting it," Jesse said. "As soon as I stopped trying, it wasn't actually that hard to control it. When I tried to hold it down all the time, it just popped out whenever I was stressed."

"Maybe you just weren't repressing hard enough."

"What, like you? With your happy childhood?"

Jack looked away. "I didn't say that."

Nothing was wrong here, in these moments. Nobody needed her to save their life. Jesse was doing just fine, with her thrift store dress, a pair of cheap sunglasses balanced on top of her head. She didn't need anything from Jack at all. That was nice.

"Hey, I was thinking of taking these outside," Jesse said, holding out the plate of crepes. "Sitting on the hill at the end of the street."

"Around here, we call that a picnic."

Jesse snorted at her. "You want to come with?"

Jack nodded. She watched Jesse bustle around the kitchen, trying to figure out the right takeout containers to pack their breakfast. She tried to think through what Belle's plan might be, what she might be up to, but it was hard to think right now. It felt like being under the river had, like she could breathe but was still drowning.

They ended up at the crest of London Hill, overlooking the river. Jesse was sitting on an old sheet they'd used as a drop cloth the week before to paint Jesse's bedroom green, but Jack didn't like the crackle of the dry paint and had sprawled out in the grass instead. It was warm out, but Jack could feel the snap in the air that told her fall was upon them. She tried to eat her crepes, but she noticed Jesse kept shooting glances at her.

"What?" Jack said at last.

"Nothing," Jesse said. She held her gaze for a long time, until she caved.

"I was just wondering if I could meet your stepdad sometime," Jesse said. "Like, he sounds really great, and mine was the worst."

Jack wasn't sure how long she sat there, perfectly still, her fingers sticky with strawberries and sugar. She could feel Jesse's eyes on her, could smell the sweet grass, could feel the city thrumming all around her. Nothing was going to move, or change, until she did. She shut her eyes and took a deep breath.

"You can't meet him," she said. "He's dead."

Jesse put a hand on her shoulder. Jack was too frozen to flick it away.

"I'm so sorry," Jesse said. "I didn't know."

"I don't talk about it."

"Well," Jesse said. "Then we won't talk about it."

Jack nodded. She looked up at the clouds. Such a beautiful day.

"He was the best dad ever—to me," Jack said. "To my sister, not so much."

Jesse's eyes grew wide. "Jesus."

"Yeah," Jack said. "And I think I kind of knew. Like, I knew they weren't good, like sometimes she hated him and sometimes she loved him, and so I just thought she was the problem. And I didn't want to understand how bad it was. But after a while, I got it, and once I knew, I, like . . . I couldn't pretend not to, you know?"

"Wow."

"Yeah," Jack said. "So I killed him."

She waited to see how Jesse would take it. She didn't say anything right away, just looked into the middle distance, like she was thinking.

"That . . . sucks," Jesse said at last.

The laughter came then, fizzling up from Jack's belly and out her mouth. She laughed until tears sprang to her eyes and she wiped them away with the back of her hand.

"Yeah," she said, still giggly. "Yeah, it really sucks!"

Jesse took Jack's hands. "It really, really does."

They sat quietly together for a long time, while Jack's laughter faded out. She felt like something that had been inflating in her chest had popped, and now there was new empty space inside her.

Jesse's weird little face was so close to Jack's now. She didn't really make a very pretty girl, not with her long face and big dumb ears. But Jesse was staring at her with a look she didn't quite recognize. The way girls looked at her sometimes, but not quite the same.

"Really?" Jack said. "That story turn you on?"

Jesse ducked her head. "Uh, not exactly," she said. "Sorry. I just like you."

"Not too much, though, right? You're not gonna imprint on me like a baby duck?"

Jesse laughed. "I don't think it's like that."

"You done this before?"

"Mostly."

Jack leaned a little closer. Jesse's breath smelled like strawberries.

"And what about your childhood true love or whatever?" Jack said. "Is he gonna come kick my ass?"

Jesse shook her head. "I mean," she said. "I'll protect you."

Jack laughed and pushed Jesse backward onto the grass with one hand. Jesse grabbed her shoulders and pulled her down, too, and Jack pinned Jesse's hands to the ground.

"You're so strong!" Jesse said.

"Yeah, yeah," Jack said. "You change your mind, you tell me."

"Yeah, yeah . . . ," Jesse said in mocking imitation, until Jack put her mouth on hers, and then they were quiet.

Afterward, they lay in the grass for a while. Jack glanced over to see if Jesse was gazing at her with that longing look girls got sometimes, but no, her eyes had drifted shut. Sleepy and smug. Good. Jack folded her arms behind her head and stared up at the sky.

She wasn't sure exactly when she'd fallen asleep, but she woke up when the angle of the sun changed, falling into her eyes. She sat up with a start. It was afternoon. Carnival was only a few hours away. Shit.

"Hey," she said, shaking Jesse's shoulder. "I've got to go. Let me drop you off at home?"

Jesse mumbled awake. "Sure," she said. "You come pick me up tonight? I'm supposed to meet . . . someone."

"Sure," Jack lied. "I might get held up, though."

"By what?" Jesse asked. "Sir gave us all the night off."

"I've gotta go visit Turing."

"They seem nice," Jesse said. "Tell them I say hi?"

Jack nodded. She had to get out of here. How had she fallen asleep? How had she wasted so much time?

She dropped Jesse off and headed uptown. The whole city was decked out for Carnival, everything bright and—

It hit her all at once. Whatever Belle was planning, it had been leading up to tonight. She'd be at Carnival.

Jack remembered Astrid's words. *You'd better find Belle before I do.* She could do that. There was still time, even with all her mistakes. There was still time to fix everything.

THIRTY

When David woke up, it was late morning, and Astrid was gone. He looked for her all through the tiny house: the kitchen, the living room. He climbed back up the stairs and knocked on the door to her bedroom across the hall, first softly, then louder, and then at last, he pushed the door open, feeling terrible, and saw nothing but an empty, messy room. Clothes draped over the back of a chair. The faint smell of mothballs. A bed with rumpled sheets. He half expected a picture of the old man on her nightstand, but it was bare, dusty except for a ring left by the bottom of a water glass.

Downstairs on the dining room table, he found a plate of cold toast and a note that said *Stay here until tonight, then come to God Street.* So she'd left him here. He wondered what could be more important than making sure he showed up to meet his destiny.

He searched the house as quickly and carefully as he could, looking for any evidence that she'd lied to him about anything. He wanted to find a trove of books of magic, or a journal where she confessed to some crime. He opened the fridge, not sure what he expected to find there, and when he shut it, he saw the RCUH pamphlet on treating prediabetes stuck to the front with a magnet. He gave up. He wasn't uncovering any great mysteries; he was just tossing the house of a middle-aged woman who'd had a crush on his father.

His father. He'd been face-to-face with him and not known who he was. David tried to imagine the life he might have lived here as a prince with a mother and father who loved each other and loved him. He could picture them both, now that he'd seen them, but every time he tried to add himself, his imagination failed. He'd always been alone.

He went back to the photo album that Astrid had showed him, and leafed through it, past all the pictures of Astrid and King Nathan, to the wedding photo of Marla. He pulled it out. She looked so loving, like she'd have forgiven him for anything. He turned the photo over and looked at the back. Nothing. No secret message between the two women. No little note to him across time and space. He felt—well, there wasn't any point in feeling anything about it.

This city was stupid and hateful, because it was dying. The place Marla had lived, the place his father had been sane and healthy and happy, the place Astrid had described, was lost.

But maybe it didn't have to be. Not if he could bring magic back.

He slipped the photograph into his breast pocket, closed the album, slid it back into place on the shelf. This place needed magic, or it was just a shit island with no laws. He didn't know much about anything except this one very specific sub-field of physics, but about that, he knew a lot. This was what he could contribute. He could fix things, and he could do it tonight.

He started walking back toward the university. People gawked at him as he passed, but for once, it barely registered. It was like the reverse of what had happened after he'd fought Jack; then, he'd felt like nobody could get in his way. Now, he knew anyone, at any moment, could do whatever they wanted to him. The only choice he had was whether he wasted time worrying about it.

When he arrived, he found that his key card didn't open doors anymore, so he followed a gaggle of students in through the hospital lobby's sliding doors, figuring he could get it straightened out later. He caught a few weird looks on his way upstairs, but no one stopped him. They were afraid to.

He took the elevator up to the ortho floor, planning to cut across the skybridge. But as he passed a half-open door, he heard someone call out, "Min? Are you out there?" He kept walking. A few moments later, though, he heard it again. "Min? Come back!"

Worried that a nurse might come, he ducked back to the room and opened the door. "Hey," he said. "I'm not Min, but—"

He froze. In the bed was a little girl, her body wrapped in bandages, hooked up to monitors. She was surrounded by presents: a stuffed unicorn, piles of books. And he recognized her. He'd seen her playing with her sister in the skywalk.

"Where's Min?" she said. Her voice was faint. "Have you seen her?"

Cold horror seized him. He backed out of the room. "She's coming," he whispered. "Just go to sleep, and she'll be right back, okay?"

He left the wing at a brisk walk, careful not to attract any more attention. He was going to get magic back, and then he was going to use it to burn this place to the ground.

When he got up to his office, the door was open, the room empty except for the bucket and mop that had been there before him. He found some of his things in the trash room on the twelfth floor, including his copy of *Planned Magic* and the poetry book. They were the only things he kept.

They hadn't gotten to his dorm room yet, and that opened with an old-fashioned key. So he holed up in there. They'd probably find him eventually; he was hard to miss. But he only had to wait it out until night fell.

He was scared to leave the room when he finally crept out. It had been claustrophobic, but at least he knew what was in every part of it. He knew how to control it. When he stepped into the hall, he felt an almost overwhelming wave of panic and had to go back inside.

He closed his eyes and promised himself he'd die before he let himself be arrested ever again. That made him feel a little better.

He picked up the book of spells, tucked it into the gap in his waistband, and put a jacket on over it. Then he went and knocked on Seth's door. Seth answered it, startled.

"David?" he said. "You're back!"

Seth was wearing a spangly jacket with no shirt on underneath, and he'd combed glitter into his scraggly chest hair, and into his eyebrows, too. He looked . . . good, David thought, although the thought had to travel a long way, through the thick cloud that hovered around him all the time since Astrid had bailed him out.

"Where have you been?" Seth asked. "They said you got arrested, but when I went down to the police station, they said you weren't there."

Seth had gone to find him. That was something. David stood up a little straighter.

"They tried to hold me without charging me," David said. "They let me go. I came back here, but . . ."

"Yeah," Seth said. "They had a meeting about it. Lang's teaching your sections. Are you okay?"

"I don't want to talk about it," David said.

Seth stepped forward, as though to hug him. David wanted that, but not enough to overcome the wave of nausea at the thought of being so close to another person. But at the last second, Seth stopped, and the nausea was replaced by deep loneliness.

"You've been a good friend to me," David said. "And I haven't been a good friend to you. But I need a favor now, and if you do this for me, then later, when things are better, I'll be the best friend you ever had."

Seth shook his head. "You don't need to do that," he said. "What do you need?"

"I need you to come with me to Carnival," David said. "I need to go there tonight to meet someone, but I'm . . ." He nearly choked on the words. "I'm scared to go alone."

He could see Seth's hand fluttering at his sides, could see Seth straining toward him and away at the same time. Why was everyone so damn afraid of him?

"Hey, I was going anyway," Seth said. "Get in here. I'm almost ready." He gave David a once-over. David could only imagine that he looked like hell. "Do you want me to, uh—"

"No," David said, and Seth flinched. "That's too much. I'm just going to go like this."

Seth smiled. "I'm sure your date will recognize you."

"I'm kind of hard to miss."

Seth half laughed. To David, it sounded at least a little like a yelp. But he stepped aside and let David into his room.

THIRTY-ONE

It was late afternoon when the nameless girl crept out of the basement and into the darkened bar. The guard let her in with an embarrassed nod. "You saved my ass last night," he said. "Thanks, T."

She nodded at him, feeling sheepish. "What are you up to?"

"Getting my costume," she said. It was only *technically* a lie.

"Pshew, going to Carnival?" he said. "I dunno, aren't they after you?"

"I'll be fine," she said.

She slipped inside. The bar was still and empty, everyone having gone to Carnival except for a man at each door, armed with guns and pagers to call everyone back in case of trouble. It was beautiful in here when it was quiet. Without everyone constantly smoking, the walls emitted a chilly damp. She sat down at the bar for a while. She was going to miss this place. She'd been hoping for more nights chatting with Agnolo, even if he was going to slap her shoulder and call her *my boy* or *good man*. She raised an imaginary glass to him.

She went through the storage closet, looking for something that might disguise her a little bit. The police had already seen her body, and the coat barely concealed her. She needed a big cloak, or some kind of makeup, or something—

And then she thought of the girls' dressing room.

She'd never been inside before, although she'd read books that had described stage dressing rooms before, and her glimpses inside had confirmed that it was a miraculous place. Her hand shook as she opened the door.

The room had a lingering smell of sweat and hairspray. The walls were lined with mirrored vanities, some with lights around the edges, some with lamps set up nearby. A few of the girls' dress forms still had costumes on them. They must be planning to come back here to get ready. They'd probably be here soon. She'd have to be quick.

She started casting about for anything she could use as a cloak, a hat, a mask, but one of the costumes kept drawing her eye. It was a dress the color of butter, and attached to the back, a pair of enormous golden wings made from tissue paper and wire. They were so large and so expressive—she felt one, and realized that as large as it was, it was hollow on the inside. As light as the wing of a bird. On the table beside that dress form was a wig on a plastic head: black hair in a braided halo, interspersed with seed pearls.

She stared at herself in the mirror. Her hair was growing in thicker and darker. She wondered what she was supposed to do as it got longer; it seemed almost brittle. She thought about Jack's hair, cropped close to her head, so that you could see individual scars that ran from her face into her hairline. Another thing she would never see again, after tonight.

On impulse, Turing reached down, picked up the wig from its stand, and slipped it on. It was a little crooked as she turned back toward the mirror; she was trying to adjust it when she saw the door open behind her.

Hannah stood there, wearing her street clothes. She had a ring of keys in one hand. Turing turned and flinched. She saw the other girl's eyes narrow, and she reached up and hastily pulled off the wig, careful not to hurt it even as she did. And then she watched Hannah's face change from angry to—something else.

"I'm sorry," Turing said.

Hannah set down her keys and her bag, took off her jacket. She stared at Turing quizzically.

"You . . . like to dress up?" Hannah asked. "Is that what this is about? Some of the guys who come in here are like that."

Turing shook her head. "Not exactly," she said. "I just . . . I've always wanted long hair."

"You're not taking care of yours," Hannah said. "You need to condition it, or it'll keep breaking."

"Is that what you do?"

Hannah shook her head. She reached up and tugged on her own long dark hair. It came tumbling off into her hands. Underneath, Turing saw, Hannah's hair was short, tight curls, like hers, but glossy.

"I really thought that was your hair," Turing said.

"Hah." Hannah looked at her quizzically. "Your mom never had a wig?"

"I don't have any parents."

Hannah cast her eyes toward the ceiling, looking around as though asking God, or the hidden cameras, why she was being put up to this. But then she set down her wig on the table and took the one Turing held from her hands.

"You want to wear a stocking cap under that," Hannah said briskly. She stepped over to a dressing table and picked up a thin sock of mesh. "And pins, to hold it on. Or it'll slip when your head gets sweaty."

The daughter of the river stood frozen. She wanted to run out of the room. If she started running now, maybe she could make it to the river before anyone saw her.

"Hey," Hannah said. "Look, I'm trying to tell you it's okay."

Turing could feel the tears bubbling up at the corners of her eyes.

"Oh my god," Hannah said. "Don't get weepy about it. Sit down."

Turing sank onto a stool. Hannah sat down opposite, her elbows propped on her knees, studying her.

"So, you have no parents, you live in the river," Hannah said. "And you want to be a girl?"

"I . . . yes," she said.

"Does Jack know?"

Turing shook her head. "I haven't told her."

"You're in love with her, aren't you?"

"She means a lot to me."

"Well, I should've known something was going on when she showed up with a boy," she said. "Sorry, you know what I mean."

"She's wonderful," Turing said.

Hannah looked sad then.

"I don't know you," she said. "But you should be careful. She's not going to take care of you."

"She doesn't have to," Turing said.

"She should!" Hannah said. "Look at you. You're all alone—" Hannah paused. Her eyes darted around suddenly like she'd just thought of something.

"You know what? Hell with it," Hannah said. She went over to her dress form, took off the wings, and laid them across a chair. She unzipped the butter-colored dress, pulled it off of the dummy, and held it out, draped across her arms.

The daughter of the river could not believe what was happening to her. She took the dress, stiffer and scratchier than it had looked on the mannequin. But Hannah was staring at her expectantly.

"Well," Hannah said. "Put it on."

Turing stared until Hannah turned around. And then she scrambled out of her clothes and into the dress as quickly as she could. When Hannah turned around, Turing watched her eyes flicker for a moment, and then she nodded.

"I can see it," she said. "You'll need makeup, though."

"Why are you doing this?" Turing asked.

"I don't know," Hannah said. "I made this dress back when I was still in love with Jack. I thought she'd see me in it and it'd make a difference. But it won't." She shook her head. "I don't need this; I know how to take care of myself. But you're so—exposed. Your heart's just out there. You need some armor."

The daughter of the river wanted to cry. But she had to be brave. She was being given an extraordinary gift. And she knew enough of stories to know that an extraordinary gift required extraordinary graciousness.

"I'll never forget this," Turing said. "If you ever need anything from me, just ask." She hoped she would be alive to keep that promise.

Hannah laughed. "Okay."

Hannah sat Turing down at the table and painted her face.

When she was done, she took a nylon cap and a handful of pins from a drawer, smoothed the cap over Turing's hair, and put the wig on, pulling it on from front to back, arranging the hair, pinning it into place. When she was finished, Turing glanced at herself in the mirror.

She looked . . . different. Nothing had changed, but everything had. She held her head differently, turning it from side to side slowly, to make her hair fall in different ways. For a moment she was transfixed. And then she remembered what she had to do that night.

Well, if she died tonight, at least she would die beautiful.

CARNIVAL

All at once it was the evening of Carnival, and time snapped to attention. In the great hollow caves beneath the city, the fairies chittered in their nests. In the high towers of the University Hospital, undergrads did their makeup in rows in the dormitory bathrooms. Downtown, Rex and Agnolito fought over a can of body spray. Beautiful girls and boys and monsters readied themselves for a night of portent: drinking water, eating dinner, tacking notes to the doors of professors and bosses saying that they were feeling kind of under the weather and wouldn't be able to make it in tomorrow. The city buzzed like a tree full of cicadas, with the thrumming energy of possibility. And now, we will step quickly through what is to come.

THIRTY-TWO

When Jack had left, Jesse went into the bathroom and got down the electric clippers that Jack used for her crew cut. Jesse carefully parted their hair to one side and shaved a wide stripe from ear to temple. They ran their fingers over the stubble. In the mirror, they tried to half change, to hold a middle shape for a moment, neither boy nor girl. It held for a second. A good look, Jesse thought. Then it slipped, and they laughed and got dressed. Fiddled with makeup, wiped it all off. Sprayed on some of Jack's dark, woody-smelling cologne. Ate some leftovers. Kicked back in Jack's chair and watched the ceiling fan turn.

Jesse waited for a long time for Jack to come back. The sun set. Jesse tried not to feel slighted. Of course Jack would stand her up. She'd done it to Hannah a hundred times, hadn't she? She did this to everyone. Jesse tried to imagine that Jack must be up to something important, or she wouldn't have flaked. But . . . maybe that wasn't true.

Eventually Jesse heard the distant sounds of the party starting up. Well, they weren't going to miss Carnival because of Jack. Fuck no. They laced up their boots and headed out.

On the walk, Jesse spotted other people heading for Carnival, dressed in bright costumes and carrying things: handles of liquor, giant puppets on sticks, musical instruments. Jesse fell in behind a brass quintet as gradually the street became more and more decorated with strings of lights and paper lanterns and old banners and flags, some with big fancy crests on them—although Jesse noticed that with these, the crests had been slashed with big red X's.

Staring upward, they nearly got hit in the head by the tail end of a massive snake marionette. The man holding it looked embarrassed and handed Jesse his half-eaten popsicle. Jesse took it without hesitation and slurped on it, tasting cherries and liquor.

Jesse ambled along, trailing the crowd, but stopped just short of the mouth of an alley that rang with a familiar voice. Astrid. Jesse stopped and peered in.

Astrid knelt on the ground, ignoring the puddles around her. In front of her was a man in a greasy black raincoat—Nathan, the man from the bus, the one that had looked so familiar to Jesse that first day. His face was bloodied on one side, a paper crown hanging haphazardly off one ear. But Nathan didn't seem upset. In fact, he looked almost young, and he smiled indulgently as Astrid dabbed frantically at the blood with a wet handkerchief. As Jesse watched, the man laughed, and pulled Astrid down into his lap.

"Nathan, stop it," she said, swatting at him.

"You can't stop true love," Nathan said.

Jesse was transfixed—it was like watching a play. Nathan wrapped his arms around Astrid, and in the dim alley, it was hard to tell if her mouth was open in laughter or grief.

And then all at once, Nathan's face changed. He suddenly looked his age again, and tired.

"Was I a good king to you?" Nathan asked, his broken front teeth making his voice whistle. "Was I a place you wanted to live?"

"You were never a king or a place to me," Astrid said.

Jesse leaned back and away from the alley, feeling like they'd seen something they shouldn't have. They waited until another gaggle of partygoers passed and slipped in among them. Time to go to Carnival. Time to go find their date.

THIRTY-THREE

Jack had found an alley narrow enough that she could brace her back against the wall and walk herself up. She was now perched in the crevice, high and hidden enough that no one on the street seemed to see her. She wrapped her jacket closer around her, fumbled in the pocket, came out with a cigarette. She cupped her palm around the lit end to hide the cherry while she watched the street for action, for signs of Belle.

The best thing, of course, would be to grab her while no one was looking. The girls, without her, would have no idea what to do. If Jack could just get hold of her, maybe she could lock her up somewhere until the time for her stupid plan, whatever it was, had passed.

She scanned the crowd, looking for any of the Bodwell girls. It was hard at Carnival, though; almost everyone had a mask, or a costume, or a wig. After several minutes of watching, she still saw no sign of any of them, or of Belle. And then, on the street below, she saw a woman dressed as an angel—a huge set of papier-mâché wings, gold paint, a long trailing gown of cheap, cream-colored satin and a braided crown of hair. But the angel stopped, and looked up at her with familiar eyes, as though knowing Jack was there all along. Turing.

Jack motioned for him to look away, and carefully crab-crawled back down the wall, and slipped out of the alley to his side.

"You shouldn't be here," Jack said. "Why aren't you at Sir's?"

"There's something I have to do tonight."

His eyes met Jack's, and something in her flipped over. She steadied herself. He was cute in drag, that was all. She didn't have time to think about this now. People were going to get hurt tonight. She needed to focus.

"What are you doing?" she asked.

He looked sober. "Someone is going to try to become king tonight. I have to stop them."

"Are you sure?"

"Yes."

She nodded. "Okay. Why?"

"Because kings kill monsters. And I can't let that happen to anyone we know."

"Huh," she said. "Well, how will you know him when you see him?"

"Well," Turing said. "I'm looking for someone who's trying to come into power. Who's trying to kill monsters. I think that they'll become obvious."

Jack felt cold inside suddenly.

"Kill monsters," she said leadenly. "And then you're gonna do what? Kill them?"

"I don't want to," Turing said. "I want to stop them. I don't want to kill anybody."

Of course he didn't. Jack felt a surge of anger, but wasn't sure where to direct it. Fuck this whole situation. She wished Belle had told her the plan. Then she wouldn't have gotten to know him. Now, something in her had turned over. And she couldn't go back.

"T," she said. "I have to tell you something."

The crowd surged around them, and they almost bumped into each other, but she caught herself in time. She didn't need to be touching him right now. Not when he was about to hate her.

"It's my sister," she said. "I think she's who you're looking for. I think she's trying to become king."

"Why do you think that?" Turing asked.

"Because she killed those cops," Jack said. And she told him everything she knew.

"The girl with the braid."

"Yeah."

"You've been protecting her."

"Yes." Jack felt like she'd had her insides scraped out.

Turing nodded slowly. "It makes sense now."

"I couldn't let her go to jail," Jack said. "Not after everything she's been through."

Turing seemed to be thinking.

"She's not the king," Turing said. "I've seen him. But if he brings back magic, she'll be able to use it?"

"She'll probably take credit," Jack said.

"And she'll kill more people?"

Jack's face burned. "Yeah."

"Then we have to stop her."

"We just—we can't kill her," Jack said. "She's all I have."

Turing's face took on some new look that Jack didn't understand.

"Jack," he said. "You know that's not true."

Jack looked into his eyes. Looking at him too long made her

stomach hurt. She'd told him she wasn't a good person, and he'd said that was fine. And he meant it. She'd told him she'd protected the woman trying to kill him and he was still here in that stupid beautiful white dress, looking at Jack like she was made of stars even though she didn't deserve it.

It made her furious.

"You're not my family," she said.

"I know that—"

"And you're not my fucking boyfriend."

Turing was silent. Around them, the crowd rustled and jostled but Jack couldn't hear them. Turing's face fell. And Jack thought, far too late, of Jesse, of people who weren't what they looked like. Had she always known?

"Turing," she said, feeling like a fool, "something you want to tell me?"

"No," Turing said. "I understand."

Turing was turning away. Jack tried to grab at her wrist, but couldn't bring herself to touch a woman she'd just hurt. "Wait," she said, feeling like a desperate animal.

"We don't have time," Turing said. She tossed her head, the pearls in her hair catching the light and gleaming like tears. "Let's find your sister."

THIRTY-FOUR

Jesse wandered through the crowd. They studied faces, getting a lot of smiles in response—everyone around here was always so friendly to them, so easy with them. This was a good place to be. The best place. Jesse slipped shapes, and kept walking, getting more and more distracted by drunkenness and the crowd. God Street was full of beautiful things: giant papier-mâché sculptures, tents selling fortunes, girls in spangled gold dresses and boys in tight pants. Jesse turned slowly to ogle, trying to walk forward at the same time, and ran into someone in a heavy brocade dress and a porcelain mask.

"Jesse!" The figure flung out its arms and embraced them. "I'm so glad you came."

"Belle?" Jesse couldn't see her face under the mask, or her blond hair under her high, powdered wig. "What are you wearing?"

"This is the traditional Maiden costume," Belle said. "They're very old and very precious. All my girls are wearing them tonight."

"Oh," Jesse said. They vaguely recalled Belle talking about the print shop as a collective, so it was a little weird to hear her say *my girls* like that. "I didn't recognize you at all! I'm glad I ran into you."

"I've been looking all over for you! You shaved your hair! It's cute. Come on, let me show you something."

She tugged Jesse by the hand through the throng of the crowd. "Are you hungry?" she asked. "Do you want another drink?"

"I'm good," Jesse said. A vague worry was creeping into them. "Have you seen Jack?"

"Not yet," Belle said. "I'm sure we'll catch up at some point."

"I didn't tell her we were going on a date," Jesse said. "I hope she's not mad."

"Oh, Jack's always mad about something," Belle said. She tipped her mask up to flash Jesse a smile. "Well, if you don't feel safe with her, you can always move in with us. I'd love to have you."

She winked at Jesse, and slid her mask back down. "Come on!" she said, her voice muffled. Jesse followed.

Eventually they came out to the center of God Street Market, to the empty fountain with its slab of ugly gray rock. Belle pointed.

"This fountain used to flow with magic," she said. "Did you know about that? People would come and dip their wounded parts in here and be healed."

"I didn't," Jesse said.

"It even flowed for a while after the last king was deposed and his wife killed," Belle said. "Astrid ordered it stopped so that we wouldn't waste the magic. That's why she walks with a limp. She had to set an example for everyone else."

Jesse wasn't sure where all this was going. They felt dizzy. That popsicle had probably been too much.

"You know," Jesse said. "I'm kind of thirsty."

Belle tipped her mask up again, and took them by both hands. And she leaned forward and kissed Jesse.

It was shocking, and the hard edge of her mask collided with Jesse's forehead, and she didn't seem to care. Belle was pressing her lips into Jesse's as hard as she could. It didn't feel like a kiss, either, not tender, not exploratory. Jesse felt their whole body go rigid. They pulled away.

"What are you doing?" Jesse said.

Belle looked angry, frustrated. She quickly tried to mask it and look remorseful, but Jesse had seen it. They knew that look. It was the same one Paul had whenever he called Jesse useless.

"Wait, was that not right?" Belle asked. "Jesse, I'm so sorry. I thought you meant . . . oh, wow." She looked down at the ground, but didn't let go of Jesse's hands. Instead, her grip got harder. "Did I hurt you?"

"I think I'm gonna go," Jesse said. They started to walk away, but Belle grabbed on tightly. Jesse was suddenly aware of other women in heavy brocade dresses and masks, circling through the crowd like sharks, converging on their location. Jesse glanced back at Belle, whose face was still a perfect mask of regret and shame, and whose hands still clutched at Jesse's wrists like talons.

"Let me try again," Belle said. "I'll do it right this time. Jesse, please. I need to make this right."

Jesse wrenched away from her, pushed past one of the women in the heavy dresses who was closing in on them, and stumbled out into the crowd. As soon as they were away from Belle, they felt a little better, until they saw two more of the women heading in their direction. They looked left, right, looking for any escape—

And then, from the corner of the street, they saw a familiar face in the crowd.

He was tall, taller than Jesse remembered—but then, it had been a long time ago. He had short auburn hair, brown skin, freckles. He was alone. Jesse ran to him, and a jostle of the crowd sent them colliding with each other.

"Sorry," David mumbled, and then he looked down, and their eyes met.

And the crowd, the women, Belle, and every other thing that Jesse had been worrying about melted away.

THIRTY-FIVE

David and Seth got off the bus in the Old City. The sun had just gone down and the street was clogged with the kind of darkness that cannot be alleviated with light. They were walking now up Carver Alley, toward God Street.

The darkness was stained bright by the street lamps, crowned with skull faces that leered down at them, and by strings of multicolored lights that blurred everything into a golden haze. The smell of fried dough was overwhelmed by the smell of grilling meat, overlaid again by the perfumes and the colognes and the stink of sweat. Bodies packed the street, bodies dressed in mantles of black feathers and cat's eye masks and frothy pink dresses and angry snarling boar's heads of papier-mâché. David felt something then, in the pit of his stomach. Pressure. He wasn't sure where it was coming from but he could feel it all around him, a sensation like being suffocated. He tried to concentrate, keep his wits about him. He had to find this girl that Astrid had told him to look for. Or failing that, he had to find Astrid.

David felt intensely uncomfortable in the shops on God Street. Everything was too short for him; he loomed over most of the people here and dwarfed the little doorways. He hunched as they walked. But it was also the people: As he passed, the older ones turned their heads and gave him perplexing looks. He wondered if they were recognizing him, the way the DVD stand woman had.

This was where the witches lived. At Carnival, the cities mixed, but this was Old City territory.

"It's dangerous here," David said, turning to Seth, and realizing, to his horror, that Seth was gone. David looked up. He thought he saw Seth moving away through the crowd, several yards ahead, a small bobbing slicked-back hairdo starred with little flecks of glitter. He started trying to push his way after him. And that was when he saw the boy.

Their eyes met at the same time. A skinny white kid with a half-shaved head, in a goofy shirt. David knew him immediately. And more than that, he knew that he'd seen him in the city before. He just hadn't known, had told himself that he was imagining things.

The crowd was jostling him in a way that felt dimly wrong; it had gone quickly from a party to an uneasy throng. Someone elbowed him in the side trying to squeeze past. He didn't care. He and the boy met and stood facing each other.

"David," the boy said. "Do you remember me?"

David had a horrible, sick sensation.

"I got on the bus," David said. "I said I was coming here to wait for someone. And they asked for your name. And ever since I can't remember it."

The boy shook his head. "It's Jesse," he said.

"Jesse!" David laughed.

It all came surging back. He felt like a kid again in the woods behind Jesse's house in Chicasaw. The awful dread that hung over him lifted just a little.

"I still have your postcard," Jesse said. Jesse! He could remember his name now.

"Did I see you in the street a week ago?"

"I saw you, too! But then you were gone—"

They got closer and closer to one another. It felt natural, magnetic. And then Jesse was shoved from behind, and stumbled into him, and David caught him. He was so small, so light, that David laughed, and Jesse laughed a little bit, too.

The two of them felt it at the same time: both their own bodies meeting, but also something else. It wasn't coming from them, but power was surging up into them, running through them. A ring of blue light expanded out around them rapidly, like a supernova, burning the air. It knocked over the people closest to them and kept going, energy that was also matter, moving against or through people with seeming indiscrimination, burning without burning, until it vanished into the distance all around them.

"What was that?" Jesse asked.

"I think," David said slowly, "I think we just brought back magic."

David became aware that the crowd around them had ceased being anonymous. Everyone was looking at them. And then the hands came. People reaching out to pluck at his sweater. Someone got down on their knees in front of him and grabbed his shoe, brought their face down to kiss it. Women were stroking Jesse's hair. Hands and more hands, pressing close around them. They liked him now, but how long would it last? He felt panicky and angry, imagined throwing up a wall of fire around them all, severing hands and tongues and whatever else they were rubbing on him—

Jesse grabbed his hand. "You okay?" he asked. "Wow, you're real sweaty."

"I gotta get out of here," David said.

Jesse nodded. "Hey, everyone!" he called. "This is great but we need to go for a minute. Everyone just . . . be nice to each other, have a nice evening and we'll be back in just a—" He started pulling David by the hand through the crowd, smiling and touching people's hands and faces as they passed. Behind them, the crowd closed in on itself, and glancing back, David saw people stroking each other's faces, kissing passionately, falling to the cobbles tangled in each other's arms. Jesse pulled David forward like a kid, not seeming to notice.

THIRTY-SIX

The daughter of the river slid away through the crowd, flinching away whenever anyone touched her. She wished her skin would fall off, that she would be allowed to dissolve into liquid and slip through a gutter. She'd made a fool of herself. Jack had seen right through her. She'd been wrong, she thought, all those times when she'd dared to think that Jack felt some flicker of what she did. Jack just pitied her. Like Hannah pitied her. Like everyone else who was too brave to fear her. She blinked back tears as she turned sideways and tightened her ribs to pass between bodies. Agnolo was wrong. Nobody could love what she was.

Dimly behind her, she thought she heard someone yelling after her. *Turing. Wait. Don't walk away from me.* But it was so faint that it was hard to tell.

The daughter of the river, whom people called Turing, struggled through the crowd. The heavy papier-mâché wings on her back kept catching on people's costumes and she feared they would tear. And then she saw a familiar face for just a moment. She was lifting her porcelain mask to get a breath of cool night air. She really did look like Jack, but if you'd made Jack's face cruel. The girl she'd seen at the river's edge was the girl who'd been waiting on Jack's steps was the girl Jack had talked about in the diner was the girl who was trying to be the king. It was like getting caught in a current underwater and turned upside down, until you didn't know which way the air was.

As Turing watched, the girl slid her mask back into place and began moving decisively through the crowd, heading for a group of other women dressed in those same heavy brocade dresses. And she was tugging someone by the arm. The skinny girl from the nightclub, the one who had smiled at her and pointed to their eyes.

Turing eased her way through the crowd as fast as she dared, cursing this costume's heavy wings and her own clumsiness as she knocked into people over and over again. And then suddenly she stopped short of a break in the crowd, an area cleared by the women in brocade. She teetered and took a step back as though she'd found herself at the edge of a cliff.

"Turing!"

She turned to see Jack panting at her side. Jack's eyes were wild. Turing pointed to the masked girl she'd been following. "There's your sister," she said. The women in masks had formed a tight phalanx. There was a current of malice in the air, a static charge. The crowd was pressing closer, trying to get a look at what was going on in the circle. They bumped together, and Jack caught her by the wrist.

"About what I said," Jack said. "I didn't—"

The wave of magic swept through the crowd, all around them people falling to the ground, but the daughter of the river didn't feel the impact and Jack didn't seem to, either. She looked around, and found they were two of the few people still standing. The third was a woman in a heavy brocade dress and a mask. Her blond braid unfurled like a banner.

Jack's sister looked at the daughter of the river. With slow deliberation, she took off her porcelain mask and tossed it down. It shattered on the cobblestones. Her face underneath was like Jack's, but colder. Like what Jack was always trying to be, Turing thought. What Jack wished she was.

"Monster," Belle said, pointing a long finger. "Magic has been restored to the city. As the rightful king I challenge you."

The daughter of the river looked down at herself. The jostling of the crowd and the wave of magic had torn Hannah's beautiful paper wings, and her own arms were visible underneath in the wire framing. Her gown looked ragged and shabby suddenly. There was nowhere left to hide from her fate. She was going to have to face her.

"You can't be the king," she said to Belle. "You don't have the Maiden. That's not now that works."

"You don't know that," Belle said. From somewhere in her dress, she produced an old piece of copper pipe with the ends stopped up: a wand. The whole shaft of it crackled with blue fire.

And then, all at once, there were police. They'd crept through the crowd, and now dozens of guns were trained on her, on Belle. But Belle's eyes didn't leave hers.

"You killed those men," Belle said. She wasn't talking to Turing, though, but to the cops and the crowd, projecting her voice like a stage actor. "And someone has to stop you."

She wondered if the police would move forward. They didn't. They stood and watched. She wondered if each one of them was weighing who they thought had done it. The small blond woman with the wand? The hulking monster like something from the bottom of a bad dream?

"You need to back off, Belle," Jack said, turning to her sister.

"No, Jack," Belle said. "You can't hold me back anymore."

Belle didn't seem to care now that Jack was in danger. And as sorry as the daughter of the river felt for herself, she felt sorry for Jack, too. After all, she knew what it was like to love someone who didn't love you back.

The nameless girl started walking forward, her dress trailing over the cobbles. Turing put up her hand, not sure what she planned to do—snatch the pipe from Belle's hand? Grab her and hold her still? But there was no walking away from this. Everything was leading to this. It had always been leading to this.

She felt something hot and bright explode into her side—a shot that ruptured her papier-mâché wings. And then she was falling.

THIRTY-SEVEN

When she heard the first gunshot, Jack grabbed Belle and tackled her to the ground. The makeshift wand went flying out of Belle's hand, skidding across the cobbles. She threw her body over Belle as they hit the cobblestones, trying to block bullets or batons or stomping feet. The crowd was panicking overhead; they stepped on Jack's hands as they tried to scatter. Cops fired wildly. A can landed on the ground near Jack, spitting smoke; she batted it away as far as she could, still spinning, still spitting, until suddenly it was stopped by a black button-boot, and it burst into a cloud of butterflies. Jack glanced upward. Astrid.

She was wearing a dress of faded black silk, patched with black embroidery, and her hair was pulled back in two tight braids. She didn't see Jack; she was looking elsewhere in the crowd, scanning for something. And then she spotted what she was looking for. Jack's eyes followed her.

Belle swore and struggled free from under Jack, kicking her away. Jack let her go. She'd spotted what Astrid was after.

Turing lay among the remnants of her ivory dress, draped over the lip of the empty fountain, her wings trodden to paste and tangled wire. She was bleeding, but Jack couldn't yet tell how badly. Astrid strode toward her, no longer limping. Oh yeah. Magic was back.

Jack glanced back at Belle, doggedly crawling after her shitty wand. Still chasing her stupid plan when around her everything had changed. Jack saw her grab it, scramble to her feet.

"Astrid!" Jack yelled. "Belle's here!"

Astrid's head snapped around. Jack ducked. Astrid spotted Belle, and headed in her direction. Jack wanted to sob with relief. She ran, low, to where Turing lay sprawled. She knelt. Turing's eyes flickered open and met hers. She was alive. A wound in her side was oozing blood into her dress.

"Grab on!" she said, and Turing grabbed her hands and staggered up, her wings ripping off as she stepped into Jack's arms. Jack slung Turing's arm over her shoulder to support her. She looked around. They needed to get out of the crowd, get to shelter. Turing's blood was wetting Jack's shirt now.

"What about your sister?" Turing asked. She sounded vague and hazy.

"Magic's back. She'll live," Jack said. "How do you feel?"

"I didn't stop the king," Turing said.

"She didn't kill anyone tonight," Jack said. "Maybe that counts."

Jack felt Turing sag a little at the news. And then Turing lifted her head, her wig tipping back from her eyes.

"She didn't have the Maiden," Turing said. "She's not the real king."

The crowd surged around them, someone stumbling back at high velocity until the wall of bodies nearly knocked Jack and Turing off their feet. Jack braced herself and hung onto Turing, who sagged down around her waist.

"Wait," Turing said. "I have to stop the king."

"You're not stopping anyone," Jack said. "We have to get you some help."

She kept walking, shuffling around jostling bodies. That was how they would get out of this. One foot in front of the other.

THIRTY-EIGHT

David and Jesse were pressing their way out of the crowd when they heard a crack. David wanted to believe it was fireworks, but then people started screaming and pushing. Panic filled his throat.

"Which way?" he asked.

Jesse pulled David down a side street, and to David's surprise, it was suddenly quiet and empty. It was incredible, he thought, how there could be a riot, with guns and magic, happening right over there. And over here, it was calm. It was a normal night in a normal city. The sounds of the crowd were a faint rumbling.

"You okay?" Jesse asked.

"Yeah," David said. "Let's . . . stay out here for a while."

They kept walking, far from the sounds of the sirens that rose from the carnival. David had Jesse by the hand, and he didn't want to let go; that hand felt so perfectly designed to interlace with his.

"I remember you knew all these secret places," David said. "Like that dry culvert where you had a bag of snacks hidden under a rock."

"I got really good at finding places to hide," Jesse said.

Through adult eyes, it all looked different. David sighed.

"Why didn't you tell me?" David asked. "You could've come and stayed with us, or something, if you'd told us."

"That's not how it works," Jesse said. "I know that's what people want to think, but that's never how it works. I mean, your parents probably moved to get you away from me."

"I mean, kind of," David said. "To get away from your stepdad, mostly."

"What did he say to them?"

"I don't know," David lied. It was too ugly for this moment. David leaned over and wrapped an arm around that small waist. Jesse tucked himself into David's side. David's body. "I . . . never stopped thinking about you."

"I sorta thought I'd made you up," Jesse said. "You weren't there for very long and you were so, like—magical."

David grinned.

"Magical, huh?" he said. "Me?"

"Yeah," Jesse said. "I think that's the word."

"But you got my postcard?"

"Yeah," Jesse said. "I still have it."

They were walking on the Boulevard of Statues now, lined on either side with rows of stately houses in different states of decay, draped with ragged, faded bunting for Carnival. Jesse pointed across to a statue on the grassy median, the first in a long row of statues: a man holding a cane aloft like he was directing a marching band.

"This guy was some kind of performer," Jesse said. "He did magic by twirling that cane. Jack said he was, like, the eighth king. King Simon."

"Jack?" David asked. "You know her?"

"Yeah? How do you know her?"

"She kicked my ass in a fight once."

"You were in my bar!" Jesse said. "I didn't know you'd been there. How did we keep missing each other?"

David shook his head in disbelief. "We weren't supposed to meet yet," he said. "So we couldn't."

It was all like being in a dream, in that it made no sense. David closed his eyes and reached down inside himself, through the layers of muscle and bone and atom and soul, to that river of light that Astrid had shown him. When he reached it, he was nearly shocked by its saturated deep blue. So much of it! It seemed like it was flooding, and when he opened his eyes, he realized he could see it everywhere around them. Magic, more magic than he could possibly have imagined, everything tinged with it around the edges.

"What's wrong?" Jesse asked.

David took Jesse by the hands.

"We did it," he said. "We really did it."

"Did what?"

He wanted to show him—her—Jesse. Wanted to show Jesse what they had done, together.

"It's power," he said. "We . . . catalyzed a reaction." He pushed his glasses up his nose. "And that reaction unleashed a kind of force. A kind of energy. People call it magic, but only because they don't understand it."

"Magic," Jesse said. "What can we do with it?"

David smiled. "Anything we want."

He turned and put his hand on the statue. It was made of bronze, corroded green. He reached down inside of himself and pushed magic out into the world, and—

The fire blazed in his hand, and the statue began to ripple with heat and started to melt. The man's torso leaned forward drunkenly on his waist, the metal groaning. David groaned, too, and pulled his hand away. He'd wanted it to be special, to come naturally. He'd wanted to—

And then Jesse was taking his hand, and holding it, and laughing a little at him.

"Hey," Jesse said. "Let's try it together."

Jesse laid their hands back on the statue, palms up, and stared into David's eyes. "What do you want to happen?" Jesse asked.

"I want it to . . ."

And then, from beside them, he heard a thumping sound. And when he could bring himself to look sideways, he saw that the statue was tapping its cane against its pediment. *Thud, thud, thud,* as though to music. And David waved his hand in time with the tapping, and then—there *was* music.

And the eighth king of River City descended from his pedestal, twirling to music that came from nowhere at all. The metal wasn't hot, hadn't turned red. This wasn't anything like the magic he'd done before. There was no rational explanation for this.

David looked back at Jesse. They clutched each other's hands and grinned wildly. Magic, real magic, was in the world.

And then Jesse's face clouded.

"My friends," he said. "We can't just leave them. That crowd was intense."

David nodded. He felt almost dizzy. They had so much power. They could—

"We need to stop them," he said. "Before anyone else gets hurt."

As he said it, he heard something behind him. A heavy metallic clanging that got louder and louder.

He turned and saw a bronze horse.

It was big even compared to David, and he had to lean back and crane his neck to see its rider, a giant in a frock coat with a face frozen in an expression of haughty cruelty. For a moment, David felt the way he had at the police station, that icy terror sweeping through him and chilling him instantly. Especially when the rider moved, swinging one leg over the saddle to land on the street with a stone-shattering *boom*. David let his hand flood with blue fire, moved to block the statue's path toward Jesse, who had turned to stare.

And then the statue held something out to David. The reins to his horse.

David took them. They were made of metal but hung fluidly from his grip. And with grinding and showers of sparks, the rider lowered itself to one knee in front of him. A show of fealty.

"Jesse," David said softly. Jesse came to his side. She—he— gripped at his sweater with one hand, staring at the statue on the ground before them. "Who is this?"

"King Mahigan, I think," Jesse said. Of course it was.

"King Mahigan," David said. He reached behind him, pulled the book out of his waistband, and held it up. "I have your book."

The stone man laced the fingers into a stirrup. He looked up at David. And David knew what he should do.

He placed one hand on the cold metal flank of the horse, put one foot up into the stirrup formed by the giant. And then the giant stood up, and David was moving rapidly up into the air alongside the horse; he flung a leg over its body and suddenly he was astride, holding cold metal reins, the city beneath him, where the statue of King Simon was taking Jesse by the hand, spinning them in his grip. And from behind him again, he heard the rumble, and turned.

Every statue of every horse and mounted rider stood there, at his back. A cavalry of bronze kings.

David raised one arm over his head. He needed a sword. He closed his fist around an imaginary hilt, and from his hand sprang a blade of crackling blue fire.

THIRTY-NINE

Jack scanned the crowd, looking for an exit. People were pressing tightly around her, and every now and then someone would make a grab for Turing. Jack snarled at them. They were barely making any headway; they hadn't even cleared the square.

And then at once, Astrid was there. One of her braids had come undone, and her dress had a new tear in the silk. She was holding Belle's copper wand.

"Astrid," Jack said. "I know you won't help me. But I need you to help her. She's hurt really bad."

She realized that Astrid wasn't looking at her, but was staring at Turing as though she'd seen a ghost. Her face was hard, horrified.

"Put it down, Jack," Astrid said. She snapped her fingers, and two men came forward, arms out to take Turing. Jack hesitated.

On her back, Turing slumped. Jack shifted her weight to keep her up.

"I won't ask again," Astrid said. And something told Jack that helping wasn't part of the plan.

"Fuck you," Jack said.

"I was there when that was born," Astrid said. "It's not a person. It came out of Queen Marla choking the life from the prince."

Jack's mind raced. "She's one of Marla's kids? Are you stupid?

All this talk about the Maiden, and you never thought it might be the *princess*?"

"It tried to—"

"She was a child! And you want me to let you kill her?"

"Not me," Astrid said.

Jack stepped back and back as Astrid pressed forward. She could get her gun out, but she'd have to drop Turing. She could try to run, but they were surrounded on all sides. And then she felt her heel strike something hard. The base of the fountain. They were back where they'd started. Fuck magic, if it was like this.

Astrid looked like she was calculating. And then she said a few sharp words. A glowing bubble rose from the ground around her, Jack, and Turing. Jack tried to shove through it and found herself staggering backward, nearly falling down.

"Put her down," Astrid said. "Or I'll make you."

"What the fuck, Astrid?" Jack said. But Astrid didn't seem to hear her. She was talking to herself.

"I can't believe it," Astrid said. "This is perfect. The very monster that tried to kill him when he was born."

Jack shifted Turing's weight just enough to free up her arm, and reached for her gun. Astrid glanced down, almost casually, and raised two fingers in a snipping motion. Jack felt a prickle along the scar on her right arm, and then a sudden lightness, and then nothing. She looked down at her arm on the ground, still holding the gun. It didn't hurt. It didn't feel like anything at all.

The men snatched Turing from her. Astrid directed them to lay her on the slab of stone in the middle of the dry fountain. Jack clung to Turing's skirts, clambering up onto the rock with her, not sure what to do except be there.

"Fuck you," Jack said to Astrid. She was close to sobbing. "You're supposed to be this noble revolutionary, and now you're just like *Oh, can't fight fate?*"

Astrid shook her head. Her usually-irritable face had softened into a slight smile.

"I made a mistake," she said. "I thought I knew what I was doing. But I lost everything. And now, I'm getting it all back."

From outside the bubble, Jack heard the crowd begin to roar, or possibly, to scream. And piercing through the din, a loud, rhythmic clanging that got closer and closer.

FORTY

The daughter of the river began to think that she might possibly have an idea of what her name was. There was a Z in it. The crookedness of Z was good, a sound she loved to say. She thought she'd like the sound of it in Jack's mouth, too, now that Jack was rescuing her. Zara, perhaps. It was a good name for a girl.

She had a moment of blurry recognition, of a face she remembered from nightmares, dreams in which a woman picked her up and then dropped her from some immense height. Then, a loud noise, and sudden, bright light.

And then, at last, she saw him. The king.

He rode a metal horse twice her height, and there were a dozen more behind him, with massive riders of bronze. He dismounted, and the boom of his feet on the ground shook the earth. He was blurry around the edges with blue, and he was so tall that she couldn't get a clear look at his face. But in spite of the certainty that pulled at her like a magnet, he didn't seem to her like a mad king who would destroy cities. His shirt was stretched in the front as though someone had grabbed it. He held a rod of blue light in one trembling hand.

She tried to straighten up, but it felt like her back had become bent around Jack, and anyway, when she moved, a throbbing hot pain shot up from her hip through her spine. Oh yes, she'd been wounded. He craned down to look at her. The fairies were right;

it was the boy from the university. He was no older than her. He had soft chubby cheeks and freckles. The look in his eyes was not murderous intent, but fear and confusion. And what's more, he seemed to recognize her. His gaze flickered over her—not the way that people usually looked at her, sizing her up as though she might kill them. He looked as though he were trying to place her. As though she were a long-lost friend.

FORTY-ONE

Jack saw David's arm moving before even he seemed to notice it. She wedged herself between him and Turing.

"Back *up*," she said. "She didn't do anything wrong."

"She's lying," Astrid said. "This is the monster who tried to kill you when you were a baby. And she killed those two men."

David turned his eyes on Jack.

"You," he said. "Get out of my way."

"Astrid is lying to you," Jack said. "Turing's not trying to kill you. You have to believe me."

"Why should you believe her?" Astrid said. "She sent you to jail to protect that thing."

David's eyes narrowed.

Everything seemed to slow down as Jack's body flooded with fear. She thought about what she'd said to Jesse earlier that afternoon: If she found herself in a position to die, she'd be surprised. And she recognized now that Turing had always moved like someone might kill her at any time. From the moment Jack had crawled to Turing on the street, Jack's odds had gone down, but Turing's had gone up.

Jack took a deep breath. "Yeah," she said. "I did. And if you want to kill me, go ahead. I'm your monster. Kill me and take your fucking throne and leave her alone."

With the fear gone, all that was left was stillness. She shook her head at David. Or rather, she'd been shaking it this whole time, and had only just now become aware of the decision she'd already made.

David raised his arm and brought it down. The rod of flame hurtled toward her, and as it did, she raised her one remaining hand to shield Turing's face.

She expected it to dissolve her. Instead she caught it.

It hurt, it burned, but she could feel it dying in her grip. She slowly forced her fingers shut around it, squeezing it, shrinking it, until it burst in her hand and dissipated.

She looked down at her hand in astonishment. And then she remembered that earlier today, she'd kissed the Maiden. Some small bit of magic had clung to her.

"Huh," she said.

David took a step back, startled.

"David," Astrid said. "Strike now. David. You are so close to restoring everything."

And then Jesse flung herself forward, between Jack and David. She reached a hand back, slid it over Jack and Turing, as though caressing them both. Jack felt her body fill with strength. Perks of the Maiden's love, she guessed. Well, she wouldn't complain.

"Run," Jesse said.

FORTY-TWO

Jesse stared David down as Jack staggered to her feet. He looked startled, angry, pained. He conjured another rod of fire, but let it hang limply from his hand. He stared at Jesse in disbelief.

For a moment, the mob around them was still. And then everyone lunged inward, toward Jack and Turing, with a frothing vengeance that startled Jesse. They were trying to grab Turing, to get them back onto the slab.

"Help me!" Jack said. She was trying to heave Turing onto her shoulder. "Jesse, I need you!"

Jesse glanced at David. He looked like he'd seen death. The surging of the crowd was making him nervous. Jesse could feel his unhappiness radiating off of him. He needed to get out of here. He was hurt. He was scared.

"I can't," Jesse said. "Run, I'll find you later." Jesse pressed through the crowd to David and caught him by the hand. They weren't going to let him go, not now that they'd found him. No matter what he'd been about to do. He hadn't meant it, Jesse told themself. He'd been scared.

Hands, dozens of hands, reached out to them, grabbing at David's clothes and snatching at Jesse's hair. Jesse struggled to hear what Jack was saying as the mob closed off a wall between them. Jack seemed to be swearing at them. Jesse waved helplessly. What could they do?

"We have to get out of here," Jesse said to David, taking his hand.

They pushed and shoved, begged and pleaded, looking for any gap in the crowd. People wanted to be near them, and rushed in to fill any available space. It felt futile and helpless, until David, exhausted, held up the rod of blue light in front of them. It crackled menacingly, and people got out of its way. David gripped Jesse by the hand, and they shoved forward, using the rod to threaten their way through the crowd, until they broke free of the mass and ran for several blocks. Jesse pulled them down an alley, and they hid behind a parked car as people streamed past, looking for them, hoping for them.

At last, they stepped out. And when they did, there was Belle.

Jesse winced when they saw her. Her brocade dress was in tatters, the skeleton of her hoop skirt exposed. She'd lost her wand from earlier, but it didn't matter: She glowed and crackled with magic. In one hand, she held a dagger that looked carved out of stone.

A few people had spotted them again and were pointing and waving to others to join. The crowd was coalescing around them again. Jesse felt raw panic. This was horrible. This wasn't how it was supposed to be.

"Jesse," Belle said. "Listen to me. If we keep doing it the same way every time, nothing will ever change. Don't you see? Can't you understand?"

Jesse shook their head. "Get away from us. Please."

Belle raised the dagger as David slashed at her with the sword of blue fire. The flame dissipated when it struck the dagger.

"Fucking bedrock," David muttered, and kicked Belle in the

chest. She fell backward. Jesse heard a crack as Belle's head hit the stone.

And something in Jesse cracked, too. And to their surprise, out poured—happiness.

Jesse was filled with joy that overflowed through their body and radiated out into the world around them. Everything hummed with it, a joy so bright and aching that not everything it touched could survive it. They spun their arms wildly, flinging joy in all directions. Their joy would destroy anything too flimsy to hold up, and everything strong would bear the weight and would become imbued itself with that joy, until the whole world burned with their love.

This was satisfaction. This was catharsis. This was how things were supposed to be.

With a clang of hooves, the bronze cavalry appeared behind them. David mounted his steed again. He was so beautiful up there, his face from that angle so hard and stony that people who saw it threw themselves to the ground weeping and tearing at their clothes in shame, apologizing for everything they'd ever done that might have harmed him. Jesse reached out and touched some of them on the shoulders, and they wept harder, their mouths stretching into grimaces as their hearts filled with remorse and relief.

Nothing could stop King David now. He had Jesse, he had a steed, he had an army made of every king who had ever come before him.

Except for one king, Jesse thought for a moment. They thought briefly of Nathan in the alley with the paper crown listing off his head. Of Astrid kneeling in front of him. Why was there no statue of Nathan anywhere in the army behind them? Why had he come to Jesse on the first day and told them—what? To feel their way down to the river? And something else, too? What had he said? *You have to stop the wheel?* Who would ever want to stop something that spun so beautifully?

"Jesse," David said. "We've won. Get up here."

David reached down a great hand, and Jesse caught it and was pulled up onto the saddle in front of him. Cheers, wild cheers! They began to proceed down the street. The band of revelers grew larger and larger, turning from a stream into a river as wide as God Street, as they rode. They started downtown, toward the heart of the city.

As they passed the place where Turing and Jack had been, Jesse looked for them. But all she saw was Astrid, who had climbed onto the roof of an abandoned car to watch them pass. When she saw them, the old woman dropped to her knees.

FORTY-THREE

The crowd around Jack and Turing lost interest and dissipated almost immediately once Jesse and David bounced, and flowed on with them toward some other scene. Someone was yelling at Jesse and David. Jack thought she might recognize Belle's voice. No time to think about that. Turing was safe for now, if they could get out before the crowd changed its mind.

Turing stirred and groaned. Jack struggled but couldn't pick her up with just one arm.

"Turing," Jack whispered. "Turing. Wake up. I need you."

Turing opened one eye. "Zara," she said.

"What?"

"My name's Zara."

Jack laughed a little.

"Okay," she said. "Here's a deal. You survive this, I'll call you whatever you want."

"No," Zara said. "I might die. Say it now."

"Zara," Jack said. "Get on my back."

Zara oozed herself over Jack. Jack struggled to keep her grip; Zara's dress was slippery now with blood. Jack dragged their collective weight down the street, her back aching. "Zara, Zara, Zara." She stopped saying it, but the name repeated in her mind like the drumming of rain.

Jack trudged as fast as she could with Zara slung over her body.

She carried her down an empty alley, crossed an empty street. It was amazing how easy it was to outpace a riot once you got out of the crowd. The noise receded behind them so quickly that soon it was like they were in another world entirely.

"Your sister," Zara said faintly.

"Don't worry about her," Jack said.

They reached the riverbank. Jack lowered Zara to the ground beside the river. Zara's tentacles reached out instinctively toward the water. They gripped the bank and began dragging her in. "Whoa," Jack said, and put her weight on Zara to pin her to the earth.

"Let me go into the river," Zara said.

"You've been shot. We need to get you to a doctor." Jack glanced around. "I don't know where we'll . . . I don't know."

"I'm the monster, Jack," Zara said. "If I don't go, the king will find me, and he will slay me."

Fuck. Jack gritted her teeth. How was she supposed to know that kid had been the king? And she'd gotten him thrown in jail, and he'd come out looking for blood. She'd fucked up, and now Zara was paying the price. What was the fastest route to not fucking up anymore? What was the move that ended with Zara safe?

"You really think if you go in the water you'll be okay?" she asked.

"I think so."

"Okay," Jack said.

She helped Zara get right to the edge of the river. And when Zara rolled herself off into the water, Jack caught hold of her, and fell, too. The river closed over their heads with barely a ripple.

Under the water, there was no light. Under the water, there was little air. Under the water dwelled the stories.

Jack and Zara sank to the bottom together, their bodies twining around each other. Zara could breathe; Jack held her breath, wondering if she could swim for the surface with one arm, wondering what it would be like when she finally let go and took the water into her lungs. Well, there were worse ways to die than in the arms of the woman you loved.

She held on for as long as she could, until she was dizzy, until she wasn't sure if the darkness around her was the river or her own blood pounding in her temples. She breathed out her last air. And then she breathed in the river.

It burned, it felt like being split in two, but she didn't die. Instead, she could see again. Down there in the water, she could see the story.

It floated like a ghost in front of them, a shimmering ribbonlike creature as big as the island itself. Half real: real enough to hurt you, ephemeral enough that any weapon you wielded against it would simply slide through and past. It was like a serpent, or a flatworm, and its glowing body a screen, projecting scenes of things that had happened before, and would happen again, and again, and again.

Once there was a monster that lived in the river.

Once there was a maiden, pure of heart.

Once there was a hero, come to make his fortune.

Once there was a witch, distributing help and harm for purposes all her own.

Every breath of dark water was agony, and Jack struggled to see clearly around the red blotches at the corners of her vision. She reached for Zara's hand, caught it, and squeezed it as hard as she could, clinging to something that felt real. Not like this behemoth in front of them.

And a voice in Jack's head whispered, *Hello, hero.*

I'm not a hero, thought Jack. I'm the fucking monster. You dumb . . . whatever you are. I wrecked everything, hurt everyone, to help myself. Is that what a hero is?

The creature's whole body rippled. Jack realized it was laughing.

You're perfect.

FORTY-FOUR

Zara floated in the dark for a long time, until a voice spoke to her.

"My child," it said.

She tried to open her eyes and found that they were already open—it was just terribly dark, as dark as the inside of eyelids. She opened her mouth to speak and water rushed in and out. So she tried to think, as hard as she could. It was hard to think; all she could manage was *who*.

The darkness all around her. It was different from the place under the river, with that cold, alien light. This dark was warm. Like a hug.

"I never got to meet you," the darkness said. "I knew I had a daughter, but I didn't learn your name."

Zara, she thought.

The warmth around her grew stronger, pressing in on her. It didn't hurt.

"Zara," the voice said. "That's a good name for a princess."

Zara could barely think now. The idea of a question. Exhausted. Sad.

"I know it hurts. But I need you to do something that no one else can do."

That was easy. *Anything*. Anything at all for this warm voice, this quiet dark.

"Zara," the voice said. "Please. Save your brother from what he's becoming."

EPILOGUE

On the morning after Carnival, the disparate parts of the city came back to life one by one to find that it was winter. Night drained from the city like water at low tide, leaving behind its flotsam of torn streamers and crushed paper cups, party hats, lost eyeglasses, buttons ripped from shirts, hairpins that had sprayed the street like shrapnel from the explosions of elaborate hairstyles, a severed arm holding a gun. In the alleys and in tangled sheets, half-dressed bodies and smeared faces opened, turned, reached out. Anyone who had gone to bed with someone else found their bed empty, with no lingering warmth, no dent in the mattress to show where a body had lain.

On the morning after the collision of great lovers, everyone else in the world woke up alone and cold. Painted bodies and battered faces shivered, and dug themselves deeper into their beds, and slept with uneasy dreams. Seth woke up on the floor of a janitor's closet, face smeared with chalk. Hannah rubbed eyeliner across her face and crawled from her blankets to close the window.

The disjointed parts of the city began to check in with one another. It took days of long, slow morning, in which each day felt like a continual sunrise, days in which getting out of bed at all was a struggle through fog. The Old City, with its crumbling brick houses, called out to the New City, with janitors and cooks and secretaries sent out as emissaries. University? *Here.* God

Street? *Here.* London Hill? Canal Street? Museum on Cemetery Hill, where no one goes for fear of disturbing the past? *Here. All here.*

And beneath the streets, in rivulets and veins, known mostly to witches but felt by everyone, the magic flowed.

In the pre-dawn light, Belle woke up behind a garbage can.

She had crawled there, she guessed, and then fainted. She stared down at her legs, sprawled out before her. At least one of them was broken. All her girls had scattered when the police arrived. She sucked in a breath, although it hurt. She felt too young for everything she'd done. The words in her mouth, which she'd felt so sure of at the time, now sounded ridiculous to her.

She tried not to cry. Every bump in the pavement hurt. She felt feverish and nauseous. But she had to get home. The girls would be waiting. They'd be scared.

She started to drag herself toward the mouth of the alley to look for help, to call for someone, anyone. But then she felt it in the air around her, in the ground beneath, seeping into her hands. The magic was back. How had she forgotten?

She started with her legs, wincing as the broken bones knitted and the swelling bubbled up and then vanished. Then the bruises on her arms and ribs, then the flecks of glass in the palms of her hands. Finally, she made herself a quick little disguise and slipped it over her head.

She crawled out of the mouth of the alley, walking on hands and feet until she could find a wall to help herself stand. She felt weak, but blooming fast. She felt like she might fall in love with the first person she saw. She felt free.

She began striding toward Bodwell Street, aiming for home. There was so much to do. She began tallying up the ledgers in her head, the way all witches do instinctively: Chastise the girls for running. Begin teaching the witch ones some better magic. Start fortifying the Bodwell School and gathering supplies—

At the intersection of God and Bodwell, she ran into a statue.

It was one she recognized: one of the old kings, wearing old-fashioned clothes. It was ill-maintained, streaked with oxidation and bird shit. She hadn't realized how big it was because the pedestal made it so far away—it was at least twice as tall as she was. It stood perfectly still, its feet planted solidly in the concrete.

Belle squinted as she got closer.

It happened so quickly that she barely had time to react. When she did manage to plant a hand on its surface and scream the word, the blue flame licked across its surface and then dissipated. Local earth, she thought, under the bronze. Interesting.

It picked her up in giant's hands and flung her down. She felt a jolt as her back hit the edge of the sidewalk—and then nothing. She looked down at her legs. Why weren't they moving? She started to dip into the magic, but there wasn't much time.

It bent over her, almost tenderly. She saw its hand reach down for her neck, tried to bat it away, but could not fight its grip. "Why?" she asked.

She got no answer.

An hour later, an old man with a wild white beard, half-blind, wandered by and saw Belle's body. He glanced around to see if anyone was watching. Finding no one, he shuffled over and knelt beside her. She lay in the street, curled up like a child in bed.

Her face was turned north, toward the river. Her eyes were open.

The old man kissed his own knuckles and muttered something. Then he got to his feet with painful deliberation. He turned slowly and shuffled away, holding his battered head with one hand.

ACKNOWLEDGMENTS

Writing is not a solitary act. All these people wrote this book along with me in ways big and small.

Thank you, Chris and Kaia, who wandered through the city with me in 2011, speculating about what those tiny doors set into the walls could possibly be.

Thank you, Christina, who showed up at a Halloween party dressed up as Eleanor from my first book before it was even out, making me suddenly feel like a real author. I want to live up to the generosity you have always shown me.

Thank you to my agent and my editor, Jen and Trisha, brilliant women who deserve everything for their patience and passion.

Thank you to my authenticity readers, Kat and Rashid, for telling me the truth.

Thank you, Toni Morrison and Leslie Feinberg, for writing first and best about some of the things I struggle with here.

Thank you, Carol and Cass, for being my mothers.

Thank you, Anna and Jake and Khan, for being my family.

And finally: thank you to my colleagues in United Campus Workers of Virginia, who have demonstrated extraordinary courage this year in the face of great adversity. I am so proud to be with you.

ALSO BY ROSE SZABO